D1390752

WITHDRAWN FROM
THE LIBRARY

UNIVERSITY OF
WINCHESTER

KA 0105618 2

THE DARKER PROOF

ff

THE
DARKER PROOF

Stories from a Crisis

Adam Mars-Jones
and
Edmund White

faber and faber
LONDON · BOSTON

First published in 1987
by Faber and Faber Limited
3 Queen Square London WC1N 3AU
Reprinted 1987 (twice)
This new edition, with two additional stories,
first published in 1988
Reprinted 1988

Typeset by Goodfellow & Egan Cambridge
Printed in Great Britain by
Richard Clay Ltd Bungay Suffolk
All rights reserved

'Slim' © Adam Mars-Jones, 1986, 1987
'An Executor', 'A Small Spade' and 'The Brake' © Adam Mars-Jones, 1987
'Remission' © Adam Mars-Jones, 1988
'An Oracle' © Edmund White, 1986, 1987
'Palace Days' © Edmund White, 1987
'Running on Empty' © Edmund White, 1988

'An Oracle' was first published in *Christopher Street* and later in *Men on Men*
edited by George Stambolian, published
by New American Library, New York.

'Slim' was first published in *Granta* and later appeared in *Mae West is Dead*,
published by Faber and Faber.
'Remission' was first published in *Granta*.

*This book is sold subject to the condition that it shall not, by way of trade
or otherwise, be lent, resold, hired out or otherwise circulated without the
publisher's prior consent in any form of binding or cover other than that
in which it is published and without a similar condition including
this condition being imposed on the subsequent purchaser.*

British Library Cataloguing in Publication Data
Mars-Jones, Adam
The darker proof. — New ed.
I. Title II. White, Edmund
823'.914[F]   PR6063.A657/

ISBN 0-571-15188-4

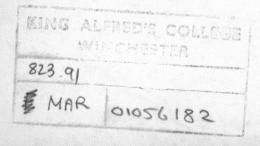

KING ALFRED'S COLLEGE
WINCHESTER

823.91

MAR   01056182

Contents

Slim

Adam Mars-Jones

I don't use that word. I've heard it enough. So I've taken it out of circulation, just here, just at home. I say Slim instead, and Buddy understands. I have got Slim.

When Buddy pays a visit, I have to remind myself not to offer him a cushion. Most people don't need cushions, they're just naturally covered. So I keep all the cushions to myself, now that I've lost my upholstery.

Slim is what they call it in Uganda, and it's a perfectly sensible name. You lose more weight than you thought was possible. You lose more weight than you could carry. Not that you feel like carrying anything. So I'll say to Buddy on one of his visits, Did you see the local news? There was an item about newt conservation, and then there was an item about funding Slim research. But newts first. What's it like talking to someone who's outranked by a newt?

Buddy just looks sheepish, which is probably best in the circumstances. Buddy would rather I avoided distressing information. He thinks I shouldn't read the papers, shouldn't upset myself. Even the doctors say that. If there was anything I should know, I'd hear it from them first anyway. Maybe. Yes, very likely. But whenever they try to protect me, I hear the little wheels on the bottom of the screens they put round you in a ward when you're really bad, and I'll do without that while I can.

Buddy's very good. That sounds suitably grudging. He

3

tries to fit in with me. He doesn't flinch if I talk about my chances of making Slimmer of the Year. He's learned to say *blackcurrants*. He said 'lesions' just the once, but I told him it wasn't a very vivid use of language, and if he wasn't a doctor he had no business with it. Blackcurrants is much better, that being what they look like, good-sized blackcurrants on the surface of the skin, not sticking out far enough to be picked. So now, if the subject comes up, he asks about my blackcurrants, asks if any more blackcurrants have showed up.

I do my bit of adjusting too. Instinctively I think of him as a social worker, but I know he's not that. He's a volunteer attached to the Trust, and he's got no qualifications, so he can't be all bad. What he does is called *buddying*, and he's a buddy. And apparently in Trustspeak I'm a string of letters, which I don't remember except the first one's P and stands for person. Apparently they have to remind themselves. But I've decided if he can say Slim and blackcurrants to oblige me, I can meet him halfway and call him Buddy. Illness is making me quite the internationalist: an African infection and some dated American slang.

Buddy may not be qualified, but he's had his little bit of training. I remember him telling me, early on, that to understand what was happening to me perhaps I should think of having fifty years added to my age, or suddenly having Third World expectations instead of First. I suppose I've tried thinking that way. But now whenever I see those charity ads in the papers, the ones that tell you how for a few pounds you could adopt someone in India or the Philippines, I think that maybe I've been adopted by an African family, that poor as they are they are sending me what they can spare from their tainted food, their poisoned water, their little lifespans.

Except that I'm not young by African standards. Pushing forty, I'd be an elder of the tribe, pretty much, and the chances of my parents still being alive would be slight. So I should be grateful for their being around. They've followed me step by step, and now I suppose I take that for granted. But I didn't always. Before I first told them about myself, I pinched the family album, pinched it and had it photocopied. It cost me a fortune, and I don't know what I thought I wanted with a family album and no family, if it came to that. But at the time I thought, no sense in taking chances. Maybe if they'd lived nearer London, if I'd seen them more regularly, it wouldn't have seemed such a big risk. I don't know.

My African family doesn't have the money for photographs. My African family may never even have seen a photograph.

I've been careful not to mention my adoption fantasy to Buddy. No point in worrying him. And touch wood, I haven't cried while he's been around. That's partly because I've learned to set time aside for such an important function. I've learned that there is a yoga of tears. There are the clever tears that release a lot in a little time, and the stupid tears that just shake you and don't let you go. Once your shoulders get in on the act, you're sunk. The trick is to keep them out of it. Otherwise you end up wailing all day. Those kind of tears are very more-ish. Bet you can't cry just one, just ten, just twenty. But if I keep my shoulders still I can reach a much deeper level of tears. It's like a lumbar puncture. I can draw out this fluid which is a fantastic concentrate of misery. And then just stop and be calm.

I used to cry to opera, Puccini mostly. Don't laugh. I thought the best soundtrack was tunes, tunes and more tunes. But now I cry mainly to a record I never used to listen to much, and don't particularly remember buying: *Southern Soul Belles,* on the Charly label. I find records far more trouble to put on than my opera cassettes, but *Southern Soul Belles* is worth it. It has a very garish cover, a graphic of a sixties soul singer with a purple face, for some reason, so that she looks like an aubergine with a beehive hairdo. The trouble with the Puccini was that you could hear the voices, but never the lungs. On *Southern Soul Belles* you hear the lungs. When Doris Allen sings 'A Shell of a Woman', you know that she could just open her mouth and blast any man out of the door. Shell she may be, breathless she ain't. There's a picture of her on the back cover. She's fat and sassy. She could spare all the weight I've lost. Just shrug it off. Her lungs must be real bellows of meat, not like the pair of wrinkled socks I seem to get my air through these days.

I treat myself to *Southern Soul Belles* every day or so. I've learned to economize. Illness has no entry qualifications. Did I say that already? But being ill – if you're going to be serious about it – demands a technique. The other day I found I was writing a cheque. I could hardly lift the pen, it wasn't a good day, not like today. But I was writing everything out in full. No numerals, no abbreviations. Twenty-one pounds and thirty-four pence only. Only! I almost laughed when I saw that *only*. I realized that ever since my first cheque book, when I was sixteen, I've always written my cheques out in full, as if all the crooked bank-clerks in the world were waiting for their chance to defraud me. Never again. It's the minimum from now on. If I could have right now all the energy I've wasted writing every word on my cheques, I could have some normal days, normal weeks.

One of the things I'm supposed to be doing these days is creative visualization, you know, where you imagine your white corpuscles strapping on their armour to repel invaders. Buddy doesn't nag, but I can tell he's disappointed. I don't seem to be able to do it. I get as far as imagining my white corpuscles as a sort of cloud of healthiness, like a milkshake in the dark flow of my blood, but if I try to visualize them any more concretely I think of Raquel Welch, in *Fantastic Voyage*. That's the film where they shrink a submarine full of doctors and inject it into a dying man's bloodstream. He's the president or something. And at one point Raquel Welch gets attacked and almost killed by white corpuscles, they're like strips of plastic – when I think of it, they *are* strips of plastic – that stick to her wetsuit until she can't breathe. The others have to snap them off one by one when they get her back to the submarine. It's touch and go. So I don't think creative visualization will work for me. It's not a very promising therapeutic tool, if every time I try to imagine my body's defences I think of their trying to kill Raquel Welch. I still can't persuade myself the corpuscles are the good guys.

One thing I find I can visualize is a ration book. That's how I make sure I don't get overtired. Over-overtired. I suppose my mother had a ration book before I was born. I don't think I've ever seen one. But I imagine a booklet with coupons in it for you to tear out, only instead of an allowance for the week of butter or cheese or sugar, my coupons say One Hour of Social Life, One Shopping Expedition, One Short Walk. I hoard them, and I spend them wisely. I tear them out slowly, separating the perforations one by one.

In a way, though, it's not that I don't have energy, it's just the wrong kind. My head may be muzzy but my body is fizzing. I suppose that's the steroids. But I feel like an electric razor that's been plugged into the wrong socket, I'm buzzing and buzzing but I'm not doing any work. It's so odd having sat at home all day, when your body tells you you've been dancing all night in a nightclub, just drinking enough lager to keep the sweat coming, and you're about to drive home with all the windows down, smelling your own sweat. And sleep.

I can't work. That should be pretty clear. But I've been lucky. I'm on extended sick leave for a while yet, and everybody's been very good. I said I had cancer, which I do and I don't, I mean I do but that isn't the problem, and while I was saying *cancer* I thought, All the time my Gran was ill we never once said *cancer*, but now cancer is a soft word I am hiding behind and I feel almost guilty to be sparing myself.

Suddenly *cancer* had the sound of 'interesting condition' or 'unmentionables'. I was curling up in the word's soft shade, soothed gratefully by cancer's lullaby. Cancer. What a relief. Cancer. Oh, that's all right. Cancer. That I can live with.

Sometimes I'm asleep when Buddy visits. Sleep is the one thing that keeps its value. He presses the buzzer on the entry-phone, and if I haven't answered in about ten seconds he buzzes again. I know the entry-phone is a bit ramshackle and you can't hear from the doorway whether it's working or not, but when Buddy buzzes twice it drives me frantic. I don't need to be reminded that I'm not living at a very dynamic tempo right now. I'll tick him off one of these days, tear off a coupon and splurge some energy.

Then Buddy comes pounding up the stairs. Sometimes he smells of chlorine and his hair's still damp from swimming, but I suppose it's a bit much to ask him to slow down, to dry off properly and use cologne before he comes to see me, just so I don't feel bruised by his health. I'll bet his white corpuscles don't need a pep talk. Crack troops, no doubt about it. I'll bet he drinks Carling Black Label.

I watch too much television. Television isn't on the ration.

Buddy's breaking in new shoes, which creak. Why would anyone crucify his feet in the name of style – assuming liver-coloured Doc Martens are stylish in some way – when comfortable training shoes are readily available almost everywhere? It's a great mystery.

Buddy likes to hug. I don't. I mean, it's perfectly pleasant, it just doesn't remind me of anything. It was never my style. I'm sure the point is to relieve my flesh of taboo, and the Trust probably gives classes in it. But when Buddy bends over me, I just wait for him to be done, as if he was a cloud and I was waiting for him to pass over the sun. Then we carry on, and I'm sure he feels better for it.

He's still got a bruise above the crook of his elbow, from his Hepatitis B jab. I really surprised myself over that. I wasn't very rational. He wasn't sure whether to have it done or not, and I almost screamed at him *Do it! Get it done!* If I'd had a needle handy I'd have injected him myself, and I don't think getting my own back was my only motive. I remember Hep B. That was when illness came up and asked me what I was doing for the rest of my life. That was before there was even a vaccine.

The back of his neck is something I tend to notice when Buddy visits. It always looks freshly shaved. He must have a haircut every week or so, every couple of weeks anyway. As if he would feel neglected unless he was being groomed at regular intervals. Neglect is what I dream of. I long for the doctors to find me boring, to give me one almighty pill and say Next please. But my case history seems to be unputdownable. A real thriller.

My grooming standards are way below Buddy's, but perhaps they always were. There's not a lot I can do about that now. If the Princess of Wales was coming to pay me a visit, if she was coming to lay her cool hand on my forehead, stifling her natural desire to say Oh Yuk – I'm with you there, Di – I might even trim my fingernails. But not for Buddy. Fingernails are funny. They're the only part of my body that seems to be flourishing under the new regime. They grow like mad. But the Princess of Wales isn't coming any time soon. I happen to know that now, now as we speak, she's opening a new ward in a newt hospital. A new *wing*.

I think I'm entitled to a home help. I believe that's one of the perks. But I'd rather go on as I am. Buddy told me a story about a man he visited for the Trust – I'm sure he's recovered by now, ha ha – whose mother was jealous of his home help. Just for that, she said, just for Slim?

I couldn't believe it. I'm still not sure I believe it. But then Buddy explained that the mother was eighty-five, and when her son started saying, Sometimes I feel better but I never feel well, she must have thought, What else have I been saying all these years, fat lot of attention you gave me.

I think Buddy was making again the valuable point that getting Slim only involves being exiled from the young, the well, the real.

Buddy is always offering to wash up, but I'm happier when I don't let him. He doesn't do a great deal to help me, in practical terms, anyway. Tessa next door changes my sheets and does my washing, and Susannah still expects to hear my dreams, even the grim ones. It was Susannah who first suggested Buddy. She felt I was cutting myself off from real kin, that even if I was saying the same unanswerable things, Buddy would return a different echo. I even suppose she's right. I've earned my friends, but Buddy I seem to have inherited, though God knows from who, and whether he served them well.

I sometimes talk to Buddy as if he was the whole Trust gathered in one person. I'll say, My father says you're not reaching him. Why are your collection-boxes massed in London? Why do you insist on appealing to an in-crowd?

But then I let him off the hook and say, Mind you, my mother thinks that anyone collecting for Slim research in Eastbourne or Leamington would get a few swift strokes from a rubber-tipped cane, if nothing worse. And my father chooses to give love and money direct.

Cutting out the middleman, says Buddy. He smiles. He doesn't have a Trust collecting box, of course. I'm not sure I've ever seen one. In fact, on this visit he's brought me a package. It's in a plastic bag, and it seems to be a foil container with a cardboard lid, and foil crimped down around it. I'm very much afraid it's food.

I've fed Buddy once or twice, used a shopping voucher and prepared a simple but exhausting lunch. Those times it has seemed to me that Buddy eats suspiciously little. I mean, he eats more than I do, he couldn't not. And I'm not the best judge of healthy habits. But somehow I expect an earthier appetite. It's certainly true that a little company at table can make me eat more than I usually do, without even noticing, while any sort of greed will inevitably sicken my stomach. So does that mean Buddy is obeying another mysterious Trust directive, and suppressing his true eating self? Perhaps he filled up with food before he came, or perhaps he's going to dive round the corner the moment he leaves, and into a burger bar. Before he leaves I open my mouth to say, Here's some money for your real lunch, but I manage to close it in time.

And now he's returning my hospitality. Go on, he says. Open it. You don't have to eat it now. It'll keep good for a few days. Not that it contains any preservatives.

He has written a few deprecating comments about his cooking on the lid of the container. There's no wishing it away. I edge up the rim of the foil and see inside a startlingly pure green. On the green lies a row of small cigars.

Fresh lamb sausages, he explains, with mint and parsley, on a bed of green pea purée. An old family recipe, that appeared quite by chance in last week's *Radio Times*.

I lower my nose over the container and breathe in the smell, trying to think that it is a bouquet of flowers that I must express thanks for, from someone I like and want nothing to do with, rather than a plateful of food that will stiffen in the fridge unless I am stupid enough to eat it, in which case I will most likely be sick.

Thanks. Can you put it in the fridge for me?

But Buddy has more to say about his choice of recipe. They're skinless, he says. I thought that would be easiest for you.

He's right, of course, with my teeth the way they are now. But I'm sure I haven't complained, I'm sure I haven't moaned to him. Perhaps my habit of dipping biscuits in my tea – not to be looked for in a man of my class – is a dead giveaway to a seasoned Trust volunteer. Next time I feel the need to dunk a digestive I'll be more discreet. I'll do my dunking behind closed doors.

The doctors are trying to save my teeth at the moment, and the last time I went to pick up some prescriptions they were being altogether too merry, it seemed to me, about the dosage that would do the trick; 200 mg, one of them was saying, that sounds about right. And the other one said, Yeeeees, in a kind of drawl, as if it wasn't worth the trouble to look it up.

Buddy is still expecting something from me. Thanks, I say again. That looks very nice. Yum yum.

Kid gloves are better than surgical gloves. Perhaps I should say that to him. That would give him some job satisfaction. I'm sure that's important.

Buddy puts his present in the fridge and heads for the door. He stops with his hand on the handle and asks me if there's anything I want, says if I think of anything I should phone him, any time. He always does this on his way out, and I suppose he's apologizing for being well and for being free to go and for being free to help or not as he chooses. There is nothing I want.

He clatters down the stairs. I remind myself that he clattered up them, so there is no reason to think he is moving as fast as he can and is planning to put a lot of space between me and him, now that his tour of duty is over.

I could check, of course, if I move to the window. I could settle my mind. I could see whether he skips along the road to the Tube, or whether he's too drained to do more than shamble. Maybe a trouble shared is a trouble doubled.

I try to resist the temptation to go to the window, but these days it's not often that I have an impulse that I can satisfy without asking myself whether I can afford what it will cost me. So I give in.

Buddy is moving methodically down the street, not rushing but not dawdling either, planting his feet with care like a man walking into a wind. I know that when I tear out and spend one of my shopping coupons and go out on to that street, I look like a man walking into a wind tunnel. I can see it in the way people look at me.

I look down on Buddy as he walks to the Tube. In the open air the mystique of his health dissipates, as he merges with other ordinarily healthy people. No one in the street seems to be looking at him, but I follow him with my eyes. There is something dogged about him that I resent as well as admire, a dull determination to go on and on, as if he was an ambulance-chaser condemned always to follow on foot, watching as the blue lights fade in the distance.

An Executor

Adam Mars-Jones

Of course the flat was empty. Gareth made noise on the stairs and crunched the key harshly into the lock, as if he had just bought the flat, and wanted the lock to know all about it. No one on a simple errand, no one who felt that his right to be there would go uncontested, would go to such trouble to avoid seeming furtive.

His business was with the bedroom, but he turned lights on in the flat generally, so that the lighting pattern as seen from the street would express matter-of-fact occupation rather than a late-night lightning raid on an intimate chamber.

It was unlikely that anyone was looking at the building, which was in poor condition and had an untenanted air. When in recent months an old friend of Charles, full of good wishes but not quite brave enough for a visit, sent a bunch of flowers instead, the delivery squad returned the bouquet to Interflora, saying that a mistake had been made: the property was derelict. Charles passed this story on almost with amusement. He was spared the irony of physical decline in immaculate surroundings.

Gareth made a tour of the flat, putting off his errand. He was used to running errands: that was one of the reasons he had been installed in Charles's life. But this errand was a little different. The rooms looked unfamiliar with the central lights on; Charles had favoured softer lighting, from table lamps fitted with bulbs of modest wattage.

The sofa was still overlaid with a laminated tablecloth, for the benefit of Charles's cat Leopold. Charles had become expert at what he called 'riding the symptoms', blotting out all the reasons for misery and concentrating on something he was looking forward to, even if it was only a broadcast on Radio 3, two days distant, that he was planning to record on tape. He could keep depression at bay on his own account, but he couldn't extend the same service to Leopold, who responded to negative emotion by pissing on the sofa. So Charles would prepare for bad patches by covering the sofa with a waterproof tablecloth, and Gareth had learned that the placement of the tablecloth was the best indicator – indirect as it was – of Charles's state of mind.

The more orthodox place for Leopold's toilet was a long wooden tray, like a shallow unpartitioned knife-box, that fitted into a recess just inside the kitchen door. Gareth glanced at it. The shavings of impregnated wood that filled it were still swollen with urine, although Leopold had already been in Haywards Heath for a few nights, with Charles's parents, where by Christmas – Gareth couldn't help imagining – his name would have been simplified or changed altogether.

Leopold's routine with his box was to climb regally in and turn right round – he was no small cat, and the manoeuvre was far from simple – so as to face the room. Being so near to the kitchen door, he could in fact be seen from most of the sitting-room. Charles would always stop what he was doing, even if he was in mid-sentence or on the phone, and lock eyes with Leopold. Excretion in cats involves the hoisting of the tail and the adopting of an intellectual expression. Charles, who found even the word 'cat' consoling and would sometimes say it a number of times in a row, got pleasure from watching Leopold at his business. Leopold's blink rate accelerated a fraction, but he showed no other sign of self-consciousness. He never failed to turn round again, through a full circle, to survey the reeking wood scrolls, with the calm of a master diplomat – a diplomat retaining his composure when served with a hideous local delicacy. Then he left the box, with just the token backward paw-scrape in passing of an indoor cat, who has never in his life had to regard the burying of waste as a serious feline project.

Gareth wondered why Charles took such pleasure in spying on Leopold's visits to his box; perhaps because this was his pet's nearest approach in the day to a moment of embarrassment. If shame got no purchase on Leopold then, it never would.

Even the most earthbound moments of Leopold's day took place on a plateau of calm self-absorption that Charles was unlikely, in his day, to achieve, however rich the pickings on Radio 3. Gareth hoped this thought never occurred to him while he watched his cat at squat, blinking slowly back at him. But envy must have been a factor in his watching, since the contrast between Leopold's unforced motions and Charles's own, which called for a large plastic bag full of dressings from Clinic every fortnight, was very great.

Moving from that corner of the kitchen, Gareth had an urge to inspect the freezer compartment of Charles's fridge. He had set himself the task of clearing it out about a month previously, and had got to work with his fingers, with a knife, and finally, without much more success, with fingers, knives and a kettle. It was not the simple enterprise it had seemed at the beginning. He had suggested it because it seemed less servile than doing the washing-up, which Charles apparently found embarrassing and which in any case only amounted, these days, to a couple of cups and small plates. Cleaning out the freezer compartment was a more ambitious programme, but one that ran no risk of imprinting his personality on the kitchen in a way that Charles might find jarring.

It might even stimulate Charles's hunger to have the

various freezer treats and Lean Cuisine delicacies that friends had brought him liberated from their moraine of crusted ice, where they looked as appetizing as mammoths in a glacier. Gareth brewed a pot of tea and started work, kneeling in the cramped space of the kitchen.

Leopold started pestering him from the moment he opened the fridge. Leopold could grasp the idea of food, and even the idea of food-not-his, but the idea of removing food from a box and returning it a few minutes later was clearly beyond him. Charles moved a chair to the corner of the kitchen and sat there with Leopold held in his lap, but Leopold wouldn't stop squirming, with a violent patience that suggested he was being gentle with his master, now that their strengths were so nearly equal.

In the end Charles took him to the window and pushed him out on to the window-box, lowering the window to leave only a crack open, through which Leopold tried to thrust his head until the skin of his face was pulled back, and his eyes were turned into vertical stripes hidden among his other markings.

Some of the ice in the freezer compartment was granular, as if it had formed from frost, while other parts – particularly between the top of the freezer compartment and the fridge proper – were clear and smooth. Neither type was particularly easy to dislodge, though the granular was attractive while he worked away at the smooth, and the smooth held the promise of a sudden breakthrough, a major yielding of encrustation, which seemed unlikely while he was scraping at the granular.

Watching Charles slumped in his chair, even without Leopold's tiring presence, Gareth knew he was longing for the bed. His bed was the natural home for the day's troughs: sitting in a chair was peak activity, not to be sustained beyond a short period. Gareth fell back for a moment from his relationship with Charles into routine, into pity, until he was recalled by the intervention of his knees, which were hurting, and of his hands, which were numb with cold where he hadn't burnt them on the kettle. He himself was dying for a sit-down, and would look with favour on any proposal that entailed slumping on a bed.

He prepared to make the suggestion himself, but a minor breakthrough in the ice-face forestalled him. A cylindrical fragment of ice from near the back came free. Then he saw that it was a small vial, of something that remained perversely liquid even at these temperatures. The label was bleached and faded as well as encrusted with ice, but the name of the product seemed to include a stylized lightning bolt. He looked enquiringly at Charles, who chose that moment to gather himself for the walk to the bed, without meeting his eyes.

The phone rang, and at that point Charles did look round, to signal his unwillingness to answer it. Gareth thrust the little bottle back in the freezer compartment, and picked up the phone.

At one stage, Charles had taken to letting the phone ring, or unplugging it from the wall. His parents had accepted this practice meekly enough, but his friends had overruled it. Phoning each other up for news, they touched up their worry until it became chronic. Then one of them would volunteer, or be deputed, to call on him at the flat. Charles was encouraged to feel that cutting himself off from those with a claim on him was a permissible stratagem for the worst hour of a bad day, but not for a bad day in its entirety.

Having Gareth screen his calls, when the phone rang during one of his visits, was a luxury that even Charles's friends would be prepared to accept. In practice, though, however much he shrank from the phone when it rang, he always interrupted Gareth's mumbled explanation that he didn't feel up to talking. He would reach across for the receiver and start to speak with a tiny new access of energy.

The voice on the phone this time was rich and smooth. The phrase *rich and dark, like the Aga Khan* arrived in Gareth's mind: he had seen it on an old advertisement in an antique shop, used to promote Marmite or Oxo or Bovril. The voice said only, but with an immense confidence, 'Charles?'

'Who is this please?' asked Gareth. 'Charles doesn't feel like talking.' He was already passing the receiver across, anticipating the little ritual of refusal, then acceptance of the social world. The instrument was between them when the caller announced his name: 'Andrew Gould'.

Charles gave a tight shake of the head, and finished his interrupted journey to the bed. Gareth, caught by surprise at a time when he thought his switchboard duties were over, stumbled through the rest of the message. He promised that Charles would call back when he was feeling better, and hung up.

Charles was now wrapped up in his colourful coverlet, rummaging through a drawer that lived on the floor by the bed, where he kept his collection of cassettes. Gareth knew he should resume his assault on the freezer compartment, but found himself putting it off. He knew that just by sitting there he was silently pressing Charles for comment.

'Shall I let Leopold in?' he asked. The cat was still intermittently trying to squeeze himself into the room.

'Yes, do,' said Charles. Leopold streaked in, but showed no interest in the kitchen. Instead he hopped up on to the bed, and settled in the crook of Charles's knee.

Charles continued to clatter through the cassettes with his fingers. 'Andrew has been away. Not far away, but far enough. In prison in fact. You may have read about him in the Sundays a while back. They put him away for dealing drugs, but he seems to have carried right on. That's what the papers said, anyway. But he's out now.' He held a cassette up, to read its label. 'I broke off with him, years ago now. Wrote him a very sensible letter. For once. Even I could see he was bad news, utterly bad news. So I told him it just wasn't my style of suicide.' He clicked the cassette into the lolling mouth of the cassette player and pressed the button to play it.

'So will you phone him back?'

'Probably.' He leant back against the pillows, lifting Leopold up in a sort of momentary hammock of blankets. Leopold put his claws out for safety, but withdrew them when he was returned to bed level. 'Otherwise he'll only phone back. And I expect he needs help. He always needed help, come to that, help hot and strong, help here and now. But now he may really need it.' He gave a small smile. 'Put it this way. If the virus has missed out on him, it's missed a great opportunity.' A soft wall of music built up behind him. 'And that seems out of character.'

Gareth had not resumed work on the fridge that day; but now he took another look at the freezer compartment. The futile food was still there; ice had grown back to shroud the packets. He reached towards the back, and pulled out the little flask. It was stuck to the back wall, and brought a little ice away with it. He held it up to the light, and shook it gently. There seemed to him something actually obscene about its liquidity at this low temperature, its continued willingness to vapourize if its stopper were pulled, its frozen obedience to desires that had long since, themselves, evaporated.

He had put off his errand long enough. He turned off the lights in the kitchen and the sitting-room, and entered the bedroom. He tried to remember the exact words of Charles's instructions. He was to remove what Charles had described, using a wry all-purpose comic tone that would have done at a pinch for reproducing a Monty Python sketch or a Goons routine, a Gumby or a Bloodnok, as 'kinky relics'. The idea was to spare Charles's mother, the most likely person to clear up Charles's possessions. Responding to Charles's request,

Gareth had to stop himself, there in the hospital, from using the posthumous word 'effects'.

Charles had made these stipulations not as it turned out on his final visit to hospital, but at a time when he had the first bodily conviction of death not far off. Gareth had noted down his instructions, and was all set to carry them out the next morning when Charles telephoned, having rallied in the night to an extraordinary extent. He was discharging himself, and wanted Gareth to contact his mother, who should now visit the flat rather than the ward. She should of course bring Leopold back from his exile.

In his instructions on that occasion, Charles had mentioned a leather waistcoat and some chaps, the leather overtrousers zipping up the inside leg that American motorcyclists had adapted from cowboys, and had had borrowed from them in their turn. There were also two pairs of leather trousers, one of which could be exonerated in the name of fashion. The other, of inferior hide and with a large rip at the knee, had to go. In Charles's sock drawer was a cap that would, apparently, break a mother's heart if found there.

He felt, as he approached the bedroom at last, more guilt even than grief. He felt, too, like a case history from Krafft-Ebing: *Deflections of the Amorous Impulse, Appendix I. A Fetish Burglar.* Perhaps Charles had removed the things himself on his last return from hospital. That would make life a little easier for Gareth, though he could hardly visualize Charles in his weakness making the journey down three flights of stairs, laden with hides, and taking them to a skip, however near to home.

The waistcoat was easy to find in the wardrobe, and the chaps, neatly arranged on a hanger, were unmistakable. Did people say, a *pair* of chaps? Certainly they said a pair of kippers, and that was what the chaps really resembled. They looked filleted, as if they would need to be reconstituted in some way – soaked overnight, say – before they would be of any use. Without legs to fill them out, they looked peculiarly useless and desiccated. They didn't even have the familiar hang of trousers in repose.

Gareth slid them off the hanger and tucked them into his saddle-bag – he had come well equipped – next to the waistcoat. On the next hanger along in the wardrobe were the two pairs of leather trousers. He had no difficulty in discriminating between them, restoring the innocent pair to the rail in the wardrobe and tucking the guilty ones away in his bag.

There only remained the sock drawer and the hat. He located the sock drawer after a couple of false starts, but nothing lurid leapt to the eye. It seemed like an ordinary crate of bananas, he thought unsteadily, no tarantulas any-where. Some of the socks were stridently coloured and others were widowed, but that was the worst thing you could say about the sock drawer. Then a little rummaging dislodged two caps that had been tucked away at the back.

One of them was a tall little cap with a downward-tilted peak, made of a grey felt-like material and modelled on the Confederate uniform cap from the American Civil War. What erotic message might this be sending? The other was of a black shiny material, but more like plastic than leather. In shape it was like a postman's cap, or a traffic warden's. If it had been severely plain, or else adorned with chains or some barbarian insignia, Gareth would have felt confident that this was the object that Charles's mother must not find. But round the brim, every few inches, were little polyhedral buttons that seemed – the light in the bedroom was not good – to be made of trans-lucent red and yellow plastic. These seemed to put it out of the sexual running. It seemed hardly likely that Charles would invest in something so cheap-looking; Gareth remembered him saying that the chaps came from New York, and were good of their kind. But perhaps the second cap's aphrodisiac aura was profound, unaffected by the tackiness of its materials.

Only for a moment did he think of taking them both. That would have been exceeding his instructions, and it somehow seemed important not to take anything unnecessarily away from this bedroom, which was suddenly becoming a museum. He could see, here on a chair, a shirt of his that he had given to Charles, neatly folded and probably never worn by him. Gareth liked the shirt, had talked himself into parting with it on the grounds that its sleeves were too short, but would gladly have gone on wearing it in all weathers with the sleeves rolled up. It had probably been fingered by Charles only for a few moments since Gareth had washed it and handed it over, but it had passed absolutely into Charles's possession. It didn't occur to Gareth to reclaim it.

Likewise in the sitting-room he had seen not one but several books he had lent to Charles. They had been announced as loans and not as gifts, but he couldn't imagine taking them away, not just the one with the bookmark tucked in it, but any of them. Although these rooms would soon be cleared out, perhaps in a matter of days, everything in them was becoming somehow definitive.

He hesitated still between the hats. Then he noticed something else tucked away in the sock drawer. It was a wallet of scuffed black leather, with a zipped compartment for change, on a chain that ended in the sort of spring-loaded clip that the belt-loops on Levi's 501s seemed to feel incomplete without. On the front of the wallet was an emblem in macho embroidery, a yellow-winged eagle with a yellow scroll above it, reading HARLEY-DAVIDSON. He picked it up and unzipped the change compartment. Inside were a receipt from a building society's automatic cash-till and the ticket stub from a dry cleaner's.

This biker wallet was in some way exempt from the embargo that lay over the rest of the flat. Gareth felt free to take it away with him, although he had no real expectation of using it. He didn't tell himself that it was something that might upset Charles's mother; it would do no such thing. In its unfamiliarity it had none of the power to hurt her possessed by Charles's oldest, tattiest shirt. In a sense it belonged with the leather clothes, but they at least had been chosen, or even made, to fit Charles; this had no similar link. They were sombre in their pretensions to masculinity; this was simply preposterous. It was an object designed for rough times and the open road, but destined for a succession of sock drawers, Charles's and now Gareth's, with occasional expeditions to the shops in the high street, and no likelihood of ever coming near a motorcycle.

He came to a decision about the hats. The balance of probability implicated the black cap in sexuality, and cleared the grey. He put the black one in his bag, slipped the wallet into the pocket of his coat, and returned the grey cap to the sock drawer.

Then he remembered a further item of instructions. He was to remove a volume of pornography, which lived under something Indian in the sitting-room. That was all he could remember, the words 'under' and 'Indian'. Under an Indian print? Under an Indian book? He couldn't be sure. At the time he had been too busy making Charles's requests seem ordinary to pay the necessary attention. He had said, in a worldly way, 'It's a brave man who goes on a long journey without destroying his pornography.' The moment he said it, he had realized that it had the ring of a morbid fortune cookie, and he tried to think of ways to take it back, or to transform it into some other kind of statement. But Charles seemed unaffected. Gareth thought that perhaps only people on the skin of misfortune can be encouraged to forget or be brutally reminded, spared by tact or pained by tactlessness. Charles was well below the surface.

There seemed to be nothing Indian in the sitting-room at

all. There was only a limited number of things for an object to be placed under, come to that, and he looked under them all. He hoped that Charles had disposed of the book himself, during his last days in the flat, or else that the hiding-place would be as impenetrable to everybody else as it was to him. This failure to complete his mission made him nervously unwilling to leave. He was able to get moving at last only because his bladder was asking him to urinate, and using Charles's lavatory would have been obscurely a trespass. He turned the lights out, and stumbled down the stairs in darkness. Then the thought came to him that one of the *rugs* in the sitting-room might be Indian. It seemed unlikely that there was anything underneath them, but he had to go back and check, whatever his bladder had to say about it.

The rugs might well have been Indian, but were concealing nothing but dust and cat hairs. By now the demands of his bladder were insistent, and overrode his qualms about using Charles's lavatory.

Yet he was right to be reluctant: he had been able to foresee the other rooms, and prepare himself for Charles's absence from them. The lavatory hadn't entered into his calculations. He was always on his own in that room, after all, so there was no reason to expect any especial sting of absence to be felt there.

Once inside the lavatory he was able to keep his eyes away from Charles's last massive issue of dressings, but there were limits to his self-discipline. He couldn't help expecting the noise of the flush, as it died slowly away, to be replaced by the continuity that Charles borrowed for his life, as it faltered, from the radio. He found himself listening out for an aria, a sonata, or at least a sonorous précis of the events of Act III. He had braced himself to face absence in the rest of the house, but not to have absence sneak up on him here.

After this small fresh climax of loss, he trotted down the stairs with relief, and without any more nagging thoughts about failing exactly to obey Charles's instructions. He had done everything he could. In fact as he left the flat and turned his thoughts to his new destination, a wholly different set of feelings and expectations cut in. He wasn't satisfied, exactly, with what he'd managed to do in the flat, but it was behind him now, and he found himself becoming for a short time at least an altogether more purposeful person, although his errand for Charles was over. Now he was on a different style of errand, one that filled him with a certain anaesthetized confidence.

A taxi was passing the entrance of the building as he emerged from it, and he hailed it. He would not have been particularly surprised if a taxi had been waiting for him at the foot of the steps, the driver patiently reading an evening paper.

He gave the name of a hospital which contained a ward not in theory given over to a particular illness. The secret was not particularly well kept. Children on the main road outside would shout, 'Fifth floor! Fifth floor!' at suitable men visiting the hospital, in hopes of being rewarded with a grown-up's mysterious tears.

In the taxi, he relaxed. He had no fears of being late. He had the strong feeling that nothing could happen without him at the hospital. However unwillingly, he was deputizing, and his authority though borrowed and temporary was real.

He made his way directly to the ward. For once the lift was waiting on the ground floor, and contained no wheelchairs or wheeled baskets of linen. On the fifth floor there was, as always, a notice requesting visitors to ring the bell and wait to be met by a member of staff, but he ignored it. Tonight he could not imagine being challenged. There had been a recent hardening of attitude among the staff, since the popular press had discovered that this floor of the hospital was not a ward at all, but a unique horizontal mine of horror stories, all of them with morals. The patients' notes were no longer hung outside the doors of the rooms, but on the ends of the beds. There was a chance that even the most public-spirited reporters could be deflected, if they had to penetrate the rooms in order to riffle through the notes at the foot of the beds. But tonight Gareth couldn't imagine being challenged, even if no one who knew him was on duty.

He looked through the glass window in the door of Charles's room before he entered. Charles's mother, he could see, was sitting at the side of the bed. She was leaning forward and seemed to be offering her son a last flower, from which, eyes closed and with only the most sluggish movement, he was turning away his head.

Charles had always complained about her failure to grasp the concept of 'treats'. Illness had separated him into two distinct bands of personality, as if illness were a centrifuge and Charles a hitherto cloudy solution. He was now a child who understood affection best in terms of presents, as well as a sophisticated adult, with an adult's full-sized contempt and impatience, who knew the child better than anyone else.

Charles had forfeited the idea of pleasure except as episodic, and needed to have emotion properly dramatized in objects. His mother, however, came on her visits to the flat and to the hospital empty-handed, while he hinted with increasing crudity that she could do better. Finally he had sent her down in tears to the hospital shop, to buy something, anything, a potted plant, if she was to have any prospect of exchanging another word with him. After that she performed better as a bringer of trivial gifts.

Only with a great effort of will had Gareth been able to stop himself from bringing presents, but his overriding priority was a different one and he needed to keep himself in a category separate from friendship.

Gareth entered the room and tucked his bag away carefully in a corner, unnecessarily concerned to make sure it didn't tip over and spill its contents. At this range he could see that the object in Mrs Hartly's hand was an oxygen mask, though he hadn't been mistaken in thinking that Charles was slowly turning away from it. She would follow him with it as he turned, until he arrived at the end of his neck's reach and turned back towards her again. She would follow his head with the mask as it moved slowly back towards her. Charles's gesture much impressed Gareth, being both instinctive and opposed to survival. It seemed to show a sort of vegetable will, as though a flower was turning consistently away from the sun.

Gareth was acutely aware that Charles was badly shaved, with crumbs of stubble in some areas of his face and sore-looking patches elsewhere, and that this bad shave was his doing. It had been the first and last time he had shaved Charles, the day before. As a wet shaver himself, he had failed to get the measure of Charles' electric razor. He had failed too, or so he assumed, to give Charles a sense of himself as groomed.

Charles's mother turned her head to see Gareth, without loosening her grip on the oxygen mask, and without any real change in her expression. She reacted as if he was returning after a short absence; she incorporated him directly in her preoccupations. 'He won't wear this,' she said submissively, indicating the oxygen mask. 'He won't keep it on his face. I put the loops round his ears, but he just shakes it loose.' She seemed to be asking for guidance.

Gareth felt uncomfortable with any approximation to the role of adviser, since he would not have enjoyed having her hear the advice he had tendered to Charles over recent months – not advice as such but cumulative suggestions, hints that Charles should keep an open mind on some issues (but only in a certain way).

He had detected in Charles a suppressed desire, which every fumbling phone call from his mother brought nearer the surface, to backslide into reconciliation with his family.

He was not especially estranged from them in the first place, as such things go, but illness seemed to be a cue, in the popular mind and therefore in his own when tired, to relapse into absolution. People whose ill health could be guaranteed not to dissipate entered a special category so far as their loved ones were concerned, in which without ever apologizing they were forgiven, as if repentance was actually a stage of physical collapse.

Quietly Gareth had opposed this programme. He had pressed Charles to resist a creeping amnesty which came into effect without even being announced. A person with limited energy owed none of it to anyone. Playing Camille was an exhausting role; only a healthy person should attempt it. Being Camille was something else again, and no audience was entitled to watch.

He had kept chipping away with these arguments from day to day, and when Charles finally said, without actual prompting, that he couldn't help having a child's mobility, and a child's strength, but it would be a nonsense to aim at a child's submissiveness as well, Gareth had felt enormous relief.

There was quite enough presumption, he now felt, in the part he had played. He found it impossible, now, to imagine intervening between the two people in the room with him. If he had committed the impertinence of interfering with someone's destiny, perhaps that was only because he was well placed to do it. He had better not compound the impertinence by seeking to advise Charles's mother. He leant over, all the same, to hear her better. He decided that she was speaking so softly in order not to be heard, not by Charles – that must surely be an extinct fantasy – but by the nurses. He found it hard to read her expression, since he had only seen her in extremity and had no idea how she functioned in real life.

'They said he's chain-stoking,' she said. 'What does that mean?'

'It's a type of breathing.' Above the faint hiss of the oxygen mask and its compressor, he could hear a rasping of irregular breath.

'Well, what has it got to do with chains or stoking? At first I thought they said *chain-smoking*, and I almost laughed. Because he never has. As you know.'

Gareth had a reflexive impulse to correct her by rephrasing her statement in a more appropriate tense – 'No, I know he never did' – but fought it successfully. 'I think perhaps it's someone's name,' he said. 'Chain-Stokes. Or perhaps it's two people's names. Chain and Stokes.'

'You wouldn't think it'd take two people to hear someone breathing, would you?'

'No, not even if they're doctors.'

Mrs Hartly winced. She seemed to be upset by the implication that Gareth had found in her joke, that doctors were not necessarily superior beings. He felt the need to backtrack. 'It's a particular sort of breathing.'

'Yes, I can hear that,' she said. She was slow to take his comment as placatory.

'It means there's not far to go,' he said, as gently as he could.

She was quick to take this comment as inflammatory. 'That's not for us to say. It's not up to us.'

This was true, strictly speaking, and certainly served to shut Gareth up. But he couldn't help feeling that two recent events in Charles's life, quite apart from the new breathing, pointed to closure: his being received back into the Catholic Church, and his asking for an obliterating dose of pain-killers.

It depressed him that Charles, having placed no hopes in the shredded safety net of family, should have clutched at two others, faith and anaesthesia. He also felt an emotion almost like pique that the dispositions he had scribbled down in his diary a few weeks previously, at the time of the kinky-relics conversation, no longer applied. The choice of priest to officiate still held good, but Gareth would now have to withhold an announcement to which Charles had given much weight, weight represented by underlined capitals in Gareth's diary: DID NOT DIE A BELIEVER. He felt his custodianship of this not-quite-final testament, this redundant intimacy, as oppressive.

There was a knock at the door, and after a few tactful seconds a nurse came in. That at least was what, a few moments later, Gareth realized had happened. At the time, his attention was so tightly focused, underneath his other preoccupations, on the man in the bed that it didn't immediately occur to him that the soft knocking could have any other source than that body on that bed. He found his head jerking towards the bed, giving him a twinge in the neck. Only when the nurse made her rustling entry did Gareth properly interpret the sequence of events. From the expression on Mrs Hartly's face, she had experienced a similar moment of disorientation.

The nurse's voice was gentle. 'We need to turn him now,' she said. There was a second nurse behind her. 'You can come back in just a minute.'

She spoke directly to Mrs Hartly. 'Do you want us to wake your husband, and Charles's brother?' Gareth knew that Mr Hartly and his son Arthur were being put up in a room down the corridor. Mrs Hartly shook her head.

Gareth led her by the arm along the corridor, to a small waiting-room that contained two old travel magazines and a vase of dried flowers. He waited for her to sit down.

'Sally and Jerome said they'd try to look in later on,' he said. It was meant to sound like a peace offering, though if there was any little rupture between them Mrs Hartly seemed to have forgotten it. His sentence came out, in any case, trivially social.

'Charles has such wonderful friends,' she said. Irony

didn't seem to be in her conversational nature, but still there was something faintly accusing about her tone, as if having friends was just another estranging refinement of her son's personality.

The nurse came back to them. 'You can go back in now.'

The atmosphere in Charles's room had undergone a change. At first Gareth thought that the nurses had opened the window. He looked over at the window, but it was closed. Perhaps they had opened the window and then closed it. Then he realized that the change was profound, and in Charles. His head was turned away from the door, and his eyes were now half open.

Gareth moved round the bed so as to be in Charles's line of vision, if any, but without approaching too closely to him. Mrs Hartly followed him. Charles's half-open eyes gave him a look, a sly look, that was not in his repertoire as a person. Gareth for one was terrified, not of death as it might happen to him, but of whatever had been substituted in Charles's body for the familiar. He found that he was holding his breath. If he breathed at all he was afraid that he would speed up his breathing, breathe faster and faster and then collapse. When he had reached his limit of endurance, he let go his breath. At the same moment Charles too breathed out, breathing out his tongue a little distance as he did so. It took Gareth a few moments to realize that Charles was leaving him to inhale on his own.

Charles's mother grasped Gareth by the elbow but made no nearer approach to the bed. 'I'll get the nurse,' Gareth said. 'No, I'll get the nurse,' said Charles's mother. They stayed where they were. Gareth was very willing to take the cowardly option, but could not at the minute remember which it was. Was it cowardly to avoid being alone in the room with someone who was dying if not actually dead? Or was it brave for either one of them to leave, and miss any possibility of being with Charles at the moment of a vital transition?

He realized that if it was brave to fetch a nurse, it was a bravery that claimed too much status for himself in the event. He had better go. 'I'll go,' he said. Mrs Hartly let go of his elbow but stayed exactly where she was, as if retreating would be a betrayal of her son, but advancing more than she could manage.

On his way out, Gareth noticed that the flap of his saddle-bag had fallen open. He closed it nervously, but dared not waste time by actually strapping it shut.

The doctors' room was empty except for one of the nurses who had turned Charles, in a way that now seemed to have been decisive, to have given some mortal enzyme its signal. She had a cigarette in her mouth and was looking at a list of patients on the wall, their names written in marker-pen on a sort of white blackboard. There was a sponge in her hand, and Gareth couldn't help thinking that she was just about to wipe someone's name out. He knew she might just as easily be changing a room number, or the name of the doctor assigned to a particular patient. Then the appalling idea came to him that she had already rubbed a name out, and that the name was Charles's. He had to check the list for Charles's name before he could speak, and it took him several moments to find it.

Even if she had been about to make some final deletion, the nurse had the grace to put the sponge down, and stub her cigarette out with a single gesture, thumb down and twisting in the ashtray. On the way back down the corridor Gareth tried to explain what had happened, until he realized that the nurse wasn't listening. Either she was thinking of something else, or she dealt with illness on a level deeper than narrative.

Charles's mother was still standing in the same spot, but Charles had moved, in the sense that he could no longer be said to be on a borderline of any description. The nurse walked rapidly to the bed, and closed his eyes. She said, 'It's over. He's gone. He's dead,' leaving a little pause between each version of events, so that the phrases seemed like three separate wedges of increasing thickness, for opening a crack. Then she tried to lead Mrs Hartly from the room.

Mrs Hartly stayed where she was.

'My son,' she said, then cleared her throat. 'My other son. And my husband. They're in room 25.'

'I'll bring them,' promised the nurse. 'But why not come along to the doctors' room, and we'll have a cup of tea.'

Charles's mother almost smiled at the weakness of this lure. 'I'll stay here till they come,' she said.

The nurse went on her errand. Tactfully she ushered Charles's father, and his elder brother Arthur, into the room, and then withdrew. Gareth would have liked to do the same, but found himself installed at the heart of a family group. Mrs Hartly was already talking, saying 'There was something strange about his breathing, and I left the room so the nurses could turn him, and when I came back he wasn't breathing, or he breathed just the once, rather. It must have happened while they were turning him, but they didn't say anything, and I was out of the room. That's when it must have happened.' She seemed to focus her sense of the injustice of the death on its manner and its moment, as if a returned Charles, dying slowly here and now, would have left her satisfied.

Her husband held her stiffly and said, 'It's no one's fault, baby. It would have happened anyway.' But when he had fully absorbed her impulse to cry, he was unable himself to contain it, and then it came round to Gareth. Charles's father stepped sideways from his wife as he started noisily to cry, and reached his arms out wide. Gareth, startled, hugged him, and could see over his shoulder Arthur moving to embrace his mother.

He wondered, and was ashamed but kept on wondering, if he was receiving Mr Hartly's emotion because that way, passed on outside the family circle, it would have no repercussions: if the emotion was to be discharged, rather than expressed. But he himself had feelings to hide, notably his spasm of selfish terror when he entered the room and saw the changed Charles, and he was glad enough to be treated with warmth, whatever its source and exact composition.

The nurse, who had perhaps been watching through the room's square porthole, tapped and came in. On this second attempt she was successful in tempting the bereaved group down the corridor to the doctors' room. This time, Gareth was careful to pick up his saddle-bag, and strapped it shut at last.

Gareth helped the nurse with the kettle and the rituals that devolved from it, the fetching from a cupboard of a carton of milk, the scraping up of the last spoonfuls in a sugar bowl. Even those with no love for tea and coffee as drinks are compelled to admire them, in crisis, as generators of trivial catechism. Gareth established who liked what and how, and how they liked it, and prepared the drinks. Only at the last minute did he spot that the milk, which he had not taken the precaution of sniffing, was floating in small bricks at the top of each cup. Carefully he ferried the cups in convoy to the sink, poured them out and started again. He tried to give the impression by his calm and concentration that he always made a round of dummy cups by way of rehearsal, or that cups of tea and coffee were like pancakes, and the first one always a failure. He thought he could feel everyone's eyes on him, and his hands were shaking by the time he brought a fresh carton of milk from the fridge. When he had finally delivered the hot drinks, he sat back in silence.

'This foul illness,' said Arthur suddenly. 'This bloody illness.' 'It's an awful thing,' said his father, and Mrs Hartly just said, 'Terrible.' Gareth felt nearer to peace than he had been since he had arrived at the hospital. Listening to this moment of acceptance between denials, he could feel almost at ease.

The nurse said in a business-like voice that there was

business to be done, but that this was no time to do it. It was too late at night for a death certificate, so they would have to come back the next day. It made sense to do everything then. 'The best thing you can do is have a good night's sleep,' she said, and made her tone sufficiently prescriptive for them not to protest, as if she was speaking from a vast body of medical knowledge uncontaminated by common sense. As a group, the family went back to Charles's room, and then returned as a deputation to give Gareth formal thanks.

It distressed Gareth to think of the three Hartlys in a huddle in the room where Charles lay dead, discussing forms of thanks. He had an image of them as people wrangling over a tip, for a porter who has carried bags unduly heavy, or unreasonably far.

'You've been so wonderfully kind,' said Mr Hartly. 'We all owe you so much. Living away from London as we do, it hasn't been easy, but it was a comfort whenever Charles said you had paid him a visit. I hope you can come to the funeral. I don't know when it'll be, we'll let you know. But it won't be complete without you. . . I mean, I hope you'll come.'

Again Gareth caught the oddly social tone, and guessed at the reason for it. They were operating under conditions of intimacy without familiarity, trust but no knowledge.

Arthur Hartly gave Gareth a double-handed handshake and his own few words of thanks. It seemed to Gareth from the faint sidelights he had gathered from Charles's conversation that Arthur was a reassuring disappointment to his parents. He had not stuck with either one career or one wife, but they were grateful to him for remaining intelligible in his faults. Charles had baffled even in his virtues.

After the Hartlys had gone, Gareth threw away their plastic cups, predictably full of cold liquid, and the nurse put the kettle on again. Gareth tried to remember if she was called Angela or Eileen. He was too tired to manage it. Was it Angela that had the red hair? If so, this was Eileen. The nurses' schedules changed from time to time, just when he had got used to them, and a new set of shifts, a new set of relationships, would be there to baffle him. On this point he could feel that he had the beginnings of a patient's ritualistic querulousness, demanding that the nurses be the same every night, and three clean pillow-slips before sleep.

He was exhausted. 'Bad day?' he asked.

'Just awful,' she said as she dropped tea-bags in the pot. 'We're all very down. We lost number 11 earlier on. He was twenty-six.' She poured tea without waiting for it to brew. 'That's my age. We're going to have an extra Support Group meeting.' She drank from her cup. 'We need it.'

Gareth blew on the surface of his tea, not really because it was too hot but because he couldn't think what to say. Selfishly he resisted the widening of context from Charles's single death to include other lives and other deaths, and it took him a little while to absorb what the nurse had said.

In the past he had socialized somewhat with nurses, not with this particular batch but with others met in similar circumstances. He had enjoyed the cheap meals in China-town, in restaurants where all the main courses cost £1.50 and the threads of meat hidden among the noodles could have been anything. But he found their taste in entertainment baffling. They loved films, and so did he, but their preference was for the soppy or else for the horrific. After a day at work, dealing patiently with the failures of the body, they enjoyed a romance, in which reality was made up of emotions, and the body only a house for emotion.

But they also favoured brutally violent horror films, which made Gareth sweat and keep checking his watch, waiting for the film to be over. After a day at work, dealing patiently with the failures of the body, they seemed to relish seeing flesh mauled, mangled and generally beaten about, treated as if it was fully as sacrosanct as pizza, and with no one – or at least someone else – to clear up afterwards.

There was a creaking from the door by the lift, and Gareth turned to see Charles's friend Sally, who to judge from her dress had been to a dinner party. 'I'm sorry I'm so late,' she said, 'and Jerome couldn't make it, I'm afraid.'

Gareth had a sudden horrible vision of a long conversation – long even if it lasted only seconds – in which he struggled, against the grain of social reality, to introduce the fact of Charles's death. He tried to say, 'I'm afraid I have bad news,' but that would be usurping the medical style, and it seemed in any case cruel to draw out a long-expected announcement. So he said simply, 'Charles died a while ago.'

Sally burst into tears, said 'Thanks a lot,' with what seemed to him bitter resentment, and stretched out her arms to be embraced. Gareth hugged her, thinking that in her place he would have hugged the nurse, hugged a passing stranger, hugged anyone rather than the person who had passed on the news as he had.

Soon she quietened down, and said, 'I don't know why I'm crying. All the way up the stairs I was saying, 'Please God let him die tonight, please God let him die tonight.' She tightened her grip on Gareth's shoulder, with an appeal that was almost amorous. 'Can I see him?'

Gareth had no authority, and no idea either, but he could see over Sally's shoulder that the nurse was nodding assent. He said, 'Of course,' and then modified that to, 'I'm sure you can, isn't that right, nurse?'

He escorted Sally to the door of Charles's room, and waited outside. He didn't want to look in through the porthole, nor be seen through it. He paced up and down a bit, but the soles of his shoes made startling squeaks from contact with the rubberized flooring, and it seemed sensible to avoid that in a place where the few sounds that weren't sombre were sinister instead.

When Sally came out she said only, 'There'd just better be

an afterlife, that's all.' Already she seemed quite composed. 'Will you call me a taxi?'

The appeal to his gallantry gave him his cue to leave the hospital; without it, he might have stayed there until he passed out. He hadn't thought of making a move, though nor had he given a thought to where he would sleep if he stayed. By leaving the hospital he would be cutting one more fibre in the ganglion of desperate experience that bound him to Charles, and he was grateful to have the rupture disguised by Sally and her errand. He picked up his bag from the doctors' room, and they took the lift down together. He decided, once they had hailed a taxi, that he might as well share it with her, so they travelled together to Sally's flat in Camden Town. Then the taxi took him on home alone.

Gareth had come across one of the few of the city's cab-drivers uninterested in conversation, at a time when he needed distraction and was willing to work for it. He tried what were in theory foolproof openers, about getting the Knowledge, about the inconvenience to the driver of London cabs, hot in summer, cold in winter, awkward turning circle and ruinous price (£15,000 these days, wasn't it?). But the driver seemed willing to give up the prospect of a tip if the loss at least won him some silence.

Finally Gareth gave up, and slid shut the glass compartment between himself and the driver. Leaning against the upholstery, he found himself murmuring the phrase, 'I'm all right,' with different readings and emphases, as if he were giving individual answers to a whole battery of voices – tender, anxious, exasperated – that were asking him how he was.

He was all right. He was thrown back, as Sally's perfume dispersed from the cab, on memories of Charles, and particularly the last part of their kinky-relics conversation. 'Get rid of them for me, would you?' he had said. 'Just throw them away.'

'Well, let's not be hasty,' he had said. 'Wouldn't you rather I gave them to someone who would appreciate them?' In itself this was the weakest of suggestions, prompted only by the primitive need to meet gesture with gesture, to say for instance, 'That'll look lovely in the bathroom, thanks so much,' of a plant that won't live to see the weekend. But he had also felt, and did still feel, that for Charles to throw anything away at this stage of life was in some degree an act of self-rubbishing. He was anxious to prevent that if he could.

'Yes, all right,' Charles said, with the minimum of breath.

'Well, I don't have to. It really is up to you.'

'No, I'd like you to.' Charles's voice was stronger. 'Do what you can, anyway.'

Gareth now felt himself bound by this wisp of a promise. But he recognized that there was such a thing as excess of scruple. When in a dimly lit street not far from where he lived he saw the huge yellow hulk of a skip looming up, he tapped impulsively on the glass and asked the driver to let him down.

It took no great ruthlessness to cast the leather trousers into the skip, among the broken chairs and broken bricks. They were acknowledged to be of low quality, and the tear at the knee made it impracticable to pass them on. The verdict on the cap was no different: heads varied in size to an almost absurd degree, and he had in any case never seen such a cap before, even in Earls Court, so he felt safe in judging its second-hand value as low.

But as he picked it out of his bag to sling after the discarded trousers, something small and heavy fell out of the cap and dangled at the end of a wire. He squinted at it in the poor light. It was a metallic package which he eventually identified as a battery. Wrapped around the first wire was another, ending in a wedge of cardboard the same size as the battery top, with a small raised ring of metal on it, clearly for electrical contact of some kind. Gareth pressed the cardboard against the top of the battery. To his horror, the polyhedral buttons round the cap, red and yellow, lit up and started flashing in a festive sequence, like so many oranges and lemons in a fruit machine, flashing out the good news of a jackpot.

The hat was clearly no item of darkness, but a souvenir of a birthday party in Oxford, or of Mardi Gras 1975. He had chosen the wrong hat. Asked to remove incriminating evidence, he had left the gun and taken away a fruit bowl.

There was no going back for it now. He disconnected the battery, and threw the cap into the far end of the skip. As he walked the short distance home, he excused himself by thinking of his state of mind, and how much stress he had been under, must still be under. If he could find the right word for his state of mind, he could excuse himself. But what was the right description? Was he blank? Hysterically calm? Simply sad? He felt no affinity with any of these descriptions. But if he couldn't name his state of mind, perhaps he was guilty of neglect after all. Still he couldn't do it. Was this the burn-out he had heard so much about? His own responses seemed to him pinched and ungenerous, but he dimly remembered that too as normal.

There remained in his bag the chaps and the waistcoat. There had never been any question of throwing either of them away. Back in his flat, he hid them, but not where he would have hidden a secret thing of his own. They were a secret, but they were someone else's secret, and he put them in a second-order hiding-place. He stowed them under his bed, in other words, and threw there also Charles's keys, which were no secret of any sort, but which he couldn't bear either to throw away or to leave anywhere that he could see them. Not having a sock drawer as such, he put the biker wallet among some shoes that he didn't expect to wear any time soon, so that an interval would pass before it could mug him with memories.

He had assumed that he would fall asleep instantly, but just as he was dropping off he thought *I'm falling asleep*, as if it was something he was dreading as well as counting on; in any case the idea of sleep, solid and specific, for long moments blocked off the thing itself.

Mr Hartly, as promised, gave him due notice of the funeral service. Gareth didn't know the area where the church was, and spent some time trying to find it, losing his sense of direction and failing to co-ordinate reality with the map. He found his failure in this respect entirely galling. Apart from anything else, it was not the sort of confusion that Charles ever felt, and he found himself mourning with an almost ridiculous timeliness the loss to the world of Charles's particular cerebral strengths, that enormous brain laid low by a know-nothing mould. Charles had an unerring sense of spatial relations: he could remember maps, could visualize a route from Johannesburg to Seoul, and could memorize a grammar or a family tree with equal ease. Consequently he displayed a dazzling command of languages, and a mild but definite snobbery which Gareth found dismaying, but would have been unable to imitate – so meagre was his memory for cousins and collaterals – even if he had admired.

Wandering through the streets, with his mental compass starting to spin whenever he thought he had got it fixed, Gareth at last arrived at the church and the funeral. Mr Hartly shook his hand warmly as he made his entrance. Arthur's handshake a few seconds later was even warmer and firmer, and contained an extra squeeze that represented apology. Immediately following the apology was the statement that made it necessary: 'I wonder if I can ask you, my parents and I have been thinking, not to mention the cause of death?' His smile was urgent. In imagination Gareth snatched back his hand from Arthur's with its compounded pressure; but still it remained there, while Arthur continued to mould it to the shape he wanted. Arthur went on to explain that some of the relatives were from the country.

It seemed to Gareth that they might as well have put a trapdoor under his pew and flushed him down into the crypt, as invite him and then, once he had arrived, ask him to suppress his reason for attending. He wondered how far the Hartlys had thought things through. Was he really supposed to use the time, while the ritual part of the event went ahead and before the social element took over, to construct an inoffensive basis for his relationship with Charles? Since people spent a fair amount of time at funerals asking each other precisely how they came to know the dead person, he would have to devise a whole false history. The effect was to isolate him altogether. It was hard not to feel he was himself being treated as a contaminated agent, who must be prevented from infecting the healthy with unwelcome knowledge.

Consequently he looked on the ceremony with a cold eye. It was apparent, for one thing, that there was a tension between the versions of Charles being perpetuated by his family and by his friends. The friends had arranged for an expensive soprano – announced as such by the usher who escorted Gareth to his place – to sing an anthem. She was stationed for effect in the organ loft at the rear of the church, so that when she rose to sing, the people gathered beneath were offered a choice between two diverging identities. They could continue to look ahead of them, and be defined as a congregation attending a rite, or they could shift round in their seats ever so slightly, indulging themselves in a better hearing or an oblique view of the singer, and slide into being an audience at a concert.

The Hartlys and their immediate neighbours continued to face ahead of them. Those friends of Charles who had come up with the combination soprano/Mozart sat sideways in their pews without embarrassment. Most of the people in the

church, as the singing went on, moved slowly out of alignment with the altar, though a handful whose attention was
drawn bit by bit to the organ loft fought the attraction, like
iron filings choosing between two magnets, and turned their
heads to face forward once more.

The Catholics in the congregation stood and sat and knelt
with practised smoothness at the appropriate points in the
service, not needing to be prompted by the priest. The others
were more ragged in their drill, seemingly puzzled by the
artificial informality of the priest's commands, which were
always phrased with the question 'Would you like to . . . ?'
Sometimes he started on a prayer without inviting the
congregation to stand, so that the faithful rose to their feet
and the less well trained wobbled upwards when they had
regained their bearings, and once they were satisfied that
standing was not fervent in itself. For most of the time,
standing and sitting seemed morally neutral activities to
these non-Catholics, and admittedly they were part of a
customary social range: people stood up on formal occasions
when a newcomer arrived, sat down when told to by their
hosts. Kneeling fell outside that range, and so some non-
Catholics contrived a kneel that said 'I don't mean this, I'm
just being polite', leaning forward and resting their elbows
on the back of the pew in front, but bringing their knees no
nearer to the floor. Gareth half-expected to see people crossing their fingers behind their backs as they mouthed Amens
to the prayers, falling back on the less adult way of doing
things and not doing them at the same time. It was an
extraordinary tribute, he thought, to pay to something that
had no power over you.

Less calmly, almost with a twinge of hysteria, he thought
that what with the choice between sitting, standing and
kneeling, plus the errors of rotation introduced by the
soprano, Charles in his box was probably the only person
present whose posture was beyond criticism.

Gareth had the unbeliever's high standards for religious services. It seemed to him that if a funeral service was to be effective as ritual, it required no element of the personal. And if it wasn't effective, then no element of the personal could save it. So when the time came for the funeral address, he was thoroughly prepared to be unmoved. He resented the intrusion of secular consolation into sacred, and although he asked for nothing better than secular consolation this was not a setting in which he could imagine receiving it. He did think it extraordinary, nevertheless, that a man speaking to a large audience on a subject of great interest to them all could offer them a version of the dead man, a roll-call of qualities broken up with small humanizing anecdotes, that sentence by sentence excluded them. It was like a sophisticated effect of theatre lighting, in which a stage-wide dazzle of illumination faded almost imperceptibly to a dim spotlight trained on the speaker, narrowing to black-out.

The priest threw Communion open to all comers, whatever their denomination, saying that all were welcome. This didn't prevent the approach to the altar rail from being an occasion for politeness and deference, the exchange of neutral smiles and the allowing of ladies to take precedence on their way to the Host. But perhaps it inspired the last communicant, a young rockabilly with a quiff and something that clanked on his jacket, or possibly his belt. He sauntered down the aisle just when it seemed that the sacrament was over. Communion was being given in one kind only, but the rockabilly seemed not to have grasped the nature of the set-up. He received a wafer from the celebrant and then stayed where he was, as if there might be more on offer, something perhaps to wash the wafer down. His model for the eucharist was apparently the buffet lunch. He seemed to Gareth the living spirit of try-anything-once as he waited there for service. In the absence of a chalice, he seemed willing to settle for seconds of wafer, brown perhaps as a change from white. The celebrant gave him a look that remained grave and formal, but was nevertheless the nearest possible priestly approach to a frown. The rockabilly returned to his seat with a shrug.

After the service Gareth turned down an invitation to the funeral itself, although the invitation seemed sincere and included the offer of a lift to the crematorium. But it seemed to him that to go any further was to lay claim to belonging to an inner circle of bereavement, and he could not then avoid the question of how he came by so much grief. The fact that he did want to spill his secret, and denounce the little knot of refusals that was to blame for its being a secret, only turned it into an act of virtue not to attend, and so not run that risk.

He went instead to the buffet lunch that Sally had arranged for after the service. There were not many people there when he arrived, perhaps because there was an unstated assumption that people should attend both service and cremation to merit the lunch.

Gareth brewed himself a cup of tea in a kitchen crowded with last-minute preparations; Sally's helpers concentrated on arranging food on plates, and left him largely alone. He strayed from room to room, wondering if by his very cup of tea he was being pretentious about the damage he had suffered, making it look as if he alone was still in shock, in need of hot restoring drinks, and not trusting himself with alcohol. Certainly all the other lunchers, as they arrived, helped themselves to wine from a sideboard or asked for whiskies or gins.

The first person to arrive that he properly recognized was an actress called Amanda (Amanda Pitt? Amanda Palmerston? Something resonant, anyway) with a mane of hair and huge hoop earrings. Gareth moved across to her immediately, hoping she was going to be the person he Got Back this time. It was late in the day to be Getting someone Back, but not perhaps too late. He couldn't help seeing these things

49

in terms of exchange. Otherwise in the assignments he took on he was simply setting himself up for loss. If he could get someone back, establish a friendship with someone he would not otherwise have met, then there was something he could set against the wear and tear. So he had found himself, for instance, gazing across a rain-drenched crowd in Highgate Cemetery at a handsome man crying into the shoulder of a man reassuringly less handsome; or striking up a conversation in a hospital lift with a chain-smoking woman whose visits happened to coincide once or twice with his own.

Amanda seemed to have the makings of the person he got back this time. For one thing, she was wearing with a sort of defiance the hiking boots, brown with vivid red laces, that she had worn when she had done a sponsored walk in aid of research into the illness. Every sidelong glance from the more greyly dressed made her prouder and more vivacious, and she bubbled over with talk.

Gareth was aware of his voice rising in volume, out of its own animation and from competition with the other talkers in the room. He tried to rein himself in, since he and Amanda were breaking almost with every sentence the taboo laid on Gareth by Arthur Hartly at the beginning of the service. There was a sort of satisfaction to be had, or so he found, in defying human pressure, after months spent railing against nature's strong extinguishing push.

At the same time his gaze kept returning, all the time he was talking with bright defiance to Amanda, to Mr Hartly's head bowed down in the act of receiving sympathy, and to the bald eroded hinge where he must always have set his parting. At this distance only pity was operative, a pale wash of background feeling; at closer quarters stronger and more personal emotions would come to the fore.

Gareth's view of Mr Hartly, over Amanda's shoulder, was abruptly blocked by a slackly handsome man in his thirties, who stood there with an air of expectancy and of suppressed triumph of some sort. Idly, thinking that this man was perhaps waiting for an opportunity to chat with Amanda, Gareth wondered what might account for this air of triumph, of vindication. This person must have surprised others by performing some action assumed to be beyond him, and had surprised himself into the bargain. Looking more closely, Gareth thought that the action assumed to be beyond him might well be shaving without help, or at any rate shaving without a shaking hand doing damage to the neck above the bow tie. Gareth was slowly coming to realize that this person was waiting to speak to him rather than Amanda, coming also to feel a strong dislike in anticipation of their talk. The man's face and manner were carefully controlled, but he was like an actor who has played a drunk, night after night, month after month, in a long-running play. A sort of blur had settled on every gesture, and when he spoke, on every intonation.

'Your name is Gareth,' he said, 'and mine is Andrew Gould. Am I interrupting?' Amanda with tact retreated, depriving Gareth of his chance to ask for her phone number, or give her his, and so make sure that he got her back. He called after her that she could reach him through Sally, and she nodded brightly as she moved towards the drinks table.

Andrew Gould was not a possible candidate for getting back. Gareth bristled with antagonism before he had even properly begun to speak. 'I'm one of Charles's oldest friends,' he said, 'and from what I hear you've been very good to him.'

'I'm very glad I met him,' Gareth said.

'Well, I'm grateful to you,' said Andrew Gould, on exactly the proprietary note that Gareth had hoped to deny him. 'I'm one of his oldest friends, but I haven't been able to do as much for him lately as I'd have wished. But we always kept in touch.' He produced from his pocket a weathered postcard bearing a single line of Charles's handwriting in its last, most ragged phase: *I think of you often with much fondness.* 'He sent me this.'

Gareth by now was in a rage of disgust at the crassness of brandishing this postcard after a funeral, as if it was a testimonial. From the smoothness of Andrew Gould's gesture, it seemed that he had produced it more than once already. Beneath Gareth's feeling of disgust was a feeling of betrayal that Charles should have made even so mild an overture after what he had said about Andrew Gould. He buried the feeling of betrayal under the disgust, and then felt the need to work on the disgust also.

His first impulse, of course, was to denounce. But Andrew Gould's bid for status was so shameless that it made any conventionally harsh response seem itself unbalanced. Gareth tried to muster his charitable resources. There was little point in specializing in one brand of misery if it made him sneer at every other sort. There was nothing to be proud of about kicking away someone's crutches and shouting, 'See! You can't stand up!'

The alternative to rudeness was leaving the party altogether. Andrew Gould seemed to have much more to say, and to be beginning to say it, but Gareth affected to catch someone's eye, at the same time thrusting his teacup ahead of him, and then following it as if it had a massive momentum. He murmured, 'I'm late, I'm afraid, I must be going,' while still possibly within earshot.

He coincided with Mrs Hartly just inside the doorway of the flat, and struggled to find something to say to her. 'How is Leopold?' he asked, adding irrationally, 'Charles's cat, I mean.'

'Well, of course he misses his master,' she said meekly. 'I think animals understand so much, don't you?'

'They could teach us a lot,' he said on his way out. It was the blandest thing he could think of to say, but still it had an all-purpose asperity that he would have taken back if he could.

Mrs Hartly wrote him a letter a few days later, a letter that began 'Not being good with words . . .' She thanked him one more time for the help he had given Charles, said she knew he liked music, and wondered if he would care for a tape or a record from Charles's collection.

Gareth had not of course expected to profit in any way from being assigned to Charles, but had visualized things in terms of the non-acceptance of a piece of furniture, perhaps an antique mirror he had always liked, with a pelmet and little velvet curtains, rather than the non-acceptance of a record or a tape. He had the feeling that his stake in the mourning was being scaled down, though if he put his mind to it he could make a case for his deprivation being the more intense. Everyone else, after all, had memories of Charles that antedated the illness. They at least had good years to set against the bad, and a mellow auditing of accounts to hope for.

In practice, he knew that things didn't work like that, not for anybody. With the person gone, the memories attached to the person died their own small sort of death. They had no independent existence, any more than Christmas tree lights had a function when the Christmas tree was gone. Sooner or later they had to be tidied away. Gareth wrote to Mrs Hartly saying that he had never had much time for contemporary music, but that listening to Charles he had begun to think that perhaps he should think again, so perhaps – if she really wanted to give him something – a record or tape of contemporary music would be a suitable token. He was a little mortified to hear nothing from her after that.

It distressed him more that Amanda hadn't phoned him. It began to look as if this time he wasn't going to get anyone back. He phoned Sally and asked for Amanda's number, but Sally didn't have it. Amanda wasn't in the directory, certainly not under the name he remembered. He thought of going to the library and leafing through *Spotlight* until he saw her picture, and contacting her through her agent if need be, but that seemed pushy even to him.

He was left with the chaps and the leather waistcoat under his bed. Sometimes while making the bed he would step in a slithering puddle of hide, an unexpected texture which took some moments to identify. He had not abandoned his intention of passing them on to some appropriate party. It didn't seem particularly odd to him to take his obligation so seriously. If gay people like himself and Charles had unacknowledged unions and divorces that made no social echo, it seemed reasonable enough that they should dispose of their property, when they could, in their own way, with by-wills and sub-testaments separate from the public arrangements.

He himself had never found it possible to wear clothes that had once belonged to someone else. He had snapped up bargains once or twice in Camden Passage or the Kings Road, and not been able to bring himself to wear them, once he had got them home. And yet here he was, proposing to find a new owner for a dead man's sexually implicated clothing. He had argued himself into finding this reasonable. It was partly that leather was non-porous rather than porous, and might be assumed to take on less of its wearer's substance than a textile would. One of the belt-holes of the chaps was a little ragged, true, and had lost its ring of metal reinforcement. But the clothes were impregnated, as it turned out when he sniffed at them, with no essence more carnal than mothballs. But beside that, it seemed to him that black leather could not take on associations because in some way it *was* associations. Even its practicality was largely a matter of symbolism: a leather jacket didn't keep its wearer dry in wet weather, it just turned him into a person who found an umbrella's protection insulting. Leather was less a fabric than a set of meanings. To sum up: anyone who bought black leather was buying its image, and made no addition to that image during his ownership.

The new owner would have to be slightly built, like Charles even in his prime. Gareth tried the waistcoat on, idly, for size, and found it was taut across the back even if he kept his shoulders hunched together. He made no attempt to try on the chaps, which would have been much too short as well as tight at the waist and in the leg.

As a volunteer, Gareth was entitled to a month off after a death. It seemed like a macabre bonus for seeing someone off. There were regular support-group meetings for volunteers, and he supposed he should give them another try. When he had first heard about these meetings, he had assumed they would be events in the style of encounter groups, and had thought that on balance he would rather be traumatized than embarrassed. But he went along, and as he came to want something from the meetings, he began to think that a little psychobabble would come in handy. There was something about the phrase used at these sessions, 'Any other business?', that failed to draw out confusion and trouble. There was, admittedly, an elderly man in a corner who remarked, at every meeting Gareth had attended, that the Chinese ideogram for *crisis* combined the ideogram for *danger* and the ideogram for *opportunity*, but he found he didn't warm to that approach either. His attendance had never been regular.

More promising than the prospect of exorcizing his difficulties in front of his equals was the hope of showing off his competence, to someone who would be impressed by it. At one time new recruits for voluntary work had gone for weeks, or even months, while waiting for their rudimentary training – a baffling medical lecture, some tips on law and social services, a few bouts of simulated counselling – without contact of any sort from the organization to which they had pledged their time. This had happened to Gareth. A new arrangement was now being tried, whereby a new volunteer was assigned to a seasoned one, whose job was to make the newcomer feel he belonged, even before the baffling lecture, the tips and the counselling.

To date he had only talked on the phone to Adrian, the young man assigned to him. On these occasions he greatly overplayed his *savoir-faire* and expertise. He didn't deny, in fact he strongly emphasized, that this was an area where no one had any answers, where there were only degrees of amateurism: you couldn't hope to do no harm, you could only hope to do less harm than good. But the absence of answers could also mean that everyone had an equal claim to be considered an expert, and a little experience could be made to go a long way.

He had been startled when it had come out, in the course of one of their conversations, that Adrian was only a year younger than himself. He had assumed a much larger gap between them, though this imagined gap was only in part chronological. It was as if there was a death virginity over and above the regular one, and those who had lost it looked on those who still had it with envy, and no inclination to take them seriously.

His own losing of the death virginity was made more definite by the way he had seemed to seek it out. He met death half-way, if that was ever a possible way of meeting death.

But this time he thought that he and Adrian should actually meet. He hoped to benefit from this himself, but passed it off as a favour to Adrian, who seemed pleased and even flattered. Perhaps he had wanted a meeting earlier on, but had been shy of suggesting it. 'It's like having a substance when you arrive at school,' Adrian said, rather fancifully, 'you know, an older boy to show you around. Substances and shadows.' Privately Gareth thought that this was a school where the old lags were more shadowy than the new boys, where it was exactly substance you lost as you learned.

Between them they agreed on a place to meet, a newly opened coffee shop run as a co-operative and radiant with correct attitudes. Just before he rang off, Gareth asked Adrian what he looked like. He didn't really think they would find it hard to locate each other, even in a gay milieu where everyone had a generalized alertness to signals, and everyone looked expectant most of the time; but he was feeling a late-flowering curiosity about Adrian, now that he was about to be more than a voice on the phone.

'Well, let's see,' said Adrian. 'I'm not tall and I'm not fat, in fact I'm definitely on the skinny side. And I've got red hair. And I'll be wearing a leather jacket. Will that do?'

That would do. Gareth felt something almost like excitement. Here was his chance to scoop up the waistcoat and chaps from under the bed, and to set about finding them a new home. It seemed to him that no one could be offended by the offer of a leather waistcoat; he had noticed them being worn as fashion items by a number of men, of no particular denomination. Then, when the waistcoat had prepared the way, it would be possible to ask a question about chaps, a trickier question admittedly but a safe one, he thought, in the atmosphere of good will by then prevailing. He realized that it was perfectly possible that he would still be curator of the chaps at the end of the day, but he had high hopes of seeing the back of the waistcoat.

He arrived at the café ten minutes early and sat sipping a coffee, wondering if its high price represented a radical policy of paying food workers a living wage, or a further tired attempt to milk the pink pound. His attention was caught by something at the edge of his vision, and he turned his head to catch a glimpse of a man with a cruelly foreshortened arm, a neat row of fingertips arranged where an elbow would have been expected, trotting downstairs to the basement. He was shocked and embarrassed by this evidence that underneath his relaxation, his air of being different and accepting difference, he was constantly patrolling the boundaries of the normal.

He was still more shocked when the man returned from the basement, where the lavatories were, advanced towards him, smiling, and was Adrian. Adrian explained that he had been afraid he was late, and had run the last part of the way. Hence his sweaty face and hence also, Gareth assumed, the leather jacket draped over his arm rather than worn, as he queued in his turn for coffee.

Separate detonations of social shame combined to produce a firestorm of embarrassment in Gareth. For one thing, it shamed him that his first reaction was brute disappointment that Adrian was not after all going to take Charles's legacy of leather off his hands. In second place, he bitterly regretted having asked someone with a deformed arm to describe himself so as to be recognized, forcing him to crank through a whole series of redundant distinguishing characteristics, to produce a self-description of what must have seemed enviable anonymity. Then too he was ashamed of the thought that occurred to him when he realized that this was Adrian: *your disability will be a real asset when you're dealing with people who are so sick. You'll be such an example to them.* There seemed to him to be something wrong with this thought in logic, as well as in feeling, and he filed it away for worrying at on a later occasion.

Adrian, meanwhile, was very much at his ease, and so by degrees became Gareth. Adrian's little fingers began to fascinate and, oddly, to charm him. He tried to find a way of both watching them and not watching them that wasn't a furtive stare, but Adrian had perfected a calm that imposed no conditions. Without showing off exactly, he demonstrated the dexterity of his fingerlets. Having torn the top off a sachet of brown sugar crystals, for pouring into his coffee, he folded the sachet, using only his fingers, into a delicate pleated concertina. He watched his fingers, as they worked, with a cool appreciation shared with a greater warmth by Gareth, also watching. It was only when they were narrowly defined as fingers, Gareth thought, that they must be marked down. As toes, which they more closely resembled, they were clever and extraordinary.

'I think I'll train for the phone lines,' Adrian was saying. 'I'm not brave enough to do that sort of thing face to face. I don't know how you do it. Of course I may turn out to be too much of a coward even for the phones. I may end up stuffing envelopes. Making cups of tea.'

Even before Adrian had disqualified himself from doing voluntary work face to face, Gareth had puzzled out why he would in fact be at a disadvantage. Someone like Gareth could offer someone like Charles company, and a sort of queasy second-hand knowledge. He could offer advice, not all of it useless, not all of it stupid, and get in return a look that said, unmistakably, 'easy-for-you'. It was an important part of his assignment to receive that look; Adrian would inhibit it. But more than that, people like Charles had to develop a ramshackle, post-Modern bravery, that had nothing in common with previous braveries except purpose: a series of bargains from a position that ruled bargains out. Adrian's all too traditional version of the virtue would be disheartening and even irrelevant.

He was distracted from these thoughts, and still further from what Adrian was actually saying, by the passage past their table of the café worker who had served them their coffee, now wearing black rubber gloves and carrying a tray of dirty crocks. His expression was seraphic, as if this cyclic demotion - the co-operative workers performed all the tasks in turn – was freighted with revelation, like a king's visit to the abattoirs that supplied the royal kitchens. But Gareth could only be reminded, by the rubber gloves, of the cleaning staff in what he would continue to think of as Charles's hospital until it acquired another set of associations. The cleaning staff had been robust and cheerful, but had not come close to the bed, perhaps for fear of disturbing Charles. They had spent a lot of time polishing the radiators.

Adrian was still talking. He had moved on from material that was familiar to Gareth, about how he came to volunteer, to an interrogatory note that forced him to focus. 'Why do you do it? You personally. Have you . . . lost somebody? Perhaps I shouldn't ask.' His voice became hesitant and tactful.

Gareth floundered. 'No. I haven't. I don't know.' He shifted his coffee cup and adjusted the little vase next to it, which contained a single tiger-lily. 'I heard once, maybe it was on the radio, that you should never run uphill from a bear. A bear's front legs are short, you see, so it can run even faster up a slope than it can on the flat. But going downhill, a bear has real problems.' This was turning into an unenlightening anecdote. 'That's what you should try to do. Run downhill.'

'Never run uphill from a bear,' said Adrian. 'Right, I've got that. How does that help?'

'Well, I just think . . . people try to escape from this thing in the obvious way. Run uphill. You have to do something different. You have to walk right up to it.'

'Run downhill from it, you mean.' Adrian was doing his best to help.

'Well, yes.' He gave a snort in spite of himself. 'I haven't worked out a method of doing that yet. So in the meantime I walk right up to it.' He had to admit, now that he was trying to rationalize his position, that it held no particular water. If it was irrational to think you were immune from disaster as long as you ignored it, it was irrational in a different way to go right up to a slow terrible bear that nobody knew anything about, and think you could buy a little safety on your own account, just by surprising it for a moment.

'Perhaps you could blow up its nose,' Adrian suggested.

'You know, like animal-trainers do. Breathe up its nose and tame it.' By now Gareth was wishing he'd never mentioned bears in the first place. He should just have said that yes, he had lost someone, when Adrian asked. That way he would have seemed a little more heroic, and a lot less confused. 'Rather you than me,' Adrian was saying. 'I think I'll stick to the phone lines. That's close enough.' He picked up his leather jacket and shrugged himself into it. 'Wish me luck.'

'I'm sure you'll be good at it.' Gareth was being more than merely polite. But being attached to the same organization, while it encouraged camaraderie, ruled out real friendship, and Adrian didn't quite qualify for getting back. People needed to feel the same downward suction to have the same need to claw themselves upwards and out.

Gareth shouldered his saddle-bag with resignation. When he got home he slung the whole bag under the bed, without bothering to unpack it. He tried to forgive himself. Even at his point of maximum embarrassment with Adrian, he had at least not actually mentioned the waistcoat.

The saddle-bag was still under the bed when the phone rang two days later. A voice said, 'You don't know me,' in a way that was embarrassed rather than sinister. 'But I'm the friend of a friend.'

'Go on.'

'He's abroad at the moment, is Andrew, but there's something he asked me to find out.'

'Who is this Andrew?'

'Andrew Gould. He was a great friend of Charles Hartly, as I'm sure you know, and he needs to know something about Charles's estate.'

Gareth was puzzled. 'I'm not a lawyer, you know.'

'Yes, I know.' The voice cleared its throat. 'But there are things that belonged to Charles that Andrew thinks won't have been dealt with by lawyers. He thinks there may have been special arrangements.'

'What sort of things?' Gareth had a dim idea.

'Some clothes.'

'Go on.'

'Some leather clothes.'

'And?'

'Charles wanted Andrew to have them.'

'How does he work that one out?'

'Pardon?'

'I said, how does he work that one out?'

'Well, they were old friends.'

'And how about you? Are you an old friend of Charles's too?' He couldn't stop himself from sounding bitter.

The voice hesitated. 'No.'

'Did you know him at all?'

'I met him.' The voice was defensive. 'Look, I don't know why you're being so heavy about this. It's got nothing to do with me. I just said I'd ask a question.'

'All right. Ask your question.'

'Do you know anything about what I'm talking about?'

Gareth found himself unable to lie. 'Yes.'

'What do you know?'

'I know that Charles had some leather clothes. And I know he asked me to dispose of them for him.'

There was a short silence. 'So . . . have you got them?'

The conscientious part of Gareth, a part unaffected by anger, took over. 'I got rid of a pair of trousers and a cap.' He stopped himself from going into details about the mistake with the cap. 'I still have a waistcoat and a pair of chaps.'

'Well, that's something. Andrew will be pleased to hear that.'

'But what makes you think he has a right to them?'

'I told you, Charles wanted him to have them.'

'I don't think so. He asked me to get rid of it all. And I said, Why not give it to someone else instead? And he said, Fine.'

'So it's up to you, is it?'

'It seems to be, yes.'

'Well then, Andrew has rights. Charles wanted him to have them.'

'You keep saying that.' It maddened him to be dealing at so many removes: in the first place with the husks of a dead man's obsession; with the friend of a friend, perceived by him as an enemy, and in any case through an intermediary; with a voice on the phone. But still with live issues of loss and possessiveness. 'You haven't said anything to convince me yet.'

'They were old friends. They had been lovers. They went back a long time. And they bought that leather together.'

Gareth had a mad impulse to ask for the receipts. Then he gave up. 'Then perhaps he'd better have it. But not because Charles wanted him to have it, because he didn't. Because he let me decide, and it might as well go to Andrew as anyone else.' He managed to suppress the surname, to grant Andrew at least the bare minimum of status. 'Not because Charles wanted him to have it.'

'He'll be pleased to have it anyway. Should I tell him to phone you when he gets back?'

'No. You started as a go-between, you may as well carry on.' His voice softened in spite of his instructions to it. 'I'd like you to. Tell me when you want to pick up the stuff. But make sure you tell him . . . ' He didn't finish the sentence. He realized by now that any attempt to stamp the gesture with his meaning, and no other, was more in the nature of a murder than a resurrection.

A Small Spade

Adam Mars-Jones

Bernard adjusted quickly and well, so well in fact that he began to think it said something rather odd about him. Or perhaps it was something to be proud of. After he had met Neil a couple of times, he told friends that he was willing to act as a support group for this sweet-seeming stranger, this so young stranger, so far from home. He also said that if you were going to offer support, it might as well be to someone you fancied. Then he started to cut down on the self-mocking pronouncements altogether, partly because he was seeing less of his friends, and more of Neil.

The circumstances of their meeting smoothed the adjustment. The place was a pub in Nine Elms which hosted an evening, every two weeks, for people who had been exposed to a virus. The great advantage, of course, was that the subject of illness, or potential illness, could be taken for granted and need never be mentioned, except where the context demanded. It could also be taken for granted, human nature permitting, that no further risks would be taken by the people who gathered there.

Consequently it was Bernard who needed to do the explaining. When it came up in conversation that he was negative in the matter of antibodies, he felt almost exposed as a fraud, as if he had been caught stretching his legs after sitting in a wheelchair, explaining feebly that there had been nowhere else to sit. In theory, those evenings were for anyone who put a high priority on healthy sexual living, but Bernard thought he could detect a whiff of disapproval – not from Neil – for the relatively assured future which branded him as not a serious person.

Neil was from New Zealand, very tall and young enough to make Bernard uneasy, twenty-four as against Bernard's thirty-two. He had been told of his antibody-positive status two months before his projected trip to London, and had not let it upset his plans. He wrote home more regularly than he would have otherwise, that was all, or that was what he said was all. He made sure that he didn't look any skinnier, in the photos he sent back to his parents, than his naturally skinny self.

Bernard found Neil's calm eerie, and guessed that Neil found his awkward animation wearing. But he took the trouble to write his phone number on the back of a raffle ticket – raffles for relevant charities were a big feature of those evenings – and to tuck it into the back pocket of Neil's jeans as he left. An absurdly elevated pocket. Neil laughed and went on talking, to a softer, furry-edged person whom Bernard thought was probably much more his type.

He was right in this assessment, or at any rate he learned later that Neil had gone home with this other person; any fidelity in their relationship was likely to be approximate, and that was all very grown-up and reassuring. But Neil had phoned the next week.

At close quarters, once he got to know him, Bernard could see that Neil made more concessions to his doubtful health than frequent letters home; but they were concessions that somehow suited Bernard. If Neil was tired, he lay down and made no apology for it. If he was hungry, he ate right away. Bernard enjoyed this programme of snacks and siestas during the time they spent together. It was never an effort to take a nap, or at least a lie-down. It was odd, but not unpleasant, to be the older man and have the junior energy.

He ate whenever Neil ate, and if he didn't imitate Neil's moderation that wasn't really an issue. Long before this illness had shown up, love affairs had been divided for him into the ones that made you fat and smug, and the ones that made you skinny and neurotic. He was quite content, for a change, to put on a few pounds.

He found Neil's profession harder to adjust to than his compromised health. Neil worked as a hairdresser, and hairdressers in Bernard's mind were necessarily fatuous people, whose fatuousness extended to their choice of lovers. Never mind that he himself had regular haircuts at an establishment which, if not exactly up-market – it stopped short of consultations, conditioner and cups of coffee – charged at least enough money to command respect for those who had earned it. Bernard's prejudice remained. To compensate for it, he announced Neil's profession in conversation far more often than was necessary, as if unless he kept mentioning it he might be suspected of a liaison with a royal duke. This went on until a friend asked, without malice, 'Which hairdresser do you mean, the one who cuts your hair or the one who messes it up?' Bernard found himself blushing almost to the point of haemorrhage, and promised himself to do better in future.

Neil did yoga every Wednesday, with a group of similarly affected people, and swam several times a week. Bernard joined him in the swimming when he could fit it in. Neil had a relaxed antipodean style of crawl, but his stamina was only moderate, so Bernard could outswim him, though not by the same generous margin that he outate him.

Neil's shortness of breath was also noticeable in bed, where it had, again, a reassuring aspect. Hearing his lover's breathing return to normal after climax so much more slowly than his own, Bernard was at least free of fears that he was being sexually humoured. On a purely cardiovascular level, Neil's experience was the more intense.

He worried about Neil, of course, seeing him only two or three times a week, but then worrying had always been the great romantic privilege, and it was a pleasure not to have it resented. He thought that perhaps romance always had a basis in fear; it was just that this time the fear was clearly defined, and external.

Bernard's worry for himself took the form of an increased superficial cherishing of the body. He had begun by shaving more carefully than usual on days when he would be seeing Neil, and put plasters on any cuts he incurred even if the results were unsightly, until Neil confessed to a labour-saving preference for at least a hint of stubble. Now Bernard stayed unshaven on the days of their meetings. His growth of beard was modest, so he could skip a day without particular comment from his colleagues. He was spared the routine questions of whether he was growing a beard, as if that was a matter of educational policy and might be controversial.

Bernard kept his worry within bounds when, as now, Neil was late for a meeting. Neil wore no watch; his character had been shaped to some extent by a late strain of New Zealand hippyism, based round sunshine, cheap dope and free rock festivals in remote areas. Giving up Smoking, with the capital S, when he found that the habit was immunosuppressive, was the hardest sacrifice his new status had yet required of him.

Bernard had bought the tickets for the train, and spent the time while he waited for Neil trying to identify gay couples engaged on the same ritual as himself: the weekend in Brighton. He hadn't himself visited Brighton since he was a schoolboy, and hadn't made an expedition with Neil any further than the cinema. It seemed to him, as he spotted couples mustering for their expeditions, that he could spot at least as many fun-hungry types stepping out of trains from Brighton, intent on the opposite ritual, of getting back in the sexual swim.

70

At last he saw Neil moving towards him, at a pace too slow to be described even as an amble. At first he had found this exaggerated leisure of pace irritating; there seemed to him little point in being an agile man of six foot four if you moved more slowly than someone plump and four foot tall, in a hobble skirt. But gradually he had retarded his own speed of walking, and Neil had slightly accelerated, not so much to meet him halfway as because the cooling air made sauntering less and less rewarding a style of motion. Already in early November there had been days, apparently, as cold as New Zealand ever got, and Neil had a respect edged with panic for the colder months to come.

He was carrying, all the same, only a small nylon holdall. Neil had a flair for travelling light, and had much to teach Bernard, who was ballasted by any number of magazines and library books, in that department. Neil was proposing to tour Europe late in the coming spring with very little more luggage than he was carrying now, and Bernard was persuaded he would manage it. He might even still be carrying the same book, *Grandchildren of Dune*, which he wasn't actively reading but carried as emergency rations, a sort of literary pemmican. His home library was equally basic: *Budget Europe*, *On Death and Dying*, and a grainy-paged paperback of pornography entitled *Black Punk Hustler*.

Any discussion of Neil's European trip, or the possibility of Bernard's changing jobs, or – as they started to trust each other's interest – a party a few weeks off, required the formal closure, originated by Neil but now spoken by either one of them, of the phrase: 'Oh, we'll be well over by then.'

Neil carried his liking for paring things down, for travel-ling light, to the point of naturism. He had found, after a couple of months in London, a couple of swimming pools, one in Stockwell, one in Hornsey, which held weekly naturist swims, for men only. At one of these sessions, Neil had met someone who had subsequently become his land-lord, in the upper reaches of the Bakerloo Line.

Bernard and Neil had agreed to meet at midday, without reference to the times of trains; Neil's strong preference was for relaxation over efficiency. By the time that Neil arrived, a few minutes late, they had in fact missed the first train of the afternoon; they would have to wait half an hour for the next one. Bernard was a little irritated, in a way that gave him fresh evidence of the satisfying disparity of their temperaments, and looked around for one of the espresso-and-croissant stalls that nowadays brightened some of London's main line stations. Victoria seemed to have escaped such brightening, and offered only hamburger-joints, without the distorted grins and hair-trigger service, honed against their competitors, which made such places in high streets entertaining.

Neil took it in his slow, unhurried stride. He ordered a fish sandwich and a cup of hot chocolate, while Bernard settled for coffee. As Neil raised his cup to his lips he said, 'Nice to have two days free, eh, before it all starts again. It's been flat stick all week.' Bernard had a mild romantic fetish for that mid-sentence *eh*, which for all he knew was a mannerism Neil shared even with the sheep in New Zealand, but was unique in his experience.

Neil singled out the idea of the weekend for praise and appreciation because it was a characteristic of his new job; he had been fired from his old one – where he had worked on Saturdays but had Wednesdays off – for being antibody-positive. He hadn't announced the fact, but a colleague had spotted a badge with the phrase Body Positive on it, when Neil had unzipped his holdall to retrieve a pot of yoghurt for his lunch. Neil's colleague seemed enlightened, and men-tioned several friends of his as being in the same condition. He promised discretion. Then one Thursday, after Neil had dealt with a couple of clients, he was summoned to the basement by the manager. Did Neil have something to tell him? Neil was mystified and asked what this was all about. Then the manager said that three juniors had left work in tears the day before, and had phoned in to say they weren't willing to work with him any more (their mothers seemed to have played a part in this decision). He asked if Neil denied being a 'carrier'. The money that Neil was owed, plus a week's wages, was ready in an envelope, so he didn't even bother to argue. He had to leave on the spot, walking out through colleagues who seemed to be focusing on their clients rather more narrowly than usual. He took with him a fleshy-fingered little cactus that Bernard had brought him, and entrusted it to a friend who worked in the salon of Dickins and Jones.

Again, Neil reacted to this disturbance with relative calm. He was angry for about an hour, depressed for about a day; he swam a little more than usual, slept a little more than usual, ate a little less. The sentence that took the longest to break down into inoffensiveness was the manager's last word: 'It was very foolish of you, you know, to pretend you didn't know what I was talking about.' But it was Bernard who worked the incident up into a party-piece, and into an indictment of hairdressers. He couldn't help feeling that Neil was overdoing the British phlegm, or perhaps it was yogic indifference. There was such a thing, he knew, as burying toxic waste so deep you poisoned the water table. It was a possibility he sometimes mentioned to his current affairs class.

Neil seemed free of poison. In fact he looked a little different today, in a way that would prompt Bernard, with anyone else, to ask if he had had a haircut. But life for Neil was one continuous haircut; he and his co-workers were forever giving each other trims in the quiet times between busy times. Over the months Bernard had known him, his hair – black with a haze of grey at the crown – had followed a general trend from crew cut to a fuller look, but with countless adjustments and accents. His beard went from stubbled to almost full, before being trimmed recurrently back.

Bernard had to admit, though, that Neil was by some way the least narcissistic person in the salon. It seemed to him that the other employees, male and female, straight and gay, would have done any work that involved their being surrounded by mirrors. If being a butcher had met that condition, most of them would be wearing blood-stained aprons by now, pleased to have themselves to themselves in the mirrors, without human competition.

Bernard checked his watch all the more because Neil did without. He started to get restless when they had fifteen minutes in hand before the train, exaggerating the effect on their progress of Neil's slow pace. Neil consented to set off at last, using his tongue to press the last of the hot chocolate from his whiskers. Then it turned out that of the two trains to Brighton every hour, one was departing from Croydon, so that repairs could be carried out on the line. This was the one they were now set on catching; they would have to take a suburban train to Croydon to meet it. Bernard shepherded Neil on to the platform, where Neil found himself a baggage wagon to sit on.

Almost immediately an abraded voice on the Tannoy announced a change of platform. Bernard couldn't make out the message itself, but could reconstruct it from its instantaneous effect on their fellow travellers, who picked up their bags and ran. By the time he had convinced Neil that this was more than a piece of random British eccentricity, and that, yes, you had to play hide-and-seek with the trains in this country if you wanted to get anywhere, they were at the rear of a long queue, backed up outside the entrance to the platform proper.

There were few free seats left on the train when they

reached it. The nearest they could get to sitting together was to be in sight of each other, occupying aisle seats, with two rows of passengers intervening. Bernard could see a newspaper sticking out of Neil's holdall, but was too far away to identify it. Neil bought a different paper every day, and was never satisfied, since he had to confront the highest concentration of distressing nonsense about the illness that threatened him, if he was also to find a reasonable minimum of the stories he liked (royalty features, pop gossip). Whatever his particular choice this Saturday, he wasn't reading it. His eyes were almost closed. He might very well be meditating, or practising autogenic training. Or just falling asleep in the normal manner of people on trains. Bernard had a book with him, which a strange isotope of loyalty would have prevented him from reading if Neil had been sitting next to him, so he turned their separation to good account.

At Croydon there was the same co-ordinated rush to the waiting train. Neil trailed behind without embarrassment, and Bernard forced himself to accept the idea of standing for the rest of the journey. In fact, this new train was much longer than the suburban one, and they were able to find seats in the buffet car, which was deserted. After about ten minutes, Bernard walked down the car and found to his joy and amazement that the buffet was staffed. The steward was standing in the shadows rather, and doing nothing to advertise his presence; perhaps he had eased up the grille of the buffet inch by inch in its groove of grease so as not to attract attention. But he was certainly there, and even on duty. When his bluff was called, he was willing to dispense refreshment.

Bernard knew he had no prospect of explaining to Neil his sense of the extraordinariness of this coincidence of serving-counter and steward, but his heart was wholly lifted by it. For the first time he had the sense that this outing would be a success, and he almost pranced back along the buffet car, carrying another coffee for himself and another hot chocolate for Neil.

'It's made with soya milk,' he said as he put Neil's cup down.

'Really?'

'British Rail have always used soya milk. And the bread for their sandwiches is made from bulgar wheat. That's why people are always complaining about the catering. People just aren't ready for progress.' As he spoke, Bernard adopted a patently ironic tone so that Neil could know he was being teased.

The tease was undermined by the fact that Neil was no doctrinaire vegetarian, as the fish sandwich at Victoria rather tended to prove. He ate meat when it was prepared for him, and his avoidance of it when he could choose had more to do with being poor, and disliking cheap cuts smothered with sauces, than with any moral stand. He no longer bothered to explain the distinction, and acknowledged Bernard's teasing only with a broad smile. As Bernard noticed a little guiltily, he did remarkably little teasing himself.

Bernard had no idea why he teased Neil, or anybody else. Perhaps it was some evolutionary leftover, like an appendix, and he should only worry if it filled up with poison.

As the train approached Brighton, Neil became more and more perky, though he was too accustomed to ocean from New Zealand – and blue ocean at that – to be more than moderately pleased when the sea hove into sight. At the station he vetoed Bernard's suggestion that they buy a map, but this turned out to be less hippyish a gesture than Bernard first thought. He had looked at a friend's map the day before and thought he had a reasonable idea of the general layout of the town.

They set off in the direction that Neil indicated, at his preferred pace. The day was bright but with a chill to it. Neil was wearing gloves, but fingerless ones which emphasized his long, beautiful fingers, and the jacket of a suit inherited from his grandfather, long enough for him and actually a bit broad in the shoulder. It was rather too thin for the weather. Neil's grandfather, by dying when Neil was six, had given him his only example of a dead person, with the result that death seemed to have acquired the status of an optional event, almost a distinction. After a few minutes Neil fished out a knitted woollen watch-cap from his holdall and put it on. Bernard was wearing an identical cap, bought for £1.80 from Laurence Corner at the same time as Neil's, and he found growing in him the urge to take it off. He was content to be part of a couple, but he strongly resisted being part of a matching pair.

Since Neil rolled his cap down to cover his ears, while Bernard rolled his up into the smallest practicable shape, so that it clung to the back of his head only by fibrous tension, they were already taking steps to differentiate themselves. There was very little chance of their being mistaken for each other. Still Bernard unzipped his jacket and wore it open, as if the effort of sustained walking had warmed him up, and under cover of that pretext took off his cap a few minutes later. He took long refreshed breaths of sea air. He scrabbled at his hair with both hands to restore it to a roughly human contour, so that it looked at least like a loved haystack rather than a despised one.

They had only penetrated a few yards into Brighton before they were offered their first second-hand clothes shop. In theory Neil's needs were the greater, since his wardrobe was scanty and his fear of winter real, but it was Bernard who dived in and started riffling through the racks. Neil had set aside the coming Saturday, rather than this one, for buying The Winter Coat, an item for which he had drawn up almost arctic specifications. Half-heartedly he tried a couple of coats on, but each time asked Bernard to feel their weave and weight. Would this one be an adequate defence? How about this one? Bernard didn't want to swear to it, not being in a hurry to shoulder blame at a later date. Neil had shopped impulsively for The Winter Boots and was regretting it. Neil's feet were size twelves, and The Winter Boots were size elevens; their waterproof days were over already. But size twelves never showed up in sales, and even size elevens – or so Bernard gathered – weren't common enough to pass up.

Bernard bought a string vest of sea island cotton after trying it on in a changing-room so small – a dirty curtain held a little away from the wall – that it reminded him of the dressing-rooms for the school play now in rehearsal (*Twelfth Night*, with Viola and Sebastian played by a pair of Pakistani twins, their resemblance not yet botched by puberty). This was not a welcome thought, since he was supposed to be devising the costumes for it – *designing* was too grand a word for what he had in mind, which would include found objects and black plastic bin-liners as important elements. But however modest his responsibilities, today would have been a logical day to devote to them.

A little further into town, the moment Brighton made any sort of impersonation of a resort, Neil started taking photographs. He didn't waste film on views, but took a couple of photographs of Bernard. More important was for Bernard to take the camera from him and to take photographs suitable for sending home. He gave Neil plenty of warning, so that he could blow out his cheeks a little, and push out his tummy. He was holding weight well, as far as Bernard could see, but from Neil's parents' point of view there was no such thing as overdoing it.

For the first photograph Neil puffed out his cheeks almost to bursting point, until laughter broke his lips open. But he was undoubtedly happier when the camera contained a good stockpile of fat photos. He could put the camera away and start enjoying himself on his own account, and not for the benefit of a mantelpiece in Auckland.

Neil liked to look in the window of every hairdressers they passed, which in a town as dedicated to grooming as Brighton seemed to mean crossing from side to side of the street more or less non-stop. He got satisfaction of some sort from what he saw through these windows, but made no comment. Bernard tried to decide whether he was simply gloating over these people who had to be cutting hair when he was free, or checking the tariffs to reassure himself that his Brighton equivalents earned even less than he did. The only certain thing was that he wasn't engaged in industrial espionage. He wasn't serious about hairdressing, and Bernard took comfort from that. It enabled him to construct two categories of hairdresser, the casual and the committed, with all the stigma attaching to the committed.

Neil was casual about his job, but well short of slapdash. Bernard had seen him more than once cutting a little girl's hair, kneeling on a towel by the chair – a chair made in Japan, for no known reason – although there were stylists much less tall, whom Bernard thought would find the job less awkward. Patiently, he cut the merest centimetre from her hair, combing her soothingly, so that she seemed not to realize she was no longer crying, though her posture was still sulky and she still held her doll in the combined crook of her elbows.

But he certainly had no great respect for his profession. The only hairdresser he admired was a friend called Joel, now working freelance, and that was because of what he managed to get away with. Joel still used the pair of scissors he had had at hairdressing school, the cheapest pair of Ice Gottas on the market, and turned up for magazine shoots – he did make-up as well as hair – with an old plastic bag bearing the motto 'That's the Wonder of Woolies', full of Outdoor Girl cosmetics. The magazines put different names for the cosmetics next to the pictures they printed, but then they did that anyway. But Joel's great achievement, so far as Neil was concerned, was to give ordinary cuts at enormous speed and inflated prices to a few selected clients in his own home, a small, shabby and disorderly flat. It was one thing to do a bad job in a pretentious salon, quite another to do a bad job – and get away with it – where the client could see his old tea-bags and underpants. Once, Neil and Joel had been about to go out for lunch when a client arrived whom Joel had forgotten. She wanted highlights, and Joel obliged in ten minutes, rather than the usual three hours, simply combing the lotion on to the hair. The results, according to Neil, were highlumps rather than highlights, and Joel charged £55 for his labour, but the client was highly delighted.

Among the hairdressers of Brighton were health-food shops and whole-food cafés. Bernard and Neil chose one that looked quiet, The Pantry, for a sit-down and a snack. It was narrow, with chunky tables of rough wood, and crammed with self-consciously tacky 1950s artefacts, some free-standing, some stuck on the walls, and some even hung on utility coat-racks: advertisements, sculptures, jokey ashtrays given a different status from the working ashtrays on the tables. In a tiny alcove there was even a mobile disco, twin turntables with a microphone attached, though it was hard to imagine anyone dancing there. Queuing for food was quite awkward enough in the cramped space, and a lot of apologiz-ing went on even with relatively few people ordering and collecting food. Perhaps the disco was only kept there off duty, and was set up somewhere else; but it was difficult to imagine any of the helpers – three women of different generations and perhaps actually a whole-food dynasty, a matrilineal succession of carers – acting as DJ. The youngest, an early teenager, seemed to have her duties confined to clearing up and, to judge by the frequency with which she dropped things, would not be trusted with the boxes of scuffed singles sitting next to the disco.

When Neil had finished his salad and Bernard his wholemeal lasagne, they carried on towards what Neil's homing instinct or memory for maps told him was the historic city centre. Neil had picked up the word 'historic', which he used with deliberate lack of discrimination, from his least favourite client, an American woman who would smoke a cigarette and put on make-up while being blow-dried. Neil's boss had followed his usual practice of over-charging tourists, but this tourist was not to be deterred from returning, and always asked for Neil. He punished her by taking on this particularly hated element of her vocabulary.

Brighton showed no great increase in historical interest as they walked on, but to judge by the air of escalating chichi they were on the right track. Finally they came in sight of the Pavilion, which they had agreed on as their obligatory piece of sightseeing. It had for the time being a complex façade of boards and scaffolding, but was still open for business. By taking the tour they would be treating Brighton as a city in its own right, not just as a collection of gay-oriented businesses with a reasonably pleasant climate.

There was no tour of the Pavilion as such. If there had been, or if they had invested in one of the expensive guide books from the gift shop, they would have been given a definite idea of the Pavilion to accept or reject. As it was, they had to come to their own conclusions. It dawned on Bernard, as they entered a ballroom containing a grand organ, that he was now in one of the most piss-elegant environments in the world. 'This is certainly historic,' said Neil.

'Worse than that. In its own way it's actually Otaran.' Otara, as he had gathered from Neil, was some sort of Maori heartland, and therefore a sort of New Zealand shorthand for tackiness. Neil himself, of Yugoslav blood and unpronounceable surname, had been the only white person in his class at school. All the Maori boys were called Rangi, or so he claimed, and all the girls were Debra. He had ended up

81

saying things like, 'J'wanta come down the Spice Inviders in my Veliant?' Thereafter, he had fallen in eagerly with his friends in their dismissal of anything Maori, though he had also had one or two affairs with Maoris not called Rangi.

Neil seemed thrown by Bernard's borrowing of a Kiwi expression, as he was on the rare occasions when Bernard said *obliverated* to mean drunk, *rapt* for pleased, *crack a horn* for acquire an erection. Neil's own accent, if his family were telling the truth on their occasional phone calls, was now pure Oxbridge. 'Well, I don't know, that place we had lunch was Otaran. This place is a bit different.'

'What then?' asked Bernard.

'This place is . . . Papatoetoan.'

'What's that?'

'Papatoetoe. It's not as far as Otara.'

Bernard laughed, and they moved through the preposterous rooms in a rare daze of unanimity. It turned out that there was an alarm system installed in the Pavilion, which gave off a series of electronic yelps if anyone infringed on the velvet rope, or even approached the edges of the aisle permitted to visitors. Each time the yelping sounded, the guard in whatever room it happened to be would intone, 'Please don't touch. Keep your distance.'

In one room the guard, who wore a stylized moustache, was young and busy with his eyes. Bernard nudged the rope, so as to make him deliver his recorded message. Then he couldn't help murmuring to Neil, 'What are the odds he turns up to a bar we're in tonight? Except he won't be saying *keep your distance* then, I'll bet.'

'Keep your distance, please don't touch,' said the guard again, as someone else triggered the alarm. Neil was normally resistant to Bernard's line of banter, but this time they were on a wavelength, and he laughed, in one little burst and then another.

They passed through to the kitchens, where Bernard saw

the first things he actually admired, the endless rows of copper pots, all the way up to Moby Dick fish-kettles; the lids were sensibly provided with their own handles, raised above the rest of the lids for coolness' sake. Neil found further fuel for his laughing jag in a stuffed rat caught in a trap, and displayed under one of the kitchen tables. It was almost absurdly unlifelike, perhaps to avoid frightening schoolchildren, and the plastic fruit and veg on the broad pale-scrubbed tables would be a suitable diet for it.

Once the Pavilion had loosed its historic hold on them, they started to think about finding their hotel. There Neil's memory for maps, however impressive, couldn't be expected to help them. Bernard remembered the address as Derbishire Place, and they asked passers-by where that was. No one knew. Bernard didn't check the advertisement in *Capital Gay*, from which he had got the phone number. One reason for his reluctance was the name of the hotel, which was called Rogues. He had phoned another hotel first, advertised in the same journal but with a nudge-free name. It was full. He had asked the receptionist to recommend another establishment, relying on impartiality now that distortions of rivalry could be discounted, and it was then that Rogues was suggested. With a heavy heart he made the call, and would have put the phone down if he had been offered the Scallywag Suite, or been told about the cheap cocktails during Naughty Hour in the Vagabond Room. He wanted to stay in a hotel called Rogues every bit as much as he wanted to have a lover who was a hairdresser, though he hoped for similar compensations once the sacrifice was made.

Another reason for wanting to leave *Capital Gay* in his bag was the sheer depressingness of the paper itself. This was hardly the paper's fault; the journalists did their best to make up jaunty headlines. But every week there were more obituaries, and the obituaries became more flippant. The conventions of obituary-writing, either that death had set the seal on a long and useful life, or that death had cut off young promise in its prime, began to break down now that untimeliness was becoming the rule. Many of the casualties were too young even to be promising. The boss of a gay business wrote of a dead employee, in the issue that Bernard was keeping in his bag, 'He told us he did not expect to live after Friday. Punctuality was never his *forte* and it came as no surprise to us that he was 2¾ hours late.' The dead men weren't ready to die. The obituarists weren't ready to write obituaries.

Derbishire Place continued to ring no bells with the people he asked about it. When people asked what exactly he was looking for, hoping that would give them a clue, Bernard became very tight-lipped, while Neil gave him what was not a look of forgiving superiority, but which if fed and watered would grow up to be one. Finally they gave in and bought a local map from a stationers, but Derbishire Place was missing from it, along with all other places beginning with Derbishire. He went back to the stationers to check other maps of greater price and detail, but Derbishire Place was missing from them all.

At last Bernard fished out *Capital Gay* for the lowdown on Rogues. The address turned out to be Devonshire Place, which was not only marked on every map, however rudimentary, but which they had passed a few streets back.

Devonshire Place was a steep little street, and Bernard felt quite tired as they reached its upper end. To his relief, the frontage of Rogues was plain, its name appearing only on a small brass plaque. He had been bracing himself for black balloons and pink neon. The man who opened the door was a further relief. He was wearing socks and sheepskin slippers, and underneath his green polo-shirt could be traced in relief the outline of a thermal vest. Not for the first time in Bernard's experience, but much to his reassurance, gay life promised the depraved and delivered the cosy.

Their host led them into a lounge with a television, which was showing the omnibus edition of a soap opera which Neil followed, without fanaticism. It seemed to be one of the few British programmes which wasn't exported to New Zealand, and that gave it, in Neil's eyes, a slight extra kick. Their host left them at the mercy of the television, and promised them a cup of tea in a couple of shakes. They sprawled on the sofa, and Neil gave Bernard one of his trademark kisses, an amorous stubbled plosive full on the ear. In a world where bodies had unrestricted access to each other, this would come near the bottom of Bernard's list of favourite gestures. He braced himself for the detonation. In essence, he thought it was about as erotic a gesture as dropping a firework through someone's letter-box. But he could not now afford to despise any permissible act, and he had worked on his reactions until the symbolic sensation gave him pleasure. Now, on the sofa, he welcomed it.

'Who's that?' he asked, pointing at the television screen. 'Is that what's-his-face's boyfriend?'

'Don't know.'

'Didn't you see it on Tuesday?'

'Yes.'

'Well, who is it then?'

'I don't know.' Seeing Bernard's expression he tightened his hug a notch or two. 'Don't worry, I'm not going gaga before my time, I'm not getting the dementia. If I am I've always had it. I've always had a short attention span.'

'You have?'

'Yup. I think I've had a little snooze in every film we've been to, and you didn't notice, eh?'

'Can't say I did.'

'Maybe your attention's not so hot yourself. And if you work out who these people are, don't bother to tell me. I'm not that interested.'

'Do you think we can turn it off?' The lounge might in theory be the guests' terrain, but it was full of the landlord's presence, not to mention his cigarettes and two planks of a KitKat, half-unwrapped from their foil.

Before they could decide, the landlord came back with the promised tray of tea, a register and some leaflets. He needed some details for the register, and offered in exchange a map of Brighton with its gay attractions marked in. A number of venues had been deleted; it was, after all, off-season. There were, though, still places to go, and the hotelier made out little passes for them, vouching for their status as bona-fide visitors, with which they could get in free at a number of key nightspots. Then he left them to their tea and the television.

A little later he returned with two bulky keys, and showed them to their room. Rogues was a modest private house lightly disguised as a hotel; Neil's and Bernard's room, at the rear of the first floor, corresponded to the master bedroom of most terraced houses. There couldn't, Bernard thought, be more than three other rooms.

The underside of the door scraped on the thick carpet, almost to the point of sticking, as it opened. Inside were posters of exhibitions at the British Museum, and a colour scheme of striated greens hinting at leafy bamboo and derived from the Brighton Pavilion. It occurred to Bernard that there must be easily one or two hotel rooms in Brighton untouched by the Pavilion in decorative scheme, but he accepted that they would cost rather more than the others, and would need to be booked some months in advance.

The hotel owner padded out and left them alone, and they tried out the bed. Neil was unswervingly loyal to his futon, but Bernard had no great love for it. This was a little squashy, squashier than his own at home, but it would do. Neil seemed to think so too, whatever his stated position: he fell asleep almost immediately. Bernard tried as a general rule not to bombard him with concern, and had managed not to ask him, earlier in the day, if he was tired. Now he began to feel, from the avidness and depth of Neil's sleep, that he should have been more tender.

Bernard wondered if perhaps at some stage he and Neil would have to decide whether 'antibody-positive' was not now an understatement of Neil's condition. Perhaps that was a secret they were keeping from each other.

Neil was curled sweetly against him in sleep. Neil's sexuality seemed to Bernard altogether caressive rather than penetrational; that was certainly the role he played with Bernard, and the role Bernard played with him. Neil had called him 'cuddly' on one occasion, meaning fond of hugging, until Bernard broke it to him that in Britain cuddly was just a friend's word for fat, so would he please retract it. Neil had even given Bernard a teddy bear for his birthday. Bernard had slept with it one night, so as to atone for his embarrassment when it was handed over, and so that he could mention its usefulness without lying. He was rather appalled to wake up freezing in the middle of the night, still clutching the bear, in a shipwreck of bedclothes. The bear's stitched smile had a vindicated smugness about it.

At an earlier stage, of course, Neil's persona had been a little different. About five years previously, while still in his teens, he had gone through a phase of anal shenanigans; that must have been the time of his exposure to infection. He still had a sharp nostalgia for oral sex, which was not these days categorized as particularly risky; but Bernard hesitated, and seeing his hesitation Neil changed the sexual subject.

Bernard rolled quietly off the bed and went for a walk. He would have liked to find a café where he could have a cup of coffee and read, but the only café that was at all promising seemed to be mutating in some mysterious way into a wine bar. It had been open until a little while before, it would be open in a little while to come, and even now it was not exactly closed; but when he suggested to the waitress that he sit in a quiet corner with a book and a cup of coffee, she wouldn't hear of it.

Thwarted of his civilized interlude, Bernard walked down to the sea front, then headed back to the hotel, not wanting to experience anything too distinctively Brighton without the partner that the whole weekend was arranged around.

Neil was stirring when he returned to the hotel room. He rolled slowly off the bed and started doing yoga exercises, hardly even opening his eyes. Bernard took his turn at lying on the bed, but after a moment he couldn't resist peering over the edge at Neil's smooth complex movements, and the quickened roughened breathing that went with them. He felt like an Indian scout creeping to the edge of a cliff to spy on the war games of a rival tribe.

There was one exercise that particularly appealed to him. Neil lay on his front and stretched back his head, arms and legs, giving his body a bowed shape and a resemblance to a parachutist in free fall. Bernard had an impulse to lean over and tickle one of the elongated feet, themselves sharply bowed, outstretched below him, an action which would have shattered Neil's calm – he was extremely ticklish – beyond the power of any mantra to reinstate. It was only a distantly mischievous impulse, like a sceptic's urge, at a seance, to contact a long-dead and cantankerous relative.

Neil finished the tempting exercise, and moved on to the next. Yoga was known to benefit the immune system. It was agreed between Neil and Bernard, without any basis in evidence, that Neil was unlikely to have been exposed, as long ago as 1981 and as far from the centre of the gay world as New Zealand, to the full grown-up horror of the virus. It was much more likely, surely, that he had encountered some nasty intermediate form, some mid-mutation that was no fun to have aboard but bore no real grudge against him.

There were factors that worked against this theory. Neil had had affairs, in that distant period, with not one but two airline stewards. He was some way from the capital of danger, but he wasn't exactly in the provinces. Bernard had an image of airline stewards (flight attendants, whatever euphemism you cared to choose) as sheer vectors of sexual transmission, their buttocks a blur all the time they weren't actually handing out soft drinks and headphones. He reacted with relative sanity to press coverage of the illness, screening out the idiocies and focusing on the few scraps of undistorted information, but he had a little obsession of his own. If any political party had included in its platform the compulsory fitting of chastity belts to airline stewards, he would have thrown his full electoral weight behind it.

Neil finished his exercises, and lay back on the floor in feigned collapse. He was hoping for a hug to revive him, but Bernard thought he could offer him something better. The advert in *Capital Gay* had mentioned a shower in every room. It was simply a matter of locating the fitted cupboard that contained it. He strode towards the cupboard nearest the window and flipped the door open. Inside were the dark green tiles and gleaming fitments he had been hoping for.

Neil was pleased, and only took a moment to take his clothes off as he walked across the carpet to the shower. Bernard noticed again his furry thighs and the dark skin tone (Yugoslav blood) that he had at first assumed was a tan, and would fade. His preferred colour for his own skin was slug-white, and he still felt the same spasm of involuntary sympathy for tanned flesh – artificial or the real thing – that he could feel for the flayed tissue of a crocodile handbag.

Neil used soap only once a week, and washed his hair only about as often, in marked contrast to his colleagues at the salon. This was down-under hippie simplicity, to be sure, but it was also mild superstition. In his teens he had suffered so terribly from acne that he had become little short of a hermit, dropping out of school and shunning company. He had once been beaten by his Physical Education teacher for refusing to take his shirt off. Now that he was clear of acne, except for the high-water mark it had left on his shoulders, he left his outside alone as far as possible. Acne had affected him profoundly, or to put it another way, on the surface; the virus in his bloodstream seemed to have changed him less. He seemed surprised, even now, to be a survivor of acne. He had suffered nothing worse at the hands of the virus, so far, than the loss of a margin for error, once the defining privilege of youth. He remained calm when possible treatments of the virus came up in conversation, but his voice took on a glow when he mentioned Roacutane, the desperate drug that had finally seen off his acne. He said he would be willing to endorse Roacutane on television, make a pilgrimage, carry a placard in the street, testifying to its healing powers. At the time it had made his bones ache, turned his lips yellow and given him bleeding from the nose and the rectum, but he regarded that as the smallest of payments. Roacutane had made his skin dry where once it had been extremely oily, but he was grateful to have working skin back, of whatever description.

A fan had switched itself on when Neil pressed the light switch to the shower, but steam was still drifting into the room. Bernard remembered, then put it out of his mind, that Neil had had one anomalous outbreak of acne after Roacutane, which suggested that his skin was having its ability to police itself undermined in some way.

Neil emerged from the shower with a small towel round his waist, dripping shamelessly on the carpet. He lay down on the bed after the briefest period of towelling, enjoying the hotel guest's privilege of treating the facilities to mild abuse. He beckoned Bernard towards him.

Bernard hung back a little. He had brought no finery for the weekend, but he had no intention of getting what he was wearing wet, just as they were going out to dinner.

Neil tried a different nuance of flirtation. 'Do you want your fashion show now or later?'

Bernard thought for a moment. 'Later.' Neil had promised

to show him the costumes he had devised for the gay
naturists' fancy-dress party, to be worn by his landlord and
himself. The theme was Rude. Bernard was proud that he
had kept his curiosity within bounds, so that Neil would
satisfy it without making him wait too long. In fact his mind
was ablaze with the need to know what Rude Naturist Fancy
Dress could actually look like.

Neil didn't seem displeased by the prospect of a few more
hours' mystery-making. 'Get dressed and go to dinner, eh?'
he crooned up from the bed.

Bernard entrusted the choice of a place for dinner to
Neil; it turned out to be a lengthy business. There were
plenty of restaurants to choose from, but it seemed silly to
walk into the first one that offered. Bernard had spotted on
his walk a place that offered Genghis Khan barbecues, served
by waitresses who seemed – from a peer through bottled
glass – to be dressed in rags of Mongolian cut, but once that
option was discarded, it was a matter of choosing from the
competitive clamour of good taste, and deciphering a plausible menu from pages of scrawled French. Most of the
restaurants, which after a few minutes seemed almost continuous, had permanent menus in their windows and black-
boards with the daily specials out in the street, so a certain
amount of cross-indexing was called for.

Finally Neil plumped for a place that seemed spacious.
They were immediately shown up a narrow staircase to an
upper room full of little tables; it turned out that the main
dining room had been booked by a large party. One benefi-
cial side-effect of the cramped conditions was that they had
to sit with their legs meshed together, in a way that would
have got them thrown out of the main dining-room.

Neil ordered a rare steak, mildly to Bernard's irritation,
since he had vetoed a number of places that had appealed to
him personally, on the unstated grounds that they offered
nothing to vegetarians, beyond salads that might just as well

have had stencilled on their drooping leaves No Fun But Good For You. Bernard ordered mussels. He had a weakness for meals that needed to be processed as much as eaten, for spare ribs and artichokes, for foods that needed to be eaten with your hands, for dishes that left a satisfying pile of debris. It gave him a sense of occasion to be engaging in an almost adversarial relationship with food, instead of simply placing it inside him.

As he levered open the savoury hinges of the mussels, like a philistine breaking the spines of first editions, he became aware that another hinge, Neil's knee, was pressing against his trouserfork with a force that went beyond affection. Bernard looked up, startled. Neil laid his knife and fork down neatly and leaned forward, putting a hand on each side of the table. His voice was dark with anger, angrier than Bernard had ever heard it. 'Do you hear what those people are saying?'

'No. Which people?'

'Behind us.'

Behind Neil were two ordinary-seeming middle-aged couples. The only fragments of conversation he had heard from that quarter had concerned schools and horse riding.

'What are they saying?'

'Listen.'

Bernard did his best to screen out the sounds of crockery and actual eating, the thick soundtrack of conversation. He thought he was able to focus on the offending quadrant of chat. The sentence he thought he heard was: 'And then of course that starts off a chain.'

'I think they're talking about moving house,' he explained, 'you know, someone makes an offer for a house, but they can only come through with the money if someone else buys their house, and they're in the same position. So it's called a chain, and sometimes people can get snagged up for ages.'

Neil was still gripping the table, and his voice had not lost rage. 'That's not what they're talking about.' Bernard couldn't help dropping his eyes to Neil's plate, wondering if this aggressiveness was what happened when a habitual vegetarian dabbled in rare meat. The idea, as he could see as soon as it was fully formulated, was ridiculous, and in any case Neil had made only minor inroads into his steak.

'So what are they talking about? Why are you so angry?'

'They're talking about a certain . . . infection and its – what do you call it – methods of transmission.' He relaxed the grip of his fingers on the table. 'They're full of ideas. Ignorant fuckers.' He rested his hands on his lap for a moment, then took up his knife and fork again.

Bernard, finally, was in touch with his anger. 'That's outrageous. That's the last thing we need to hear.' Now that he had started to feel anger, he felt the need to work it up into action. He couldn't stop the virus itself from playing goose-berry, but there was a limit to what he had to put up with. There was no reason why he should sit back while these people broadcasted their idiot editorials. 'Do you want me to talk to them?'

Neil gave a small smile, his mouth full of his steak's unaccustomed juiciness. 'Don't bother.' Bernard was forced to realize that if he made any protest, the people he ticked off would feel only that their rights were being violated: their right to make no distinction between public and private, their right to have the world remain as it was advertised to be. He returned reluctantly to his mussels, which had cooled off almost as quickly as Neil had, and were nowhere near as appetizing as they had been when he had last looked at them. They were no longer sending up steam to signal their deliciousness.

Neil's burst of temper hadn't lasted long, but it was still out of character. His personality held very little of the aggressive. Only in one family story that he had passed on to Bernard was there a trace of hostility mixed in with the warmth, and even there the aggressiveness was sweetened and made palatable. As a boy he had dreamed that New Zealand was stricken by a famine. At a family conference it was decided that they should eat Neil's elder brother Robin – who had been weeping quietly throughout – since he was made of trifle. Neil and the others took small spoonfuls from the place they felt would be least painful, just above the hips.

Bernard pushed away the graveyard plate of mussels. 'I'm stuffed,' he said. 'How about you?'

Neil looked startled. 'I'm not too stuffed, I've still got some inergy left,' he said. He used the same pinched vowel that made the word 'sex' on his lips sound like the number after five. Bernard didn't grasp for a moment the reason for Neil talking about energy, when he himself was asking about food. Then he remembered that 'stuffed', in the Kiwi lexicon, meant tired rather than full.

'I'm not stuffed either. What I meant to say was full up. Could you manage something else? I saw trifle on the menu.'

Neil seemed indifferent to trifle, in a way that suggested he was still upset about their fellow diners, who were now greeting the sweet course with a round of hushed exclamations, gasps of complicity in sugar and resolutions to take exercise. One of them was saying, 'As long as I ride enough, I don't have to worry. It just shakes off.'

For form's sake, Bernard enquired about the composition of the trifle. Neil would touch only teetotal trifle, since for some reason possibly to do with the virus, alcohol and sugar collaborated to make his teeth sing at the time, and screech the next day. The message came back from the cook by way of the waitress, who gave a proud grin, that the trifle was full of good things. 'You could wring the sponge out and fill a liqueur glass with it,' she said. 'A real Saturday night treat.' Bernard asked for the bill, and they left.

The nearest gay pub marked on the map that their host at Rogues had given them was called The Waterman. As they entered, their novelty ensured them the equivalent of a ticker-tape welcome. The Waterman had the usual amenities of a gay bar that had evolved stage by stage from a straight one, that is, no chairs, so that turning round to stare involved no violence to furniture. The pub was too crowded for conversation actually to stop, but everyone there gave them an aggressively searching look in their first ten seconds in the pub. Bernard knew the commercial gay scene well enough to realize that interest and approval were often signalled with a coldly accusing stare, but it still seemed strange to him. You would have thought that The Waterman was playing host to a convention of bounty hunters, he thought, who couldn't help comparing any unfamiliar faces with the Wanted posters in their minds. Neil and Bernard felt Wanted all right. It wasn't particularly pleasant.

When they had been served Neil took a single sip from his orange juice, narrowed his eyes and said, 'This should give you some idea of gay life in New Zealand. Imagine this being the only bar in Auckland. Those boys over there, eh, the cream of the local talent.' He nodded his head towards a group of bleached-blonds in multicoloured tracksuits, drinking gin and tonics. 'About the same number of punch-and-pricks.'

'What are punch-and-pricks?' asked Bernard, wondering if this was a word from the Kiwi lexicon or a term of gay argot that he was too old to be familiar with. It turned out to be professional slang.

'Punch-and-pricks? You know,' he lowered his voice significantly as a man passed between them on his way to the lavatory, 'hair transplants.'

'How do you rate that one?'

'Five out of ten.' He leaned forward against Bernard's ear, so that he expected a public version of Neil's trademark kiss. Instead he murmured, with the same moist intimacy, 'Yip yip yip.'

'What's that mean?'

'Don't look now.' He nudged Bernard's head into the appropriate alignment. '*Keep your distance*, remember? *Please don't touch?*'

Neil was right. The attendant from the Pavilion, now wearing jeans and a check shirt, was standing guard, with the same paranoid glint, over a pint of lager. 'Sharp eyes,' said Bernard. 'You must have been pretty good in Ye Olde Kiwi Gay Bar.'

Neil didn't deny it. 'Well, you don't want to drag home anyone too soft or tragic. Not with your friends watching. And they didn't have anywhere to go either.'

The man who had been identified by Neil as a punch-and-prick paused on his way back from the lavatory. He was short enough for Bernard to be able to see his head from above; for Neil this was presumably the normal angle of vision, since he was so tall and spent his professional time hovering about people's heads with scissors. The punch-and-prick gave a broad smile. 'When you've had enough of these tired provincial queens,' he said, 'come over and talk. I'm with friends. You'll like them.'

There wasn't a lot Bernard could think of to say to that. Neil nodded amiably. When they left the pub, a little later, on their way to a nightspot marked on the map from Rogues, they could only hope not to be too visibly passing up this invitation. Given Neil's height and the pub's single exit, which meant passing near where the punch-and-prick and his party must have set up their rampart of masculinity, there was not much chance of their going unnoticed. At least they could hope that the punch-and-prick wouldn't turn out to be the owner of the club they were heading to now, or the little free admission vouchers from Rogues might not be enough to smooth their passage.

Vouchers or no, they had to wait quite a while on the steps heading up to the club. Bernard spent the time inveighing against the name of the club, Stompers. Why did every place that offered even the mildest pleasure after dark need to call itself by some idiot plural: Stompers, Bumpers, Bangs, Rogues, Spats? Why did pleasant pubs called the Churchill Arms install a few spotlights and reopen as Churchills? Did it bother Neil as much as it bothered him?

Neil said, 'I can live with it.' Bernard was about to back up his objections when he realized he was only inches away from one of his classroom tirades, against crimes like Grocer's Apostrophe (Apple's and Pear's). He shut himself up.

The vouchers from Rogues, which Bernard had been nervously locating in his pockets at intervals throughout the evening, turned out to entitle them only to half-price admission. This would have taken the gilt off the gingerbread, except that no one waiting on those narrow stairs, after being buzzed through the street door, could have been expecting gilt or even gingerbread. There was something eerily familiar, Bernard thought as he explored with a drink, about the layout of the club, its chain of undersized rooms. Then he realized that like Rogues, the nightclub was the smallest possible conversion from a terraced house. He had been briefly fooled by the staircase, which caused them to enter where the top landing would have been.

The upper bar had taken the place of a back bedroom; the lower one was substituting for the front parlour. Eventually Bernard and Neil found their way to the disco dance-floor, which had once – perhaps even recently – been a kitchen. Bernard was pleased to see that the oldest man in the club was dancing with the best of them, was dancing in fact even when he was the only one on the little dance-floor, though he seemed to need little twists of tissue paper stuffed in his ears to make the experience bearable. From time to time he adjusted the paper-twists to block out more of the music that gave the dancing its excuse, before going back to his interpretative movement.

Bernard kept examining Neil for signs of fatigue. The whole visit to Stompers was something of a token gesture, to prove to themselves that they had gone to Brighton and done the whole bit, and he didn't want Neil tiring himself out for a gesture's sake. He asked Neil to dance as a preliminary to suggesting that they might as well think of going home, but neither of them was particularly light on his feet. Neil, when he danced, betrayed the awkwardness he must have had in school photographs – assuming they had such things as school photographs in New Zealand – towering year after year above the massed Rangis and Debras. Bernard for his part was kept well below his normal modest level of competence by thoughts of the primal kitchen which the disco had supplanted. The kitchen lurked reproachfully under the thin crust of night-life. He tried to make up his mind about what exactly the DJ was replacing. Would it be the fridge or the draining board?

When they had finished dancing and were sweating lightly in the kitchen passage, Bernard suggested they go back to the hotel. 'Do you want to?' asked Neil.

'Yes, why not.' Bernard was moved partly by consideration for Neil. Neil suffered from social strangury, though the word he used was *piss-shy*. He was unable to urinate in public; even taking turns in the bathroom with Bernard after sex, he couldn't perform at the bowl with Bernard there. He needed a couple of minutes to himself before his inhibited duct opened up again.

Bernard was pleased by this foible in such a sturdy naturist, Neil's bladder living by a more reticent code than his pelt's. But by now it must be several hours since he had been to the lavatory, several hours of taking in liquid without any alcohol to drive it off. He had been for the last time in the hotel before dinner, using the shared facility with a little difficulty.

Back at Rogues, Neil made no obvious dash for the

bathroom; in fact he insisted on putting on his fashion-show at last. Bernard obediently faced the window while Neil undressed, and then made intricate adjustments. Bernard thought he could hear a snapping noise, either of elastic or some sort of fastening, as well as the faint dry swish of material on skin. Then Neil announced, 'You can turn round now.' His costume was worth waiting for. Rude, naturist, fancy dress; it fulfilled all the requirements. Neil was wearing a jock-strap with the pouch cut out, so that his genitals dangled freely; the jock-strap was held up – though this was purely a visual touch, the elastic waistband being perfectly adequate – by a pair of braces. Hanging diagonally across his chest, in the manner of a beauty-pageant sash, was a strip of towelling that Bernard recognized as being a strip cut from a corporation swimming towel, bearing the woven legend BOROUGH OF CAMDEN 1986. Neil advanced towards him to be embraced. 'It's wonderful. Really,' Bernard said. 'And is your landlord's just the same?'

'Yes. Except he's Mr Borough of Islington.' Neil's embrace became more rhythmic; he rocked their combined bodies from side to side. Bernard needed to do some marking, and broke the embrace to say so. 'I should have done it earlier on,' he said, 'I know. But I can't work on trains.'

Neil made no protest. He took another shower, calling from the misty cubicle that it wasn't a cold one, not by a long stretch, while Bernard did some perfunctory, guilt-appeasing marking. Then Neil brushed his teeth with his usual thoroughness. Bernard had conscientiously left his toothbrush at home, so as not to do the same through force of habit. Neil's gums had a tendency to bleed, and even when they weren't affected Bernard had been led more than once to the ultimate inverted-Judas gesture of withholding a kiss. Sometimes his tongue stood aside from a kiss even when he wanted to involve it. Neil, it had to be said, even at his most passionate,

99

was not a great one for tongue-stabbing, and his reticence increased, understandably enough, when thrush made his saliva soupy.

Bernard's fear of going to the dentist had not long survived the onset of the health crisis. It had been quite a big fear until then, and he sometimes wondered where it had gone. It seemed likely that he had the same total quantity of fear in him, only now it was salted away in little packets rather than gathered in a single large consignment.

The dentist had become tolerable once Bernard had realized that kissing was the only possibly dangerous thing he intended to go on doing. The safety of kissing seemed to be assumed and disavowed almost by turns in the publications he consulted, but either way it was only sensible to have his mouth's defences regularly seen to. He had confessed to his dentist that he avoided brushing when he was going to be kissing soon after, expecting to be told not to be so silly. He had been disconcerted when the dentist had said that of course there was only a possible risk when his partner was 'shedding virus' (whatever that meant), but yes, brushing the teeth could abrade the gums and lead to bleeding. Brushing was a necessity in the long term but did involve a tiny risk, a really tiny risk, in the short. Not brushing before, er, intimate contact might be a realistic precaution.

So it was that Bernard smelled mintiness and freshness on Neil's breath, and Neil smelled whatever Bernard had been eating. This hardly seemed a fair exchange, except that the smell of toothpaste had come to seem definitely sinister to Bernard, even when he was brushing his teeth in the morning, in total security.

Bernard was still hanging over his marking, but had not been taking it in for quite a time. Neil, meanwhile, was already asleep. Bernard packed away the pile of exercise books, turned out the light and went to join him. He approached the bed from the near side, but as he lifted the duvet and prepared to slide in he encountered a large, heat-filled leg. He went round to the other side, but Neil was there too. He had the habit, when he went to bed before Bernard, of stretching out like a starfish, or at least of occupying the diagonal, so that Bernard would be certain to wake him.

When Neil reached a deeper level of sleep, Bernard knew, his personality would change, would lose this responsiveness. He would turn into a warm elongated bobbin and gradually wind the bedclothes around him, winding the warmth off Bernard. He was the last person on earth Bernard would have suspected of being a blanket-fascist, but there it was, you could never tell.

Bernard nudged his way into the bed, triggering Neil's reflexes of welcome. Neil shared his hoarded heat. His body offered a wide variety of textures, not just the ghosts of acne on his shoulders and the back of his neck, but the little fleshy pebbles seeded across his face and forehead which he said the doctors called *molluscum* – a term which Bernard refrained, as an act of love, from looking up in the medical encyclopaedia. On Neil's back were the extraordinary parallel scars he had acquired as a schoolboy athlete, his speciality inevitably the highjump since it involved a modified fall from his embarrassing height to the enviable equality of the sandpit. Once he had practised a Fosbury Flop over a barbed-wire fence, and the long striations of scar tissue on his back were the result.

Neil's scars had a sentimental value for Bernard. Neil had mentioned them in an early conversation in a way that Bernard had found inexplicable. Then he realized that Neil was disposing of embarrassment in advance, and was anticipating, consciously or unconsciously, a conversation in which the subject would necessarily arise if it hadn't been dealt with already: a conversation in which both of them would be naked.

Lower down on Neil, the textural variety continued. He invariably wore bedsocks; night for him was always a cold country no matter what the temperature of day. Since mid-October he had taken to wearing two pairs, and no amount of central heating could coax his feet out of their coverings.

Neil's embrace was semi-conscious now, but Bernard couldn't resist asking, 'Neil, is there anywhere you've been in the world where you haven't worn bedsocks?'

Neil grunted faintly into the pillow but admitted it. 'Yeah.'

'Where?'

'Hawaii.'

Something else struck Bernard as odd. Neil hadn't actually been to the bathroom since they had got back from the disco. 'Neil . . . have you had a piss since we got back?'

Neil grunted again. 'No.'

'I thought you'd be dying for one.'

Neil thought for a moment, still muffled against the pillow. 'Is that why we left so early?' He struggled to the edge of the bed. 'I need a piss now anyway.'

When he had come back and settled back under the duvet, Neil said, with a deliberateness that was almost the same as sleepiness, but not quite, 'You really piss me off when you decide things for me like that.' His voice slowed down and lost definition. 'That really makes me . . . ' on the edge of sleep, he found the appropriate Kiwi word, '. . . ropable.'

'Now you know that's not the way it works,' Bernard said. 'It's not me that pisses you off, it's you that pisses you off. Remember Re-birthing? You told me that was the whole principle of the thing. Taking responsibility.' There was no answer. 'So what you mean is, you really piss yourself off when you let me decide things for you like that. Isn't that right?' Even while he was saying all this he was wondering why he was fighting so dirty, using heavy ammunition – and more to the point, irreplaceable ammunition – in the smallest little squabble. He could only hope that Neil was fully asleep.

He waited a few moments for a reply. Then he stretched out next to Neil, turning his back so their buttocks touched lightly.

He still wasn't satisfied that Neil was really asleep. There was only one way of telling for sure. Thanks to some aberration of the New Zealand educational system, Neil spoke good German, while Bernard was only now studying the language at an elementary level with an evening class. Neil didn't waste his academic advantage. So now Bernard breathed a simple sentence, knowing that if Neil was less than deeply asleep he would inevitably surface to correct Bernard's pronunciation, which he found laughable in its exaggeration. *'Der Friseur liegt hinter dem Lehrer,'* he murmured, but making the consonants clash like sabres in a duel. There was no answer, and this time Bernard was satisfied. That made it official.

Bernard himself slept well, except for a dream which had no characteristics until he diagnosed it as a dream, and decided to leave it. Then it became intensely confining. He tried twisting his arms and legs to be free of it, but they were dream arms and legs, and powerless. He started to cry out instead, and was so afraid they would be cries only inside the dream that he kept on making them. He produced, in reality, four low shouts. Neil put his arms round him and said, 'I'm here.' Bernard was now fully awake, while Neil had surfaced only long enough to give out that single breath of reassurance.

Bernard lay awake for a while, thinking that in Neil's place he would have wanted to give reassurance too, but the phrases he would have used for the job were 'Neil . . . Neil . . . Neil' and 'You're having a nightmare.' Not very helpful. It would never have occurred to him that it would bring comfort to say, 'I'm here.' But Neil's sleeping self seemed to include, as well as the blanket-fascist, a sweetly competent disperser of nightmares that Bernard could only admire and find mysterious.

He was woken in the morning by what he thought was rain,

until it turned out to be the sound of Neil getting his money's worth out of the shower. The time was 10.15. He stretched under the duvet, remembering what the hotel-owner had said about breakfast. Breakfast lasted from nine to eleven. 'So I'll turn the toaster on at five to,' he said.

'Oh, Neil and I were thinking of having an early breakfast and going for a walk.'

The hotel-owner nodded. 'Yes, people do say that.'

Bernard protested feebly. He didn't know whether the implication was lechery or laziness. He remembered a friend telling him about a weekend in Brighton with a new boy-friend, when they had broken a bed on their first night. The landlord had been very understanding. The next night they broke the other bed. Bernard wondered if perhaps he should reassure this hotel-owner that his furnishings and fittings were likely to survive the weekend. He settled for simple repetition. 'Oh, I think we'll have breakfast early and go for a walk.'

'See you then, then,' said the landlord politely.

Neil had dried himself by now, and returned to the bed. Bernard hugged him. 'When I heard you in the shower, I thought it must be rain.'

'Rain, eh? In England? At a weekend?'

'It was a wild idea and I bitterly regret it.'

'Have you looked out of the window?'

'No.'

'Raining. Just thought you'd like to know.'

Bernard took his turn in the shower. By the time they reached the dining-room, it was a little before eleven. Their host made no reference, even with a smile, to the planned walk, didn't for instance produce plates of shrivelled food, vintage nine o'clock. It was some consolation that the other breakfasters – there were only four of them – were just being served their test-tubes of orange-juice, and so couldn't have been down much before them.

After breakfast, Bernard settled the bill. They could still take their walk, but now they would have to take their bags with them. It seemed a good idea, all the same, and when Neil had wrapped around his neck his collection of Oxfam-shop scarves they set off down the hill to the seafront.

They took a turn along the promenade. One bus shelter in two seemed to be open to the sky, asserting in the teeth of the evidence that a resort once favoured by royalty could never run out of sunshine. Looking out to sea from the promenade, they could see the weather being formed some way offshore. Beyond a certain distance, the sky was an undifferentiated grey. On the near side of an invisible barrier, clouds appeared and were driven towards land. It was bad weather, but at least it was new weather, and there was some status in that. At least they had got to it before anyone else.

Bernard wanted to get down to the gravel beach, not because he wanted a paddle or a chance to make gravel-castles, but because somehow there was no point in going to Brighton and doing anything else. Neil hung back, either because the sea shore didn't meet his spoiled southern-hemisphere definition of beach, or because the going under-foot would prove too tough for what was left of The Winter Boots. 'We could have a swim, though,' he suggested. Bernard stared. 'In a pool,' Neil added.

'On a Sunday?'

'Why not?' Neil was optimistic.

'We'll have to break in.'

'I don't think so.' Neil held up the map. 'We can try, eh?'

It took them a few wrong turns, all the same, to find the swimming pool, but when they got there it was open. It was also called The Prince Regent Swimming Centre. 'Isn't that just as piss-elegant as you'd expect,' said Bernard as they queued for tickets. 'Other people have pools. The Prince Regent has a Swimming Centre.'

'I think it looks stunning. There's a water slide.'

The changing rooms were certainly well equipped. Because of their bags, Neil and Bernard had to use a relay of lockers, locking each key in the next compartment along to avoid pincushioning their trunks with safety pins.

Besides the water slide, the swimming centre had a separate diving pool, and a supervised lane for serious swimmers. Neil and Bernard included themselves in this category, and had the goggles – guaranteed against misting and leakage – to prove it.

Bernard admired Neil's efficient unflustered crawl, his progress through the water in a series of easy windmilling shrugs. Once, as they passed each other in opposite directions, Neil slid his hand between Bernard's legs, breaching lane discipline for a moment in order to do so.

Afterwards, when they had dried and dressed themselves, Bernard said, 'I enjoyed that.'

'Yes, there's nothing like a swim.'

'I don't mean that, quite. I mean when you touched me.'

Neil smiled. His face had a badger's-mask look to it, from where his goggles had left their shape on his skin. 'I couldn't be sure it was you. So I had to touch up everybody in the pool.'

When Bernard regained his bearings after leaving the pool, he realized that they were only some little way from The Pantry, where they had had such a pleasant snack the day before. Why not go there again, or try it anyway? If they were now in a town where swimming-pools were open on the Sabbath, perhaps they had been transplanted bodily to a universe where – in spite of its resemblance to Britain – anything you wanted might be had when you wanted it. Neil fell in with this suggestion, and Bernard obliged him by falling in with his lazy pace.

The Pantry was indeed open, though almost empty. The only addition since the previous day was a lavish spread of Sunday papers; the only subtraction was the middle generation of the staff. Today the old lady served, and the young girl once again cleared up.

Neil had a small salad and an orange juice – he always asked simply for 'juice', but he was now in a country where no one would think of looking for juice in anything but an orange, or rather a can of orange juice. Bernard ordered a coffee and some garlic bread, which took a little time to arrive. When it did, it repeated, he felt, the triumph that the mussels had had the day before, until they were obscurely sabotaged by the people at the next table: the bread was thick, the way Bernard liked it (and Neil didn't) and so saturated with garlic butter it might have been injected with it, like a Chicken Kiev.

Neil had already nearly finished by the time the garlic bread arrived, but Bernard felt no need to hurry. 'I should have had this before we had our swim.'

'And got cramp, eh?'

'Maybe, but at least I would have had a lane to myself. *Headlamps* of garlic.'

Neil leaned sideways and down, then sat up again with a yelp. Bernard said, 'What's the matter?' Neil said, 'Splinter'. Bernard gave a smiling wince of fellow-feeling and returned to his colour supplement, slightly smeared as it was with garlic butter. He licked the last of the butter off his fingers, enjoying his last tastes of it. When he looked up, there was still pain on Neil's face, and he was still inspecting his hand. 'Is it a bad one?'

'It's in a bad place, anyway.' The splinter had run under the nail of his left index finger. Neil held the hand out to him. The splinter seemed to have gone all the way to the back of the nail. Most splinters are like small spears; this one was like a small spade, as Bernard could see through the pale shield of Neil's fingernail before blood obscured it.

Bernard said, 'What were you doing, exactly?'

'Looking in my bag for the map. To see how far we are

from the station. Only I didn't get as far as my bag. I must have got caught on the bottom of the table.'

Gingerly, Bernard patted the underside of the table, which was rougher even than the unpolished top. He thought for a moment. 'We need a pin.'

'Well, I haven't got one.' Neil was pressing down on the tip of his nail, to prevent any issue of blood, in a way that looked particularly painful.

Blood in general, and blood like Neil's in particular, had acquired a demonic status over the few previous years. Before that time, blood seemed largely a symbolic substance, and people's attitudes towards it signs of something else. Being a blood donor involved only a symbolic courage, and squeamishness about blood was an odd though perhaps significant little cowardice. Now blood had taken back its seriousness as a stuff. Bernard spent needless thought worrying about what would happen if a drop of blood landed on the table, as if the customers had the habit of running their tongues along the lacerating wood. They would need to be pretty quick off the mark anyway, to have any hope of putting themselves at risk.

'Could have been worse, eh?' Neil said. 'I could have had a nosebleed.'

'I'll see if there's someone here with a pin,' Bernard said. The grandmother of the establishment was in a kitchen full of steam and the smell of burnt toast. Bernard tried to explain his need for a pin, but succeeded only in flustering her. He glimpsed, meanwhile, a bottle of bleach on a shelf by the sink, which a sense of responsibility to the public would oblige him to use if Neil shed his blood at all widely.

The young girl slipped in through the swing door and watched with a neutral interest. Bernard found himself missing that intermediate generation of staff, the competent mother–daughter who would make everything all right.

The grandmother produced at first some tiny forks with

wooden handles, designed for the convenient handling of corn on the cob, and then a safety pin, which Bernard carried in sombre triumph back to Neil in the eating area.

Neil was still pressing his nail down, and had managed to prevent any real leakage. 'We'd better not do it here,' Bernard said. 'Put people off their food.' In fact the few people in the cafe were stubbornly focused on their plates and Sunday papers, but Neil followed Bernard obediently back to the kitchen.

Now for a change Neil pulled up the end of the nail, with a shiver of pain, and Bernard used the safety-pin, trying to skewer the splinter and draw it out. The field hospital established in her kitchen seemed to distress the grandmother more, if anything, than impromptu surgery would have upset her customers. She kept fluttering up to them from the stove, and saying, 'Are you sure you shouldn't go to the hospital?'

'We'll get the splinter out first,' said Bernard, speaking with false confidence, 'then we might get the hospital to take a look.'

He tried to peer under the rim of the nail, hoping to see the contour of the splinter again. By working the safety-pin gingerly from side to side, he was able to snag the thin stem of the splinter. Neil's hand gave a little jerk as the pin started to pull on the embedded fragment. Bernard tried to move his hand as slowly and smoothly as possible. Neil gave another involuntary pull, and the narrow part of the splinter broke off, leaving the rest of it lodged in the quick.

Bernard pulled out a chair for Neil to sit down, and told the grandmother what she had been telling him for some time. 'I think we'd better go to the hospital. Is it near? Walking distance? Do you have a car?' He thought driving them to hospital was the least she could do to atone for the dangerous roughness of her table, but she shook her head in answer to the question about a car. He was surprised when she took her coat from the back of the kitchen door and put it on. 'We're not on the phone here,' she explained. 'I'll ring from my daughter's.'

'Does she live in Brighton?' Bernard asked, aiming at a joke.

She didn't smile. 'Just round the corner. I'll be back in a minute.' She murmured something to the girl, before she left, about being in charge.

The girl, all the same, chose to stay in the kitchen rather than attend to her customers. By and large they were patient Sunday customers, but every now and then a little self-righteous queue built up, and she would have to venture out to serve them.

Bernard's worries had transferred from spilled blood, no longer a risk now that Neil's clotting agents had started to work, to the safety-pin. He shouldn't leave it without some attempt at disinfection. He could pour a little bleach over it, before the girl came back in. Or might Neil be offended? Then again, if he had been a smoker, he could have lit up, and held the match flame under the safety pin just for a few seconds, before blowing it out.

The girl came back in, and Bernard abandoned any plan of eliminating contamination on the premises. Her grand-mother – if they were in fact more than professionally connected – came back the next minute. She hung up her coat and offered to make tea, on the house. Bernard only regretted that they had paid when they had ordered, and so had no opportunity of expressing emotion by withholding payment. Neil wanted to be ready for the taxi when it arrived, so they sat in the eating area, at the table next to the door.

There was no sign of the taxi. 'If this was America,' Bernard said, 'they'd be so afraid of being sued they'd treat us a lot better than this. We'd have a chauffeur to the hospital, I dare say.'

'If this was New Zealand,' Neil said, 'they'd polish the

tables in the first place.' He had wrapped a paper napkin round the finger.

Again Bernard tried for the light note. 'Not much point in going to a veggie restaurant, eh, if the furniture goes and bites you.'

His impatience got the better of him and he stepped out on to the pavement to greet the taxi when it arrived. There were infuriating numbers of taxis rushing past already, but none of them so much as slowed down. They all seemed to have their signs illuminated, and Bernard tried frantically to flag them down, feeling that this emergency justified the breaking of his promise to the taxi that was on its way.

The taxis ignored him anyway, but not from solidarity. It became clear that Brighton was not a town where taxis could be hailed. They had to be ordered, and if they had an illuminated sign on top, that was to say 'I am a taxi,' not 'I will take you where you want to go.'

After several frustrating minutes, Bernard went back into The Pantry. He swept into the kitchen and announced that it was now twenty-five minutes since the taxi was called, not consulting his watch in case the true figure was less impressive. He bullied the grandmother until she offered to phone again, reaching once more for her coat on the back of the door. Bernard caught sight of the safety-pin on the table and picked it up, murmuring hollowly that he'd better take it along in case there was more he could do on the way to the hospital. As the grandmother left, he took a seat next to Neil near the door.

'How's it feel?'

'Not bad.'

'Hurt a lot?'

'Not much.'

Bernard hadn't seen him often enough in situations of ordinary adversity to know whether the stiff upper lip was a reflex or a performance. Then the grandmother knocked on

111

the window next to them, and pointed at a cab that had drawn up at the kerb.

The taxi-driver needed some convincing that he was picking up the right party. Bernard began to feel that a telephone call was not enough to secure a taxi in Brighton; you needed a letter of introduction. But once the driver was satisfied that he had got hold of the right people, he drove them rapidly and without conversation to the hospital, which was a little out of town to the east. As they passed, Bernard recognized the street that Rogues was in.

The hospital was shabby and far from new. An old lady was having difficulty in opening the door as she left; automatic doors were clearly a thing of the future in this part of the world. The casualty department was full of glum waiting people. Bernard pressed a button at the reception counter, which was unmanned, and a receptionist appeared after a few moments. Neil advanced his finger towards her, and she said, 'That looks nasty.' She took his details and told them to take a seat.

After a while, a nurse came timidly down the line of seats, calling a version of Neil's awkward Yugoslav name. Her despairing intonation suggested she spent most of the day calling out names that their owners regarded as parodies of the real thing. She took a look at Neil's hand, and said it looked nasty. Bernard was impressed by this prompt response into thinking that the health service was not quite as clapped-out as it seemed, until the nurse told them it would be at least an hour and a half before they were seen to.

Neil smoothly settled down to writing a letter to his parents in New Zealand. He expressed to Bernard his relief that it wasn't his writing hand that was affected. Bernard tried to settle with a book (there wasn't the desk-space necessary for marking) but found himself unable. He looked round at the rows of silent, passive people waiting to be attended to. After the hotel and the disco, both trying hard to pretend not to be bourgeois homes, it should have been refreshing that the hospital made no attempt to be anything but what it was.

He stood up, and asked the receptionist where he could find a toilet. Across the corridor, she told him, with a slightly furtive intonation that was explained when Bernard realized they were staff toilets, not in theory open to the laity. On his way back from using them – they seemed no more sophisticated than the usual ones, and demanded no extra skills – he spotted a hot-drinks dispenser. This too was labelled Staff Use Only. One of the items it offered was hot chocolate, so Bernard searched through his pockets for change. A pair of shoes strode through the corridor, and stopped behind him in a way he felt was intended to pass a message. They had the acoustic properties unique to white lace-ups worn by a trained person. For an absurd moment he thought he was going to burst into tears. He straightened up, and stopped the search in his pockets, which had so far yielded only copper coins and the safety-pin – in the closed position, mercifully – that he had planned to dispose of so responsibly. He trailed defeated back to the seat next to Neil's.

Neil's letter was reaching its closing stages, with the phrase 'Bernard says hello'. Neil passed the biro across to him and he wrote, embarrassed, 'hello', wishing either that he could embellish this message a fraction with something more personal, or that he could be excused from contributing at all. Out of the corner of his eye he could see that Neil was writing *Bernard saying hello* in brackets after his word of greeting. It seemed like a schoolboy's letter home, but he had to admit that Neil currently held the monopoly on adult calm. It was Bernard who had the schoolboy restlessness.

He had intended to wait at least until Neil had finished his letter, but found himself asking prematurely 'Are you going to tell them?'

Neil didn't need the meaning of the question clarified, 'I

don't know,' he said. Normally he was scrupulous about disclosing his antibody status, with the result that he was still waiting, after four months, for a dentist's appointment. If when Neil's appointment arrived – and it was still likely to be several months off – any work was necessary, Bernard knew that the dentist would use a low-speed drill to make sure he didn't volatilize any saliva, which might then be inhaled. Perhaps that was why, Bernard thought, it was taking so long for Neil's turn to come round. He could imagine the dentist spending hours on every filling with his hammer and chisel, murmuring behind his mask that people got these things out of proportion, when a few simple procedures were enough to eliminate any risk.

Bernard said, 'It shouldn't make any difference, should it, whether you tell them or not?'

'But Brighton is a provincial town, eh?'

'A provincial town full of gay men, mind you. You're going to have to make up your own mind.' He hoped it didn't sound as if he were washing his hands of the matter. His private preference was for telling them – whoever 'they' turned out to be – but he didn't want to make Neil feel like a danger to health, quietly being quarantined.

'I doubt if it matters anyway.'

Towards the end of the stated time, another nurse, who turned out to be a doctor, paid a visit. She kept her hands in the pockets of her white coat, while Neil dutifully held out the finger. She peered through her glasses at it, then looked over the top of them and said, 'Come with me, please.' Neil followed her, and Bernard included himself in the expedition. They went to a room full of little cubicles.

The doctor, though only about Bernard's age, had a feathery growth of hair on her upper lip, which looked oddly touching in spite of its incongruousness. It was like an adolescent's moustache, a shy fanfare of hormones. She kept her hands in her pockets so long that Bernard expected them to be warty, or at least covered in hair, but when she did at last bring them into the open, and touched Neil's finger, they were sightly and even shapely. She put them back in her pockets immediately, in what was clearly the defining posture of her profession. Then she said, 'It's fairly clean, but I may have to cut the nail.' This at least made a change from calling it nasty. 'How long since you had a tetanus injection?'

'Years.'

'Two years?'

'Ten years.'

'You'll be needing one of them, then,' she said. Neil looked uncomfortable. 'And I have to move you again, I'm afraid, to where I keep the long-nosed tweezers. Don't worry,' she said, perhaps seeing Neil's expression. 'I'll give you an anaesthetic. Follow me, please. Your friend can come too.'

They followed her along the corridor to Minor Surgery, where Neil and Bernard had to take their shoes off. As he took off the ragged Winter Boots, Neil said, 'Perhaps someone will steal them, eh? With any luck.' Then he turned to the doctor, and said 'I'm antibody-positive, you know.' Bernard assumed that Neil was urged to frankness by the doctor's willingness to have Bernard along. A relaxed worldliness could be deduced from that. 'I see. That's unfortunate,' the doctor said, frowning as she washed her hands.

'In what way?' said Bernard truculently, assuming that she would now make difficulties about operating on Neil.

'My dear man, you hardly need me to tell you that. It's unfortunate because it makes life so very difficult.' She coaxed Neil on to the operating table.

Bernard's anger still had some momentum to it. 'I think anybody who doesn't work with people who are antibody-positive should be sacked on the spot, not because they're prejudiced but because they must be incompetent to be taking any risks.' He paused for breath.

'Funny you should say that,' said the doctor, and then

when Bernard was preparing to ask, 'Why so?', 'That's just what I think myself.'

She helped Neil to push his finger through a sort of stiff cowl of material, so that it was singled out for surgery. Deprived of its fellows it looked almost amputated, even before the doctor had unpacked the case where she kept her long-nosed tweezers.

Sheepishly, Bernard fished the safety-pin out of his pocket and strolled over to a vivid yellow box labelled Contaminated Sharps. He dropped it into the hole in the top, feeling a bit ridiculous but reminding himself that it was, after all, contaminated and it was, after all, sharp. The doctor was unwrapping instruments, individually wrapped in gauze, from a sterilized tin box. Bernard noticed that although she was already wearing surgical gloves, she put on another pair from inside the box. 'Is that necessary?' he asked, with a slight return of his earlier truculence.

'It's routine,' she said. 'Rubber gloves don't stay sterile for ever, you know. I could have taken the first pair off, but this seemed more sensible. Now shut up,' she said, without heat. 'But you can hold the patient's hand if you like.'

She began to unpack her long-nosed tweezers. Neil turned his head resolutely away, and Bernard locked glances with him. They stayed like that for a little while, like people trying competitively not to blink, then Bernard started flicking sideways glances at the fingernail. The doctor said, 'I'm putting the local in now.' Bernard could see her sliding two needles, one after the other, into the top of the finger. Neil blinked a few times rapidly in succession, and Bernard could feel his hand-grip tightening in spite of itself.

After some probing, the doctor said, 'No, this won't work, I'm going to have to cut the nail.'

'Cut as little as possible, eh?' said Neil,' I've got a full-head bleach to do tomorrow morning at 10.30.'

The doctor gave a little laugh. She seemed to find this

ambition amusing. 'We'll sort something out with the nurse, see if we can't get you a light-weight dressing of some sort.'

Bernard stopped taking his sideways glances, having no wish to see Neil's nail being cut. The two locked glances again, like pieces of heroic statuary. In a moment, the doctor said, 'All done.'

Bernard did the talking. 'How much have you cut?'

'The tiniest sliver. Take a look.'

Bernard kept his eyes where they were. 'Will you be able to reach the splinter?'

'I already have. All done, I told you. Take a look.' She was holding out the stub of the splinter in the mouth of her long-nosed tweezers.

Bernard could feel Neil relaxing against him. He tensed up again when the doctor said, 'Nurse will give you a tetanus injection.' She took off all her rubber gloves, scrubbed up, shook hands pleasantly and left.

Before doing any injections, the nurse fitted Neil with a light-weight dressing, as promised, and told him to go to a casualty department in London in a few days if he needed another. Bernard put his arms round Neil's neck while the injection was done. It occurred to him how stupid he was not to have done it earlier. A local anaesthetic involved having a needle stuck in you just as much as an inoculation did, but somehow the word 'local' made it sound trivial, something you shouldn't need to be helped through. A tetanus jab gave cowardice a wider scope, and Bernard took advantage of it.

Down the corridor there was a telephone which did not, for a wonder, bear the message Staff Use Only. Bernard used it to call a taxi, while Neil climbed awkwardly into his jacket.

It was already fully dark, although not as late by his watch as Bernard had expected. Neither of them knew the times of trains, but they went straight to the station, prepared to take their chances.

'How's it feel now?' Bernard asked.

'Not too bad. Throbs a bit. They say it'll be worse tonight when the local wears off. I may need a sleeping tablet, but we got off pretty lightly, eh?'

Bernard had to agree. They had got off lightly. He had underestimated the amount of practice the hospital would have had with this whole new world of risk and stigma. But he still felt damaged, and found it hard to be cheerful for Neil's benefit.

There was a London-bound train waiting in the station, already very full. There were only isolated seats free, so once again Neil and Bernard sat apart, though visible to each other.

Bernard was grateful for their separation. He needed time to recover independently, always assuming the damage was reversible. The train filled up still more before it pulled out of the station, so that there were people standing, who intermittently broke his view of Neil. From what he could see, Neil had his eyes closed, was asleep or meditating.

The train was a slow one, and stopped at every station it saw. Work on the track diverted it, and at least once it stopped – to judge by the absence of lights – in open country. Near Bernard there stood a woman dressed for a party, complete with bunch of flowers, and a harried mother, come to that, but Bernard felt no inclination to give up his seat. He felt he had a claim on it that outranked theirs. He was still in shock, apparently, though nothing had happened directly to him.

Something had happened to him all the same. He knew that love starts off inspired and ends up merely competent. He didn't resent that. That was bargained for. But he hadn't foreseen, in all his mental preparation, that the passage could be so drastically foreshortened. A tiled corridor filled with doctors and nurses opened off every room he would ever share with Neil. He had always known it was there, but today the door to it had briefly been opened.

He thought with nostalgia of the time when people had got so exercised about who loved who, and how much. Now it was simply a question of what character of love would be demanded of him, and how soon. It was as if he had been pierced in a tender place which he had thought adequately defended, by a second splinter, not visible. The word *sick*, even the word *death*, had no power to match the fact of hospital. As with the first splinter, he had managed to break off the protruding part, but not to remove it. It gnawed at the nail-bed.

The Brake

Adam Mars-Jones

Sex brought him a number of things, all of them more useful than pleasure. His first memory was sexual, and not only that but it had a significant element of endlessness, of continuous quest, as was pointed out to him in later days by a psychiatrist with whom he had an on-again, off-again but not altogether unfulfilling affair.

In the memory, he was in a swimming pool with some of his father's army friends, and he was diving between their legs. They stood with their legs apart, laughing, and he dived through the underwater arches they made. Once or twice he tried to hold his breath and keep swimming, so as to swim through a second arch without surfacing, but the excitement was too much for him and he had to come up for air. His mouth making bubbles, he bumped upwards against the keystone of the arch. When he broke the surface at last, coughing and waterlogged, the laughter was louder than ever. As soon as he got his breath back he dived again.

For his eighteenth birthday, his father gave him a copy of *Battle Cry* by Leon Uris, saying it would teach him everything he needed to know about being a man. But when, the day after his eighteenth birthday, he announced his intention of joining the army, his father wouldn't hear of it. Even his mother wasn't so set against it, but his father was angry in his dismissal of the plan. That was his father all over, spelling out in detail what would win his approval, man to man, and then shooting him down in flames when he tried to put it into practice.

It didn't take much thought – and this was long before he met the psychiatrist – to work out that his first memory couldn't possibly be his first, or anything like. It was actually embarrassing, when he tried to establish which of his father's postings brought with it the privilege of a swimming pool, to realize how much older he must have been than he instinctively thought; and still he couldn't take the label 'first' off the memory of diving through the arches, seeing in close-up the muscly flesh goosebumped under its scattering of hair. Logic could strip the memory of its claims to antiquity, but could do nothing to lessen its force. In that sense it kept first place among his memories.

With very little effort he could summon up a memory that must be earlier, and had its own sort of formative power. As a child, he was ready and willing to play with any toys that he was given, or that his playmates owned, even the educational ones, but there was one toy – toy was too small a word really – that he couldn't bear to share, and with which he established an almost erotic relationship. It was a construction set, but unlike Lego or Bayko its materials were grown-up; scaled-down of course, but still very much the real thing. Lego was pleasant to fiddle with, and he enjoyed making the nipples on top of one block snappingly engage with the hollow underside of another. But the houses it made were clumsy and uniform. Bayko was even worse. You had to start by sticking rods vertically in the baseboard, to the shape of the house you were building, and then you slid panels of bricks grooved at each edge down between the rods. You didn't build the roof, you just popped it on like a hat when you'd done everything else. And then all you got for your work was a house like the one his family lived in at the time, with a red tiled roof and one futile bay window.

In any case, he'd seen a house that looked a lot like theirs being built. It was on the way to school, and he passed it every day. He looked closely every time he passed, but there was never any sign of vertical rods. He thought Bayko was probably a cheat, but he wanted to be sure. He dragged behind his mother when the workmen were coming close to the roof level, just in case they put the rods in at the last minute, down through the bricks, to make them stronger. But he never saw any sign of them.

Contemporary Brickplayer was different. All it was was a baseboard and a box of tiny bricks of a dark pinky grey, and a packet of mortar mixture that you made up with water. You didn't have to plan anything and the pieces didn't need to fit together at particular angles. The only limit to your constructions was the binding power of the mortar, and there was no arguing with that. But you could cantilever things out until your building slowly, voluptuously, prised itself apart.

Often he would put a brick in his mouth as he started to play, as if the sour tablet was a sweet, not the crunchy sort of sweet or the chewy sort of sweet, but a sweet like butterscotch that you just moved around your mouth, sucking and sucking, until it faded away. Except that the bricks from Contemporary Brickplayer never faded away. Each new part of his mouth, as he shifted the brick, drew out its inexhaustible flavour of baked clay.

He would build and build until he had used up all the bricks, mixing more mortar when he needed it. And then when there really were no more bricks in the box, and none that had fallen out where he could find them, he would take the brick out of his mouth and add it regretfully to the complex structure on the baseboard. Because of its long immersion in saliva, it had a different colour from the others and stuck less well.

Demolishing the building was almost more fun than building it in the first place. All you needed was warm water, which dissolved the mortar, so he persuaded his mother to let him do it in the bath. He would sit in the hot water and simply hug his building. Everything would slide together in his arms. Then after a few minutes in the water the bricks would be clean and separate again, ready to be used. If his mother was watching, he would let the water drain away, pack away the bricks, and then have a bath on his own. If she wasn't, he liked to let the mortar-rich water dry on his skin in crusty patches.

Contemporary Brickplayer gave him a temporary second skin of greyish powder, which he shed on the sheets, much to his mother's irritation, but sex gave him a second name, one that didn't wear out but eventually replaced the first one for most purposes.

If his father had been more enthusiastic about his joining the military, he might have been able to put off, perhaps for years, tentative steps in a different direction. After that rejection, it took him a long time to understand his father's motives, and what was really expected of him.

There was a life that the army would have saved him from, a life that would save him from the army. He found himself not much later on the brink of visiting a gay bar, the only one in the town where he lived. He stayed on that brink for a remarkably long time. He passed the pub a number of times, and went defeated home. The entrance was down a flight of steps, and he looked longingly down them as he passed.

When he did go down those steps at last, the image that accompanied him was not the image of his parents, whether angry, shocked or horribly understanding. It was the image of his two little sisters, six and eight years younger than himself, though if he had really run into them it would have been easy to pretend he was just visiting another pub. His sisters' feeling for him was not far short of adoration. In the image that he carried downstairs with him, they were clinging on to each other and weeping in bafflement.

Not that he got any further than the bottom of the stairs

that time. As he paused there at the bottom before pushing the door open, he could hear a complex noise of layered conversation that was nevertheless the silence between two records on the juke box. This complex noise excited him. It must contain a voice that would speak to him. But as he was about to push the door open, the next record came on. Its first word was 'Stop!', followed after a dramatic pause by the words 'In The Name of Love'. Startled, he turned and ran up the stairs, and went home.

The next time he tried, the Supremes were off-duty on the juke box and he was able to break through the imaginary cordon of weeping sisters. On his first visit, there was no voice that would speak to him, perhaps because he stood very still and kept his eyes fixed firmly on his beer glass.

On later visits, he was talked to, and he talked grudgingly back. He was full of suspicion of the men who owned these voices. He was unwilling to tell them his real name. His parents were well known in the area, so there was some dim sense to this precaution, though his parents were not so well known as to make it worth anyone's while to hang around gay bars on the off-chance of ensnaring their next of kin. There was no rational reason, in any case, for withholding his first name as he did. The name was Gregory, which was hardly distinctive enough to betray him. To each person he spoke to, in the weeks following his first visit, he gave a different Christian name, as if by this discretion he could avoid having the successive burly boys who sat on the same stool and ordered the same timid drink identified as a single customer – a customer who was fast becoming a regular.

He could have been a David, he could have been a Walter. He had used those names in conversations that he had taken great care should not lead anywhere. His withholding of himself, in fact, was so long-lasting that his parents, if the object had been women and not men – and if they had known about it – might well have worried about him, thinking him underpowered or otherwise troubled.

But he was Roger when he took the fatal step of giving a man his telephone number. By dictating a handful of numerals he dragged himself from sexual pre-history. He was horrified even while he did it, but it never occurred to him to falsify a digit. The logical consequence, of course, was that a man would phone his parents' house, wanting Gregory but asking for Roger. The next night he hovered by the phone, ready to snatch it up, irritated that his parents seemed to be exchanging secret smiles at his behaviour. The call came the following day. Even a year or two later he would have been able to anticipate such a phone call almost to the minute, but when it came he was lying on his bed, relieved and regretting relief.

The man on the phone was confident that his call had been hoped for; he kept the suspicious woman who answered talking for a little while, long enough for Gregory to reach the phone red-faced with the idea of arousal. He became Roger as he reached for the instrument. In time, only the people in the house at the moment when he grasped the receiver, his parents and his sisters, continued to call him Greg.

His schoolmates had used the word 'roger' in a sexual sense, but it never occurred to him that this meaning might have a wider currency. He thought it was purely a school word, like a teacher's nickname. When, later on, he first realized that the sexual sense of his name had escaped its school context and was at large, when someone showed it to him in print in a dictionary, he experienced a bolt of shame, perhaps the very bolt that had been missing from the moment of losing his virginity. He had named himself after a piece of taboo slang.

Later, with some mental effort, he constructed a different rationale for the name. 'Gregory' actually contained 'Roger', albeit back to front. All he had done was set it free from its confines, reading his name against the grain of his parents' intentions. In fact 'Roger', in the moment he had chosen it to present to an attractive stranger, and before it acquired the power to change his life, had seemed to him to have a vaguely military association. It was the crisp, telegraphic, masculine way of saying, I understand. I obey. That the military association still had the glamour testified to the continuing influence of his father.

No shame derived from his initiation into sex, but a desperate embarrassment hedged it about. Before leaving the house on his assignation, he had left on his bedside table an envelope, with an inscription instructing that it should be opened if he didn't return that night. He imagined he had no preconceptions about what was about to happen, but at the same time he couldn't visualize anything but returning home. The sex he had with himself led on to sleep, but he couldn't imagine the tense business of traffic with others having the same drowsy consequences. At most he was collecting the keys of the new house of adult sexuality. He wasn't moving in.

Inside the envelope was his partner's phone number, and strict instructions that his parents should not call the number, but pass it on to the police and let them investigate. In later life it amazed him, not that he had had so little trust in his first lover – or in his parents for that matter – but that he had had so much in the police.

In fact, he woke up to the smell of bacon. He pulled on his clothes in a fever, and rushed out of the bedroom, almost colliding with his host, who was carrying a breakfast tray.

'Got to go,' he muttered, and ran out of the house.

When he got home, there was no need even to go upstairs. It was immediately obvious that his note would still be there, unopened. Breakfast was in full swing, though he couldn't help noticing that marmalade here stayed in the jar it was bought in, while on the tray he had run past a little earlier he had seen a glass dish containing a dainty mound of orange, and a fluted spoon like a miniature shovel. He said something about staying over with a friend, and his sisters immediately started asking when they would be allowed to stay the night with their friends. If his parents detected a particular satisfaction in his manner that morning, they probably decided that Gregory had become a man at last, and only hoped he had been careful. In fact, Roger was thinking how strange it was that you could take your life in your hands, and still wake up to a cooked breakfast.

He saw the man for whom he was Roger a few times, and through him was introduced to a small provincial circle. In later life, he forgot them wholesale as people, and remembered them only as the sources of particular catch-phrases that arrived in his mind, if not actually on his tongue, at long but never predictable intervals. Who was it would murmur when flustered, 'Not a pot washed nor a sausage pricked, and all these Spanish captains in the town'? Who was it sang softly as he shaved, 'How much is that doggie in the mirror?' Who was it used the phrase 'doing the cooking', which seemed at first so casually domestic ('Who does the cooking?', 'I'll bet he does the cooking') to describe a sexual role? There was one man he would remember whenever he heard the word 'hard-on', who had given it the fastidious plural 'hards-on', like someone correcting 'court-martials' to 'courts-martial'.

He liked them, and was grateful to them, but everybody already knew he didn't belong there. He could feel their valuation of him reluctantly rising, though they were also puzzled by him. He wasn't sexually aggressive, but he had none of the pliability of personality they valued in someone his age.

Staring coolly at himself in the mirror, he had decided that the blue of his eyes was his only physical asset (in fact his eyes were much more attractive when he wasn't using them to stare coolly). So he decided to wear nothing but blue jeans, and a narrow range of shirts, all of them incorporating blue as an important element, to point up his only physical asset. In later years, he wondered if his life would have been different if he had had, say, brown eyes. Would he have worn only brown velvet trousers, for instance? But his life would have been different if he had had brown eyes anyway. At least, after his single fashion decision, he was never diverted into dressiness, and his choice of uniform was historically fortunate, if not actually prophetic.

Meanwhile, his other fantasy, the one that started in the bath, had also come out of the water, and taken feeble amphibian steps on land. He was slow to realize that there was a profession that corresponded to the sensations he had experienced in the bath with the bricks. It was only when he saw, on television, film of Frank Lloyd Wright in old age scampering spryly over the Guggenheim Museum while it was being built, that he saw how it was possible to leave the bath, and go on playing for a long lifetime as if you were still there. 'Architect' and 'architecture' became words that took on any amount of glamour – the excitement that was meant to attach to 'marrying and settling down' as well as to 'satisfying career'.

There wasn't much he could find out about Wright at short notice, and none of it was necessarily true; but it was all promising. Wright had started off building wind-mills for his uncles. He had affairs with his clients' wives. You could hire him to build you a house, but that didn't give you the right to change the furniture round.

He had feared that when he first sat in front of a drawing board all the excitement would drain away, but instead it seemed to concentrate on the point of his pencil. He came to enjoy the drawing as much as he had ever hoped to enjoy a finished building. He had a particular soft spot for axonometrics, where the workings of a building, the secrets of its surfaces, were laid out as if from above and to the side: the point of view of a nosy helicopter, or a low-flying god.

In his early architectural drawings, even those submitted for examination, the buildings seemed to float in a depthless pink space, and there might be an effigy of Frank Lloyd Wright on a pediment, engaged in some complicated transaction with a group of boys and dogs.

It was architecture, and his pursuit of it, that brought him to London, but once he was there it wasn't architecture that took up his attention. He began to find that he had a strongly sexual charm, that he could make men find him attractive more or less by wanting them to. He was suspicious of this charm, and used it as little as possible. Rather later, when he got a credit card, he used that too, as little as possible, and for the same reason: not because his credit was limited, but because it seemed not to be. His credit limit on the card was extended every time he exceeded it, and it seemed to him that the settling of an account so long deferred could only be devastating, when the final sum was called in.

At first, he found gay life in London baffling, congested and chaotic, but then he had the same first impression of London driving. It wasn't long before he was threading his way through the slums and squares with confidence, and with pride in his knowledge, the mental maps he had built up.

He was lucky enough to arrive in a sexual capital at a time when a thick neck was considered a major asset, and a thick waist a minor defect, in some settings even an aphrodisiac. He fitted the metropolitan model of attractiveness far better than he had ever fitted the provincial. Ten years before, he would have been an anomaly even in London.

He made no modifications to his style of dress. At first, he went to a barber's where his hair was trimmed with clippers to a No. 1 on the sides and a No. 3 on top. Later, when more pretentious establishments, actual salons, offered similar cuts, now become fashionable, he transferred his custom.

The atmosphere as such didn't do anything for him, but he loved to have his head massaged by a junior's stiff fingers while he was being shampooed. He went almost into a trance, loving this impersonal caress. Any too sensual or tender move in bed had the opposite effect, making him tense and suspicious.

He stayed clean-shaven even when gay fashion moved on to facial hair. He grew a beard just once, and kept it only long enough to receive his first compliment on its fullness, before he shaved it off.

The sharp focus that city life brought to his sexuality had brought with it disillusions as well as enchantments. He was more or less at ease with a fair repertoire of sexual acts. He no longer prepared himself – it embarrassed him to think about it now, cursing his provincial beginnings – for oral sex, or 'giving someone a blow job', by ranging on the bedside table two glasses, one empty and one filled with water.

He had come to a better understanding of himself, in certain specialized departments. He had assumed for a long time, on the evidence of what nude magazines he was able to obtain, that he was mildly undersized genitally. He was slow to gather from his sexual partners that there was something satisfactory about his equipment, and slower yet to twig that its satisfactoriness lay in disproportion. His penis ('cock') was a healthy average, while his testes ('balls') were unusually large.

But there was a bad news too. As a sexual mechanism he functioned smoothly on his own, but he was never able to come with anybody there. He could perform only in rehearsal. In his early sexual career, he was able to fool himself that release would come for him when he found more compatible partners, but here he was, established in a milieu that put a high value on him, and only confirmed in dysfunction.

He tackled the problem, with considerable enterprise, on three simultaneous fronts. In the first place, he started to chase heterosexuals. The theory here was that since for him the chase was everything, the conquest nothing, he could only gain by spinning things out. There was no play, after all, in reeling in fish that wanted to be caught, so he would learn to cast more widely.

He soon made the dismaying discovery that even straights could be landed. He was always forthright about his desires, and never made the mistake of going in for that David-and-Jonathan rubbish. Straight conversational skills lagged a long way behind gay, he was under no illusions about that, but he was willing to make sacrifices. The trouble was that all too often the opposition collapsed. He would just be setting up an enjoyable pattern of drinks, long phone calls and expeditions to the cinema, setbacks and concessions, when the specimen chosen for his unavailability would raise his beautiful, elusive face - he always went for conventional good looks, on the principle that lookers would be more used to admiration, and better at resisting it – and murmur the dreaded words, 'You've won. You know you've won. You can do anything you like.'

He was always going too far, and getting away with it, that was the trouble. He would be sitting on a sofa looking over an architectural book, the sort that seemed naturally to spread over four knees, and without preparation he would lean down and slowly take off his shoes. He would say softly, 'If I take off my shoes, that doesn't mean anything. But if I take off my socks,' starting to do so, 'that means I'm staying the night.' He would draw out the sock-striptease as long as he could, waiting for an interruption and a protest he imagined as inevitable. Then he would look up, and see instead a pair of eyes shining with more than their usual glitter, and an Adam's apple bobbing nervously under the hang of a classic jaw.

Coarse-fishing of this sort was all very well, but he seemed to spend an undue amount of time trying to throw these prize catches back, so that he could start again, separated by a goodly length of line from his thrashing prey. At least until the setback of their surrender he had their unattainable images to rehearse with. This was a different sort of sport, but still he thought of it as playing himself rather than playing *with* himself: playing himself like a fish, on both ends of the line this time, reeling himself in and then letting himself run, playing himself until he was exhausted and dangling, then letting himself off the hook, to slip back into the water.

There was another way out of his erotic cul-de-sac. Being the passive partner in anal intercourse ('getting fucked') was a problem-solving activity to someone in his circumstances. It was respectable for the person taking this role not to ejaculate: orgasm was as often as not only the signal that a sexual event was over, that some exchange had been consummated, and being penetrated was good enough evidence of that.

Since he was socially aggressive, and free of the mannerisms which made some poor people seem like victims of their sexuality rather than exponents of it, there seemed often to be an extra fillip given to his partner by his willingness to receive advances of this sort. He was quite happy to grant them their triumph, for the benefits he derived from it.

Inevitably, though, as he came to think, his body thwarted him, by growing a cyst in its, in his, back passage. Surgery didn't dampen his ardour, but certainly diverted it to other channels. The habit of sex stayed with him: he picked someone up the day after he left hospital, on his first tottery walk to the supermarket. For a long time, he remembered returning to bed in the middle of the night, from a session at stool which had made him weep with pain, and looking down on the peaceful sleeping face of this stranger – until he had to laugh instead, at the momentum of his habits, and the fringe benefits they continued to bring him, whether he wanted them or not.

His third line of attack took up the slack. Simply put, it

involved refusing no advance whatever, on the offchance that he might stumble, even at this late date, on what really turned him on. In practice, he found that his willingness had limits that were beyond his power to negotiate. Having his hands handcuffed, tied or confined in any way, was unendurable; it gave him the precise physical sensations of drowning. Most other things he tried.

He picked people up or was picked up by them, at all hours and in all settings. Once, taking his mother to Sadler's Wells (his sisters had both married young and had a son each, so she had time on her hands), he linked eyes with a Mediterranean-looking stranger over cups of sour coffee in the Lilian Baylis Room, and had a piece of paper bearing the stranger's name and telephone number slipped into his hand, with secret-agent slickness, as he queued with his mother to resume their seats after the interval.

So too he found himself on one occasion lying on thick carpet in a luxurious flat, with a cashmere scarf tied loosely over his eyes by way of a blindfold, while his host applied something, something feathery, to his scrotum. The scarf felt wonderful against his face; it returned his breath to him, slightly warmed and lightly scented. He imagined the end of it wafting up and down with his breathing, rolling and unrolling, like a snorer's beard in a Disney cartoon. He thought he could even cope with bondage if it was done with cashmere. Cashmere bondage. Was there such a thing? What a nelly thing to be thinking. His host, who had an actorish voice, was perhaps an actor whose income was earned doing voice-overs for advertisements, said, 'This will sting, of course.' He lay there, trying to match the voice to a particular product. Ice cream? Holidays? 'Why should it do that?' he asked lazily. Just then, signals from his scrotum arrived at the brain. 'Well, nettles do, you know.' *'Nettles?'* He squirmed, but the sensations when they reached him were only as sharp as curries are, to a palate unused to spices. 'It has to be the young leaves, of course,' the voice went on, 'the earlier in the season the better.' The voice became sad. 'The season is terribly short.' The cashmere soothed as if it had been turned into a dock leaf, even as the nettles prickled him, and his scrotum took on an amorous glow. His host's voice came from higher up, almost as if he had used the little set of library steps and was consulting the big dictionary on the top shelf. 'There's even a verb, to urticate. To thrash with nettles. Well, thrashing is too strong a word. What do you think? How would you describe it?'

As time went by, he developed a ground rule: sex must always happen at his place, not anyone else's. Since by now he rented a small flat in Earl's Court, and frequented pubs in easy reach of it, this was not a very restrictive stipulation. He decorated the interior in olive and grey, with accents of pastel, to general admiration.

The flat was small enough for tidiness to be forced on him. Its only glory was an outsized bath, both long and deep, which he could share in comfort with anyone of less than grotesque dimensions. He was doing so, one day, and scrubbing the muddy back in front of him, which belonged to a rugby-playing geologist, when a voice from the general area of the taps said languorously, 'Until you've been well fucked in a hot spring, you haven't lived.' He went on to describe a field trip he had taken with his lover, during which they had sneaked down a ladder into a bubbling cave of hot mud. Roger went on scrubbing mechanically – the water took on a grey-brown tinge from the mud – but this lustful fervour awoke no echo. The conversation chimed with his two obsessions, the men in the pool and the bricks in the bath, and that was why he remembered it (though he wasn't to know that). But he always pursued them separately. The only links were verbal: the word *erection*, and the word *built*, always his adjective of preference for men he found sexually attractive.

There were, here and there, dissenting voices to the life he was evolving for himself. One lover lost his temper when Roger left a party they had gone to together, without telling him. Roger, unusually for him, had taken a few puffs of a joint, and felt suddenly sleepy. His escort was deep in conversation, and he hadn't wanted to interrupt, so he went home. He had only been there five minutes when the phone rang, and there was the lover, ranting. The dope that had softened Roger had only made him ratty. 'You know what you are?' he shouted, when Roger had explained his leaving, 'you're a control freak. Would it have been so terrible if you'd fallen asleep on the sofa? I'd have woken you. I know what its, you're afraid of losing control. Tell me I'm wrong. You can't bear to let go, can you?' He sounded as if he was going to say something else.

'And another thing . . .' There was always another thing with this one. 'Do you know how oppressive it is being in that flat with you? You've tried to imprint your personality on that place so hard I'm surprised you haven't written your name on the walls just to be sure. Look, I like you, I'd even like the flat if you weren't there. But with you there, it's horrible. It's like . . . it's like being in the cinema and having someone read you the book of the film at the same time. Don't you see?' This was presumably a bid for the status of psychologist, and the staking of a deeper claim in Roger's life. But that was the moment when the lover acquired the prefix *ex-*. Roger hung up.

Other people who were less than taken with his way of life at least had professionalism to back up their distaste. The doctor to whom he took his first case of gonorrhoea said, 'Look.' Roger always said that in the 1970s he had gonorrhoea fifty times, clearly a Homeric figure. But he also always said he had seen *Some Like It Hot* twenty-five times in that period, so if you assume a constant ratio (that he contracted gonorrhoea twice for every time he saw *Some Like it Hot*), that is still quite a population of gonococci. Still quite a record of mucopurulence. Still quite a little pile of pills. 'Look,' said the doctor, 'you can burn the candle at one end. You can have a good time with your . . . cock,' (he said the word as if a penis was in itself a morbid growth) 'or you can eat too much, drink too much, smoke a lot, take drugs. But you can't do both.' Roger knew the doctor was beyond the range of his sexual charm. He could tell a closet case when he saw one. 'You need to put the brake on. If you don't, something else will. Lungs. Liver.'

He could only manage to feel guilty about the smoking. For a time he kept a record of smoking in his diary, so that the habit would become conscious, and so breakable. He would make vertical marks for the first four of every five cigarettes and a horizontal one for the fifth, to make a little gate. The plan was to fence off the habit, in due course, altogether. But the result was not to cut down his consumption of cigarettes. All he did was to incorporate into the bad habit a gesture of ritual repentance, which made the habit itself more durable. Some days his consumption actually increased, when his design sense made him smoke more cigarettes to complete a little gate towards the end of the day, puffing his way towards symmetry.

Sometimes he got the impression that he needed to defend his appetites even to gay friends. They seemed to need their share of explanations. He thought it wasn't the amount of activity as such, though perhaps it was that too; but it was really the variety that offended them, compulsive search without compulsive object. If he had responded only to boyish blonds or to older men, they could have excused the number of boyish blonds, the number of greying ex-athletes. If he had restricted himself to one-night stands or doomed passions that too would have been helpful.

He left his friends to their puzzlement, but privately he explained things to himself. He wasn't to blame if his needs were greater than other people's, if he was less efficient at converting sexual experience, into whatever sex became once converted. He remembered a magazine article about a toddler who dismayed his parents by dipping his food into a bowl of salt at every meal. They worried so much that eventually he was admitted to hospital, just for observation. After a few days, he died, and it turned out afterwards that his body had a severely impaired ability to absorb salt. The kid had compensated instinctively, and the bland hospital diet had killed him. It all went to show, Roger thought, that sometimes you had to shut out what other people said, and listen to your body. He was good at that. If his friends chose to live on a hospital diet all their lives, that didn't bother him. He would eat just as much salt as his system demanded.

This would have been a stronger argument if he hadn't had a sweet tooth as well as a salt thirst. At least his craving for sugar was seasonal rather than constant, but that actually made it more dangerous. Sometimes in autumn, tea and coffee with his usual dosage of sugar began to taste very sickly, and sweet foods lost all of their charm for him. It was an effort to keep on eating them. But if he gave up sugar, as his body seem to want him to do at this point in the year, other things changed too. His temperament quietened down, and he started looking for a lover – the only absolute requirement was good circulation, warm feet for cold nights – to nest with. He would be fond and even tender for the winter months. But then all it would take was three doughnuts in April and he would be off, crackling with aggressiveness, stepping out of the partnership as if it had never existed. The lover he left would not be much consoled to learn that it was not him personally that was being abandoned, since it was not him personally that had been chosen. The lover would be mortified, if anything, to find he had collaborated with an instinct not so much of romanticism as of hibernation.

Roger didn't want to go through that again with anybody,

and in any case he did no work at all during those snuggling winters. So he laid down, in September, in October, a good mulch of ice cream, pastry, chocolate, until he drove the yawns out of his bloodstream. His body would finally come to its senses and cut itself, unprompted, another slice of cake. Then he knew he would be spared another winter without work.

His private life was complex and contradictory: professionally, Complexity and Contradiction became his architectural watchwords, after he discovered Robert Venturi's Museum of Modern Art monograph on the subject. This, and later Venturi's *Learning from Las Vegas* – which like most architectural books was physically too large to cruise with, while *Complexity* could fit a pocket with a little bending – became his bibles, the best sort of bibles since they set out to multiply heresy. He continued to admire Wright, but extended his susceptibilities. He looked with favour on historical references, irregular curves, erosions, the creative use of interstitial space. He broadened his tolerance for eccentricity. He loved, for instance, Peter Eisenman's House V, with its upside-down dummy staircase formally balancing the functional one – so useful at moments of reversed gravity. He enjoyed too the slim pillar in the bedroom, whose sole purpose was preventing the residents from moving their beds together; by doing so they would lose the dawn view he had prepared for them through a slit window. That, Roger thought, was the right way to treat a client. Even better than running off with the client's wife, make it hard for *him* to have an affair with her. Make sure he's awake to see plenty of dawns.

He was in love with the profession, but he hung back from a career. Technical drawing paid his bills, or at least the interest on his credit card. He reminded himself that Louis Kahn hadn't built anything until he was well past forty, and *he* hadn't done too badly (and had died in debt).

There had always been a strong element of frustration in

his love affair with architecture. As a student, he had responded well to criticism, that is, he had listened politely while people made their comments (and not everybody liked his designs, ever) and then, when the critiquing session was over and everyone had gone, he would destroy his models (not everybody liked his designs, but *everybody* liked his models). Then came a phase when most people, almost everybody really, said they liked the designs, and still he destroyed the models, kicking them across the room in his rage at something or somebody.

He started teaching a little evening class, supposedly in Architectural Appreciation, but he soon changed that. At the first meeting of the class he announced that the course he was actually offering was A History of Horizontal Access. He wrote those words on a blackboard. There was a moment of profound shock in the room, and the sound of little dreams being punctured: dreams of taking civilized walks in a great city, making sophisticated comments on the buildings, and then finding somewhere to eat sandwiches. Then he explained that gallery access, which organizes the circulation of a residential building horizontally by way of balconies rather than vertically with internal staircases, had a particular beginning: with Gloucester New Gaol, the first purpose-built prison in Britain (1780). Gallery access was now the hallmark of council estates, and he proposed to show that the past and the present of gallery access were more than casually linked.

One person failed to reappear at subsequent classes, apparently unable to deal with the removal from the course of its element of the genteel. The others became more and more absorbed. For the last class he took them to Southwark and showed them the site of the Old King's Bench prison, which was familiar to them from contemporary prints. On the site was a council estate that closely followed the old prison in layout and contour. Roger then read to them a list of the facilities available in a prison like King's Bench (taprooms, cobblers, pie shops) and defied them to name a council estate that offered so much. These ideas were very much in the air, of course, and he made no secret of the fact from the class; he provided a full reading list. But he enjoyed the effect that he had on his students, and the identity they reflected back at him, even it if wasn't quite the identity he aspired to.

As regards his prospects of a successful career, his attitude was, rather surprisingly, like his father's, of puzzled waiting. It took him some time to realize that his father had been eighteen when he was born, that he had been a forethought as some children are afterthoughts. No wonder his father waited impatiently for him to be tied down, for him to choose a cage a little bigger than his father's – progress demanded that much – but not a lot bigger. He was almost tempted to remain uncommitted forever, out of spite, but he had an impatience of his own.

The main problem was that he couldn't decide whether he was going to have a very long career, or one so short that it was hardly worth starting. It seemed to him that there was no intermediate possibility. In his late twenties he had a pre-monitory dream, except that since he never remembered his dreams it must count as a premonition proper. In the premon-ition, which was extremely vivid in some respects, or rather had an aura of vividness without giving anything away as detail, he was in a car with another person when it crashed. One of them died, aged thirty, and the other one lived to be over a hundred. But the dream didn't specify which of them was which.

As he approached thirty, he took more rather than fewer risks, on the principle that he certainly wasn't going to die before that age. Before his thirtieth birthday he made a will, and destroyed it on the day of his thirty-first. In the interven-ing year he had been defiantly faithful to driving, but he couldn't pretend not to be glad when those twelve months were over.

In the aftermath of thirty, with the sense of a reprieve that was an almost infinite extension of life, he visited, finally, America. His preferred architects had consistently been Americans; but he had also been hearing of America for years as the gay heaven on earth. An American in The Boltons had told him that in San Francisco there was virtually a gay city within the city. 'Oh, you mean like Harrods,' he had said, and the American had gone on to explain. Americans seemed to like jokes to be clearly signalled.

'No, it's like a gay district, a gay district where you can get anything you want.'

'It still sounds a lot like Harrods. Did you know that the telegraphic address of Harrods is *Everything, London?'* The American went on looking puzzled. Americans seemed to see camp as an on/off switch, so that something was either campy or it wasn't, whereas he felt that true camp, high English camp, worked like a rheostat, providing endless gradations of frivolity. Perhaps camp was something that set in fifty years after an empire, in which case America would have to wait till the beginning of the next century.

'By the way, do you have nettles in America?'

'Nettles?'

'A stinging plant.'

'I guess not. Poison ivy, poison oak, poison sumac . . .'

'But no nettles. Pity. You're missing something. But even here the season is terribly short.'

America opened his eyes just the same. It was partly the amazement, for an architect from a soggy but stolid climate, of landing in California and finding that the buildings which weren't up to earthquake safety standards had signs on them telling you so. And there wasn't a damp-proof course for hundreds and hundreds of miles. That seemed to be the nature of the place: there could be disasters, but never disadvantages.

Leafing through a gay magazine at a bookstall, he saw that some of the personal ads incorporated stylized symbols, one of a classical column, scrolled and fluted, one of the Eiffel Tower. Then he noticed that some of the symbols were standing upright, others lying down. For a moment he thought these advertisers were expressing a preference for classical or modern architecture. It took him a few moments more to realize that these symbols represented countries (Greece, France), while each country in turn represented a port of entry to the body.

The men did their share of bewitching. On his first night in San Francisco, a man directed breath on to the ice in his glass so that it bounced up to refresh Roger's face, after they had danced. The cooling mist that rose from the glass was like a version in domestic miniature of San Francisco's chilly fog.

In American cities at that time, you weren't 'lovers', with someone, you were 'keeping company' with them. You weren't 'gay', you were 'for men', though whether the preposition was meant to be two-faced – meaning 'in favour of', or else 'to be used by' – he could never quite work out.

There were other shifts of language. It struck him forcibly over those first weeks that it was never bad form in America to call a man 'stud' if you had forgotten his name since your last meeting, or while he was buying drinks, or while you visited the lavatory; and that was quite a relief to someone who wasn't so very good at remembering names. In London, calling someone 'stud' would be a cue for incredulous laughter.

But it was the quality of American promises that most pleased him. They referred only to self-belief in the present, to the pleasure given at the time by a commitment. They had no bearing in the future. He might start talking to a man at

The Stud on Folsom Street – which had a surprisingly mixed crowd, despite the heavy-duty name – and they could have a long conversation about the dismalness of promiscuity, the importance of growing up and making adult choices, before taking each other to bed. And they could meet there again the next day, by accident, and have the same sort of conversation as before, without needing to apologize for the way their eyes ranged the room. In London, the realities of such a second meeting would be the same, but as a social experience it would be almost unendurable. Here there was a healthy mixture of the rhetoric of warmth and trust, and the fact of a mutual discarding.

Culturally, the city had much to offer. He never forgot the first time he visited a restaurant called Welcome Home on the Castro. A cowboy strode lazily up to him and murmured not some gruff warning about the breakfast bar not being big enough for the two of them, but 'Good morning, honey.' He turned out to be Roger's waiter, and was soon telling him that the special was a sour cream and jelly omelette, with hash browns, and very good.

He found the whole display ridiculous, but he had to admit it had never seemed out of place when it was a woman delivering the routine. Retrospective guilt made him, for a few weeks, a more generous tipper to waiters in general. He would stubbornly plonk down bills while his companions referred to those serving them as 'waitron' and 'waitrix', according to gender, as if they were androids of slightly differing models.

In Britain, he had tipped modestly. But then, in Britain, if you wanted breakfast when they weren't serving it, they made you feel wrong for wanting it. Here, at Church Street Station, he could order corned beef hash with two fried eggs, over light, at any time of day or night. Even more glorious was the accepted habit of eating out at one restaurant, then moving on to another for dessert. He could slide straight from corned beef hash to the rich puddings at the Café San Marco.

He watched Cukor's *The Women* at the Castro movie house, amazed. There wasn't a man on screen, and hardly a woman in the audience. In the film, Norma Shearer's mother told her that men were shallow, that men could only see themselves in someone else's eyes, that when they were bored with themselves they just changed the eyes they saw themselves in, so the best thing for her to do was to buy some new clothes, get a new hairdo, redecorate and wait till her man came back. The men in the audience, with their new clothes, their recent haircuts (and some of them only going to the movies while the paint dried in their apartments anyway), erupted in affirmation. Roger might have expected something of the sort when Scarlett O'Hara vowed never to be poor or hungry again, but he was startled, and more than half depressed, by this public assertion of the will to pleasure.

Americans might have lapses like these, but they were free of other defects. In London it often happened that his partner would express an unhealthy interest in satisfying him. Suddenly playful, his partner might ask, 'What about you? It's your turn now.' Roger would smile lazily and say, 'Your pleasure is all the pleasure I need,' or 'Gay sex is all foreplay, don't you think?' In extreme cases he would retaliate with an onslaught of erotic distractions, nibblings of the ear and inner thigh, disguising his terror of patience as gratitude for it. Sometimes he had even pushed his breathing to an artificial peak, then given a series of low incredulous sighs. This was in its way a consummation and a release, and he didn't associate it with a phrase that recurred in the more abrasive comedy programmes, faking orgasm. He was in the wanted place, and need not apologize for the route he had taken to get there. For practical reasons, the manoeuvre was only possible when the surfaces were already slippery, so he manufactured an interest in sensual massage, and kept a jar of hand cream by the bed.

In America, his partners were easily satisfied with tokens of climax, though they would sometimes send a hand down admiringly and say, 'I can't believe it. You're still hard.'

He resisted the temptation to consummate his relationship with America by buying T-shirts from All American Boy or Hot Flash. Instead, from an authentic cowboy (Oklahoma, no less), he acquired the authentic affirmative 'uh-huh' – Basic Americanism – and the trickier negative 'huh-uh' – Advanced Americanism. He bought an authentic Schott leather police jacket, a brown one, not a pretentious black one. He had spent too much time in the past informing enthusiasts of the material that what they bought with their many pounds, labelled REAL HIDE, was a veneer of skin blasted with dye and covered with a layer of plastic. His new jacket was exempt from such sniping. All the pragmatic romance of America was summed up for him by the tag sewn into its lining, with cleaning instructions: FOR BEST RESULTS BRING OR MAIL TO Leathercraft Process, 62W. 37th Street – NY, NY 10018. Tel. 212-564-8980

From talking to American architecture students he had also acquired a new idea of his profession. The unfamiliar word they used was *charrette*, a noun they also used as a verb. A charrette was an all-night session of work, and they seemed to feel they were missing something if they didn't pull a charrette ('pull' was the correct verb, if you weren't actually saying 'charretting') every week or so. The word was explained to him as meaning 'little cart' in French: at one time students had to put their work in a cart which would drive off at a pre-ordained time. They could run after the cart if need be, and throw their work in, but if their work didn't reach the cart there could be no excuses. From the explanation as well as the word itself, charretting should be a European rather than American tradition, but his informant argued strongly for its status as American. Certainly he had never heard the word in Britain. The equivalent British words, he remembered, were *gnoming* or *grinding*; they were always words of penance and failure. In London, gnoming or grinding was a symptom of a disordered time-table or an erratic temperament. In America, charretting was a fact of life, made palatable by the imminence of worldly success, and the availability of speed of various kinds.

He had always felt himself to be different in kind from his contemporaries, more driven, less interested in ambling into a niche. In future, when there was work to be done, he would pull a charrette and glory in it, proud that he was incapable of doing the minimum. So what if his technical drawings, for instance, were absurdly over-specified, offered a foolish surplus of elegance and finesse? In due course, his commissions would stretch him. Till then, he would stretch them instead. He made some wildly ambitious large-scale fantasy drawings that took up where Archigram, in its great days, had left off, or like some Sant' Elia steeped in popular culture.

Back in London, he made two major changes in his life. One was to be grown-up at last, and join a proper architectural firm. He made approaches to one firm only, specified the maximum number of hours he was willing to work, even the minimum size of office he was prepared to consider. He made it clear that no inducements would lure him into a suit. He indicated that these conditions were not negotiable, and sat back in his chair during the interview well pleased with himself.

He walked out of the office numb, and when it finally sank in that they had accepted him he burst into tears. He sat down on the kerb, and hunched his grief down to the bumper level of the cars parked on either side of him.

He also took a lover. He didn't set out to, but then he'd always been told that that was the way it happened. It was always the least likely person, as in a classic detective story.

Larry wasn't the least likely person, exactly, but he wasn't far off: a quiet accountant with a bushy moustache and a taste for domesticity. It wasn't this that first gave Roger the idea of being lovers with him, but a sexual peculiarity. While most men, in Roger's experience, had the equivalent in facial contortion, pelvic movement and swearing, of a ten-second countdown to orgasm, Larry had a hundred-second countdown, which he reproduced exactly on every occasion. The third time they went to bed together, with the help of a judicious sniff of poppers (from the first bottle he had ever bought), Roger was able to ejaculate almost at the same time as Larry did. All he had to do was imagine he was on his own and masturbate as usual, synchronizing himself with Larry's providentially predictable countdown.

Roger was by now very good at starting a sexual relationship, and very good at ending one, usually in swift succession. He knew almost nothing of the bits in between, but he thought he should try to explore them with Larry. Now that he had finally achieved the hub of a sexual relationship, the spokes should follow as a matter of course. He had tried the other method of building up to sex, as if it was the keystone that would keep everything else in place, and that hadn't worked. Now he would start with the keystone and work downwards, see what happened.

What happened was nothing, except that Larry became very attached. For once, getting free, Roger felt a real guilt, since for once he had encouraged someone to expect things from him, things that turned out not be in his gift.

For the first time in his life he was earning properly, but he still had manifold debts to clear, and he didn't have a lot to spare. He took as much time off as he could get away with – the part of him that thrived on failure hoping to be fired for his cheek and intransigence – and travelled more widely in America.

He spent one Christmas in San Francisco, where disco

carols played in the bars and artificial snow fluttered down from the ceiling at a pre-arranged signal. The effect was of something so unlike Christmas as almost to be worth celebrating. He also heard Michael Graves lecture, in a building that made no promises about what it would do in an earthquake. Graves showed slides of his two favourite buildings: the Chrysler building in New York, and a small museum in London that Roger, to his shame, had never visited.

On internal flights in the US he always took advantage of the coin-operated insurance machines that paid out huge sums for pennies to the beneficiary of your choice, in the event of your death in a plane crash. He found it a good way of exorcizing his faint flutter of fear; he was too British to be able to take flying altogether for granted. But he also enjoyed looking through his address book for a suitable beneficiary. Some entries disqualified themselves by consisting only of a Christian name, or only a telephone number without an address. But he would start at one end of his address book, or the other, or in the middle, or at a favourite letter, and riffle through until he found an entry that was sufficiently full but rang no bells whatever. Then he wrote it down on the form. The trouble was not that people were promiscuous, he thought, but that they were promiscuous only with their bodies.

In New Orleans, he liked the way the men reserved masculinity only for the heaviest cruising. They would catch someone's eye while they were gossiping with friends, and would walk across the bar to him, shedding one set of mannerisms and assuming another, so that the person who arrived at the point of attraction was quite different from the one who had set out for it.

He liked to walk along Bourbon Street, loving the clarity of its division. On one side of a definite line, the street was clearly straight, on the other side it was just as clearly gay.

Standing there on the divide, it was impossible not to notice that straight sex was sold, and gay sex given away.

He favoured a bar called the Café Lafite in Exile, and a twenty-four-hour restaurant called The Bunkhouse. In the days he would repair to a leftover hippie establishment called Till Waiting Fills, where the curtains were never opened and dim table lamps were the only sources of light. There he could get a pot of Earl Grey tea made with a teaball, so he could pull the leaves out of infusion after a little while, and make the pot last for hours.

In all the cities he visited, there were gay baths, establishments where he could have gone to have sex without a word's needing to be exchanged. It would have been perfectly polite in such a place to explain to a partner that he had just ejaculated, so freeing himself from expectations of performance. In Britain, after all, he had used a similar ruse, using a phrase adapted from the adverts for a credit card, 'wanking takes the wanting out of waiting', to account for his supposed depletion. But he never tried such places. If he had thought this was a moral qualm, inherited from childhood, there would have been a particular joy in overturning it. It wasn't moral. But just because he couldn't build sex into his life in the approved manner, didn't mean that he could build it out.

In Houston he went to the Y, whose gym contained equipment that was new to him. He quite liked the atmosphere of some such places, their hum of sexual thwarting. In San Francisco the gyms were excessively social, and the staff always voluble with worry that they wouldn't have enough drugs for the weekend. No tension built up in such an atmosphere, and he stopped going. Even the nude gym he visited, very Athenian except for the million-dollar sneakers, palled after a time.

He had overcome British prejudices, and was sometimes willing to be told what to do by an instructor. What he had never been able to stand were the self-appointed pals who stood over him at the bench press, and cheered him on, murmuring, 'Just five more reps, guy, three, four. All the way. Five, now just one more. One more for me.' They seemed not to notice that the veins that stood out on his neck and forehead were not swollen by the repetitions, but by their gruff litany of *No gain without pain.*

'Reps' for repetitions, 'lats' for latissimus dorsi, 'pecs' for pectorals. Blood that normally went towards finishing words seemed to be redirected to rebuild muscle tissue. Except that nobody referred to the body's largest muscle as the glute ('Hey man, great glutes'). Nobody referred to them at all, though he noticed they had eyes for little else.

The piece of equipment with which he was unfamiliar involved a pair of bars that rested on your shoulders. You bent your legs and braced yourself against the machine, which pressed down on you at regular intervals. The idea seemed to be to give you a fairly intense upper-leg work-out, without the risks of free weights.

Already Roger had seen one man faint while using this machine, but all he thought was, *shouldn't work out if you're not in shape.* This seemed to him afterwards a thought that could have come from any brain in that gym. It had none of his hallmarks. He stepped up to the machine and did as he had seen others do. It didn't occur to him to read the instructions written on the machine, some of which were in red.

He passed out. Not only that, but when he came to – it was only a few seconds later – his hair was drenched with blood. He had burst a small vessel in his scalp. As the instructor helped him up, he took Roger's hand and ran his finger with patronizing slowness across the red sentences, which warned of the importance of synchronizing your breathing with the machine, and emphasized its unsuitability for the unfit.

In New York he went to bars at the foot of Christopher

Street that had no names written on their outsides, and more
decorous bars in mid-town. He could always be sure of a bed
for the night, and he could more or less rely on being bought
dinner when funds were low. But he could never quite afford
to forget which was all-you-can-eat clams night at HoJos. At
a mid-town bar he met a gallery owner with whom he would
have had his usual foreshortened affair, if the gallery owner
hadn't mentioned, during one of their first conversations, that
he ate regularly at The Four Seasons. That sentence became
the pivot round which their relationship swung. Bob, the
gallery owner, wasn't slow to realize he had power, though
he wasn't sure what sort of power he had. But he knew
enough to promise lunch at The Four Seasons, maybe tomorrow. He knew the *maître d'*, and could always fix things at
short notice. Maybe tomorrow; or maybe the day after
that. When they finally got there, with Roger wearing a Bill
Blass shirt which Bob had bought him for the occasion, and
which cost almost as much as lunch for one at The Four
Seasons, they both realized they would not be seeing each
other again. It seemed silly to Roger not to take off and hand
back his borrowed tie as soon as the meal was over, but he
didn't. He put it in the mail that afternoon. And even then he
couldn't help thinking with a kind of pride: how many
people can say they've sold their bodies for a chance of
seeing a Philip Johnson interior?

Back in London he had what felt even at the time like an
Indian summer of sexual self-esteem. This was thanks in part
to a new sit-up technique that he was taught by a young man
with a notably firm mid-section. Roger had been doing
inclined sit-ups on a tummy board, with weights amounting
to about thirty pounds grasped in front of his neck. He now
learned that this was the worst possible way to treat his
body. He should do sit-ups unweighted and on the level,
knees bent and heels off the ground. He should put his
hands on the floor behind his head, and swing forward, hold

a pose as far forward as possible and then slowly lower himself back down, feeling the tension in his stomach throughout. He was so interested in what the young man had to teach that he was disappointed when he finished his demonstration and slid into bed, but he was used by now to foreplay being the beginning of the end.

He did his reformed sit-ups assiduously, but in truth he was carrying too much weight for the exercise to modify his shape more than a fraction. But his old method of sit-ups had in fact been giving him back pain, and being free of it put much of the smoothness and pleasure back into his walking, and that was no small improvement.

In gyms in America he had seen men of towering virility use moisturizers, and for a trial period he dared to do so himself, even going so far as little pots of a more concentrated extract, specially formulated for the problem area under the eyes. All these products migrated in due course to the medicine cabinet, and then to the bin.

Even without moisturizer he had a sort of leftover attractiveness. Once, long after he fitted any definitions of beauty, however eccentric, he was driving frantically round town running errands. He was all booked to go away on holiday later that day. A police car overtook him. He was running late so he speeded up, thinking he was safe from the police as long as he stayed in their slipstream. But the police car must have tucked itself away where he failed to see it, because suddenly there it was behind him, siren screaming, signalling him to stop. The driver said, 'Do you have any idea what speed you were going, sir?' Roger said, with all the seriousness he could muster, 'The truth of the matter is, I saw you a little while back and I thought you were a good-looking man. I couldn't think of any other way of getting your attention. Will you have dinner with me tonight?' If he'd known how to bat his eyelashes, he would probably have done it then, and ruined everything. As it was, there was a terrible silence.

Suddenly Roger thought, *Oh God, don't let him say yes*, mainly because he was booked on a flight that afternoon, but also because the policeman was not in fact his idea of a good-looking man. Luckily the policeman blushed, put away his notebook without a word and got back into the car.

He began to make significant progress professionally. The first actual work he did, inevitably, was a series of conversions. He got used to wives saying they needed more space, and husbands saying they couldn't do without their studies, even though their wives pointed out they'd done no work there for years. He wondered how long it would be before he did work that wasn't a form of counselling, offering architectural solutions to marital problems and shoring up emotions with bricks and mortar. But at least he started doing some proper teaching in drawing and design, not just the baby evening classes.

He flirted outrageously with his more attractive male students. Eventually they formed a deputation, awkward in their tweeds and cricket sweaters, not to complain of sexual harassment but to say they were on to him. They knew, they said, that he wasn't really gay, that he was just trying to catch them out. But he really needn't bother. However big an act he put on, he wouldn't trick them into a single anti-gay comment. Some of their best friends, in fact, were gay, and they knew better.

That in its way was the high point. Already in America he had heard rumours and read reports of a new sexually transmitted illness, little flickers of hysteria, and subconsciously he braced himself for more of the same in Britain. It took longer than he expected, but when it came he got more than he bargained for. Early on, when the publicity was only moderate, sowing in hatred what would later be reaped in terror, he came across a bulky questionnaire in a gay bookshop where he had gone shopping for bad-taste greeting cards. Thick as it was, he welcomed it. He bought himself a coffee and sat down to complete it. At last someone was doing something, was doing a little fact-finding.

The questionnaire was completely baffling. Almost the first question asked him to rate himself as 'active' or 'passive' on a scale of 1 to 7. It offered no definitions of active and passive. For a moment he thought it must refer to sexual practices, but no, there were detailed questions about these later on. It must mean something else. If it had offered some framework, however silly – if it had asked him, say, if his chest hair touched the ground – he would have filled it in somehow. As it was, he left it blank.

The other questions were no improvement. One asked him 'How much of the time do you get more than 50 per cent of your contacts from (a) bars, (b) clubs, (c) public toilets, (d) parks, (e) . . .' He was willing to spill all the beans he could, but the question stubbornly refused to make sense.

The question about sexual practices wanted to know if he indulged in Lindinism, which could only mean, he thought, having sex while doing the Lindy, a popular dance craze of the 1940s. Some time later he realized that this must be a misprint for Undinism.

An entire page invited him to rate his relationships as 'faithful', 'fairly faithful', 'not faithful' and 'don't know', from the point of view of each participant. A postscript told him to put the letter C against one of these relationships if it was continuing. The C seemed like a gold star for good work, and it seemed to him that it was possible, in spite of what teacher implied, to earn more than one.

He scrawled his objections, methodological, sexological and just plain logical, all over the form, and felt more frustrated than when he had started. It took him almost an hour. If he had considered himself personally at risk, he would have projected his anger further than the sheaf of mimeo-graphed paper on his lap. But he had got used to the promise his premonition made him, that he would live longer, almost, than he wanted to.

All the same, he couldn't deny that the world was changing. For months, people seemed to talk a great deal about buses. Roger heard more discussion of buses during this period than he had heard in the ten previous years. Again and again he heard people saying 'But I could be run over by a bus tomorrow,' as a way of rejecting unwelcome advice to be careful. 'I could live like a saint and still be run over by a bus.'

For a time before there was even a rough model of the illness's operation, gay men in London expressed their fear, which still occupied only a corner of their lives, as an aversion to Americans. Roger was in a bar off Oxford Street one night when a young and very handsome American came in, announcing himself as such by a lilac sweatshirt covered with little sprinting lambdas and the slogan 'FrontRunners, NY,' even before he made the mistake of tipping the barman. People shrank back visibly; in dress and in posture he was saying, 'Hi! I come from a town where people get very sick, and no one knows how or why! Let's talk!' Roger sent his eyes in a slow half-circle across the bar: everywhere were jeans, check shirts, cowboy boots, running shoes, Robert Redford and Marlon Brando imitators. It was like a bar full of anti-Semites with sidelocks and yarmulkas.

He gave the young American a few words of advice. 'If you want people to talk to you, wear your sweatshirt inside out and put your hand out for your change when you buy a drink. And say you're from Montreal.' But when he described the incident to a friend, expecting to be backed up in his condemnation of irrational behaviour, the friend just said he had never liked Americans, so he wasn't giving anything up by not sleeping with them. He spoke as if the virus – it had to be a virus, didn't it? Didn't everything point to that? – would be refused a visa by the authorities when it applied for one, and that would be that.

He was forced to examine his own defences. Only at this late stage did it occur to him that his premonition had not yet been confirmed by anything in the world. No car crash had happened, after all. He experienced a wash of panic, the sort reserved for Greek heroes when the ambiguity in the oracle turns and bites them. It only lasted a second before he got a grip on himself. Then he forced himself to be reasonable. The premonition only told him he would be one of two people in the car crash, one of whom would die at thirty – not necessarily in the car crash. The other would live to be over a hundred, so all that was certain was that he was the long-lived one. The car crash could happen at any time.

For a while he was reluctant to give anyone a lift in his car who might be thirty or under, or to accept a lift from anyone in that category. But he felt a fool asking people their ages, one thing that had never mattered to him, so he stopped. He thought he was being egotistical anyway. If he deserved a premonition, after all, so did the other chap, the one who wouldn't live so long. Let him have a premonition of his own.

His fears subsided. The next time he had a feeling of premonition it wasn't a true premonition at all, not a warning but the leading edge of the catastrophe itself. He was sitting at his drawing table, pulling a charrette, working on a project for a competition, the first one that he felt his design solutions – in particular an elegant circulation – put within his grasp. He glanced across at the motto taped to the wall, just about the only quotation he had any time for: *All Those That Love Not Tobacco and Boyes are Fules*. The Elizabethan spelling gave it a satisfactorily delinquent air.

Then he looked down at his coffee-cup, which held a syrupy sediment, his drawing pens, the ashtray, which he had emptied at some stage but which needed emptying again, and a packet of Pro-Plus (not, he seemed to remember, his first of the night) that he had apparently finished, without quite meaning to. Then abruptly the objects seemed to change their relationships with each other, as if subjected to a complex camera movement, in a way that he would have considered artful in a film but which was downright ominous in real life. If this was a film, he thought, then it was the credit sequence of a low-budget detective thriller, which would be completed by a body slumping lifeless to the floor. He held his breath. His ears popped, as if he was in a plane just taking off.

His mind now contained the words, *This is it. This is the brake*. He wasn't conscious of thinking this thought as such, but he understood that his reference was to what the doctor had said at the special clinic all those years ago. Perhaps as a result, the sensation, when it came, was the sensation of a cable binding tight against a drum, a moving part slammed into stillness.

There was an afterwards, and in the afterwards he was able to walk unsteadily to the phone. At the hospital they kept him in for a couple of days, for tests, but they didn't exactly seem worried about him. They told him that he had probably had a mild heart attack. Subsequent investigations indicated that he had a faulty valve. It was likely to be an inherited defect, aggravated by a life-style that omitted almost nothing that was hostile to health.

The doctors seemed to him absurdly young, and their suggested surgical intervention literally childish, since it involved inflating a miniature balloon inside a blood vessel to free it from obstruction. They assured him it was a minor procedure. When it was done they pronounced themselves satisfied with him (except of course for the life-style). After the event, it was his turn to be childish: he learned there was an even more modern surgical technique, involving lasers rather than balloons, and was piqued to have missed out on it. Was there some complication he had failed to produce, which would have secured for him the top surgeon and the snazziest hardware?

He was profoundly changed by the event in a handful of ways. The doctors gave him a great deal of information, some of which made no impression and some of which struck deep. He might have expected that a potentially mortal episode like the one he had experienced would bring him closer to his parents, or at least make him reconsider his relationship with them. But those bonds were no more or less elastic than before. He did reconsider one set of relationships, but not that one. It struck deep, out of what the doctors said, that the genetic defect he had inherited was likely to have been passed on to his nephews. (It may be that his sisters were, or could be, similarly affected, but if he was told so, that was part of the information that made no impression.)

He took an interest in the boys for the first time. For the first time he felt that he had had a hand in their making, even if he had brought to their christenings not a bouquet but a blight. They became for him potentially tragic children, children with whom he shared a fate, instead of being a mild amusement, a mild distraction, a mild reproach. He became more attentive as an uncle, though also less indulgent, since he now steered them resolutely away from the junk food that was his major previous association in their minds.

The doctors told him that providing he changed his ways in almost every respect, there was no reason why he shouldn't live to be a hundred. In a sense it was what he had been waiting to hear for a long time. But just because he had been waiting to hear it, it didn't follow that he would have paid any attention to these strangers, if they hadn't been talking with the full authority of his body. They drew up a schedule for him, by which he was allowed to hold on to some vices longer than others. He was expected to tackle his diet, for instance, before he needed to do anything about his cigarette habit. The unhealthiness of his sex life was never mentioned, as if it had already stopped being an issue.

The designs that he had been working on at the time of his attack were finished, had really been finished for some time. A less driven personality would have submitted them already, but he had been unable to hand them in before the last copy date. That date now approached, and he submitted them.

His firm gave him time off. They didn't pay him or anything, but he still arranged a trip to the States (going into debt was a vice he planned to have long after he gave up smoking, even). This time he chose Chicago as his destination. He had never bothered with the city before; it had only the most moderate reputation as a sexual playground. But it contained an extraordinary variety of early modern architecture, notably by the Sullivan who had been Lloyd Wright's inspiration, mentor and employer. It was only after he had left Chicago that he realized he hadn't gone to a single bar.

He never got used to a healthy diet, skimmed milk and de-natured cheeses, bran cereals and coffee that had had its reason for living extracted at the same time as the caffeine. But he made his accommodation. In the end, he found it easier to give up men than to give up the taste, even the smell, of fried bacon.

Remission

Adam Mars-Jones

Yoghurt. Yoghurt taught me something yesterday. I was eating a yoghurt, not one I'd bought, something one of the lovers picked up for me, a really creamy one with a crust of fat, not at all my usual style of yoghurt. Maybe it was the creaminess, or maybe it was the absurd clashing of the fruits (apricot and mango, of all combinations), but I could really taste it; first thing I've really tasted in months. The fruit was only there in shreds, but there was enough juice in those shreds, juice or sugar or something, electricity for all I know, to give my mouth the feel of something vivid. And I thought – first thinking I've done in months, too, I dare say – I thought, illness is a failure, that's obvious. You don't have to be well to know that. But what is it a failure of? And at that moment, the answer seemed to be: imagination. It seemed to me then, reeling as I was from the impact of the fruit in the yoghurt, that with a little effort, with a little imagination, I could taste anything, take pleasure in anything.

The yoghurt didn't stay down, of course; it wasn't such a new beginning as all that. But what it had to teach me it taught me on the way down; on the way up it had nothing to say. And even that was a lesson of sorts. It was no more unpleasant to vomit that yoghurt than it was to throw up my usual watery potlet. Its curds were no viler as they rose in my throat. I suppose I've been following a policy of appeasement with my stomach, and that's always a mistake. I've been behaving as if my insides were just being temperamental, and if I could find some perfectly inoffensive food for them, they would do the decent thing and hang on to it. And it just isn't so. I might as well eat what has a chance of giving me pleasure. My stomach will lob it up indifferently.

At the end of all that, after I had vomited, I was – I imagine – just fractionally weaker than when I had started. I had used some energy (vomiting is hard physical work) and I hadn't managed to get any nourishment. Trying to break down the yoghurt had been, as it turned out, a costly waste of gastric juice. But in spite of that, I had had three distinct phases of pleasure – one, the taste of the yoghurt itself; two, the long, incredulous moment when it seemed that it would stay down; three, the euphoria, after it came up, of having expelled poison, of knowing it wouldn't be fizzing in my guts for the rest of the day – and only one phase of unpleasantness when it was actually coming up. In some strange way it seemed that I was ahead on the day's transactions. That's when I thought of making this tape.

It's only a cheap little secretarial Sony, this machine, but it's got everything I need. The controls are very simple; you don't even have to look at them. When things get bad, I can curl up with it under the bedclothes, a muttering foetus that can't get comfortable. [   ] If I get a coughing fit, I can edit it out, like that, by using the pause button. I've just got the two tapes, so I can change them over very easily, with the minimum of fumbling around.

There's the shits-and-vomits tape, which I'll use when I'm making the same old complaints, when I'm sicking up the same old record of bodily disasters. I'm never going to play it back. I'll just record on top of it, same old rant anyway. It's not for listening to, just for getting out of my system.

This tape is different. I've written the word *remission* on the spine of the cassette, and that's what I mean to concentrate on, every little quantum of forgiveness I can find in my body or my circumstances. I'll play it back eventually, but I'll wait as long as I can, so that I have a real hoard of positive moments to refresh myself with.

It's a bit odd, using the same channel to get rid of some experiences and intensify others. But I don't have to look further than my underpants to remember a similar arrangement.

And if there's a medical breakthrough soon, very soon – in the next twenty minutes, say – then I may not have to go back to the shits-and-vomits tape at all, just steam on with my remission. But I'll still go on thinking *remission*, however long it lasts: I'll never say *cure*. I can't be doing with that word. It makes everything impossible. It's a real obstacle to getting on with things.

What else fits the requirements for the remission tape? *The video*. Sleep is sweeter than it ever was, and I resent time wasted on anything else. But my video has taken all the angst out of insomnia. I sleep quite a lot in the day, so I'm likely to wake up in the middle of the night, quite suddenly, as if there was someone flashing a torch an inch from my eyes. Television will have packed up hours before, the sleepy-head announcer yawning after the late film (it's past midnight, imagine!), wishing all the other sleepy-heads out there good-night. There's a programme on before close-down that has the nerve to call itself *Night Thoughts*. It's on at different times depending on the schedule, but always before one. *Night Thoughts* indeed! Can you beat it? The tube trains are hardly tucked up in their sheds for the night, and there's a lot of thinking to be done before morning, unless you have a video.

I bought the video quite a while ago, and it was one of those bits of self-indulgence that turn out to be good resolutions in disguise (having said that, I can't think of any others). I thought I'd turn into an addict, and I certainly taped a lot of programmes, but I never got round to watching them. I'd just buy more tapes as they got filled up. I never got into the habit of labelling the cassettes, so now I never know what I'm watching. I watch episodes of *Hill Street Blues* from two different series, and the only way I can tell them apart is by seeing whether Henry Goldbloom has a moustache or not. Promotions and romances don't help me much with the chronology, but with Henry's moustache I know where I am. I always did like moustaches. On top of that, Henry Goldbloom is always talking suicides down from their high places, reasoning with them through his megaphone of good intentions, and I suppose that's bound to strike some sort of chord.

The great thing about the video, of course, is that I can play things as fast or as slowly as I want. The other night I watched an old episode of *The Avengers*, in which John Steed was meant to dispose of a bomb by lobbing it into the bell of a euphonium. The detonation made the euphonium uncoil, like one of those irritating party-blowers. Except that the actor was too clumsy, or too drunk, to throw the bomb properly, and it rolled under a chair. The euphonium blew up all the same, of course, but if you rewind the video and play the sequence again you can see that it had no reason to. I found the whole thing extravagantly amusing, the other night, and I played it again and again, perhaps because it was one of the few things I'd come across in some time that was in no way a metaphor of my present condition.

That can't be right. Surely I can do better than that. With the explosion, all the instrument's brass knitting unravels. What remains on the carpet is revealed as an intestine, tarnished and smoking. Good. Do better. What *The Avengers* was telling me, in an episode made around the time of my puberty, is that euphoniums end up unrolled and in ruins, even if they don't take a bomb in the bell. That's just what happens, with euphoniums. Good thought. Hang on to that.

Change the subject. *The lovers.* I have two lovers at the

moment. *Lovers* is the wrong word, but then it always is. All I can say is, these two do everything for me a lover could do, and that's pretty amazing. We treat each other as if we had a history of sex, but that isn't the intimacy that binds us. I've had half-lovers before, even three-quarters lovers, once or twice, but these two are somehow fully loving towards me, and that's worth putting down on this privileged spool of tape (chrome dioxide for a longer life).[

]*Dead parents.* Anyone whose doctors are not cheerful should try as a first step not to have parents alive. I'm not being unduly oriental here; it's not that I think it's disrespectful in some way to turn in while your parents are still around and about. But I'm sure it confuses things. There's a touch of the bailiff about parents, I've always thought, as if they were waiting for you to fall behind with the payments on your life, so they could repossess it. What a terrible thing to say.

I'm not always so cynical, but I try. Anyway, I'm sure it makes it worse, having your parents around. Not my problem. Having your parents die is unpleasant in its own right of course, and not only in the expected ways. Example: my father had this terrible rightness about him. From his hospital bed he corrected the doctors' pronunciation and finished their sentences for them. I always hated that. It makes me think, now, how robust he was in his dying, how reliable his vitality was right up to the moment that it fell away from him. But the point is that while he was alive, I didn't realize that I have a scarcely less terrible rightness myself, though everyone I've known must have noticed it. I finish people's sentences for them too – I just interrupt them later on in their flow – so I've always fooled myself I'm a good listener. And compared to my Dad, I *am* a good listener, but the people I've shut up over the years didn't know that.

The lovers are going to get a bit of a shock, when I get some strength back and start bossing them about. I think they deserve an entry of their own, while their patience has yet to be tested, while my character is still blurred by my power-lessness.

The lovers. I had a lover, of a sort, when I was diagnosed, but I soon got rid of him. I'd already placed a small ad which defined me as a Lonely Heart, which was my way of serving notice to myself that I was going to serve notice on him, and then I was diagnosed. I thought at once, that settles it (that was my first thought), I've got to get rid of him, and I did. He thought his health made him necessary to me, and I had hell's own job convincing him it made him even more of a nuisance than he was before, more of a menace, more of a pest. I couldn't carry him and illness too.

So when the magazine forwarded the replies to my ad, everything had changed, and they were replying to someone who didn't exist any more. There were only two replies, perhaps because I was never the world's most beautiful man, and my advert wasn't exactly raging with self-esteem. But I thought they deserved an explanation, and I arranged to meet them, both of them together so I didn't need to repeat myself.

By treating these strangers well after behaving so badly to someone who thought he was close to me, I think I was exercising in some final way the prerogatives of vigour. That's how I've worked it out since then. It was a choosing spree, and now my choices are made.

All the same: it wasn't as easy as I thought. I felt a terrible lurch when I started talking, and I had something like an anxiety attack. Perhaps it was simply grief for the person who had placed the ad and wasn't around any more. It's hard to be sure what it is you're having when you know your body is scheduled to fail you piecemeal – and your mind doesn't have a lot to look forward to, come to that – and you experience a sensation of intense heat and horror. Whether it was only an anxiety attack or what, I wasn't able to stay as long as I'd meant to, and I stumbled out while their drinks were still half finished. And a couple of hours later they phoned, the two of them, to ask how I was, and to say they'd like to help me in any way they could, if I'd let them.

If I try, knowing them as well as I do now, I can probably reconstruct the conversation that led up to their phone call. But I don't care to analyse something that has become so necessary to me. I answered. They offered. I accepted. We've developed some useful routines.

Diagnosis broke me up, the way a plough breaks earth, and all the recent growth, rooted so lightly, was pulled right up. But I was left all ready for seeding. When they phoned – it was Rory actually holding the phone and doing the talking – I remember I said, 'Let's get one thing straight. I have never depended on the kindness of strangers.' Then I had to break it to them that what I was saying was Yes.

The lovers. Leo and Rory, my lovers, my lions. They pay their visits separately; I know they meet up at least once a week to arrange their timetables. They used to visit in the day, but now they know that day isn't really the time they're most useful. They used to be great soup-merchants, the pair of them, but they soon got sick of eating their own soups. Now Rory helps me with housing benefit, which is much more important. Leo has a car, and Rory doesn't, so it's Leo who stays the night, assuming he's free, when I have a clinic appointment in the morning. If it's Rory keeping me company, we take a taxi.

The taxi costs money, of course, but I prefer Rory's company at the clinic. Leo gets very tense, and I more or less have to look after him. Rory is different. I've been particularly unwell for a few weeks, and the hospital wanted a stool sample. That's not easy when your stools move at a hundred miles an hour, like mine do at the moment. With a straight face they gave me a little pot with a screw top, as if what they wanted collecting was a butterfly and not a bowel movement.

Rory wasn't with me that day. Anyway, I tried. Day after day I'd go to the lavatory with my little pot, but I was never quick enough. It was as frustrating as my train-spotting days as a boy, when I would stand by the main line in the early morning mist as the express thundered by, trying to read the number on the engine. Anyway, I got my sample at last, and took it along. After a week, I went back for the results, and they told me the sample had leaked and couldn't be used for analysis. They hadn't phoned me, of course, to say so. Didn't want to depress me, I dare say. So they gave me another pot and sent me back home again, to wait for the express.

These grumbles shouldn't be on this tape at all – they're classic shits-and-vomits stuff – but it all leads up to Rory and why he's good to have around. When I'd got my second sample to the hospital and they'd analysed it at last, the doctor prescribed Dioralyte, which she said I have to take every time I have a loose bowel motion. She added, 'It comes in three flavours, avoid the pineapple,' and I could catch Rory's eye and know that he was feeling the same tickle of amusement at her phrasing. The doctor pinched the skin of my arm to see how dehydrated I was, and we both watched the little swag of raised flesh she left, which took a good long time to fade. If they'd told me about Dioralyte earlier on, of course, I wouldn't be dehydrated in the first place, but you can get it from the chemist even without a prescription, so it's not the sort of thing that holds a highly trained person's attention.

Or she can be explaining about *cryptospiridion*, the guest in my gut, and be saying, 'It produces nausea in the upper tract and diarrhoea in the lower, you see, because the whole intestine is implicated.' I can look at Rory and know he's thinking what I'm thinking: *Implicated? It's up to its bloody neck.* Leo would just sit there squirming, willing her to change the subject and talk about something nice.

I wish I'd had Rory with me when the doctor – the first doctor – asked me his three little questions. Did I receive anal intercourse? On occasion I did. He made a note. Had I visited Central Africa? On occasion I had. He made another note. Had I received blood there, by any chance? I seemed to remember something of the sort, when I was weak and confused from hepatitis. As I came out with the last of my answers. I could see the doctor's lips framing a word that looked like 'Bingo', and it would have been handy having Rory's eyes there for mine to meet.

Not that Rory's perfect. When we first heard about *crypto*, he and I, when she first mentioned the name, he blurted out, 'Oh dear, that's a stubborn one, isn't it?' I couldn't resist saying, 'Thanks a bunch, that's all I need,' just to see him flinch, though it really doesn't make any difference to me. In fact I'm glad he knows what he's about, if he does, so I don't have to worry about him the way I worry about Leo.

It's at night that Leo comes into his own, and not because he sleeps in the buff. He has a beguiling little body and all that, hairless and pale-skinned, but it's really only memory that tells me so. I let him sleep on the side of the bed away from the window, otherwise he thinks he won't sleep. It doesn't bother me which side of the bed I'm on, but with Rory I pretend I have a preference for lying away from the window. That way I know who it is that's staying over, even when I'm half asleep, just by our positions, just by feeling which side the warmth's coming from.

I couldn't really be in any doubt, anyway. Leo may wear no night-clothes, but he keeps to his side of the bed, and he turns his back on me – slowly, quietly, as if I'll be offended – when he's going to sleep. Rory sleeps in a night-shirt, but all the same he hugs me and holds me to him, which is all very nice. Just as he's dropping off to sleep, he's been known to stroke my nipple absent-mindedly with his thumb, but my nipple, quite unlike itself, inverts instead of stiffening.

There can't be much doubt in their minds about who they're sleeping with, that's for sure. The guest in my gut, the gate-crasher in my gut, sends out smells beneath the duvet. And when I have my sweats, I can't think it's pleasant for them. The sheets spread my wetness pretty widely.

I cheat them both, I suppose, by sleeping so much in the day. But it makes such a difference having a lover installed and snoring if I'm not doing much sleeping at night. And Leo is perfect, regularly breathing, just the minimal presence I need. Leo's snoring is my night-light. Sleep works on him like a humane killer, stunning him before it bleeds the consciousness out of him. If he stays up too late, he slurs his words, and then starts to doze with his eyes open, and I expect he's replying to my conversation in his head, and doesn't realize he's making no sound.

In the morning it works the other way round. He opens his eyes when I bring him a cup of tea, but it's a minute or two before he can properly hold the cup. Till then he blinks, yawns, changes position, groans and scrabbles at his hair. I know he's embarrassed that I bring him tea in the morning, but I'm solidly grateful that he sleeps so soundly, and I'll reward him in any way I can, even if it involves effort.

Rory is a much more partial sleeper, and when I get up he often joins me in front of the video. Or he'll go to the kitchen and mix up some Complan, with bananas and honey, the way I 'like' it, the way I can sometimes even tolerate it.

As he pads in, Rory asks me which series we're in, that is, are we escaping to 1982 or 1984? Does Henry Goldbloom have a moustache?

I tell him what year it is in the violently reassuring world of *Hill Street Blues*. Sometimes Rory seems to be doing a Henry Goldbloom himself, but all it means is that he's skipped shaving for a day or two. He gets rid of the growth before it has a real prospect of changing the balance of his face. It's a shame, he's got a great thick growth of hair right up his neck – what we used to call a poor man's cravat – so he actually looks a little odd clean-shaven.

It's wonderful of him to keep me company, I know, but I wish he'd go back to bed. Sometimes I put on a yawning routine, and we both go back to bed again, then I sneak out and go back to the video. It's not him I mind, it's the company he brings with him. If I can slide out of bed without waking him, I can get half an hour uninterrupted in front of the video. But when he gets up, and especially when he starts moving with a sort of muffled purposefulness round the kitchen, a gnawing and a churning wake up too. The gnawing is hunger and the churning is nausea, and wouldn't you know it, the gnawing is exactly in the middle of the churning, so there's no way I can get to it. So what with Rory and the Complan and the gnawing and the churning, it gets to be too much of a huddle round the video, and my view of the screen gets blocked off.

Lower levels of illness. I'm supposed to have mellowed: that seems to be the general verdict. I don't believe a word of it, myself. What really happens is different. There's an awkward interval, when you're ill but not yet conditioned by illness. You're far enough down to be spending all your time below ground, but every now and then you come across shafts of something very like daylight. That makes you impatient and hard to deal with. Things get easier, for other people at least, when you don't have moments of real vitality to show up the false. By now it's second nature for me to follow the cues I get from Leo and from Rory, and not to hang around waiting for my own spontaneity. Only if that draining away of impulse is mellowing can I take credit for it.

The new, eroded me – but for form's sake we'll say *mellow* – the new mellow me has learned to put up with a lot of goodness from people lately. I had to get Rory to pay for this tape recorder, for one thing, and for everything I needed for quite a while. I could have given him cheques, of course; all it would have cost was a little embarrassment if I'd needed help writing them. But he didn't mind waiting for his money. I have this memory thing, you see. I have trouble remembering how to spell, particularly the last part of words for some reason. The words are all there, but I can't seem to spell them. That's what makes this recorder such a good idea. But it also means I can't remember the code number for my cashcard. I hadn't written it down, so I couldn't tell it to Rory. If I'd been up to it, I would have gone to the cashpoint myself, just to see if there was still some memory in my fingertips when I stood in front of the machine. As it was, Rory went for me. I told him he could take his revenge for every time the machine has been out of money on a Saturday night, or swallowed his card without provocation. I told him to mash the keys just as hard as he liked, all three times the machine gave him a chance of getting the number right. Then the card was swallowed up, and my bank sent me a replacement, and by the next post the new number for it. This time I gave the number to Rory to look after.

He's earned my patience. He tries to get me to lie down when I eat, as if that was going to help me hang on to my food, when all it means is more trouble being tidy when I throw up, but I forgive him for that. I know he means well even when he mixes me up some Dioralyte the moment I've had my *loose motion*, though I'm quite capable of throwing up the Dioralyte on the spot, before it's even properly gone down, just to make it clear that my system discriminates against digestion impartially, from both ends of the process.

These days I keep my mouth shut when Rory talks about diabetes. His dad is diabetic, but so what? When Rory talks about it I get rather too clearly the feeling he's trying to teach me something. He tells me diabetes used to be a fatal illness, and that insulin is the crudest sort of treatment you could imagine: just a matter of smashing up bits of animals and

injecting them into you, but that's enough to change everything. I want to say, wasn't there a film about the heartbreak
of diabetes in that season they had on the box, just recently,
of socially concerned American dramas (made for TV, naturally)? I'm sure I taped some of those. Instead I listen to
what Rory has to say about his father. Before too long I'll ask
Rory if he thinks there might be something of the same sort
coming my way, some sort of vinegar-and-brown-paper job,
some way of jury-rigging the body, just to show him I've
been listening.

Eroded as I am into mellowness, I've even learned to have
mercy on Leo. We were in bed the other night, but for once
he wasn't sleeping, for the very good reason that every time
I lay down in bed I was having an attack of coughing. I tried
sitting up in bed for a while, and then gradually sliding
down to horizontal, but you can't fool a cough that way. I
was trying it one more time just the same, when there was a
knock on the door. It was very late, and we were both
surprised. Leo put on a shirt and went to answer it. When
he came back, he took off the shirt and got back into bed
without explaining. I asked him who it was, and he said
it was someone delivering pizza who'd got the wrong
address.

'At this time of night?' I asked him.

'Yes.'

I didn't even know you could have pizza delivered around
here.

'What address was he looking for?'

'Don't know.'

'Did he find where it was?'

'Don't know.' We lay there for a moment, and Leo turned
slowly over in bed, away from me.

Suddenly I had the idea that what I wanted most in the
world was pizza. A sudden flow of saliva even soothed my
cough for a moment. I suppose it was partly because it was so

late, my nausea was deeply asleep, and for a moment I had a clear view of my hunger. And then the pizza seemed so near, so ready on the other side of a door. So I said, 'Leo, this may sound silly, but could you go out and see if that pizza man is still around? If he is, tell him I'll take it off his hands. I'm not fussy about toppings. I'll even pay full whack.'

Leo dragged himself slowly out of bed, put on the shirt again, some trousers and some shoes, and stumbled across the room towards the door. Then he came back and sat on the bed. He told me then that he'd made it up about the pizza. When he'd opened the front door there was a man there in dressing-gown and slippers, holding out a bottle of Benylin, that heavy-duty cough stuff, and saying, without a lot of warmth, 'Try this.' Leo hadn't wanted to tell me. He put the Benylin somewhere where he was going to pick it up the next morning and take it away with him. He hadn't known what else to do.

Nor did I for a moment, and then I asked him to fetch me the bottle, I'd have a swig anyway, just to be friendly. The nausea was wide awake by then, so it didn't cost me a lot to be generous, just a little. Leo undressed again and fell asleep soon after that, and so did I, I think, though I woke up towards morning for a little practice hacking, which Leo slept through, and I hope everybody in the street did too.[

]*Salmon sperm!* What's the word? Milt. It's unbelievable! They just told me today. It turns out that milt is clever stuff. It has a Suppressing Effect. What it Suppresses is Replication. It's such clever stuff. And what that means is, salmon sperm is on my side. Milt loves me! And I love milt.

They're very dour about it. They say, don't build up your hopes too high. They never said that about fears. They never said don't build up your fears too high. And I'm not getting carried away. All I say is, milt loves me and I love milt! I don't even need to fellate the fish to get at it, though God knows I'd do it if I had to. They've synthesized it for me. They say, warning me, that it'll taste like metal. I say, you're wrong, it'll taste like Life. And they say, warning me, that I'll have to take it every four hours at first, day and night. And I say, nursing mothers have to put up with a lot more than that. I'll set the alarm for the middle of the night, and when it goes off I'll know what makes it worth while waking, there's no sleep so deep that I won't know. I'll know it's my Life waking me for its four o'clock feed.

They tell me it isn't a cure, as if I didn't know that. I tell them I know it could only be a poison, that's all doctors can ever give you, poison; you just have to hope that it hates you less than it hates what you've got. They tell me salmon sperm can attack your red cells, and your white cells come to that, so it might help to take some iron and vitamin B. I tell them I've always liked spinach. Oh, I've got all the answers. I just want to be able to put off the questions a bit.

Remission. Maybe I'll be able to move over to this tape for good. Shut away the shits-and-vomits tape in its little case and never need to pull it out again.[

]Remission. I had my remission.[

]I had my remission, and I didn't record it. I didn't even write anything down.[

]When I listen back to this tape, I hear myself explaining what I'm going to use it for, but I never do. I never do.[

]Some things I don't need help remembering. I remember getting the first prescription for my salmon sperm, and going along with it to the hospital pharmacy. Rory was with me that day, but he was shutting up for once. The new twist my case was taking seemed to have robbed him of his small talk. The Aussie I've always hated was on duty in the pharmacy, with his usual tan, only more so, and the stupid bleach-streaked hair, only more so. And of course the awful voice! When you're waiting your turn, eyes down or looking at the warnings on the walls for innocent things like whooping-cough, and he's bellowing instructions to the customers before you in the line, you can think he must have picked up an old copy of *Punch* from the table, and rolled it up to make his voice so deafening. Then when it's your turn you find it's even worse. He *roars* at me as he passes over the box of Dioralyte, 'Make up a sachet after every loose bowel movement,' and then tells me how many times a day I need to take my antibiotics, as if it wasn't written on the container. He seems to have a heroic notion of his job, as if he was still a life-guard back in Australia – though I think you need broad shoulders for that – striding across toasted sand and warning red-heads not to sun-bathe. Then he pushes across the salmon sperm. I'd expected it to be a liquid, somehow, a heavy metallic liquid, what with its being so new and precious and rationed. I must have been thinking, too, of cod-liver oil. So I was disappointed for a moment when it was just ordinary capsules, like the timed-release symptom-suppressors you take for a cold, except with a different paint-job, white with a thin blue belt at the middle. Then I was impressed all over again by the size of the bottle, it wasn't really big, but bigger than I'm used to, so it looked like a sweetie-jar in an old-fashioned corner shop. For a moment I thought, almost tearful with gratitude, *All that, for me?* £250 for a fortnight's treatment isn't peanuts, but why should I have been so surprised to be worth it? Then the Aussie booms out, 'You have to take these every four hours, day and night, do you understand? The best thing is to take 'em at four, and eight, and twelve. That way you only need to get up once in the night.'

And I thought, this idiot knows *nothing*; if I was sleeping eight hours a stretch I wouldn't be needing the salmon sperm, would I? I'd be holding down a job, wouldn't I, the way a paper-weight holds down a pile of prescription forms, the way you hold down yours. The week before, I'd just have let it wash over me, but this time it was as if the salmon sperm was giving me strength already, just by sitting there on the counter, so I said, 'Oh, I think I'll miss the four o'clock dose, get a full night's sleep.' I tried to make my voice campy. 'I'm not really an early morning person.' I could see Rory out of the corner of my eye, trying not to giggle.

But of course the Pharmacist From Bondi Beach looked really concerned, and he even lowered his voice, and he said, 'You really should, sir, it's important.'

If I'd had more than just the sight of the salmon sperm to give me strength, perhaps I'd have said something really crushing. But I couldn't think of anything anyway, so I just lowered my voice, all the way down to a whisper, and said, 'Just to please you, then.'

There was no holding me. I nipped into the waiting room on my way out, flashed the nurse a big smile and asked, 'Would it be possible, do you think, to trace the kind person who brings along all those back numbers of opera magazines?' Then, just as she got launched on the sort of smile that says you've made someone's day, I said, 'Because I'd really like to push him off a small cliff. That would make my day.'

I remember that day because I had only had a premonition of health. I was still outside the world of the well, that world which I understand so little of now.

I have to reconstruct those weeks, those (admit it) months, from what they left behind, like a pathologist reconstructing a dead person's last meal. I remember looking at my first capsule, with a tiny animal printed on it in blue, like the little lions that used to be stamped on eggs, and what I took to be the word WELCOME in tiny letters. I remember thinking with real fervour, *Welcome yourself*, before I saw that the L in the word was double.

I know I became impatient with Leo and Rory almost instantly. They seemed so petty and nannyish, so ignorant of the real business of life. They nagged me to take my salmon sperm, as if it was something I'd forget just to be annoying.

In fact I became very good at waking up seconds before the alarm went off for the three o'clock and seven o'clock feeds – I just had to be different, didn't I? – as if there really was a baby in the room, screaming. It should have struck me as funny when Leo struggled out of sleep at ten past seven one morning and started shaking me, convinced that I'd missed the seven o'clock feed and probably the three o'clock too, which of course he'd also snored through. It should have seemed funny, but it didn't. I suppose it was hard for them. They had suited themselves to me by an effort of will: it must have seemed ungrateful on my part to discharge myself – and so suddenly – from the intensive care I had demanded from them. But that didn't stop me from thinking what my mother used to say, poor bitch, of a piece of furniture that no longer pleased her: I'd rather have your space than your company.

Something peculiar must have happened. I stopped being feverish all the time, in that low-level way that becomes your new normal after a few months. But I entered another kind of fever; I was in a fever of health. That must be the explanation. I know I took a lot of trouble to repeat, in my new health, experiences that I'd had in sickness. That must be a very sophisticated pleasure.

I know, for instance, that in my sickness I had made a trip to Highgate Ponds. I needed to be driven, by Leo of course, and I needed to take a little rest at the unofficial gay sun-bathing area before I tottered down to the nudists' compound.

Leo and I laid out our towels on the concrete. I'd brought along a blanket and a pillow (which Leo was carrying, of course) for a little extra padding, but at least I laid the towel on top. I wasn't ashamed to strip off, though of course I was worried in case I had to run for the dingy lavatory, under the eyes of the ghastly crew by the weight-bench. But shame didn't get a look in. As far as I was concerned, this was strictly between me and the sun. I wasn't going to be done out of our date just because I could hardly walk.

I was surprised to see that Leo was shy, and kept a pair of swimming trunks on. I wanted to tempt him out of them, so I could at least look at the label and see whether they were bought from C&A or the British Home Stores.

After a while I struggled into a swimsuit myself, and walked weakly through to the pond. I was hoping that I would feel strong enough for a dip at least, which was a pretty bizarre hope. Perhaps I thought that, all other sources of energy having failed, I would turn out to be solar-powered. I lay down on the diving-board. I had been there about ten seconds, feeling the wind on me almost warm, and watching the people sprawled on the raft in the middle of the pond, when a man came out of a hut and shouted at me that sun-bathing was not allowed in the swimming area.

The trip I made in my health, I seem to think, was very different. I took bus after bus to get there, by myself. I strode past the sun-bathing area, and straight into the compound, though this time I was reluctant to take off my underwear. By then I had a little roll of tummy fat which I was very proud of, and which showed to best effect above the waistline of a pair of underpants, and I wasn't in any hurry to have it vanish the moment I took my briefs off and lay down. I expect I was waiting for someone to call out, 'Wonderful! I can't see your ribs. Well done!'

Before the sun had properly got to work I was standing up again and pulling my swimming trunks up. I went out into the swimming area, but I wasn't quite brave enough for the diving-board. The water looked cloudy, but I knew it was supposed to be pure and clean, equally free of pollution and disinfectant. I let myself down an iron ladder that had a lot of weed attached to it. The ladder wasn't full-length, as I had assumed, it stopped only a little below the surface, so I slipped into the coldest water I have ever touched. My body gasped and went on gasping. The water was unexpectedly deep, too, considering it was so near the edge of the pond.

I set out to swim to the raft, which supported what looked like the same group of sun-worshippers, but I found myself swimming instead in a tight circle back to where I started. I wanted to strike out for that floating island of health, but my body wasn't having it. My feet had no memory of the ladder, and scrabbled for purchase where the rungs were imaginary. Then I remembered, and felt for the actual bottom of the actual ladder, and managed to pull myself out.

I slumped on the jetty to recover. Not even the most officious attendant, seeing me there flat out and wheezing, could imagine I was having a sun-bathe on the sly, but the men on the raft set up a round ironic applause that I could hear even through the numbness of my ears.

I wasn't going to give up. I didn't hang around until my skin had dried off and my trunks felt cold and clammy. I went back down the ladder and swam out through the cold. The water got warmer after a while, or else it stayed cold and I got used to it. The raft was only fifty feet or so away, but that was quite far enough. I could feel the special uneasiness of swimming in water of unknown depth. As I got near the raft, all I could see above the edge of it was the soles of someone's feet, those odd sort of feet with the second toe longer than the big one.

The ladder by the raft was even shorter than the one on the jetty. In my memory, it has only two rungs. I know I had to pull myself up with what felt like the last of my strength. But when I looked round at the raft, which rocked under my weight and wasn't as securely tethered as I'd expected, it was covered with shit. I don't mean that the men there were lying in it: they were too fastidious for that, with their uniform tans, as if they'd all chosen the same shade from a paint card. But there were substantial little turds scattered all over the raft. They were bigger than anything I've known a bird do, but I couldn't imagine what beast could have got there to lay them. I was tired out from my swim, but lying in shit was too recent a memory – from nights when I improvised a pair of incontinence pants out of an old Marks and Sparks bag – for me to be able to stay on the raft. I climbed down the rusty ladder, losing my footing one more time, and swam back to the jetty. It may be that my strength was failing towards the end, but I think the water near the jetty was the coldest of all.

I know I did all that. I even remember it all, in the sense that I still bear traces of those thoughts and sensations. I remember what my body felt in its health, what it touched, how it reacted. But I have no sense of how my body felt to itself. Health was just one more thing that happened to me, and I have kept nothing from it. The tape is blank for all those weeks and months.

And now I am back in my siege of fevers. What it feels like, as always, is shame, as if this raised temperature was nothing more than a hideous extended blush, which I could get rid of if I just did the right thing. I find myself wondering what it was I did wrong, what crime my body remembers with this heat of shame. They didn't lie to me about the salmon sperm. I knew it could nibble away at my cells. I knew there was a price to be paid for the job it did. I knew it wasn't a medicine so much as a protection racket; I just hoped we could get along. I took vitamins, I took iron, I took supplements. Was there one night when I passed up a dish of green vegetables, in my feverish health, snubbing all those B vitamins, and went out instead? There must have been. I know there were times when I was too bound up in the play I was watching to remember my feed. I'd glared in the dark at people whose watch alarms went off in the theatre for too many years to commit that crime myself. And there was the terrible day I lost my bottle of capsules. I had to dash across London, whimpering, for replacements. I'd lost six expensive days' worth. To make myself feel better I asked if anyone had lost their salmon sperm before me. But I was the first.

How can I put it, to make myself feel I have made heroic

choices? Health for me is more than being not-yet-dead. It's not something you patrol; it's something you must forget to patrol or it's not any sort of health at all. That should do it. That sounds right. That must be why I didn't use this tape to hoard up bits of my health, so I could live off them at a later date.

And here I am with a body that's ashamed of itself, that's burning with remorse for something it did or didn't do, and with the word *surge* beating at my ears. They warned me what would happen when I came off the salmon sperm. A surge of virus. Virus replicating uninhibited. *Surge* is a word that sounds overwhelming even on the smallest scale, down on the cellular level. What chance do I have, against a *surge*?

Every time I went to hospital for some more salmon sperm, and they took blood, I must have known they were monitoring my levels. Fourteen. Twelve and a half. Eleven. Nine. It was more than a pit stop. And when I went below nine, and they started give me transfusions, I knew what they were about. But I tried to think, closing my eyes when the prick came in my arm, and then the slowly growing ache in it, that I was giving blood rather than getting it, that from my overflowing health I was giving freely of my surplus. Nine and a half. Nine. Eight. I tried to think I was paying my taxes, when all the time my bloodstream was being heavily subsidized. On long car journeys as a child, I remember, to stop from feeling sick – from motion, from too many boiled sweets, from my father's Senior Service and my mother's Piccadilly – I would close my eyes and try to interpret the sensations in terms of movement backward, though I don't quite know why that was comforting. I could produce a surprisingly strong and consistent illusion until I opened my eyes at a bump in the road, or when my mother asked if I was asleep, and the world came crashing back at me.[

]The lovers are back. They can deal with me again. And I suppose that really means that I can deal with them. Rory has that handsome look in the face that means he's certain to shave in the morning, and Leo smells so strongly of soap he must wear a bar round his neck.[

]They've done something very tactful with the key. I'm not very steady on my feet just at the moment, and my neighbour has a spare set of keys. She's always been a hypochondriac, can't bear to be in the room with anyone who has a cold, so I suppose it's something of a miracle that she's not returned them, or that they don't reek of disinfectant. This I noticed today, and it qualifies for inclusion on this tape. That's what this tape is supposed to be for, isn't it? Sometimes my neighbour even leaves groceries outside the door. Anyway, when Rory last came by he let himself in, and explained that he had happened to run into my neighbour outside the house. Then *Leo* let himself in next time he paid a visit, and he looked all tense and startled, as if at any moment he might be called upon to lie. So my guess is they've made a policy decision not to make me walk any more than I have to. They must knock on my neighbour's door every time they come round. For all I know, they get her to leave the key under the mat when she goes out. I think they're waiting for me to twig and get angry, but they'll have to wait a little while longer. I'll either keep it to myself or let it hitch a ride on a real grievance. 'And another thing,' I'll say, 'about the keys . . . '[

]We've started taking baths together, the lovers and I. Rory lifts me into the tub very competently, which is so reassuring it's sinister, but at least he climbs right in with me, like no nurse in the world who wants to remain in employment. Suddenly I wonder if he answered my ad – poor idiot – to get his life moving again after grief, and has to keep his teeth clenched on his knowledge. So I'm more than usually grateful that he gets into the bath with me. He sits behind me with his knees bent, so I can rest my head on his chest, and he strokes me a little awkwardly with a sponge. It's a posture

I like anyway, and now in particular I'm glad of it because it's not a position that encourages talking. We can't really see each other's faces. I think he closes his eyes in the steam, and from time to time he seems to drift off. He doesn't seem to mind that the water gets cold; perhaps he doesn't even feel it.

If there was just a little more water in the bath I'd be floating. As it is my head bumps softly against Rory's chest. Here and only here, in this limbo inside another, I remember my lover, the lover I disposed of so efficiently, dumping his body in an acid bath of resentment. What I remember isn't the friendship, which I resisted, or even the sex, which I wanted only when I wanted it, but the game we used to play when we were out together, the game he taught me and that he may even have invented, the sweetly innocent game he called *compelled*-to-fuck. One or other of us would say, 'If you were *compelled* to fuck a set number of people – under pain of death, mind . . . ' (or later just, 'If you were *compelled* . . . '). Then the other would say, 'How many?' And the answer would be, 'One on this bus,' or 'Two before we leave the Food Hall,' or 'Three before the next traffic light.' Then he would say, 'Three? You'll be lucky. That one, at a pinch. Another one? No chance. All right, the thinner of these two bobbies, the less fat I mean. That's the lot. That's my last offer. One more? Do I really have to? Let it be the one with the tie, then. Cancel that. The other bobby. If I have to.' What I remember best is the grudging lust in all its variety that he could call up on his face, as he made his protesting selections.

Sooner or later I have to tell Rory that it's time for me to get out. I start shivering, even in the water, even against his skin. He doesn't risk trying to lift me out while he's wet and slippery, so he dries himself as quickly as he can and comes back for me with a hot towel. By now I'm really shivering. He helps me stand up and pulls the plug out. He wraps the towel round me and rubs away until at last a tingle passes to me from the towel. By then I'm likely to be exhausted, and once he even had a shot at carrying me to the bed. He was staggering by the time we got there, and he didn't so much lay me down as fall with me down on to the mattress.

Leo is different, of course. He has a hard time lifting me into the bath, so I hang on to the towel rail just in case – though I'm not sure I could support my weight for more than a second or two, if he lost his grip. He puts stuff in the bath so that it's full of nutty-smelling bubbles by the time I arrive in it, which relaxes me and relaxes him too, because he doesn't have to see me naked for more than a few moments. I'd rather he joined me in the bath – the edge of the tub is hard against my shoulders – but he likes to stay where he is. Still, he's become something of a pro as a back-scrubber, and that's something. At first he used a nail-brush, but one day he couldn't find it so he used my toothbrush instead, and we've never gone back to the nail-brush. He's even brought along a toothbrush which is specifically for scrubbing my back.

He starts on my left shoulder, pressing hard with the bristles, moving his wrist in tiny circles. It's extraordinary how – even the first time he did it, and much more so now – my skin anticipates the sideways progress of the brush as he moves it across my back, so that I develop a roving itch that is always just a fraction ahead of the scrubbing. When he has reached the outside edge of my right shoulderblade, he drops his hand an inch or so and scrubs steadily back to the left again. I try to concentrate all my attention on the itch, which moves ahead of the toothbrush all the way. It's as if there was a poem written on my back that I learnt by heart in childhood. I have wholly forgotten it, but each word that I am prompted to remember sparks the memory of the next. I close my eyes. The travelling itch holds still, for once, at the extremity of my back, until the brush comes to scrub it out.[

I lose the ability to talk. My voice unravels, and speech

drops away from me like the mouthpiece of an instrument I am suddenly unable to play, a medieval instrument that I don't even recognize as a possible source of music.

When I open my eyes again, they are both there, both the lovers. Leo and Rory. Imagination is the last thing to fail me. I see them lying side by side on their fronts, their arms around each other, their faces pushed into the pillows. They turn slowly towards each other, and I see Rory trace a line with his finger down Leo's cheek. I can see a tear on Leo's skin by the tip of Rory's finger, but from my point of view I can't make out whether Rory is following its progress as it trickles, or drawing it out of Leo's eye with the gesture he makes. Rory leans over and kisses the tear where it has come to rest, and I flinch in spite of myself. Leo turns away from the kiss, so they are both on their sides now, facing the same way.

Rory sets up a gentle motion of the hips, which Leo's hips take up. A terrible rattle of protest and warning bursts from me, behind clenched teeth. Their hips are in rhythm now, and Rory's face is pressed against Leo's neck, just as it was against the pillow a few moments ago.

I turn my head away, and see the cardboard box that contains all my medicines in their varied containers. I see also the little piles of Leo's and Rory's clothes. Their two pairs of trousers have fallen in an oddly symmetrical pattern, forming a sort of star, and I can see among the keys attached to one belt-loop a new pale-silver copy of a familiar shape. I glance at the keys on the other trousers, to locate the twin of it. But I forgive my lovers their ability to comfort themselves and each other, and I forgive myself for bringing them together, as I cross the room as quietly as I can and open the door, as quietly as I can. Then I close the door after all, walk back across the room, not worrying any more about whether I make any noise, and sit back down on the edge of the bed.

Palace Days

Edmund White

To Maxine Groffsky

"escaping" from the dangers of the
U.S. to the playgrounds of Europe.
Safe Sex = No Sex is not a motto found
within the pages

Mark & Ned. Self-imposed exiles trying
to recreate a life left behind.
Constant comparisons with N.Y.
The men who don't pop in. Who aren't
impressed by Mark's wealth. Beauty is al
When Mark Meets Majo we think he will
find happiness & security with the man of
equal age & wealth it is destroyed not
so much by Mark's HIV status but by
the fact that he has lied to him —
denied his promiscuity. But his
positive status is <u>too</u> much & all is
left is Ned.

What is Ned?
Who is Ned?
 — Son / lover?
 — Ned not afraid of positive status
 — affair with Luc

They came to Paris from New York as lovers, although they hadn't slept together in a year. Of course they kept sleeping in the same bed, and of course they would never have admitted the shameful secret of their chastity. If other people had known they weren't having sex together, they would have undervalued their love, which was growing at once more detailed and more unified every day, like an epic poem bristling with events and characters all held together through a mysterious system of balanced echoes.

Their poem, however, was more a nursery rhyme, since they had a stuffed bear they named Mister Peters and they called each other 'Peters' or 'Pete' or 'Petes' and were generally silly to the point of rapture, endlessly shouting their love from room to room. One of them would sing out, 'Do you still like me, Peters?' The other would reply, 'Petes, I *love* you.'

The truth was they were both so insecure that the ordinary discretion between lovers would never have suited them. They were willing to trade in thrice-weekly sex for hourly affirmations of love. 'You're going to leave me, I know it', one of them would suddenly announce with mock-fear to disguise the real fear. 'I'll *never* leave you, Peters', the other one would swear with mock-solemnity to take the embarrassing edge off the real solemnity.

There was almost a twenty years' age difference between

them, but when they were horsing around the apartment they scarcely noticed it. The older one, Mark, had always been considered 'immature' back in New York because the things he liked – going out every night, disco-dancing, sexual conquests, smoking dope and screaming and sobbing through pop music concerts – were the things wild, affluent kids had liked in the 1970s. Although Ned, the younger one, liked to drink, he did everything else in moderation and even when drunk he was always the one in the group who remembered where the car was parked or could explain things clearly and politely to an enraged policeman.

Living it up had been a way of making a living for Mark. He was the president of the Bunyonettes, a gay travel agency that arranged all-male tours. Forty gay guys would float down the Nile from Aswan to Luxor, impressing the Egyptians with their muscles and moustaches and shocking them with their pink short shorts and filmy, drawstring *après-piscine* harem pants. Or Mark would charter a small liner that would cruise the Caribbean and surprise the port town of Curaçao when two hundred fellows, stocky, cheerful and guiltless, would ransack the outdoor clothes market looking for bits of female finery to wear to the Carmen Miranda Ball scheduled for the high seas tomorrow night.

A computerized dating service, a rental agency for Key West and Rio, a caterer that put its waiters in shorts, T-shirts and, to emphasize those powerful calves, orange work boots and sagging knee socks – these were just a few of the satrapies in Mark's empire. Actually the whole business was run by Manuela, a tough Puerto Rican everyone assumed must be a dyke, though after two rotten marriages she wasn't into anything but money and good times. She did the accounting, hired and fired the staff, organized the trips. Mark was just there to socialize, to 'circulate' as his hostessy Virginia mother put it.

When things fell apart in '81 Mark couldn't face it. An

old room-mate came down with the disease, and Mark wrote on his desk calendar nearly every week, 'Visit Jason', but he never got over to St Vincent's until it was too late. At the bars, discos and gay restaurants between rounds of Rusty Nails, he'd look up to see the starved, yellow face of an old playmate. The short hair and moustache made him ashamed for some reason, as though God had contrived a rebuke of their past pleasures and fashions. Of course the worst rebuke to the fashion-conscious is to be no longer in style, and these eyes ringed in dark and these sallow cheeks looked like daguerrotypes of what they'd represented in full living colour just a year ago.

Of course Mark went through the motions. He was a sort of community leader. Although he knew plague talk was bad for business, that no one wanted to take a cruise on a death ship, he quickly put aside such interested thoughts. He organized safe-sex jerk-off parties, thought up themes for benefits, signed petitions for money and against bigotry, but his heart wasn't in it. He was a good-time Charlie and the times had soured.

And he felt guilty.

He wondered if he'd set a bad example. So often he'd trusted excess. He'd tripped out on acid every night in Water Island that summer of 1978, tempering the speediness with Rusty Nails and Valium. He cheerfully visited his cheerful doctor almost once a week all through the 1970s for clap in the throat, dick or bum, for anal warts, for two different kinds of hepatitis, for the syph (a night of fever and shakes after the first massive dose of antibiotics). He saw every ailment as a badge of courage in the good fight against puritanism.

He knew he was charismatic owing to his Virginia drawl, his shiny straight hair, his blue eyes under scribbled-in, black-black brows, and especially owing to his way of respecting men for their successes while never losing sight of their vulnerability, which for most of them constituted their sexuality. 'OK, Harold, we know you're the world's greatest ichthyologist but that doesn't mean your ass ain't as cute as a twelve-year-old's and how about parking it here' (he pointed to his knee), 'right here'. Without doing much Mark attracted a whole solar system of playmates around him every evening. Like a stage Irishman in London, he'd always played the Rebel Gentleman among the Yankees, for whom Southernness meant gallantry, borderline intelligence and a bibulous conviviality. He feared that he'd misled all those guys who, imitating him, had worn madras, sniffed ethyl and voted Republican – and had had sex with hundreds and hundreds of partners. All those hot athletic men came now to haunt him with their skin hung like a wet shirt on a hanger.

Mark began to change. His doctor, no longer so cheerful, ordered Mark to stop smoking: 'You have chronic bronchitis and it can only get worse. Go to Smokenders; they have a foolproof programme.' Mark had a charming way of hanging his head like a kid, pawing the floor and saying loudly with that winning Southern accent, 'Aw, Doc, give a fella a break', but the doctor, pudgy and owly after his own recent double withdrawal from nicotine and cocaine, stood firm.

Mark went to the Smokender sessions dutifully, switched to a vile mentholated brand, wrapped each pack in a paper sleeve, sat through gruesome movies of lungs, saved all his butts in one big Mason jar and compiled lists of minor, personal, non-gruesome reasons for quitting.

It worked. He stopped smoking, gained twenty pounds and went almost overnight from a young guy in his early thirties to a middle-aged man deep into his forties. He watched his father's jowly face overwhelm his own sharp features. He had no desire to touch a cigarette. But he felt that stopping smoking had turned him from a hot number into a slow-burning grouch.

Without the nicotine to counteract the effects of alcohol, he became drunk more easily. One night he was so high he couldn't get his newly fat body up the ladder to his loft bed. He slept on his couch and woke with such a feeling of drenched, panicked shame that he never again took another drink. He warned himself that if he started again he'd have to join Alcoholics Anonymous, and that dire prospect kept him sober. Of course his AA friends screeched at him he was just on a 'dry drunk', but that suited him fine as long as he stayed sober. Sometimes he did envy them. The party was still going on for them, if dry this time, whereas he was slowly withdrawing.

After he sobered up a previously unsuspected sweet tooth grew in and he became still stouter. He gnashed at Godiva chocolates and Lanciani brownies with fury, wolfing his curse.

Ned was his only consolation. Ned was sweet and adaptable without being a pushover. If people ignored him at a dinner party or failed to remember his name after he'd been introduced several times, he complained loudly. He was handsome without the loss of individuality that quality usually implies. He had teeth that weren't perfect and a queer way of cocking his head to one side which, when coupled with a confused smile, gave him a goofy, dazzled air. On bad days he was certain that people were making fun of him, and then Mark would call him Paranoid Petey. His sweetness touched Mark – every feeling that was struck inside Ned vibrated somewhere inside Mark.

They'd been introduced formally (well, not so formally as all that) by a mutual friend who'd said to Mark, rubbing his hands like a matchmaker, 'Have I got a boy for you.' That had been in late '81 when the official line had been, 'Limit the number of your partners. Know their names.' Ned was a very cute name to know, and if less was better, then just one would surely be best.

There was an old-fashioned sweetness about their love from the very beginning. At their first encounter over drinks Ned had been cooking a roast lamb and had asked Mark how to test it for the right degree of pinkness. Two nights later Mark had been entertaining three friends from Venice and had invited Ned to help out, since Ned had studied a year in Florence and sort of spoke Italian, as did Mark. Ned dressed perfectly, smiled often and kept Mark company while he washed up.

As a Southerner, Mark took social life very seriously. He couldn't endure New York insolence – the spiteful attacks called teasing, the shameless social climbing (heads poking up like periscopes over the sea of faces), the charged pairings of conspirators who ignored the mêlée around them. Mark believed in keeping one conversation (frivolous, decorous) going amongst the eight dinner guests. He believed in dressing carefully for every occasion, even schlepping to the deli. He was for stoicism rather than bellyaching, for quips rather than teasing, for light opinions rather than heavy information, dull kindness rather than rapier wit – all the values, in short, his Episcopalian mother (poor, imperious) had imparted to his rich and humble Baptist father.

Although Ned wasn't a Southerner he was a little Boston aristocrat who shared Mark's patriarchal values. Ned automatically called older men 'Sir', opened doors for ladies, instantly identified himself on the phone by name and said 'Good evening' when he got into a taxi. He also had fresh, clear emotions. If someone told him a sad story (and more and more of the stories these days were sad), Ned cried quickly and copiously. He never worried about being consistent. He wasn't the kind of stuffed shirt who decides you're only hurting bums by giving them handouts; if the bum looked pitiful, Ned would brush away tears and empty his pockets. He was a volunteer for lots of charities.

Ned specially liked Joshua, Mark's best friend, who was

well into his fifties, an English professor and a well-known critic of contemporary poetry. When Joshua was recovering from cataract surgery Ned worked for him, reading him his mail, taking dictation, preparing meals, telling him what the characters were doing on TV.

In fact for a while Ned saw a lot more of Joshua than Mark did. Mark had to settle for daily phone calls.

Joshua was a master of the art of the telephone call. Like Mme de Sévigné, who could plunge headlong into a story in the first line of a letter, Joshua would sometimes start off by singing the latest pop song or quoting the latest advertising jingle. Sometimes he'd pretend to be someone else. Mark would have an ancient sex pervert on the line wanting to join the 'Bunyonette Orgy Club', or a little kid saying, 'I'm twelve years old and I read your profile in *Christopher Street*, the gay magazine . . .'

Or Joshua would start by quoting a really juicy academic absurdity he'd gone truffling after in a learned journal. Or he'd quote from Wallace Stevens' 'The Auroras of Autumn' or discuss brim width at his hatmaker, Gélot in Paris. For such an unworldly man he was terribly *mondain*.

If he were munching something he'd give the recipe. An eavesdropper might have been startled by his instructions for grated zucchini: 'First you peel and rape six cour-gettes . . .'

In their drinking days Joshua and Mark would eat a T-bone and green beans at Duff's on Christopher Street, down a bottle of wine and then head over to the Riv on Sheridan Square, where they'd sip sweet, dangerous stingers. In the warm weather the glass walls would open up and they'd be seated almost in the midst of all the grit and clowning, the sudden updraft through the subway grate, the mammoth black men in shorts on skates, their wrists circled by glowing fluorescent bracelets, the susurrus and scent of queens from the provinces mixed in with the sweat and grunts of the local machos. When they were quite drunk Mark and Joshua would speak to each other in their version of Italian, because they'd spent many summers together in Venice and liked to imagine they were Italians, even Italian housewives who addressed one another with feigned affection as 'carissima'. Then Mark and Joshua would pour themselves into separate taxis, wave, and head in opposite directions home. There they'd call each other once more, just to say goodnight. No one could ever have fitted into such a closed corporation of a friendship, but Ned did.

Mark and Joshua had met fifteen years ago at the ballet. At first they had had nothing else in common (later their friendship itself was what they shared). For Mark the ballet was prowess, gymnastics as a foreglimpse of paradise, a way of seeing perfect men powering long-legged, long-necked women through the crosslit air. For Joshua it was Utopia. As he said, 'All these physically deformed, argumentative New York intellectuals in the audience couldn't accept any vision of society except something non-verbal and sublimely athletic.' They went at least twice a week to the State Theater and called all the performers by first names, although they didn't know them. Mark thought of Balanchine as by definition a European – a Russian who had lived in Paris – and he ascribed Balanchine's clarity and hardness to his cosmopolitan background.

As things became grimmer, Mark was summoned more and more frequently to bedsides and graves. Ned kept him happy, not through any services he performed, since they were equally sloppy and incompetent in the kitchen and Ned never hid his depressions except from what they both called 'company'. No, what Ned offered was sweetness. They'd hug each other in the loft bed and say, 'I love you, Petes.'

'Aren't we cosy here, Peters?' That was their word for happy: cosy.

And then they moved to Paris, not for any special reason

but because Mark knew that if he didn't make an effort he'd end up in St Thomas, get totally lazy, still fatter and start drinking again. Mark had heard about this really neat cooking school in Paris where the chefs worked under mirrors all morning while everyone looked up and took notes, then the class ate the results. American apprentices did all the chopping and translated the instructions into English. The Paris trip sounded appealing to Ned who'd once studied at an American brat school in Florence and had never stopped daydreaming about 'Europe', a unity that existed more in the American imagination than in any actual Frenchman's or Englishman's mind. What they didn't say, Mark and Ned, was that they hoped the party would go on in Europe as it had before in the States. It amused Mark to call Europe the 'New World', since it was all new to him. And just as Europeans had once gone to America in search of sex, in the same spirit he'd come to the New World.

They found a pretty house on the rue de Verneuil, just a few blocks from Saint-Germain-des-Prés. The street was lined with the grey, unbroken façades of severe eighteenth-century townhouses, but if you punched out the right code and pushed through the teal blue lacquered doors you crossed a courtyard filled with planters and reached their white wood house with the green shutters and the small rooms that an inspired maniac had painted floor to ceiling with *faux marbre*, *faux* malachite and putti swirling in grey and pink clouds. Despite this hectic décor, the house was charming and quieter than a cottage down a village lane, where invariably there are animals, birds, people and cars. Here there was only silence filtered through the crepitation of rain in the courtyard. Mark amused his French friends when he referred unwittingly to the stately *hôtels particuliers* in his neighbourhood as 'palais'; he was used to Italy, where even the meanest apartment block counted as a *palazzo*.

He and Ned made big fires in the fireplaces, thoroughly

enjoyed the comedy of half-learning French and took trains nearly everywhere, to Stockholm and Barcelona, Rome and Amsterdam. Mark told himself he was scouting picturesque locales for the Bunyonettes, and from time to time he took notes on prices, quality of service, sights to see and nearest gay bars.

He even enrolled in the cooking school and bought all the *batterie de cuisine* that the school had for sale. But though he took down the instructions for lobster bisque, rabbit in its own blood and lemon crêpes, he never even unpacked the crêpe pan.

They both cruised. Without discussing it they had an agreement not to bring anyone home. They'd also tacitly consented to continue sleeping in the same bed. Every night they headed out to the back-room bars where indeed the party was still in full swing. People were shorter and more perfumed and kissed more than in the old days in New York, but what the French called *touche-pipi* went on without restraint. One couldn't say the gay community in Paris was irresponsible, since no such community existed, at least not as far as Mark could figure out. They'd stumble home at two or three in the morning, shower and crawl innocently into their big bed with the old, eyeletted linen. Back home people had warned them to say they were from Canada or England, but the French weren't scared of the disease and besides appeared to like Americans. The French thought Americans were at once uncultured and wildly up-to-date and kind, although the kindness was sometimes taken as proof of stupidity. Some kid assured Mark, 'Ned est toujours gentil – et pas du tout bête!' as though good humour were usually cretinous.

Here Mark was, dashing about from the Alliance Française to the cooking school, checking out the discos and saunas, renting cars for jaunts to châteaux and running up thousand-dollar phone bills calling all his friends in New York to praise

Paris and to assure them the French were 'real shy and sweet' under that stylish Gallic disdain. He felt rejuvenated and even lost three kilos, though he had ten more to go. Joshua filled him in on the latest doings of Mister B. and Jerry, that is, the choreographers George Balanchine and Jerome Robbins.

Although Ned was twenty-eight he looked twenty and picked up Parisian styles so quickly that soon he'd become the choicest Kiki in town, hair military short on the sides and gelled high on top, jeans rolled and military boots huge. He and Mark would wander separately about in the rain for hours memorizing street names. Often they'd help lost compatriots for a moment, then vanish into the attractive mystery of being half-Gallicized Americans. Mark overheard Ned pretending to confuse 'assist' for 'attend' and 'actual' for 'present', and kept teasing him ('You big phoney') with a happy smile on his face. The happiness was that of children who laughed to see themselves in a distorting mirror.

But they couldn't get a real social life off the ground. In New York Mark had had his regulars stopping in unannounced for cocktails. There'd always been pretty men hanging out for the coke or the good times or to meet one another. In Paris people seemed to think it was sufficient to check in once a month to keep a friendship alive. And if they liked Mark and Ned and submitted with a laugh and a blush to their nosy questions in English, in French they were disdainful towards the other French guys. Everyone, moreover, thought it strange Mark and Ned knew only gays; French people kept referring contemptuously to the 'ghetto'.

So now social life was something Mark surrendered as well, along with booze and cigarettes and drugs. Soon he'd have to give up sex, no doubt, but not yet, not yet. Like the French boys he knew he said he was being 'prudent' and 'cautious', but the prudence amounted to nothing more than approaching only those boys who appealed to him, the caution to vowing not to go this far tomorrow night.

Even so Mark had much less sex, since in Paris no one knew who he was and he didn't get any free rides. In New York people admired money more than here, or rather they confused wealth with sexiness.

Ned had no such restraints imposed on him. He had that foolish grin, crazy American accent and never worked, so he was as attractive as he was available. He met someone named Luc.

'Is he cute, Petes?'

'Peters, he's just a flirt.'

'Petey, I know you're going to leave me.' Mark whispered to their stuffed bear, 'Mister Peters, he's going to dump fat old us for this garlic-smelling, lap-swimming, four-foot tall, fireball do-nothing.'

'Luc hates garlic and he has more energy than both of us. He's some sort of weird French nurse running around to old ladies at six in the morning giving them shots.'

The more Mark heard about Luc the more he worried. Ned found every banal remark Luc made 'génial' or 'géant'. He was so enamoured he was even slipping into scrappy French around Mark, who had to lay down a new rule: 'Look, Petes, no Frog in the house. I'm serious.' Ned tried to downplay his ardour but since Mark was his only real friend in Paris and certainly his best buddy in the whole world, he couldn't resist talking to him about his obsession. He attempted to disguise it as a series of complaints: 'Luc is such an egomaniac he invites three of his friends over to watch him take a bath'; 'I know you never thought I'd like opera but I'm humming it because Luc plays that damn caterwauling all day'; 'He's so absurdly macho he always insists on running the show sexually, not that I exactly mind.'

Mark realized then how fragile their love was. Since he and Ned didn't have sex, they were dependent on outsiders. The least threatening kind of adventure was one-time-only tricks, and in the old days New York would have turned up an inexhaustible supply of them. But the statistics were closing in on them and they'd die if they kept up this pace. Luc was right for Ned, but what if Ned moved out? Mark would have preferred a less possessive lover for Ned.

He thought they might already be harbouring this lazy seed, this century plant of death. Ned and Mark both believed that if they slept enough their immunities would resist the virus; they were always sinking into deep, swooning naps to the sound of the rain in the courtyard, which was like the sound of newspaper burning.

Out of deference to Mark, Ned saw less of Luc, but this very gift caused Ned to resent Mark and made the already troubled Luc crack. He sold his nursing practice, sublet his apartment and headed off to Brazil to be a Club Med GO (*Gentil Organisateur*).

To compensate for this loss Ned enrolled in a History of French Art course at the Louvre, but in June, after a year in Paris, they both realized they were as rootless as when they'd arrived. Ned was on a nodding, beer-buying basis with dozens of men in the bars, on a love-making basis with a few but with none could he go to a movie or share a secret. Mark knew only a few guys from his gym.

They made plans to spend the end of the summer with Joshua in Venice. Before going to Venice they stayed two months on Büyükada, an island an hour away from Istanbul by ferryboat. It was plenty exotic with noisy, chuckling sea-gulls on every roof, vast turn-of-the-century clapboard houses and a bay full of sailboats with varnished wood cabins. Cars were banned and the only transportation was by horse and buggy or bicycle. The houses were owned by blond Jews who spoke Ladino, a sort of Spanish, for the sultan had welcomed them to Turkey after they'd been driven out of Spain by the Inquisition. Their servants were dark-skinned, blue-eyed Kurds from the Syrian border.

The weather changed, the nights blew cool, women wore

dresses and draped cashmeres over their shoulders, boys jogged, teens danced to rock – it was a sort of parody of American summer resort life. Even the white houses with their Carpenter's Gothic details seemed like allusions to Maine or Northern Michigan. But at the same time two muezzins, one a crooning youngster, the other's voice cracked with age, called the seemingly indifferent Muslims to prayer, a sort of witch in her hut on a hilltop above a beach in a cove cooked them lamb patties on a grill and sailors in white spats with machine guns greeted the arrival of every ferryboat. A horny blonde girl up the hill fell in love with Ned and referred to Mark as 'your dad' in her perfect Istanbul American Academy English.

One night Ned and Mark were the only customers in a huge hotel dining room. Six waiters brought the plates of hors d'oeuvre and later the red fish. They were seated beside the window at a table for ten. The waves boiled up under the rocking hulls of moored sailboats and hissed over the foundations of the hotel. Lightning flickered over the coast of Asia and danced across the Sea of Marmara. Suddenly the lights went out. In the dark Mark and Ned ate sardine bits in a dilled vinegar and held hands until a gas lamp, white as daylight, was placed inside a metal circle above their heads.

They were the only two single men in this community of commuting husbands, pregnant wives and children, this warm, puling nursery. Everywhere – in the gardens overflowing with flowers, the grounds of the Greek Orthodox church or of the new synagogue, the exclusive beach club – kids were playing or floating past on whole flotillas of bicycles. Boys in jeans and T-shirts, coasting on bikes, hitched rides by hanging on to the fender of a hired buggy. The only people who noticed Mark and Ned other than Ned's horny admirer were the gold-toothed men modernizing an old mansion. The foreman beckoned them into the garden and presented Ned with a pink rose and Mark with a red.

The truth was that without friends or tricks they irritated each other. It turned out they needed a big modern city full of distractions and gay institutions in order to maintain their intimacy.

From there they flew to Venice, where they joined Joshua in the rambling apartment he rented in a palace on the Grand Canal. Despite the flame-shaped windows, the coloured marble façades and the turbaned heads that served as door knockers, Venice felt sleekly, plushly European after Istanbul. Maybe it was just familiar. To be sure the churning motors of the ferryboat in Istanbul, the vapura, did rhyme with the same vibrations of the Venetian waterbus, the *vaporetto*, as it was thrown into reverse approaching the pontooned stop.

Joshua looked as burnished as the city. He was tan and slim from his daily bastings at the Cipriani pool, where the rich clients were so old Gore Vidal had dubbed the place 'Lourdes'. Joshua worked every afternoon at his desk under the painted allegory of the ceiling. He listened to the soft lapping of the little *rio* under his windows. In the evening they'd wear white shirts and linen suits over that day's burn and saunter forth into Campo Santo Stefano which Joshua liked because it was dominated by a nineteenth-century Dante scholar. Their conversation, however, was anything but scholarly; it was all laughter, boys and gossip. Mark thought he was making such a mistake living in Paris and depriving himself of Joshua's good humour, always subtle no matter how exhilarating it became. This friendship was the brightest jewel in Mark's diadem.

And then Ned flew home to Boston for a visit with his parents. Just before he left he said to Mark, 'I hope I'm not making a mistake. I've never left you alone before. Peters, you're going to leave me, I know you are, you're bored with me.' That very night Mark was cruising in jeans along that dark patch between the Piazzetta and Harry's that looks out across the Lagoon towards the illuminated façade of San

Giorgio Maggiore. He saw a man with a dazzling smile leaning against the railing. Mark said, 'Hello,' and the man said, 'You must be American.'

'How did you know?'

'It's completely obvious – in a nice way.'

Mark, wary of a put-down, said, 'Actually I'm an American who lives in Paris. And right now I'm staying with some friends in an extraordinary palace where Henry James lived and John Singer Sargent – it's a real American hang-out. Wanna see it?'

'Sure.'

On the way through the echoing streets they went past the ugliest church in town, San Moise. 'Exactly who was Saint Moses?' Mark asked.

His new friend introduced himself as Hajo and said he was German. He mentioned he had become very careful given the health crisis and Mark, who identified himself as a sort of gay leader, lied and said he, too, had long been circumspect. Mark felt very self-conscious about his weight and told himself there was no reason this blond, slender Hajo in the cashmere blazer would want someone like him. Of course, Mark had to admit to himself, he *had* picked up a cute Spanish kid the night before at the very same cruising spot.

They lit the courtyard, walked past the abandoned *feltre* (the shuttered cover for the gondola on rainy days) and mounted the outdoor stone stairs to the *piano nobile*, went on up the inner stairs to Joshua's floor, closed the painted wood doors to the library and made drinks for themselves. The transistor played some old string concerto and the wake of the passing *vaporetto* slapped the steps of the water gate below.

But no sooner did Mark toast Hajo under that artificial paradise of scholarly muses bearing tomes of Petrarch and Aretino than Hajo put his drink down on the stone floor and kissed Mark, and Mark wondered if you could get high off the liquor in someone else's mouth, then he wondered how many more times in his life a handsome stranger would kiss him like this with real desire, then he wondered how much longer he'd be alive, then he wondered what this guy's angle was, why me? It even occurred to him Hajo was a gigolo Joshua had hired to cheer him up.

They went to bed and tried to eat each other alive, so hungry were they both for affection. Up close Mark could see Hajo must be more or less forty himself, and that made him feel good. Everyone assumed Mark went for nothing but kids. But it just happened that way. Twinkies were available, adaptable, ready to pack a bag and take off. Another grown-up came with a complete set of friends, habits, hesitations.

Hajo seemed to like Mark's body. Over the next few days Mark started giving Hajo a tour of his favourite paintings in Venice. Although Mark got the names and centuries all turned around, Hajo began to call him 'Professor Bear'.

Wounded, Mark said, 'Like Jerry Lewis, the Nutty Professor?'

'No, Mark, but because you know so much and your body, you look like a lovable bear, so Professor Bear, but maybe *professor* is a better word in German I think?'

'Maybe. Nobody wants to be a professor in America.'

Whereas Ned had given Mark back his childhood, the silliness and sweetness of lazy days in Charlottesville so long ago, Hajo represented middle age, but not the dimness that term suggested in English, rather the ripeness implied by the French phrase, *un homme d'un certain âge*.

Hajo was staying at the Gritti Palace in a corner room people called 'the Elizabeth Taylor suite', because she'd slept there once years ago with Richard Burton. As with most Germans his English was fluent, but more unusually he was equally at ease in French and Italian. His clothes were beautiful, not the dark, undertaker's suits Frenchmen affected on the theory that sobriety is discreet and discretion is elegant, but rather, bright Armani jackets over jeans, antique silk ties with handmade check shirts, high boots so intricately laced they suggested perversion. For someone so dandified Hajo was winningly reluctant to talk about clothes; he even blushed when Mark snooped into his closet and said, 'Wow'.

For years Mark had been the one to plan the evening, order the food, pay the bill, light cigarettes, ask questions, but now he felt himself the focus of attentions more refined than those he'd ever paid anyone. Hajo was especially gallant to Joshua, who was instantly seduced.

Hajo was a film producer and he'd come to Venice for the festival. Unlike everyone else, who stayed at the Excelsior on the Lido to be near the screenings and hoopla, Hajo preferred to live in town, at one remove.

As Mark grew to know him, he discovered so many complexities in Hajo that he despaired of ever explaining his new friend to the folks back home. Not that Hajo was full of inner conflicts. No, he was all of a piece, but that piece had strange new contours. Hajo was both a socialist and a socialite – his politics the residue of 1968, a year Americans could scarcely single out but that had marked every European who'd been young at the time, whereas his taste for *mondanités* was something he'd come to more recently and hoped to contain, like a dangerous but exciting drug habit. His picture was frequently in the paper for having escorted a starlet or ski'd with a prince, and yet he insisted that at Gstaad he preferred to go to bed early with a book and be flown by helicopter to the top of virgin trails ('That way you see all the wild animals on the way down instead of the usual Muffies and Babs').

He was really a bit like the European movie business itself, Mark came to realize. There was the Berlin Film Festival in freezing February with all those dirty, long-haired hippies in their fifties scuttling through the snow to look at movies from a leftist or lesbian perspective; and then in May there was the Cannes Festival with stars in ermine and chauffeured Mercedes and bathing beauties granting bikini sessions to photographers on the beach. Hajo embodied the contradictions but did so by finding unsuspected kindness and softness in steely international hostesses as well as a queer glamour in dour ex-Maoists who'd traded in revolutionary politics for beer and bitterness. He seemed to like everyone. As soon as Mark mentioned a name Hajo smiled his huge smile and said, 'She's great! A fabulous woman!' or 'Isn't he sympathetic? Please give him my very best.'

Among his Parisian friends Mark had grown accustomed to a low level of constant grumbling, but with Hajo everything was upbeat. He liked most movies, he was curious about most new political or artistic developments and he thought nothing of hopping on a plane to see a new ballet in Marseille or a fashion show in Milan. For several summers he'd rented a house in East Hampton, and he prided himself on his knowledge of America. His only hypocrisy consisted of pretending he'd been trying to reach someone for hours by phone. When that person answered even on the first try Hajo invariably sang out, *'Finally!'*

The America of old movies he also liked – Westerns, Minnelli musicals, the *films noirs* of the 1950s, Hitchcock – but he felt the more recent super-budget sci-fi kiddy crap was endangering the entire industry. A photo of a cowboy would make him grow misty-eyed but he could also say quite casually, 'You're lucky you live in Europe, Mark. The quality of life in America is so low. The clothes, the crime, especially the food.'

Unlike Mark's Parisian acquaintances, who all seemed to despise their jobs, Hajo loved his work. Like an American, Hajo bragged about how much he worked, even exaggerated how long and arduous were his hours, and he quite gratuitously attributed gruelling efforts to indolent Mark. ('Poor

Mark, you spend every moment studying the tourism allure –
do you say that? *allure?* – of Venice'). As far as Mark could
see, Hajo's work was much like his own, mainly a matter of
kissing babies and cutting ribbons, of 'circulating'.

Unlike an American businessman, Hajo revered art. In
Berlin he shuffled into the ugly modern opera house with all
the fat ladies in galoshes to listen to the upsetting stridencies
of *Lulu*. His big house in Grünewald was filled with the
newest German expressionist painting and Hajo had once
even been asked by the reigning genius of the moment to
find him wild hare's blood to be sprinkled over a legless,
hacked-to-pieces Steinway; Hajo had guiltily confessed to
Mark in bed one night that he'd been so busy that week he'd
settled for plain rabbit's blood from the butcher ('I pray this
lie is never revealed – even the title is *Hasenblut!*'). Mark
learned that Hajo had been faithful to his previous lover for
ten years until last June when the lover had left him for a
'phoney' Austrian baron ('It's even against the law in Austria
to use titles; you can be fined for putting *baron* on your
carte de visite').

When Mark returned to Paris, Ned was already there;
he'd enrolled at the Sorbonne. Mark couldn't help talking
about Hajo all the time. Besides, Hajo phoned twice a day
and sent by express mail unbearable tapes he'd concocted
out of all the most recent dissonant music, a quartet by
Henze, water dripping and gurgling by Cage. Ned would
come home from school and catch Mark doing sit-ups to
Stockhausen blips and bleeps. Now it was Ned's turn to
apostrophize their stuffed bear: 'Mr Peters, he's going to
leave boring old us for this arty-farty Kraut who's as old as he
is, why it's obscene, sex between two people of the same age!'

Because Ned loved Mark, he accepted Hajo. 'It could have
been worse,' Ned told the bear. 'It could have been a
gold-digging twenty-year-old Parisian, who would have
driven poor aging us out of our home, Mr Peters.' Later, over

dinner, Ned said, 'I'm happy for you. And I want you to be faithful to him – it's better for your health.'

'What about yours?'

'I think it's odd' – this back to the bear – 'that he broke up my affair with Luc and then started up with A-hole or is it Hajo?'

Love had taken Mark by surprise. He spent hours selecting post cards and sent six or seven a day to Berlin. He bought a book on German history and read it until he was thoroughly confused. He hung around the German bookstore next to his gym and even contemplated buying a beginning German course on cassettes for French speakers before he came to his senses. He dieted and exercised, hoping to impress Hajo on his first visit to Berlin three weeks hence.

He'd never been faithful to anyone before. In fact he'd preached against fidelity, which he'd considered as barbaric as female circumcision. Now he liked it because it meant he was consecrating all his energy and desire to one person, just as he was the sole object of Hajo's love. He was less fearful than before of competition. He trusted Hajo – so much so that he wondered if he'd ever really trusted anyone before.

When he arrived in Berlin in the new clothes he'd bought for the occasion with the new pigskin bag from Hermès and the big illustrated book on Jean-Michel Frank under his arm (Frank was Hajo's favourite designer), Hajo kissed him on the lips and hurried him into the waiting car. As they sat side by side Hajo kept interrupting himself or Mark in order to pull back an inch, look at Mark and say, 'Good to *see* you!'

Mark was so in love he kept losing his erection. He suffered two days over these fits of impotence until, scarlet-faced, he blurted out to Hajo, 'Look, don't think I'm always such a dud, it's just you're so great and -'

'But Mark,' Hajo said, 'I don't even notice. Don't be so complicated, Herr Professor Bear.'

In bed Hajo was slender and hairless to the point of

puerility and he slept with his head on Mark's chest. But in public places, dressed in his double-breasted jacket, outsize raincoat and high-laced boots, Hajo could be unsmilingly severe with headwaiters or ushers or drivers. In bed his face softened and he seemed to be sleepily nuzzling Mark, but out on the tense, shoddily modern Ku'damm he looked pale and lined and determined.

In the same way he seemed to like Mark's strength, his physical bulk, as a kid might like his father's, but over dinner at the Paris Bar Hajo himself would turn paternal and counsel Mark on everything from health insurance to diet. 'Don't eat pork at night!' he said, scandalized. 'It's bad enough at lunch, but never at night. You might as well eat a *sausage*!'

Like many people in the theatre and movies, Hajo cultivated superstitions about food. He wouldn't drink anything, not even water, with meals for fear the liquids might dilute his digestive juices. He ate nothing but fruit till noon, nothing but vegetables after six and never did he combine the two, but a month later it was all cheese and potatoes and spinach pasta. For cold sores he had drops of homoeopathic potions and something he called *salvia* and he told Mark he'd never in all his forty years had a shot of penicillin.

What most astonished Mark was how little Hajo knew about gay life. For years Hajo had lived with a woman, then with one man for ten years and in all that time he had been to a gay bar only twice and to a sauna only once. None of Hajo's friends was gay, although all of his straight friends knew Hajo was 'homosexual', as they said without the slightest shade of meaning, condescension or embarrassment.

'Just my luck,' Mark said, 'to find a Berliner who doesn't drink beer, doesn't eat sausage, has never been to a cabaret and never worn a garter belt.'

Hajo's house was his hobby. It was filled with French furniture from the 1920s and 30s and German paintings from the 1980s. A Turkish woman came twice a week to clean but everything was already so scrubbed and gleaming she had little to do except iron Hajo's shirts (he'd sent her for ironing lessons with a friend's maid, a Spanish woman who had once been in service to the Spanish ambassador to Vienna).

To Mark the house gave off the feeling of silk and barbed wire – the silk was the faded Kilims, the polished pearwood and pale upholstery, and the wire was the brutal paintings, those burned and anguished figures, abandoned Icarus wings and scrawled words. The cold winter light cast a haze over the plants, which were huddled in the conservatory like people waiting for the underground. The expensive furnace burned noiselessly.

For all his pride in his house, Hajo liked excitable, bohemian film people given to what Mark thought were strange political resentments against Reagan, nuclear weapons and US intervention in Central America. Mark knew from his mother never to discuss religion or politics, which led Hajo's 'Greens' to assume Mark was as ecological and left as they were.

At two or three in the morning the drunk guests would roar off through the dark, silent suburbs, Hajo would open the french doors to let in the cold night, he and Mark would empty ashtrays and load the dishwasher and suddenly their peace was restored, like the birdsong spring brings back to the garden. 'Hi,' Mark would say.

'Hello,' Hajo would reply, as their intimacy emerged from hiding. Despite the sudden noise and laughter of these visits from friends, Hajo struck Mark as a solitary, someone who preferred a night alone to read the world press for movie news, to repolish his Puiforcat silverware, to watch videos of movies about to be released or to study the paintings reproduced in the art magazine *Wolkenkratzer*.

In bed they were passionate but cautious – ardent in their kisses but afraid to exchange those fluids that had once been the gush of life but that now seemed the liquid drained off a fatal infection. In Mark's dreams Berlin itself – this pocket of glitz and libertinage surrounded by the grey hostility of East Germany – became an emblem of their endangered, quarantined happiness.

On the last night of his visit Mark stretched sleepily and said, 'You know I've never been faithful to anyone before.'

'No?'

'And I like it!' He smiled into the dark. 'There's even a Spanish kid I met in Venice just before, uh, well, a kid who's been writing me, but I was proud to write to him and say I was faithful to a guy in Berlin and, well,' he mumbled into the ominous, breathless silence on the pillow beside him, 'I've never burned a bridge before or turned down even the remotest sexual possibility, it's all so new . . .'

Hajo didn't say a word.

At last Mark asked, 'Is there anything wrong?'

Hajo said, 'Do you mean you make love with many men now, during *die Pest*?'

'No one since I met you.'

'But before? In Paris and Venice?'

Now it was Mark's turn to say nothing. Hajo went into the kitchen and came back five minutes later with something in his hand that smelled of a summer roadside.

'What are you drinking?'

'Camomile. Mark, you lied to me. You said you were a gay leader. You said you are health-conscious since a long time. Now I understand you were with a Spanish the night before you met me – that was why your nipples were too sore to touch then but never now.'

It occurred to Mark that 'health-consciousness' had become a new word for jealousy.

Hajo took more and more precautions when they made love. When Mark compared their love-making with his own heavy sex scenes of the 1970s (losing consciousness in leather harness, the smell of poppers, his legs coated in grease) he had to admit how tame a porno movie of Hajo and him would look. Yet Mark no longer felt like a sex star and he even pretended to be shocked when he heard about things he used to do at least once a week. With Hajo he felt like a conductor awakening the blare of brass with a raised hand, hushing the massed strings simply by closing his eyes. But the moment it was over Hajo wouldn't stew in their juices, not even for a second; he dashed off to wash off with a special surgical soap. At dinner he wouldn't taste anything from Mark's spoon; from even the merest brush of lips he'd draw back, as though Mark were carved out of burning ice.

Even if Mark conceded Hajo was perfectly within his medical rights, he couldn't help bridling at the thought he was being faithful to someone afraid to kiss him.

When Mark flew back to Paris, Ned announced Luc had returned from Brazil. Apparently Luc had drunk too much one night in Belém, tried to jump-start a car and had been shot in the leg by the irate and equally drunk owner of the car. Luc was in a Paris hospital. Bits of his hipbone were being transplanted into the damaged femur. Nothing, naturally, was more romantic than nursing a sunburned young lover in pain, and they'd already had sex while a sympathetic male nurse stood guard.

In the delicate cantilevering of Mark's and Ned's love, the precarious downward thrust of forces required a solid underpinning, which they had now – Ned had Luc and Mark had Hajo. But of course no one had anyone for sure, and Mark feared one day he'd lose both Hajo and Ned. Then that calculation shamed him and he sought to imagine himself splendidly alone. He realized he'd picked up the superstition that so long as someone or other was his lover he'd continue to live; to love and to live were near rhymes.

One night Mark said he wanted to read late in the guest

bedroom; the next night he wasn't feeling well; by the third he and Ned had definitely stopped sleeping in the same bed.

Hajo insisted that Mark take out a good German health insurance policy, one that would cover hospital and doctor expenses no matter where in the world he felt ill. Mark was grateful to have the policy since he knew many single men had become uninsurable. He was also touched by the attention, the sort he'd usually paid to his younger, dizzier boyfriends. But he also registered the thought that Hajo might be expecting something to go wrong with his health.

That spring Mark and Hajo spent one week out of every month together. Two of Hajo's Berlin friends became ill, one with the pneumonia, the other with the parasite in the brain. In America more and more of Mark's friends were dying or dead, and his profits were way off. When he went home to New York for a week he couldn't stay in his own apartment, since he'd sublet it. He stayed with Joshua and they laughed a lot, but Mark couldn't help but notice that he, Mark, wasn't up on the latest fads and feuds, nor was he a constant in his friends' calculations. Oh, they all liked him and if he came back they'd make room for him soon enough, but as an expatriate he didn't count as an ally, an introduction or even an ear.

On the street there seemed to be fewer gay men, or perhaps they were just less visible; they'd shaved their moustaches, put on some weight and let the holes pierced through their ears grow back. On the Upper West Side there were ten more gourmet shops and two fewer gay bars. Young heterosexuals – loud, rich and confident – swarmed down Central Park West, gaudy in leg-warmers and pink jogging shorts over midwinter tans.

George Balanchine had died and the company was performing his ballets perfectly, but now that Mark knew there would be no new dances he saw each work as part of what the French called the *patrimoine*, a sad and pompous word. All of these swans, even the cygnets, had known Mr B.; his old hands had stretched a leg still higher or relaxed the rigid circle of lifted arms into a softer ellipse. But soon there would be new troops of seventeen-year-olds and the old coolness and precision would slacken, blur. Having lived in Paris, Mark no longer believed in progress. When he looked at the tinker-toy tackiness of the new buildings at Les Halles, he was grateful Paris had been built in earlier, better centuries.

When he went home to Paris, it didn't feel like home. He could barely understand the muttered conversation of the taxi driver with his Montmartre Titi-Parisien accent. The dollar was losing value every day and anyway Mark had fewer and fewer of them. He and Ned started ironing their own shirts, buying clothes during the sales, eating in, cutting short their calls to America.

They both expected to die. 'I just hope I graduate first,' Ned said. 'I'd love to finish one thing before buying the farm.' Mark had an attack of shingles. Before his doctor diagnosed it, Mark looked at the spots across his solar plexus and panicked and said out loud to his reflection in the mirror, 'Dear God, I'm not ready to die.' The same week, after learning what was wrong with him, he read that shingles in someone under fifty was an accurate 'tracer disease', a sure sign of dangerously lowered immunities. The illness made Mark sleep all the time. He felt as though he were weighted down by wet, heavy eiderdowns. The only thing he could do was watch television, but the foreign language made him anxious. He didn't like being ill in a foreign country.

He recovered. In May when he saw Hajo in Berlin they went to the hospital for a blood test. Hajo had insisted on it, although Mark had warned him, 'You know how it'll turn out, you'll be negative and I'll be positive and then we'll break up. It's just that simple.' Hajo was sure they'd both be negative.

At that point the blood samples still had to be shipped to America to be analysed. They would have to wait a month for the results. Their doctor also gave them physicals and a multi-test, that is, they were each scratched with eight different infections. The idea was that someone with intact immunities would respond to them all or at least five or six. Mark developed only two red bumps, whereas Hajo grew all eight.

The doctor refused to give out the results over the phone. He insisted that Mark return to Berlin for a face-to-face conference. That wasn't really inconvenient since he and Hajo had planned anyway to fly together for a week to Vienna, which neither of them had ever visited.

In the interval Mark seldom thought of the disease. He had decided, almost as though it were a question of personal elegance, to be courageous. He wasn't going to complain or suffer. He was going to be very brave, no matter what happened. That was because he was a gay leader, sort of, and people expected him to set an example. His Virginia ancestors had been courageous. Anyway, he wasn't all that attached to life. He thought it was fun, but he wouldn't mind giving it up. Of course he had no idea how he'd act when worn down by the long, painful reality. He probably wouldn't have the energy to be courageous.

He begged Ned to take more precautions. Ned said that Luc had swollen glands in his neck and under his arms and night sweats. He also had athlete's foot and bad skin. They hugged their bear and Ned said, 'Peters, I guess it's curtains for us.' They agreed that if they became ill they'd travel to India and commit suicide beside the Ganges. It was Ned's idea: 'We've never been there. It would be an adventure. We should do something absolutely new. Anyway, they know all about death and cremation there – it's their specialty.'

Whereas the French were calm and rational in their responses to the epidemic, the Germans, like the English, were being driven to hysteria by their press. In France one could forget the disease for whole days at a stretch, but in reactionary Bavaria, for instance, the Minister of Health had proposed quarantining even healthy carriers. Mark was afraid their test results wouldn't be kept confidential, no matter what the hospital had said.

The sun was shining on the gilt Spirit of Victory on top of the Siegessäule the day they walked through the Tiergarten on their way to the hospital. Beds of red and pink tulips alternated around the statue of Bismarck, who stood with a sword in one hand and a drapery below the other, as though he were a portly, exhausted torero. They'd each dressed carefully and Hajo had taken the day off from work.

At the last moment Hajo decided he didn't want to know the results.

'Don't be silly,' Mark said.

'But what good are they?' Hajo asked. 'I'm afraid. If I'm positive I'll freak.' That was one of his Americanisms: 'Freak'.

'Look,' Mark said, 'we've always been careful, but I was such a slut before; I'll be positive, you'll be negative, I'm sure of it, but we'll know we must continue to be extra extra careful. If we're both negative we'll be able to fuck each other like bunnies and you'll never be able to leave me, you'll be sealed to me for life, you poor sucker.'

Their original doctor had gone off on holiday and had been replaced by a young man who'd just come back from two months in San Francisco where, he told them in his almost accentless English, he'd learned how to do all the lab work for the blood test. Then he shuffled through their reports, crossed and uncrossed his long legs. He told Hajo he was negative and Mark he was positive. He took another blood sample from Mark just to be sure, but the next day he would confirm the diagnosis. Now he said, 'We don't really know what *positive* means, but we're finding that at least a third of the positives are developing the symptoms and that percentage appears to be growing over time. There are even those who say one hundred per cent of the carriers will become symptomatic.'

'You mean die?' Mark asked.

'But there are new methods every day,' the doctor said, embarrassed or maybe vexed, as he stared at Mark's chart again.

That night they ate dinner at the Paris Bar and Mark joked with the two beefy, handsome guys who owned the place and Hajo quizzed them about Vienna, where they were from. But suddenly, Mark thought that it was all over, his affair with Hajo, his grown-up European love. It occurred to him he'd never been loved by anyone quite so thoughtful and kind and mature. Mark looked at his own fat face in the mirror over the banquette and he feared no one would ever love him again. He felt sorry for himself and he went into the toilet, locked the door and sobbed, pulled himself together and returned to their table. But that night in the big lacquered sleigh bed, under the painting of a scorched field still smouldering, Hajo went right to sleep. He was wearing shorts to bed for the first time. In the past he'd always slept bare-assed. His soft, rapid snores sounded like kindling being trimmed by the smallest Braun saw. Mark started to quake silently from thinking their beautiful love was over. He went down the hall and locked himself behind the toilet door to sob out loud, but then Hajo, skinny in his black T-shirt advertising Kurosawa's *Ran* and his baggy boxer shorts, was tapping at the door and saying, 'Mark, darling, Mark, come to bed, it will be all right, I love you, nothing's changed,' but Mark knew everything had changed, starting with the shorts.

Vienna was hot and airless and deserted. They walked slowly through the museum of natural history and looked at dinosaur bones. The famous horses weren't performing their tricks right now, it was off season, and at the opera *Die Fledermaus* was playing only to Japanese group tours; Mark and Hajo left during the first interval. The Mozart apartment was supposed to prove how poor the great composer had been, but Mark reckoned it would rent for four thousand bucks a month in Manhattan today.

They lay in the sun in their swimsuits at a public pool on the outskirts of the city. He made Hajo translate what the young people on the towel beside them were talking about. Hajo said that one young man, the one with the hair held back with red rubber bands, was recounting the plot of a story he was writing, or maybe it was a dream. Mark said, 'Perhaps he'll be a famous writer,' but he thought all of this was like a dream: the woods in the distance under a colour-leaching sun; this turn-of-the-century brick spa; the virtually naked strangers all around him, each of whom knew the best bus routes, the name of the best butcher and the date of the next concert to be given by their favourite local singing star – a whole life Mark would never fathom. Wherever they went, Mark kept murmuring to himself, 'It's over.' Obviously Hajo couldn't do or say anything. It was Mark's responsibility to break up with him. Maybe the heat as they swayed in the tram along the brilliant, nearly deserted Ringstrasse recalled summer days in Charlottesville, yes, that time he'd led an out-of-town cousin through Monticello. He and Willie Lee had stood formally, sweating in seersucker jackets, and watched the lady guide demonstrate 'Mister' Jefferson's system of pulleys by which double doors could be opened symmetrically. Some little Yankee brats had been cutting up, refusing to stick with the tour, until the mono-bosomed volunteer had said in perfect Tidewater tones, '*Thank you*. This way. *Thank you.*' Those *thank yous* had chilled the boys into obedience. The formality of that place, sweating inside a jacket, could be paired with the shadowless heat of Vienna. They stopped and stared at a Russian war memorial: the inscriptions were entirely in Russian, not a word of German, and Mark said to himself, 'It's over.'

But it wasn't. Hajo lay in his arms in the hotel room and said, 'You must forgive me. I'm such a coward, and all my German cleanness manias.'

'Hell no,' Mark said, 'it's a question of dying, not of politeness. Why should you risk your one and only life?' Their intimacy was very deep, maybe because they were both far from home in a hotel with the jaunty name, The King of Hungary.

On the television every newscast was about the Austrian wine scandal; vintners were lacing their wine with anti-freeze. Mark and Hajo made deep love - physically reserved but emotionally deep. For the first time Mark understood that the precautions they were taking weren't an insult directed against him; he'd always known that, of course, but he hadn't accepted it.

Two days after he returned to Paris he learned that Joshua had been hospitalized for the pneumonia. His doctor had been treating it as though it had been just bronchitis, but Joshua had fainted in his apartment with a high fever and the friend he'd stood up at the ballet had made the police break down his door. That same friend had waited to call Mark until Joshua was better. The pneumonia went away as fast as it had come on, but it foreshadowed, of course, a future that made Mark think of the words in that Yankee hymn, 'His terrible swift sword'.

He told Ned the news with a smile he couldn't suppress and Ned wept in his arms. They stared at the truth only a few minutes. Soon Ned was hurrying off to his class at the Sorbonne and Mark was ironing a shirt for the evening, but as the iron slid over the damp fabric and awakened wisps of steam, he thought he had too few attachments to the world. Maybe that was why he'd become such a porker, to weight himself down. He felt the circle was tightening around him. In a way he was grateful he'd lost the habit of talking to Joshua twice a day and going to the ballet with him twice a week; if their lives had stayed so intertwined Mark would never have been able to give Joshua up.

Joshua had been – *was!* – Mark's civilized friend. Mark had forgiven himself his own hell-raising, his own shallowness, because he'd been loved by this serene, subtle man. Joshua's love had vouched for Mark's value, but now Mark felt shabbier. Mark didn't know many French people well, but he doubted if any of them came in Joshua's variety – this sense of fun linked to the most lightly worn erudition, this kindness redeemed by the least malign bitchery. Anyone who lived in a circle as tight, as overbred as Joshua's needed to complain a bit; at least he always said he felt his blood had been oxygenated after a good complaining session. Who else but Joshua could hold in suspension so many different elements – his Venetian elegance, his scholarliness, his campiness, his ballet fanaticism, his passion for society (he was the most collegial of creatures). His social being was an achievement, a work of art. His laugh – his great, head-thrown-back, all-out, unthrottled laugh – announced his forbearance and hilarity in the face of experience (he pronounced it 'high-larity' and certainly his friends all got high off it).

Mark called his mother in Virginia. She was in her eighties but as starchy as ever. They seldom spoke of personal matters. She'd met Joshua several times. When Mark told her about Joshua's illness and his prospects, she said, 'You're too young to be losing your friends. That's more for folks in my league, the golden oldies.'

'Yes, ma'am, I guess you're right there. I hope you're taking it easy.'

She laughed. 'Easy? Why I'm so relaxed I'm downright trifling.' Her voice darkened. 'Now if you get sick, you come home to Virginia and I'll nurse you, you hear?'

Mark said, 'Yes, ma'am,' but he thought he'd rather make a pilgrimage to India. He hadn't come this far, moved North to live among the Yankees and then come on over here to Paris, France, just so he could end up back home in Charlottesville. He didn't want to be pitied by his father's Baptist kin.

As though she were reading his mind, his mother ('Miz Ellen', as they called her) said, 'I don't want you killin' yourself if you take sick. I'd never forgive you. In my family we fight the good fight.'

'Yes, ma'am,' he said, but he thought he didn't want to undergo the humiliation of dying amongst friends, losing his looks and powers, nor the loneliness of dying slowly amongst strangers. He'd kill himself beside the Ganges.

Mark invited Luc and Ned and another friend to a restaurant in the Eiffel Tower for dinner. As they looked down on the river valley and picked out Notre Dame in the distance, Sacré Coeur on a hill, the pale square of the Place de la Concorde just this side of the dark rectangle of the Tuileries, they watched the early summer sunlight fade and the blue blaze of streetlamps ignite, laced by swarming yellow headlights. Every moment of beauty had its valedictory side these days for Mark. He took a real pleasure in ordering a good bottle of Montrachet-Chassigny for his guests, and he suffered not the slightest temptation to sip it. He wished he were very thin and lined and dry looking, an old man with a grey pony tail and bony, Cocteau-like hands, for that look would better correspond to the way he felt.

Luc was still hobbling and he'd lost weight, but his charm was intact if too consciously dispensed in the right doses to the right recipients. They all broke up in a flood of warmth after dinner, but around midnight Ned surprised Mark by coming home in a rage. 'Here it is, a nice romantic evening,' Ned said, 'and Luc wanted to go out to a bar. I

228

know he's terribly worried about his health, he's got *champignons* in the throat – what's that in English?'

'Fungus. Thrush.'

'Oh. Anyway, he's driven. He's afraid to have sex with other people, but he can't stop prowling, and I just keep getting hurt. He thinks I should be there to keep him from being lonely, but I feel lonelier when I'm beside him, wanted but not really, you know what I mean? He's afraid of missing out on the action and he thinks we're it.'

In July Mark and Ned went back to Büyükada. They befriended a group of Turkish yacht captains who lived on board the boats moored in the harbour. Every night they pooled their food and drink and took potluck on one ship or another. Only one of the captains, a twenty-year-old named Adnan, spoke English. Adnan said, 'First we eat, then congratulation.' It turned out 'congratulation' meant 'conversation'. The conversation was all rather high-schooly questions such as: 'Tell me, do you think there will be war in the next century?' Neither Mark nor Ned had opinions on such subjects. As expatriates, they'd ducked out of politics. Reagan's senile shenanigans embarrassed Mark slightly, and Mitterrand's cadaverous looks repelled him exactly as much as his statesmanlike style attracted him, but their personalities were less real to Mark than the heroes and villains on the dubbed reruns of *Dynasty* he always watched in Paris.

Hajo visited them. He liked the kids who played on their steep, dusty road and always said, 'Allo!', their one word of English. He couldn't bring himself to look at the flies clustering on the butcher's shop meat like grape seeds on cheese, and the entire seven days he stayed with them he ate nothing but fruit and vegetables. One night Mark cut his thumb slightly with the vegetable peeler. It was just a nick, but Hajo must have noticed it. In bed, when Mark reached for Hajo's penis in the dark, Hajo said, 'Do you mind, not with your thumb, you cut it.'

Mark said, 'OK, that's it. Let's just be friends. I can't live this way.'

Mark realized Hajo was relieved. He'd been too kind to break it off himself, but he was grateful Mark had finally made a move.

Ned flew home to the States to see his parents at the end of August. Mark took the Orient Express boat from Istanbul to Venice. When they sailed into Venice at dawn, Mark stood on the top deck of the huge square ship and looked down on the palaces and churches; for the first time he was even higher than the campanile. He didn't like this sensation; it made even Venice's proportions seem arbitrary

He'd decided he'd let Joshua set the tone. If Joshua wanted to be frivolous, fine; if he wanted to talk about illness and death, fine. Joshua chose frivolity, which Mark considered gallant.

Once again, if for the last time, they settled into their old habits. They'd be awakened by the spluttering, rumbling, honking, shouting water traffic under their windows. They'd sit in the kitchen, which had been John Singer Sargent's studio a hundred years ago, and look down into the courtyard and nibble on bread rusks and listen for the furious rumbling of yet another pot of brewed espresso. Then Joshua retreated to the cool immensity of the painted library, where he sat beside a window laced with a morning glory vine and tapped at his typewriter. Joshua listened to the classical music station on his transistor and the thin reproduction of a full-bodied piece for strings floated from room to room over the lustrous floors and under the bands of pink and beige plaster layering the cornices.

Daydreaming on his bed with the door open, dozing in the middle of a day too breezy to be hot, Mark heard the radio and the typewriter, these faint life signals Joshua was emitting. Mark thought that this summer everything was just as it had been the twelve preceding summers. The only thing that was different was that this summer would end the series.

He wanted to know how to enjoy these days without clasping them so tightly he'd stifle the pleasure. But he didn't want to drug himself on the moment either and miss out on what was happening to him. He was losing his best friend, the witness to his life. The skill for enjoying a familiar pleasure about to disappear was hard to acquire. It was sort of like sex. If you were just unconsciously rocking in the groove you missed the kick, but if you kept mentally shouting 'Wow!' you shot too soon. Knowing how to appreciate the rhythms of these last casual moments – to cherish them while letting them stay casual – demanded a new way of navigating time.

Maybe that was why these days were so beautiful. Hadn't Joshua quoted the poet he was working on, Wallace Stevens, who'd said, 'Death is the mother of beauty'? Joshua had explained that eternal, unchanging beauty would seem insipid and not at all beautiful – 'a bore'.

The maids, mother and daughter, arrived at noon and began the never-ending task of washing and polishing the *pavimenti*. They preferred working together, since that way they kept each other company. Joshua liked them and he kept giving them little presents – an extra coffee pot, an old typewriter, some picture books devoted to Venetian painters. In fact, Mark noticed that Joshua was silently disposing of most of his belongings; they carried down a sack full of old clothes and left it with the garbage outside the *portone*.

Then they sauntered across Campo Santo Stefano in search of lunch. Joshua looked leaner; there was something grey and slack about his cheeks. He who'd always suffered from a writer's block was now working with greater fluency than ever before. Tap, tap, tap – the typewriter pecked its way across the page. At the pool they'd gossip. Sometimes they'd assume new characters, loosely based on their own but exaggerated towards archness. With Hajo, Mark imperson-ated an adult; with Ned, a child; but he and Joshua styled themselves as fantasy versions of themselves – them-selves disguised as bored Venetian housewives (*'carissima!'*) or as catty Milanese queens in the rag trade, which would provoke astounded laughs from the two thoroughly Ameri-can fellows within them.

The days were sunnier, the nights more ambrosial than ever before. At the Ca' Rezzonico they looked once more at the *pulcinellos* playing obscene leapfrog, but it was down-stairs, as they passed a banal Canaletto, that Mark realized these palaces had been here for centuries past and would still be here for centuries to come. Only the people came and went, supernumeraries. He wanted to ask Joshua if this Venetian eternity was a consolation or an insult, but he didn't know how to broach the subject.

Hajo called him every day from Berlin. 'I'm so glad you're back to civilization,' Hajo said. He'd been frustrated by the Turkish phones. He told Mark about his friends who were dying; Mark told Hajo about Joshua. When Hajo said that both of his friends who were ill had fooled around for years at the saunas, Mark flared up. 'If Joshua had sex ten times in the last five years that would be a lot. It's not a reward for promiscuity, Hajo. It's just bad luck.'

Mark knew they'd always be friends, but the sexual tie between them was broken now, that tension that had kept drawing them back to each other. Now Mark wondered if he'd ever sleep with another man. If he met someone new he'd have to say he was positive. In the past he'd sometimes imagined he'd end up with a woman, even father children, but being positive had scotched that little fantasy.

Although he avoided newspapers, he picked up the *Herald Tribune* one day and read that India was planning to require bloodtest results before granting visas to tourists. There went the notion of being cremated on a burning ghat.

He missed Ned.

After the regatta, Joshua decided to leave Venice. He stored a summer fan, a box of books and his beach things – 'for next summer,' he said with deliberation. He'd given away most of his belongings; this little pile was his sole lien on life. A water taxi pulled into the *rio* under the library windows. The driver, a portly, sunburned man in a starched white uniform who stood and steered with one hand, backed them out into the Grand Canal. A barge went past carrying the stacked bleachers from the regatta viewing-stand. They looked up at the new wooden Accademia bridge, downstream to the white stone lions sipping water at the Guggenheim and beyond to the gold ball above the old customs house agleam even on this cloudy day. Then, as they were pulling away, they took a last look at *their* palace and, smiling shyly at each other, pushed the tears aside.

In Milan Joshua boarded his plane for New York and Mark flew home to Paris. Mark behaved well at the airport, just as though it were a question of keeping up a good front until the company had all left. Maybe because his life had been so charmed (Ned called himself and Mark 'the brat brigade'), the hardest thing about grief was just to accept it was happening 'live' and not like a commercial on a videotape that could be edited out later.

A few weeks later Mark and Ned went to a Robbins–Balanchine evening at the Paris opera house. They were happy to be back together. They had so little money now, it looked as though they'd be going home soon; if Mark didn't make an effort his business would surely go under.

The Robbins ballet was new, but the two Balanchines were old friends, *Apollo* and the Stravinsky *Violin Concerto*. They were both nicely danced, but the somnolent audience scarcely applauded and Mark felt offended. He'd never been able to make Parisians understand that the lobby of the New York State Theater had been the drawing room of America and that we, yes, *we* Americans saw in the elaborate *enchainements* on stage a radiant vision of society.

Hadn't Robbins called his best piece *Dances at a Gathering*? The old hymn said, 'We gather together to ask the Lord's blessing.' Now there was no Lord left to ask anything of, but in the book on modern poetry Joshua was struggling to finish hadn't he quoted Wallace Stevens, who'd said that if Americans were to have a god now it would have to be art?

The last movement of the *Violin Concerto* was clearly both Stravinsky's and Balanchine's homage to the square dance, and just as clearly these Parisian dancers had never seen a square dance in their lives; nor had the people in the audience. The idea of a courtship dance held in the midst of a whole smiling world of grown-ups ('Alleman left and do-si-do') – oh, the sweetly unsensual spirit of checked, flouncy dresses and handheld Stetsons – eluded these bored Parisian performers, all state employees eager to wrap it up and head home.

Mark wept at this old mirror, leprous with flaking silver, that was being held up to reflect the straight young features of Balanchine's art. Ned held his hand in the dark and Mark spoiled Ned's silk *pochette* by blowing his nose into it.

Ned whispered, 'Are you crying for Joshua?'

Mark nodded. Seeing the beauty he'd known with Joshua so distorted made him feel all the farther from home. His muscles registered the word 'home' with a tensing, as though to push himself up out of the chair and head back towards home, to Joshua and the stingers at the Riv and the wild nights of sex and dance, but then he relaxed back into his seat, since he knew that home wasn't there anymore. Ned was the only home he had.

An Oracle

Edmund White

For Herb Spiers

After George died, Ray went through a long period of uncertainty. George's disease had lasted fifteen months and during that time Ray had stopped seeing most of his old friends. He'd even quarrelled with Betty, his best friend. Although she'd sent him little cards from time to time, including the ones made by a fifty-year-old California hippie whom she represented, he hadn't responded. He'd even felt all the more offended that she'd forgotten or ignored how sickening he'd told her he thought the pastel leaves and sappy sentiments were.

George had been a terrible baby throughout his illness, but then again Ray had always babied him the whole twelve years they'd been together, so the last months had only dramatized what had been inherent from the beginning. Nor had George's crankiness spoiled their good times together. Of course they'd lived through their daily horrors (their dentist, an old friend, had refused to pull George's rotten tooth; George's mother had decided to 'blame herself' for George's cowardice in the face of pain), but they still had had fun. Ray leased a little Mercedes and they drove to the country whenever George was up to it. A friend had given them a three-hundred-dollar Siamese kitten he'd found at a pet show and they'd named her Anna, partly because of Anna and the King of Siam and partly in deference to an ancient nickname for Ray. They both showered her with affection.

Which she reciprocated. Indeed, the more they chased away their friends, the more they relished her obvious liking for them. When they'd lie in bed watching television at night, they'd take turns stroking Anna. If she purred, they'd say, 'At least *she* likes us.' After George became very feeble and emaciated, he would ignore his mother and father and refuse to stay even a single night at the hospital and would play with Anna if he had the strength and berate Ray for something or other.

George would become very angry at Ray for not calling to find out the results of his own blood test. 'You're just being irresponsible,' George would say, 'to yourself.' But Ray knew that the test would tell him nothing – or tell him that yes, he'd been exposed to the virus, but nothing more. And besides there was no preventive treatment. Anyway, he owed all his devotion to George; he didn't want to think for a second about his own potential illness.

Every moment of George's last four months had been absorbing. They quarrelled a lot, specially about little dumb things, as though they needed the nagging and gibbering of everyday pettiness to drown out the roar of eternity. George, who'd never cared about anything except the day after tomorrow, suddenly became retrospective in a sour way.

They quarrelled about whether Ray had ever needed George, which was absurd since until George had become ill Ray had been so deeply reliant on George's energy and contacts that Betty had repeatedly warned Ray against living forever in George's shadow. What she hadn't known was how much he, Ray, had always babied George at home – nursed him through hangovers, depressions, business worries, even attacks of self-hatred after he'd been rejected by a trick.

George, of course, was the famous one. Starting in the early 1970s he'd been called in by one major corporation after another to give each an image, and George had designed everything from the letterhead to the company jet. He'd think up a colour scheme, a logo, a typeface, an overall look; he'd re-do the layouts of the annual report. He'd work with an advertising creative director on the product presentation and the campaign slogans. He'd demand control over even the tiniest details, down to the lettering on the business cards of the sales force. Since he was six foot three, rangy and athletic, had a deep voice, and had fathered a son during an early marriage, the executives he dealt with never suspected him of being gay, nor was George a crusader of any sort. He liked winning and he didn't want to start any game with an unfair handicap. George also had a temper, a drive to push his ideas through, and he wasn't handsome – three more things that counted as straight among straights.

He'd also had the heterosexual audacity to charge enormous fees. His job as corporate image-maker was something he'd more or less invented. He'd realized that most American corporations were paralysed by pettiness, rivalry, and fear, and only an outsider could make things happen. George was able to bring about more changes in a month than some cringing and vicious vice-president could effect in a year if ever. George made sure he reported directly to the president or chairman, although as soon as he came 'onstream' he solicited everyone else's 'input'.

On summer weekends George and Ray had flown in a sea-plane to Fire Island, where they'd rented a big house on the ocean side complete with swimming pool. Around that pool they'd spent twelve summers with just a phone, a little acid, and thirty hunky men. They had, or Ray had, pounds of Polaroids to prove it. Here was the White Party and the house flying a thousand white balloons and Skipper in the foreground with his famous smile, the smile that earned him a hundred and fifty dollars an hour. Dead now of his own – not hand, but leap: he'd leapt from his penthouse on angel dust. And here was the Star Wars party with George as Darth

Vader and his arm around little Tommy as R2D2, the cute kid who wanted to be a DJ but never made it though he did amazing disco tapes he sold to friends in editions of fifty.

And here was George as Darleen. Older guys hated George's dabbling in drag, since they associated it with the cissy 1950s. And the younger kids simply didn't get it; they'd heard of it, but it didn't seem funny to them. But for George's and Ray's generation, the Stonewall generation, drag was something they'd come to late, after they'd worked their way through every other disguise. For George, such a sexy big man with a low voice and brash ways, the character he'd invented, Darleen, had provided a release – not a complete contrast, but a slight transposition. For one thing, she was a slut, but an intimidating one who when horny yanked much smaller men to her hairy chest without a second's hesitation. For another, she had a vulgar but on-target way of talking over George's current corporation and reducing it to its simplest profile; it was Darleen in a drugged state who'd mumbled forth the slogans now selling seven of the biggest American products.

And Darleen had introduced a certain variety into Ray's and George's sex life, for she liked to be passive in bed, whereas George was tirelessly active. No one would have believed it, not even their closest friends, but Ray had fucked Darleen whereas he could never have fucked George. After sex they'd weep from laughter, the two of them, Ray sweaty and gold with his white tan line and George, foundered, skinny legs in black net stockings and the lashes coming unglued on his, yes, his left eye.

When George died, Ray thought of burying him in his drag, but the two people he happened to mention it to (although fairly far-out numbers themselves) drew back in horror. 'You've got to be kidding,' one of them had said as though Ray were now committable for sure. Ray had wanted to say,

'Shouldn't we die as we lived? Why put George in a dark suit he never wore in life?'

But he didn't say anything, and George was buried as his parents wished. His father had been a cop, now retired, his mother a practical nurse, and in the last twenty years they'd made a lot of money in real estate. They liked fixing up old houses, as did George. Ray had a superstition that George had succumbed to the illness only because he'd worked so hard on his own loft. George was a perfectionist and he trusted no one else to do a job correctly. He'd spent hours crouched in the basement rewiring the whole building. Everything, and most especially the lacquering of the loft walls, was something he'd done by himself, again and again to get everything right.

Now he was dead and Ray had to go on with his own life, but he scarcely knew how or why to pick up the threads. The threads were bare, worn thin, so that he could see right through what should have been the thick stuff of everyday comings and goings, could see pale blue vistas. 'You must look out for yourself,' George had always said. But what self?

Ray still went to the gym three times a week as he'd done for almost twenty years. He never questioned anything there and resented even the smallest changes, such as the installation of a fruit juice bar or a computerized billing system always on the blink.

And then Ray had Anna to feed and play with. Since she'd been George's only other real companion towards the end, she felt comfortable and familiar. They'd lie in bed together and purr and that was nice, but it wasn't a sign pointing forward to a new life, only a burnt offering to his past, itself burnt and still smoking.

He thought he was too young to have had to renounce so much. He'd always known that he'd have to end in renunciation, but he didn't like being rushed. He thought of George's long femur bones slowly emerging in the expensive coffin.

And of course he had his job. He did public relations for

a major chemical company with headquarters on Sixth Avenue. It was a gig George had found him; George had done a total facelifting for Amalgamated Anodynes. Nearly everything about the company was reprehensible. It had a subsidiary in the Union of South Africa. Its biggest plant was in South Carolina, precisely because there the 'right-to-work' laws, as they were called in the best Orwellian manner, had banned most of the unions. AA had produced a fabric for children's wear that had turned out to be flammable; Ray had even had to draft for the president's signature some very high-level waffling as a statement to the press. And Amalgamated Anodynes had a lousy record with women and minorities, although a creepy Uncle Tom headed the company's equal hiring practices commission.

Worst of all was Ray's boss, Helen, the token female vice-president. Helen was by turns solicitous and treacherous, servile to superiors and tyrannical to her staff, an old-fashioned schemer who knew more about office politics than her job.

Following a run-in with Helen a few days after the funeral (which, of course, he hadn't been able to mention), he'd locked himself in the toilet and cried and cried, surprised there was so much mucus in his head. Where was it stored normally, in which secret cavity? He was also surprised by how lonely he felt. Lonely, or maybe spaced. George had always been barking at him, scolding or praising him; now the silence was oddly vacant, as though someone were to push past a last gate and enter into the limitless acreage of space and night.

To cry he had had to say to himself, 'I'm giving in to total self-pity,' because otherwise he was so stoic these post-mortem days that he'd never have let himself be ambushed by despair. Why did he keep this job? Was it to please George, who always wanted him to go legit, who'd never approved of his 'beatnik jobs'? George had used 'beatnik', 'hippie', and 'punk' interchangeably to dramatize the very carelessness of his contempt.

Ray had grown up on a farm in northern Ohio near Findlay and still had in his possession a second prize for his cow from the State Fair; he'd sewn it and his Future Farmers of America badge to his letter-jacket. What big-city sentimentalists never understood about the rural existence they so admired was that it was dull and lonely, unnaturally lonely, but it left lots of time for reading.

He'd read and read and won a first prize in the Belle Fontaine spelling bee and another as the captain of the Carrie debating team against Sandusky on the hot subject of 'Free Trade'. His grades were so good he received a scholarship to Oberlin, where, in his second year, he'd switched his major from agronomy to philosophy.

From there he'd gone on to the University of Chicago, where he'd joined the Committee on Social Thought and eventually written a thesis on Durkheim's concept of *anomie*. His father, who wore bib overalls and had huge, fleshy ears and read nothing but the Bible but that daily, would shake his head slowly and stare at the ground whenever the subject of his son's education came up. His mother, however, encouraged him. She was the school librarian, a thin woman with moist blue eyes and hands red from poor circulation, who drank coffee all day and read everything, everything. She'd been proud of him.

But she too had had her doubts when, after he received his doctorate, he'd drifted to Toronto and joined an urban gay commune, grown his blond hair to his shoulders, and done little else besides holding down part-time jobs and writing articles analysing and lamenting the lesbian-gay male split. In the doctrinaire fashion of those days, he'd angrily denounced all gay men and assumed a female name for himself, 'Anna'. The name wasn't intended as a drag name (although later George had insisted he use it as one), but only as a statement of his position against gender distinctions. Only his friends in the commune could call him 'Anna' with a straight face.

Unlike most of the other early gay liberationists, Ray had actually had sex with other men. His affairs were shy, poetic, and decidedly unfancy in bed. Despite his political beliefs, he insisted on being on top, which he admitted was a 'phallocratic' hang-up, although nothing felt to him more natural than lavishing love on a subdued man, similarly smooth-skinned, slender, and pig-tailed.

Then one summer he'd met Jeff, a New Yorker and a contributor to the *Body Politic* who was every bit as ideological as Ray but much more muscular and amusing. When Jeff's Toronto vacation came to an end, Ray moved to New York to be with him. He justified the move to the other communards by pointing out that New York was a literary centre. 'So is Toronto!' they'd objected, for they were also Canadian patriots.

Ray had inchoate literary aspirations. For years he'd dutifully kept a journal. When he re-read it after living in New York a while, he found the voluminous self-analysis neither true nor false; the recorded ideas a good deal sharper than those he was currently entertaining; and the descriptions of nature accurate, and mildly, solidly of value.

When he looked for a job as a writer in New York, all he could find, given his lack of credentials (his PhD in philosophy counted as a drawback) was a position on *Conquistador!*, a sleazy tits-and-ass magazine for which he invented the picture captions in the centrefold ('Lovely Linda is a stewardess and flies, natch, for Aer Lingus'). The indignities (plus low pay) of that job he tried to compensate for by reading manuscripts in the evening for Grove Press and evaluating them artistically and commercially. Since he'd read little except the classics in school, his standards were impossibly high, and since his acquaintanceship till now had included only Ohio farmers, Chicago intellectuals, and Toronto gay liberationists, his grasp of the potential market for any particular book was skewed.

He drifted from job to job, ghosted several chapters of a US history college textbook for a tottering publishing house, worked as a bartender in a black-glass, red-velvet singles bar, taught one semester at a snooty Episcopalian boys' school in Brooklyn Heights, spent one winter as a stock boy at a chic Lucite boutique some friends owned, fled another winter to Key West, where he wore short shorts and served rum and coconut 'conch-outs' around the pool of a gay guest house (he saw the shells as shrunken skulls). He was hired because he'd long since joined a gym, acquired a beefy but defined body, traded in his pigtail and severe manner for a ready laugh and a crewcut ('Wear a Jantzen and a smile' as the old swimsuit slogan had put it). Naturally he no longer insisted on being called Anna. He'd also moved bumpily from one affairlet to another and had been embarrassed that most of them had ended in squabbles over money or fidelity.

Into this confusion, so rife with opportunities he was unable to see how little hope it held out, George had entered. They were both guests at someone's house in New York and when they helped out washing up their hands met under the suds. When he later tried to pinpoint what had made this relationship take and stick he thought it could be seen as a barter – George's forcefulness for Ray's beauty, say. George was homely if sexy, yet he didn't sense his own appeal and he dwelled on all his imperfections. Ray on the other hand was 'pretty' in the special sense that word acquired in the mid-1970s to mean massive shoulders, shaggy moustache, permanent tan, swelling chest. He was also pretty in the more usual sense, for his full lips seemed to be traced in light where a slightly raised welt outlined them, his deepest blue eyes contained an implosion of gold particles falling into the black holes of his pupils, his jaw had comic-book strength, and his teeth were so long and white a dentist had had to file them down once when he was twelve. And now that he was in his late twenties one could discern brown-gold hair on his chest spreading wings over his lungs like that goddess who spreads her arms to protect the pharaoh from all harm.

Ray didn't take his own beauty too seriously, though he maintained it as one might conserve a small inheritance for the sake of security. His spell in the gay commune had made him suspicious of all 'objectifications of the body' and 'commodification of sex', but his years in New York had taught him the importance of precisely these two operations. He was a bit of a star on the deck during tea dance on Fire Island, for his years of training had in point of absolute fact turned him into a physical commodity – but one he was too ironic, too human to sell to the highest bidder. That George was not at all an obvious candidate, that he was too skinny, too pockmarked, a diligent but unsuccessful dresser, made him all the more appealing to Ray.

George had a ravenous appetite to win, even in the most trivial contests, and that made him both infuriating and appealing. Ray had always been accommodating – too accommodating, he now saw, in view of how little he'd accomplished. He deplored the way George cussed out every incompetent and sent back the wine and at every moment demanded satisfaction.

And yet George's life was royally satisfying. He drove his Chrysler station wagon full of friends to Vermont for ski weekends, he was doing the work he most enjoyed and making a minor fortune, and now, to put the final *u* on parvenu, he had . . . Ray. Until now, Ray had never thought of himself as primarily decorative, but George saw him obviously as a sort of superior home entertainment centre – stylish, electric. Ray didn't like to stare into this reflection, he who'd won the Belle Fontaine spelling bee and written one hundred and twenty closely reasoned pages on *anomie*. He saw that without noticing it he'd drifted into the joking, irresponsible, anguished half-world of the gay actor-singer-dancer-writer-waiter-model who always knows what Sondheim has up his sleeve, who might delay his first spring visit to the island until he's worked on those forearms two more weeks, who feels confident Europe is as extinct as a dead star and all the heat and life for the planet must radiate from New York, who has heard most of his favourite songs from his chronological adolescence resurface fifteen years later in their disco versions, at once a reassurance about human continuity and a dismaying gauge of time's flight.

Lovers are attracted by opposites and then struggle to turn them into twins. Ray worked to mollify George's drive to win and George wanted Ray to turn into a winner. Work hard and play hard was George's motto, whereas Ray, without admitting it, wanted lots less work than play and wished both to be not hard but easy. Nevertheless, George, true to form, won. He nudged Ray into a series of well-paying jobs that ended him up at Amalgamated Anodynes. 'You must look out for yourself,' George was always saying. He said it over and over: 'Look out for yourself.' Ray would sit on his lap and say, 'Why should I deprive you of a job you do so well?' The one thing they'd agreed on from the first was not to be monogamous. Ray's ideological horror of marriage as a model and George's unreflecting appetite for pleasure neatly converged. What wasn't decided so easily were the terms under which they were to be faithful. George, who had a funny face, skinny body, and enormous penis, was always a hit at the baths; Ray, whose penis was of average dimensions ('a gay eight' meaning six inches), was more likely to attract another man for a lifetime than a night. Ray already had love, George's, but in order to get sex he had to seem to be offering love. When George would see some other beauty, as dark as Ray was fair, melting amorously around Ray,

George would break glass, bellow, come crashing through doors, wounded bull in the china shop of Ray's delicate romantic lust. Of course Ray envied George his simpler, franker asset and wished he could score more efficiently, with fewer complications.

And now, a year after George's death, here he was learning all the ways in which he had accommodated George and was still doing so, even though George had broken camp. Ray saw how in their tiny group he'd been billed as the looker with the brain, exactly like the starlet whom the studio hypes wearing a mortarboard and specs above her adorable snub nose and bikini – yet he wasn't in Hollywood but New York City and he realized that he'd fallen way behind, hadn't read a book in ages or had a new, strenuous thought.

He still had the big showboat body that George had doted on and that Ray was vigorously maintaining two hours a day at the gym, even though personally (as in 'If I may speak *personally* about my own life') he found the results caricatural and the waste of time ludicrous. And yet he was afraid to let go, stop pumping iron and deflate, sag, shrink, because if he was no longer the greatest brain he was at least a body; Some Body in the most concrete, painful sense. He looked around and realized he was still impersonating George's lover. He was even still using the same deodorant George had liked; George had had such an insinuating way of sticking his big, cratered nose into the most intimate aspects of Ray's habits. He'd made Ray switch from Jockey to boxer shorts, from cotton to cashmere stockings, from Pepsi to Coke, from ballpoint to fountain pen; like all people who make their living from publicity, George had believed that products and brand names determine destiny. Ray was still walking around like a doll George had dressed and wound up before taking off.

In the corner bookstore he picked up a remaindered

large-format paperback called *The Death Rituals of Rural Greece*, by Loring M. Danforth. He liked the way the widows resented their husbands' deaths and said, 'He wasn't very kind to me when he left me.' That was closer to the truth than this twilit grief one was supposed to assume. He liked the funeral laments, specially the one in which a mother asks her dead daughter how Death, called Haros, received her. The daughter replies, 'I hold him on my knees. He rests against my chest. If he is hungry, he eats from my body, and if he is thirsty, he drinks from my two eyes.'

When he had a Midtown lunch with Betty she told him he was in an identity crisis precipitated by George's death. 'But your real problem,' she said, warming unbecomingly to her subject, 'is that you're still seeking an authority, the answer. If you don't watch out, you'll find yourself saddled with another dominating lover; it's your passive Aquarian nature.'

Ray could scarcely believe how much his fur was being rubbed the wrong way, although he felt certain the prize had to go to Betty's insinuation that he was well rid of George. That night he found in an old linen jacket he took out of storage a joint of Acapulco gold George had rolled him – how long ago? Two years – and he smoked it and cried and ordered in Chinese food and sat in bed and watched TV and played with Anna, who kept wandering over to the lit candle on the floor to sniff the flame. When she felt the heat her eyes would slit shut and she'd thrust her chin up, like a dowager who's smelled something rude.

Even though George had been a baby, he'd fought death with a winner's determination but he'd lost anyway. Ray thought that he wouldn't resist it for long. If and when the disease surfaced (for it seemed to him like a kid who's holding his nose underwater for an eerily long time but is bound to come crashing, gasping up for air), when the disease surfaced he wouldn't much mind. In a way dying would be easier than figuring out a new way of living.

Betty must have taken it on herself to contact Ralph Brooks and suggest he ask Ray to Greece. Otherwise Ray couldn't imagine why Ralph should have written him a belated condolence letter that ended with a very warm and specific invitation.

Ray was flattered. After all, Brooks was the celebrated painter. Betty would say that Ray accepted *because* Brooks was the celebrated painter. Not that she ever accused Ray of social-climbing. No, she just thought his 'passivity' made him seek out authorities, no matter who or of what. Oddly enough, Betty's nagging, grating Brooklyn accent reassured him, because it was a voice that stylized suffering, domesticated it. 'Oy,' Ray thought when he was with Betty. She wasn't even Jewish, but she was from Brooklyn, and if he used her accent he could actually say it to himself or to Anna: 'Oy.'

Ray welcomed the trip to Greece precisely because it didn't fit in. George had never been to Greece; Ralph had never met George; Ray himself scarcely knew Ralph. They'd become friendly at the gym and worked out a dozen times together and Ralph had always asked him his bright, general questions that didn't seem to anticipate anything so concrete as an answer. Ralph, who'd worked out for years, had a big bearish body that was going to flab – exactly what envious, lazy people always say happens to weightlifters in middle age. His shoulders, chest, and biceps were still powerful, but his belly was as big as a bus driver's. Ralph said he hated the ruin of his looks, but he seemed so relaxed and sure of himself that this self-loathing struck Ray as an attitude he might once have held but had since outgrown without renouncing.

Then again Ray would so gladly have traded in his own

prettiness for Ralph's success that perhaps he couldn't quite believe in Ralph's complaints. As for the three weeks in Crete (he found the town, Xania, on the map), it would be all new – new place, new language, no ghosts. He even liked going to the country where people expressed their grief over dying so honestly, so passionately. In that book he liked the way a mother, when she exhumed her daughter's body after three years of burial, said, 'Look what I put in and look what I took out! I put in a partridge, and I took out bones.'

Betty agreed to take care of Anna. 'You must look out for yourself,' George had said, and now he was trying.

Ralph had rented a floor of a Venetian palace on a hill overlooking the harbour; at least Ralph called it a 'palace' in that hyperbolic way of his. The town had been badly bombed during the war and empty lots and grass-growing ruins pocked even the most crowded blocks like shocking lapses in an otherwise good memory.

Nothing in town was taller than three storeys except two minarets left over from the centuries of Turkish rule and allowed to stand more through indifference then ecumenism. At first Ray looked for the blazing whitewash and strong geometrical shapes he'd seen in trendy postcards from the Greek islands, but in Xania everything was crumbling brick, faded paint, mud or pebble alleyways, cement and rusting cement armatures sticking up out of unfinished upper storeys, shabby exteriors and immaculate interiors, dusty carved-wood second storeys overhanging the street in the Turkish fashion. Along the harbour a chrome-and-plastic disco, booming music and revolving lights as though it had just landed, made chic racket beside shadowy, abandoned arsenals where the Venetians had housed their warships. One of them had a stone balcony high above the harbour and two doors shaped like Gothic flames opening up on to a roofless void and a framed picture of the night sky – the half-waned moon. *not ½ full*

Ralph and Ray ate fried squid and a feta cheese salad at a rickety table outside along the brackish-smelling harbour. The table could never quite find its footing. They were waited on by a Buddha-faced boy who smiled with mild amusement every time his few words in English were understood. The boy couldn't have been more than nine, but he already had a whole kit of skilled frowns, tongue-clicks, and body gestures and his grandfather's way of wiping his forehead with a single swipe of a folded fresh handkerchief as though he were ironing something. Ray found it hard to imagine having accumulated so many mannerisms before the dawn of sex, of the sexual need to please, of the staginess sex encourages or the tightly capped wells of poisoned sexual desire the disappointed must stand guard over.

Ralph, who was shoe-leather brown and so calm he let big gaps of comfortable silence open up in the conversation, was much fatter – all the olive oil and *rosé* and sticky desserts, no doubt. A cool wind was blowing up off the Aegean and Ray was glad he'd worn a long-sleeved shirt. Ralph had helped him unpack and had clucked over each article of clothing, all of which he found too stylish and *outré* for Xania. In fact Ralph seemed starved for company and gossip and far less vague than in New York. There he seemed always to be escaping sensory overload through benign nullity, the Andy Warhol strategy of saying 'oh great' to everything. Here he took a minute, gossipy interest in the details of everyday life. Ray thought, 'We each need just the right weight of pettiness to serve as ballast.' George's death had tossed all the sandbags overboard and Ray had been floating higher and higher towards extinction.

Ralph was specially interested in the 'locals', as he called the young men. 'Now this is the Black Adonis,' he said of one tall, fair-skinned twenty-year-old strolling past with two younger boys. 'He's in a different shirt every night. And would you look at that razor cut! Pure Frankie Avalon . . . Oh my dear, what fun to have another old timer from the States with me, no need to explain my references for once.'

Ralph had a nickname for every second young man who walked past in the slow, defiant, sharp-eyed parade beside the harbour. 'This is the tail-end of the *volta*, as we call the evening *passeggiata*,' Ralph said, typically substituting one incomprehensible word for another. 'There's absolutely nothing to do in this town except cruise. In the hot weather they all stop working at two in the afternoon. Now here comes the Little Tiger – notice the feline tattoo? – a very bad character. He stole my Walkman when I invited him in for a night cap; Little Tiger, go to the rear of the class. He's bad because he's from the next town and he thinks he can get away with it. Stick with the locals; nothing like the high moral power of spying and gossip.'

Ray had always heard of dirty old American men who'd gone to Greece for the summer 'phallic cure', but he'd assumed gay liberation had somehow ended the practice, unshackled both predator and prey. Nevertheless, before they'd left the restaurant two more Americans, both in their sixties, had stopped by their table to recount their most recent adventures. Ray, used to fending off older men, was a bit put out that no one, not even Ralph, was flirting with him. In fact, the assumption, which he resented, was that he too was an old timer here 'for the boys' and would be willing to pay for it.

'Aren't there any Greeks who do it for free?' Ray asked, not getting the smiles he'd anticipated.

'A few frightful pooves do, I suppose,' Ralph drawled, looking offended by the notion. 'But why settle for free frights when for ten bucks you can have anyone in town, absolutely anyone including the mayor and his wife, not to mention the odd god on the hoof?'

For a few days Ray held out. Betty, morbidly enough, had made a tape of all the crazy messages George had left on her answering machine during his last year. She'd given Ray the tape just before he'd left and now he sat in his bedroom, wearing gaudy drawstring shorts, and looked at the harbour lights and listened to George's voice.

Ray remembered a remark someone had once made: 'Many people believe in God without loving him, but I love him without believing in him.' Ray didn't know why the remark popped into his head just now. Did he love George without believing he existed? Ray described himself as a 'mystical atheist'. Maybe that was a complicated way of saying he believed George still loved him, or would if God would let him speak.

In his New York gay world, which was as carefully screened from men under twenty-five as from those over sixty, Ray counted as 'young'. That is, some old flame whom Ray had known fifteen years ago – a guy with a moustache gone grey and fanning squint lines but a still massive chest and thunder thighs under all that good tailoring – would spot Ray at a black-tie gay rights dinner or health-crisis benefit and come up to him murmuring, 'Lookin' good, kid,' and would pinch his bottom. It was all continuing and Ray knew that despite the way his body had acquired a certain thickness, as though the original Greek statue had been copied by a Roman, he still looked youthful to his contemporaries.

In the first two weeks after George's death Ray had picked up three different men on the street and dragged them home. Ray had clung to their warm bodies, their air-breathing chests and blood-beating hearts, clung like a vampire to warm himself through transfusions of desire. He and Anna would sniff at these bewildered young men as though nothing could be less likely than a scabbed knee, furred buttocks, an uncollared collarbone, or the glamorous confusion of a cast-aside white shirt and silk rep tie. What they, the pick-ups, wanted, heart-to-heart post-coital chat, appealed to him not at all; all he wanted was to lie face down beside tonight's face-up partner and slide on top of him just enough to be literally heart-to-heart. Their carnality had seemed very fragile.

After this brief, irresponsible flaring up of lust, which had followed the sexless years of George's dying, Ray had gone back to celibacy. He thought it very likely that he was carrying death inside him, that it was ticking inside him like a time bomb but one he couldn't find because it had been secreted by an unknown terrorist. Even if it was located it couldn't be defused. Nor did he know when it might explode. He didn't want to expose anyone to contagion.

He wrote his will as he knew everyone should. That was the adult thing to do. But the paltry list of his possessions reminded him of how little he'd accumulated or accomplished; it was like the shame of moving day, of seeing one's cigarette-burned upholstery and scarred bureau on the kerb under a hot, contemptuous sun. His relatively youthful looks had led him to go on believing in his youthful expectations; his life, he would have said as a philosophy student, was all becoming and no being. All in the future until this death sentence (never pronounced, daily remanded) had been handed down.

Occasionally he jerked off with poppers and dirty magazines. Although he found slaves and masters ludicrous and pathetic, his fantasies had not kept pace with the fashions and were mired somewhere in 1972, best simulated by the stories and photos in *Drummer*. He would read a hot tale about a violent encounter between two real pigs, sniff his amyl, even mutter a few words ('Give your boy that daddy-dick'), and then find himself, head aching, stomach sticky, heart sinking, erection melting, alone, posthumous. Anna wrinkled her nose and squinted at the fumes. He hoped his executor, who was his lawyer, would be able to bury him next to George as instructed, since he only slept really well when George was beside him. Once in a Philadelphia museum he'd seen the skeletons of a prehistoric man and woman, buried together (he couldn't remember how they'd come to die at the same time). He was lying on his back, she on her side, her hand placed delicately on his chest.

The days in Crete were big, cloudless hot days, heroic days, noisy with the saw rasp of insects. They were heroic days as though the sun were a lion-hearted hero . . . Oh, but hadn't he just read in his beach book, the *Odyssey*, the words of the dead, lion-hearted Achilles: 'Do not speak to me soothingly about death, glorious Odysseus; I should prefer, as a slave, to serve another man, even if he had no property and little to live on, than to rule over all these dead who have done with life.' He'd cried on the white sand beach beside the lapis lazuli water and looked through his tears, amazed, at a herd of sheep trotting towards him. He stood and waded and waved, smiling, at the old shepherd in black pants and a carved stick in his hand, which itself looked carved; Ray, expensively muscular in his Valentino swim trunks, thought he was probably not much younger than this ancient peasant and suddenly his grief struck him as a costly gewgaw, beyond the means of the grievously hungry and hard-working world. Or maybe it was precisely his grief that joined him to this peasant. Every night he was dreaming about George, and in that book about the Greek death rituals he'd read the words of an old woman: 'At death the soul emerges in its entirety, like a man. It has the shape of a man, only it's invisible. It has a mouth and hands and eats real food just like we do. When you see someone in your dreams, it's the soul you see. People in your dreams eat, don't they? The souls of the dead eat too.' Ray couldn't remember if George ate in his dreams.

Ralph and Ray rented motor scooters and drove up a narrow road through chasms, past abandoned medieval churches and new cement-block houses, high into the mountains. They chugged slowly up to and away from a goat stretching to reach the lower branches of a tree. They saw a young Orthodox priest in a black soutane out strolling, preceded by a full black beard he seemed to be carrying in front of him as one might carry a salver. He remembered that Orthodox priests can marry and he vaguely thought of that as the reason this one seemed so virile; he looked as though he'd just stepped out from behind the plough into this dress.

The summer drought had dwindled the stream to a brook within its still green bed. At a certain turn in the road the air turned cool, as though the frozen core of the mountain had got tired of holding its breath. In the shepherd's village where they stopped for lunch a smiling boy was found to speak English with them. He said he'd lived in New Zealand for a year with his aunt and uncle; that was why he knew English. Laughing, he offered them steaks and salads, but it turned out the only food available in the village was a runny sour cheese and bread and olives.

Every day, despite the climate's invitation to languor, Ray did his complete work-out, causing the heavy old wardrobe in his room to creak and throw open its door when he did push-ups. Some days, specially around three, a wind would suddenly blow up and he and Ralph would run around battening down the twenty-three windows. At dusk on Sundays a naval band marched all the way around the harbour to the fortress opposite the lighthouse and played the national anthem ('which was written by a German,' Ralph couldn't resist throwing in) while the blue and white flag was lowered.

Although the days were cheerful – scooter rides to a deserted beach, vegetable and fish marketing, desultory house-hunting out beyond the town walls on which the Venetian lion had been emblazoned – the nights were menacing. He and Ralph would dress carefully for the *volta*,

Ralph in a dark blue shirt and ironed slacks, Ray in a floating gown of a Japanese designer shirt and enormous one-size-drowns-all lime-green shorts, neon-orange cotton socks, black Adidas, and white sunglasses slatted like Venetian blinds angled down ('perfect for the Saudi matron on the go,' he said).

At least that's how he got himself up the first few nights until he sensed Ralph's embarrassment, the crowd's smiling contempt, and his own . . . what?

Desire?

Every night it was the same. The sun set, neon lights outlined the eaves and arches of the cafés, and an army of strollers, mostly young and male, sauntered slowly along the horseshoe-shaped stone walk beside the harbour. Sometimes it stank of pizza or what was called 'Kantaki Fried Chicken' or of the sea urchins old fishermen had cleaned on the wharf earlier in the day. The walk could be stretched out to twenty minutes if one lingered in conversation with friends, stopped to buy nuts from one vendor and to look at the jewellery sold by Dutch hippies. A drink at an outdoor café – ouzo and hors d'oeuvre (*mezes*) – could while away another forty minutes.

The full hour was always devoted to boy-watching. Ray looked, too, at the wonderful black hair, muscular bodies, red cheeks under deep tans, flamboyant moustaches, big noses, transparent arrogance, equally transparent self-doubt, black eyebrows yearning to meet above the nose and often succeeding. 'Of course they need reassurance,' Ralph said; 'what actor doesn't?' These guys had loud voices, carnivorous teeth, strutting walks, big asses, broad shoulders. Ray thought they were more like American teenage boys than other European youths; they were equally big and loud and physical and sloppy and unveiled in their curiosity and hostility.

One of the sixty-year-old Americans, a classics professor in the States, was an amateur photographer of considerable refinement. He'd persuaded, it seemed, dozens of locals to pose nude for him. He paid them something. He was discreet. He flattered them as best he could in the modern language he'd pieced together out of his complete knowledge of ancient Greek. 'Sometimes,' he said, 'they say a whole long improbable sentence in English – picked up from an American song or movie, no doubt.'

Among the locals his ministrations to vanity made him popular, his scholarship made him impressive and his hobby risible, but since he always seemed to be laughing at himself in his ancient, elegant prep-school way, his laughter softened theirs. His photographic sessions he dismissed airily but pursued gravely.

Homer (for that was his name, absurdly, 'Stranger than epic,' as he said) took a polite but real interest in Ray – but strictly in Ray's mind. Ray – who expected, invited, and resented other men's sexual attraction to him – found Homer's sex-free attentiveness unsettling. And appealing. Maybe because Homer was a professor and had a professor's way of listening – which meant he winced slightly when he disagreed and cleaned his glasses when he deeply disagreed – Ray felt returned, if only for an instant, to his schooldays. To the days before he'd ever known George. To the days when he'd been not a New York know-it-all, but a Midwestern intellectual, someone who took nothing on authority and didn't even suspect there were such things as fashions in ideas.

This repatriation cheered him. Ralph had made a spaghetti dinner at home ('Enough with the swordfish and feta, already') and invited Homer. Ray's and Homer's conversation about the categorical imperative, the wager, the cave, the excluded middle astonished Ralph. 'You girls are real bluestockings,' he told them, 'which is OK for a hen-party, but remember men don't make passes at girls who wear glasses.' Ralph even seemed disconcerted by their intelligence, if that's what all this highbrow name-dropping had revealed.

After the wine and the laughter Ray thought it only natural to go on to the bar with his friends, the gay bar where they met with 'true love' every night, as Ralph said. On the way along the harbour, Ray told Homer all about his sexual qualms. 'I just don't think I should expose anyone else to this disease in case I've got it or in case I'm contagious. And I'm not disciplined enough to stick to safe sex.'

Homer nodded and made the same noncommittal but polite murmur as when earlier they'd discussed the *Nicomachean Ethics*. Then, as though shaking himself awake, he asked, 'What *is* safe sex, exactly?'

'Strictly safe is masturbation, no exchange of body fluids. Or if you fuck you can use a rubber. But I'm not worried about myself. The only one in danger where fucking and sucking is involved is the guy who gets the come.'

Silence full of blinking in the dark, blinking with lashes growing longer, darker with mascara by the second. 'But darling,' Homer finally confided, hilariously woman-to-woman, 'then the Greeks are *always* safe. They're the men; we're the girls.'

'Call me square,' Ray said, 'but that's old-fashioned role-playing – and I've never, never paid –'

Homer interrupted him with a soft old hand on his arm. 'Give it a try. After all, it's your only option.'

The alley leading to the bar was too narrow for cars but wide enough to accommodate four noisy adolescents walking shoulder-to-shoulder; one of them stepped drunkenly down into the grass-sprouting ruins and pissed against a jagged wall. Ray thought of those jagged walls in . . . was it Giotto's murals in Santa Croce in Florence? The kid had a foolish grin and he seemed to have forgotten how to aim, shake, button up. The others started barking and mewing.

Ray found the situation and the hoarse voices exciting. Had these guys come from the bar? Were they gay?

The bar was a low room, a basement grotto, one would have said, except it was on the ground floor. There were several dimly lit alcoves just off the room in which shadowy couples were smoking and drinking. The waiters or 'hostesses' were two transvestites, Dmitri, who was chubby and brunette and kept a slightly deformed hand always just out of sight, flickering it behind his back or under a tray or into a pocket, and Adriana, who was slender, with straight, shoulder-length blond hair, and who responded to open jeers with a zonked-out grin that never varied, as though she were drugged on her own powerful fantasy of herself, which made her immune. Both were in jeans and T-shirts; Adriana had two small, hormone-induced breasts, but his arms were still muscular and his hips boyishly narrow. Dmitri, the brunette, had less beauty and more vitality, a clown's vitality; he was the stand-up or run-past comic. He did pratfalls with his tray, twinkled past on point, sat on laps or wriggled deliciously against sailors, always keeping his hand in motion, out of focus. The bar was called 'Fire Island'.

At first this gay bar seemed to Ray an unexpected trove of sexy young guys until Homer explained that, technically, they (Ralph, Ray, and Homer) were the only gays, along with the two hostesses, of course. Everyone else was, well, a gigolo, although that was too coarse a word for it. 'Greek men really do prefer male company. All their bars are like this one,' Homer said with that ornithological pride all old-timer expatriates exhibit to the newcomer. 'The women don't go out much. And the men all think it's normal to get money for sex – just remember the dowries they receive. And then they're terribly poor, the sailors, five bucks a week, that's all they get. So, you take all these horny nineteen-year-olds away from their villages for the first time in their lives. Here they are, bored, lonely, with too much time on their hands, no unmarried Greek girls in sight . . .'

'Where are the girls?' Ray asked, embarrassed he hadn't noticed their absence till now.

'Their mothers quite sensibly keep them under lock and key. I myself feel an infinite reverence for the intact maidenhead. Of course you know these scandalous mothers teach their daughters to take it up the ass if they must put out; anything to stay intact. Although why am I complaining? That's my philosophy exactly.'

'So the sailors are alone and horny . . .'

'And naturally they want to party. That's how they think of it. You buy them drinks and you're a real sport. You ask them home. It's a party. The only problem is how to wean them away from their *parea*.'

'Come again?'

'*Parea*. That's their group, their friends, oh, a very useful word. If you want to pick someone up, point to him, then yourself. Say, "You, me, *parea*?"'

'And what do they call us, the faggots?'

Homer smiled and lowered his voice: '*Poosti*.'

'So we're *poosti* on *parea* . . . Don't rain on my *parea*.'

'Yes,' Homer said somewhat primly, 'but not so loud. You'll scandalize the seafood,' nodding toward a *parea* of five sailors, smiling at them with lofty politeness.

After two hours of drinking gin and tonic, Ray realized most of the boys weren't drinking at all and were just sitting over empty bottles of beer, bumming cigarettes from one another and hungrily staring at the door as each newcomer entered. Only a few were talking to each other. Sometimes they seemed to be inventing a conversation (involving lots of numbers, as even Ray could decode) and an emotion (usually indignation), but purely as a set piece to show them off to advantage to potential clients. The same tape of 'Susanna' kept playing over and over, last year's disco tune, which didn't mean much to him since it had been popular when George was already sick and they had stopped going out dancing.

He excused himself, pecked Homer on the cheek, and squeezed past a suddenly amorous Dmitri, the hefty hostess, who smelled of sweat and Chanel.

Outside the night was airless, fragrant, the sky an enormous black colander held up to the light. Since it hadn't rained in months, dust filled the streets, dulled the store windows examined by veering headlights, rose in lazy devils behind passing shoes. In a bridal store the mannequin of the bride herself was snub-nosed and blonde, her hair bristling up under her veil at crazy shocked angles as though she'd stuck her finger in an electric socket. She was flanked by curious white cloth bouquets trailing white silk ribbons. Were they held by her bridesmaids? Ray had seen a woman bringing such a bouquet here on the plane from Athens. In that book he'd read the exhumations of a dead person's bones three years after death were compared to a wedding. The same songs were sung; the words varied only slightly. Both songs had begun with the words: 'Now I have set out. Now I am about to depart . . .' Something like that.

On the corner a man was selling round green melons out of a cart. Everywhere people seemed awake and watching – from a trellised balcony, from a waiting cab, from a rooftop café. In such a hot country people stayed up to enjoy the cool of the night. Kids, calling out to one another, sped by on bicycles. In the square in front of the cathedral a whole line of taxis waited, five drivers standing in a circle and disputing – what? Soccer? Politics?

Ray turned on to a deserted street lined with notions shops displaying lace trimmings and bolts of fabric and spools of thread. At the corner an old man with yellowing hair, worn-down shoes, and no socks had fallen asleep with his feet up on his desk in an open-air stand that sold *ex votos* in tin – a bent arm, an ear, an open eye, a soldier in World War I uniform and helmet – and also tin icons, the metal snipped away to frame crude tinted reproductions of the Virgin's face. He also had long and short candles and something (incense?) wrapped in red paper cylinders, stacked high like rolled coins from the bank.

Cars with bad mufflers blatted and farted through town or throbbed beside a lit cigarette kiosk in front of the dim covered market. The cars were always full of teenage boys, but when they'd get out to buy cigarettes or to go into a bar and buy a paper, he'd see they were fat or thin, usually big handsome guys with black moustaches or the first faint charcoal sketches of moustaches.

It struck Ray that it had been years since he'd seen guys this young. Expensive, childless Manhattan had banned them. Ray imagined that he was back in Findlay, Ohio, on a Saturday night, the dark silent streets suddenly glaring and noisy with a gang in two hotrods. He forgot for a moment that he was forty; he felt he was sixteen, afraid of the hoods who'd driven in from Sandusky or even from as far away as Toledo. He was afraid and curious and contemptuous and excited as he darted along under the old trees, hoping he was invisible.

He crossed the street to avoid two strolling straight couples, and now he did feel forty. And queer. And foreign. He wouldn't even know if they were gossiping about him. Worse, he knew he didn't exist for them, he was invisible.

As he headed up the gently winding street towards the town zoo, he passed a lone young guy coming down towards him, who stared at him hard, harder and longer even than the other Cretan men normally stared. The boy spat through his teeth as they passed. He struck his heels with spark-making violence against the pavement. And then he stopped. Ray heard him stop behind him. If I turn around will he punch me?

When Ray finally turned around, the young man was standing there staring at him. 'Ya,' he said, that short form of *Yassou*, the all-purpose greeting. Ray could see he was handsome with regular features, an upper lip pulled back to show white teeth made whiter by his moustache and a black beard that he was letting grow in. He had on jeans and a denim jacket, and the jacket sleeves were tight enough to reveal well-muscled upper arms, not the netted cantaloupes Ray had for biceps, but longer, grooved haunches, the tightly muscled arms that the ancient Cretan youths had in those wall-paintings at absurdly over-restored Knossos: murderously slim-waisted matadors.

He was either very tanned or very swarthy. His hair was long and pushed back behind his ears. His slightly unshaved face (the look of the New York model who wears a two-days' growth of beard as an accessory to his smoking jacket or white silk pyjamas), his obviously American jeans jacket, and his long hair were the three things that made him look fractionally different from all the other young men in this city of young men.

He kept staring, but then when Ray looked away for an instant, he slipped into a side street. Ray wondered if he'd be jumped when he followed him. As he turned the corner, the boy was standing there and asked aggressively, 'What you want?' and his faint smile suggested he already knew and that Ray's desire was disgusting and entirely practicable.

Ray said, 'You,' with the sort of airiness that ruined Oscar Wilde, but that word apparently was not one of the boy's dozen English words. He frowned angrily.

'Sex,' Ray said, and this time the boy nodded.

'But money!' he threatened, rubbing his thumb and forefinger together. Ray nodded with a face-saving smirk he regretted but couldn't wipe away. 'I fuck you!' the boy added. This time as Ray nodded his smile vanished, a little bit in awe at the mention of this intimacy, once so common, now so rare, so gravely admonished, so fearfully practised in his plagued city.

'*Profilatikos*. You buy. Here.' He pointed to the lit cigarette kiosk on the corner.

'No! *You* buy,' Ray said, the facetious smile back in place but genuine alarm in his heart.

'You,' the boy insisted, stepping into the shadows of a building.

Now all of his teenage qualms did come rushing back. He felt his fear of and fascination with the prophylactics dispenser in a Kentucky filling station toilet he'd glimpsed once during a family trip through the Smokies. Or he remembered the time when he'd helped his mother turn back the covers for a married couple who were visiting them, and he'd seen under the pillow the raised circle of the rolled rubber in its foil wrapper. The very width of that circumference had excited him.

He said the word to the impassive middle-aged woman in the kiosk. She lowered her head on an angle, dropped her eyes, said, *'Ne,'* which means 'yes' but sounds to English-speakers like 'no'. A second later she'd fished up a box that read, in English, 'Love Party' above a photo of a woman in provocative panties, one nyloned knee resting on the edge of a double bed.

Why rubbers? Ray wondered. Has he heard of our deadly new disease way out here at the end of the world, in a country where there are only two recorded cases, both of whom were visitors to New York? No, he must have in mind the old, curable maladies. Or maybe he just wants to dramatize our roles. I don't mind. Rubbers are terribly 1958 Saturday night at the drive-in. Maybe he needs a membrane intact to suggest his own virtual virginity.

A moment later, Ray was pursuing the boy through deserted night streets under big trees, big laurels so dry their grey-green leaves had started curling laterally. Distant

delapidation
seedines of scene
no romantic pick-up

motorbikes were test-drilling the night. The turn-of-the-century mansions lining these blocks were dilapidated, shuttered, and unlit behind rusting wrought-iron balconies, although trimmed hedges proved at least some of them were inhabited. The smells of garbage on a hot night alternated with the smell of jasmine, at first sniff slightly sweet, then ruttishly sweet. The boy wouldn't walk beside Ray, although Ray thought it must look much odder, this strange parade. They turned right off the boulevard and walked up, up a hill through residential streets. The boy's Keds shone almost phosphorescently white in the dark. Ray was calculating how much money he had in his wallet, while in his heart, his suddenly adolescent heart he was exulting: 'George, I've escaped you, I've gotten away from you.'

In one sense he knew he was a slightly cissified middle-aged New York muscle queen somewhat out of her depth. In another sense he felt he was the teenage debating team captain in love again with Juan, son of a migrant Mexican worker who'd been brought to northern Ohio to pick fruit. The first confused conversation with Juan, the visit to the workers' compound, the smell of cooking chili, the sight of candles burning even by day before the tin shrine of the Virgin . . . The one thing certain was that whatever was going on in Crete came before or after George and precluded George.

As they walked along, the boy clicked a keychain, vestigial worry beads. Cats were everywhere, gliding in and out of shadows, daintily pawing black plastic garbage bags, slithering through gaps in fences, sitting on top of parked cars. Twice the boy stopped and scented the path – and now he looked like an Indian brave. Or so Ray thought, smiling at his own way of leafing through his boyhood anthology of erotic fantasies.

They reached what looked like a school-yard, dark and empty because it was summer and night, but otherwise like any school-yard in Ohio – broken concrete playing area, an orange metal basketball hoop dripping rust stains on to the wood backboard, peeling benches, a toilet with separate entrances for boys and girls, a high fence surrounding the whole. The boy scrambled over the fence in two quick steps up and a graceful pivot at the top. Ray followed fearfully, awkwardly ('Here, teach, lemme give you a hand'). The boy gave Ray his hand and produced his first real smile, as dazzling as a camel boy's (a new page in the anthology flipped open). His skin was surprisingly warm and plush and there were no callouses on his palm. Homer had told Ray that if parents could afford the luxury they preferred to shield their kids as long as possible from work. The boys, their adolescence extended well into their twenties, sat idly around the harbour at night, trying to pick up foreign girls (the sport was called *kemaki*, 'harpooning').

When they ducked into the toilet, in the second that Ray's eyes took to adjust to the deeper dark, he walked by mistake right into the boy. They both gasped, the boy laughed, maybe a bit insultingly, his teeth lit up the room. Ray started to draw away but his hand had brushed against what could only be a big erection, 'big' because of normal size; the boy's youth, the night, the danger, the fact he would be getting some money later on, all these things made it 'big'. Ray noticed the boy had already unzipped his fly. Out of eagerness?

Ray wanted him to be eager.

And then Ray, a famous beauty in his own right, a perennial hot number, hard to please, easily spooked by a maladroit cruiser, pursued throughout his twenty years of gay celebrity by hundreds of equally beautiful men, that élite corps of flight attendants, junior executives, and models – this Ray (he was trembling as he knelt) knelt before what could only be white Jockey shorts, yep, that's what they were, luminous under undone fly buttons, tugged the jeans down a notch, pulled down the elastic waist of the under-pants, and tasted with gratitude the hot, slightly sour penis. He whose conscience years of political struggle had raised now sank into the delicious guilt of Anglo fag servicing Mexican worker, of cowboy face-fucked by Indian brave, of lost tourist waylaid by wily camel boy. He inhaled the smell of sweat and urine with heady, calm pleasure. He felt like ET being recharged by spaceship transfusion.

His mouth had been dry with fear. Now the penis striking his palate drew forth a flow of water in the desert. His knees already ached where he knelt on the wet cement floor. He took the boy's limp, hanging hand and laced his fingers into his. He looked up to catch the glance, but his eyes were shut and his face blank, which made him look much younger and almost absurdly unintimidating. At a certain point Ray pressed the unopened rubber into the boy's hand. Like a child peeping through a keyhole, Ray continued to kneel to watch the boy breaking open the packet and methodically unrolling the rubber down the length of his penis. He got it going the wrong way, lubricated side in, and had to start over. Then the boy gripped him from behind and Ray felt the invasion, so complex psychologically, so familiar but still painful or pleasurable to accommodate, he couldn't tell which, he'd never known which. The boy breathed on his shoulder; he smelled of Kantaki Fried Chicken.

When Ray paid the boy, who aristocratically palmed the money without bothering to see how much it was, Ray used one of the few Greek words he'd picked up (this one at the laundry), *avrio*, the word for 'tomorrow'. The boy nodded, or rather did what Greeks do instead of nodding, he clicked a 'Tsk' between his teeth and jerked his head down, lowering his eyelids. He pointed to this spot, to the ground in front of them. Then he flashed ten and two fingers. 'You like?' he asked, pointing to his own chest.

'Yes, of course,' Ray whispered, thinking: 'These men . . .'

He told the whole story at breakfast the next morning to Ralph, who was courteous enough to appear envious. After their yoghurt and honey and the French roast coffee Ralph was at such pains to secure, they moved into Ralph's studio with its one small window looking down to the sea and the lighthouse. The studio had little in it besides a rocking chair, an old battered desk, a small kitchen table freighted with tubes of acrylics, a big, heavy wood easel and a rack for finished paintings. On the wall was a watercolour, poppies brilliant in a silky field of green and tan grasses. 'Well, it's the only solution. For you,' Ralph said.

'Oh, he's turned his envy into pity,' Ray thought, 'pity for me, the ticking timebomb, the young widow, but my "only solution" doesn't seem all that much of a hardship.'

As Ray napped in the hot, airless, late afternoon he could feel a small painful spot inside him where the boy had battered into him and he smiled to feel that pain again. 'Oy,' he said to himself in Betty's accent.

That night the boy was there exactly on time. His hair was cleaner and shinier and he'd shaved (not the moustache, of course). But he was wearing the same jeans jacket, although the T-shirt looked clean. They went through exactly the same routine, for Ray didn't want to scare him off. He wanted to build up a fixed routine, the same place, the same acts, the same price. Tonight the only innovation was that Ray pulled the kid's jeans and underpants all the way down below his knees and discovered that his testicles hadn't descended and that his ass was hairy with nice friendly fuzz. Nor did he have a tan line; his skin was naturally just this dark.

After sex the kid hopped over the fence and disappeared into the night and Ray walked home, downhill all the way through the silent, cat-quick, jasmine-scented streets. He felt sad and lyric and philosophical and happy as he'd felt as a teenager; since these encounters with the boy – strictly sexual – seemed a strangely insufficient pretext for so much emotion, he also felt something of a charlatan. 'Objective correlative.' That was the term. T. S. Eliot would have said that his emotion lacked an objective correlative.

The next night he asked him his name, which he discovered was Marco. 'You must remember,' Homer said during the *volta* the following evening, 'the Italians ruled Crete for hundreds of years. Maybe he has some Italian blood.' And again Ray had to describe his 'find', for that's how the connoisseurs judged Marco. 'Not the usual harbour trash,' Homer said, and he announced that he was going to start harpooning in the zoological gardens again, which he'd assumed had long since been fished out. Ray refused to divulge where he met Marco every night. He wanted one secret at least, his dowry, the smallest secret he could keep and give to Marco, and again he thought of that book and the way they'd compared marriage to death, or rather marriage to the exhumation of bones.

Once he asked Marco where he lived, but Marco only waved vaguely in the direction of the shanty town inland and to the west of the harbour. '*Spiti mou, to limani,*' Ray announced, which he thought meant 'My house is on the harbour,' but Marco only lifted an indifferent eyebrow, the counterpart to the Frenchman's weary '*Eh alors?*' when smothered by Americans' doggy effusiveness. That night, Ray broadened his area of conquest and explored Marco's taut brown stomach up to his chest. By now there were several white rubbers on the wet cement floor like jellyfish washed up on the bleak shingle.

By day, Ray would go swimming or motorbiking to old churches or ruined monasteries or hidden beaches, but all day long and during the endless evenings, he'd daydream about Marco. He bought a phrasebook and pieced together Greek words for that night's rendezvous.

Once Marco asked Ray if he should bring along a friend,

and Ray agreed because he thought Marco wanted him to. But the friend was a portly sailor ('Greeks go off early,' Ralph had said, as though they were a temperamental triple cream cheese, a Brillat-Savarin, say). Ray sucked them both at the same time, doing one then the other, back and forth, but his only pleasure was in imagining reporting it to the other Americans tomorrow. The boys seemed embarrassed and talked loudly to each other and joked a lot and Marco kept losing his erection and he sounded nasty and used the word *'putana'*, which surely meant 'whore' in Greek as well as Italian.

Ray paid them both and was tempted to mutter *'putana'* while doing so, but that might queer the deal, so he swallowed his resentment (yes, swallowed that, too) and drew Marco aside and said *'Metavrio,'* which meant 'the day after tomorrow' (*meta* as in 'metaphysics', 'beyond physics'). The delay was meant as some sort of punishment. He also indicated he wanted to see Marco alone from now on. Marco registered the compliment but not the punishment and smiled and asked, 'You like?' pointing to himself, asked it loud and clear so the other guy could hear.

'Yes,' Ray said, 'I like.'

As he walked home, Ray took a stroll through the zoological gardens, where there was also an outdoor movie theatre. Inside people sat on folding chairs and watched the huge screen on which a street lamp had disobligingly cast the shadow of a leafy branch. Tonight he sat outside but he could hear the end of *Querelle*, of all things, dubbed into Greek and offered to the extended Cretan family, who chuckled over the perversities of northern Europe. In the closing sequence, Jeanne Moreau laughed and laughed a shattering laugh and the caged egrets dozing beside Ray awakened and started to chatter and call. Then the house-lights came up, the families streamed out, for a moment the park was bright and vivid with crunched gravel and laughs and shouts, then car doors slammed and motorbikes snarled, the lights were dimmed and finally, conclusively, everything was quiet. Ray sat in the dark, listening to the awakened birds paddling the water, a leaf-spray of shadows across his face like an old-fashioned figured veil. The jasmine gave off a shocking body odour, as though one were to discover a pure girl was really a slut.

Ray regretted his spiteful decision to skip a day with Marco. The depth to which he felt Marco's absence, and his anxiety lest Marco not show up at their next appointment, made Ray aware of how much he liked Marco and needed him. Liked him?

There was nothing to like, nothing but a mindless, greedy Cretan teen who was, moreover, heterosexual. Or worse, a complete mystery, a stranger, a minor tradesman with whom he was only on fucking terms.

Then Ray told himself he liked his own sense of gratitude to Marco, the silence imposed on them by the lack of a common language, liked the metered doses of sex fixed by fee and divergent appetites. He liked the high seriousness of the work they did together every night. He also liked stealing bits of affection from his co-worker, whose moustache was coming in as black and shiny as his eyebrows and whose chest (as Ray's hand had just discovered) was sprouting its first hair, this young man who would never love anyone, not even his wife, as much as Ray loved him.

One weekend Ralph went off on a yacht with a Greek collector of his paintings; they were sailing over to Thera and wouldn't be back till Monday. 'Feel free to bring your child husband to the palace while I'm away,' Ralph said as he pecked Ray on both cheeks in the French manner. And indeed that night Ray did say to Marco, '*Spiti mou,*' showed him the house keys, and led him through town, walking a few paces ahead just as on that first night Marco had preceded Ray. On the street of notions shops someone hailed Marco ('*Yassou*') and talked to him, and Ray, smiling at his own quick grasp of things, didn't look back but turned the corner and waited there, in the dark. After all, it was a little town. And only last week a shepherd had discovered his son was getting fucked and had killed him, which Homer said most of the locals had considered fair enough.

Marco in his white Keds and Levi jacket came treading stealthily around the corner, noble and balanced as a lion; he winked his approval and Ray felt his own pleasure spread over his whole body like the heat of the sun.

Marco was obviously impressed by the palace – impressed by its grandeur and, Ray imagined, proud that foreigners had furnished it with old Cretan furniture and folk embroideries.

Impressed? Nonsense, Ray thought, catching himself. Purest sentimental rubbish on my part. No doubt he'd prefer lavender Formica with embedded gold glitter.

Ray, who liked Marco and wanted to show that he did, felt a new intimacy between them as he led him into his bedroom. He gently pushed him back on the bed and knelt to untie the Keds and take them off, then the smelly socks. Then he made Marco wriggle out of his jeans; he started to pull the T-shirt over his head but Marco stopped him, though he, too, was gentle. Every one of Marco's concessions meant so much more to Ray than all the sexual extravagances of New York in the old pre-plague days – the slings and drugs and filthy raps.

Ray undressed himself. He wondered what Marco thought of him, of this naked adult male body which he'd never seen before. How old does he think I am? Does he admire my muscles? Or does my role as *poosti* on *parea* keep him from seeing me?

Ray worried that the whole routine – nakedness, a bed, privacy – might be getting a little too queer for Marco, so he was quick to kneel and start sucking him, back to the tried and true. But Ray, carried away in spite of himself, couldn't resist adding a refinement. He licked the inside of Marco's thighs and Marco jumped, as he did a moment later when Ray's tongue explored his navel. Strange that his cock seems to be the least sensitive part of his body, Ray thought.

When the time for the rubber arrived, Ray thought that surely tonight might make some difference, and indeed for the first time Marco gasped at the moment of his climax. Ray said, 'You like?' and Marco nodded vigorously and smiled, and a young male intimacy really had come alive between them, glued as they were together, their naked bodies sweaty.

Almost instantly Marco stood and dashed into the bathroom, pulled off the rubber, and washed while standing at the sink. Ray leaned against the door and watched him.

In this bright light the boy looked startlingly young and Ray realized, yes, he was young enough to be his son. But his other feeling was less easy to account for. It was of the oddness that a body so simple, with so few features, should have provoked so much emotion in him, Ray. Clothes with their colours and cuts seemed more adequate to what he was feeling.

Once again Ray noticed that he was feeling more, far more, than the occasion warranted. No objective correlative. Ray took Marco up to the roof to see the panorama of the sea, the harbour, the far-flung villages, a car burrowing up the mountain with its headlights like a luminous insect. But now that the transaction was over, the tension between them had been cut.

The next night Marco came directly to the palace and Ray persuaded him to take off his T-shirt, too, so that now there was no membrane except the rubber between them. Before they got to the fucking part, Ray paused in his exertions and crept up beside Marco and rested his head on Marco's thumping chest. Marco's hand awkwardly grazed Ray's hair. Ray could smell the rank, ingenuous odour of Marco's underarm sweat – not old sweat or nervous sweat but the frank smell of a young summer body that had just walked halfway across town.

On the third and last night they'd have alone in the palace, Marco came up the steps hanging his head, not giving his hearty greeting: 'Ti kanes? Kala?' He simply walked right into the bedroom, threw his clothes off, fell back on the bed, and with a sneering smile parodied the moans and squirmings of sex.

'What's wrong?' Ray asked. Marco turned moodily on his side and Ray was grateful for this glimpse into the boy's discontent. When he sat down beside Marco he could smell beer on his breath and cigarette smoke in his hair, though Marco didn't smoke. At last, after a few words and much miming, Marco was able to indicate that he had a friend who was leaving the next morning for Athens to begin his compulsory military service and the guy was waiting for him in a bar down below alongside the harbour.

Ray pulled Marco to his feet, gave him double the usual thousand drachmas, helped him dress, set tomorrow's date back in the school-yard, and urged him to hurry off to his friend. He had a half-thought that Marco understood more English than he was letting on. For the first time Marco seemed to be looking at Ray not as a member of another race, sex, class, age, but as a friend.

Friend? Ray laughed at his own naïveté. The boy's a hooker, he told himself. Don't get all moony over your beautiful budding friendship with the hooker.

After Marco had run down the steps, the thuds rattling the whole house, Ray was alone. Definitely alone. He walked to the balcony and looked down at the harbour, most of its lights extinguished, the last waiters hosing down the board-walk. He put on his headphones and listened to George's telephone messages to Betty. 'Hi, doll, this is Darleen, now a stylishly anorectic 135 pounds. The Duchess of Windsor was wrong. You can be too thin.' Oh yes, four months before the end. 'Hi, doll, I know you're there with the machine on watching *The Guiding Light*. Can you believe that bitch Vanessa? Hi!' and a sudden happy duet of overlapping voices, since just then Betty picked up and confessed she had indeed been pigging out on the soaps and a pound of chocolates.

Ray snapped it off. 'You must look out for yourself,' George had said, and just now the best way seemed to be to forget George, at least for a while, to forget the atmosphere of dread, the midnight visits to the hospital, the horrifying outbreak of disease after disease – fungus in the throat, a bug in the brain, bleeding in the gut, herpes ringing the ass, every inch of the dwindling body explored by fibre optics, brain scanner, X-rays, the final agonies buried under blankets of morphine.

see p282.

Ray received a call from Helen, his boss, and her tinny, crackling tirade sounded as remote as the final, angry emission from a dead star. He had no desire to leave Xania. With Homer as his translator he looked at a house for sale in the Turkish quarter and had a nearly plausible daydream of converting it into a guest house that he and Marco would run.

He started writing a story about Marco – his first story in fifteen years. He wondered if he could support himself by his pen. He talked to an Irish guy who made a meagre living by teaching English at the prison nearby in their rehabilitation programme. If he sold George's loft he could afford to live in Greece several years without working. He could even finance that guest house.

When he'd first arrived in Crete he'd had the vague feeling that this holiday was merely a detour and that when he rejoined his path George would be waiting for him. George or thoughts of George or the life George had custom-built for him, he wasn't quite sure which he meant. And yet now there was a real possibility that he might escape, start something new or transpose his old boyhood goals and values into a new key, the Dorian mode, say. Everything here seemed to be conspiring to reorient him, repatriate him, even the way he'd become in Greece the pursuer rather than the pursued.

One hot, sticky afternoon as he sat in a café with a milky ouzo and a dozing cat for company, a blond foreigner – a man, about twenty-five, in shorts and shirtless, barefoot – came walking along beside the harbour playing a soprano recorder. A chubby girl in a muu-muu and with almost microscopic freckles dusted over her well-padded cheeks was following this ringleted Pan and staring at him devotedly.

Ray hated the guy's evident self-love and the way his head dropped to one side and he hated the complicity of the woman, hated even more that a grown-up man should still be pushing such an over-ripe version of the eternal body. He really did look over-ripe. Even his lips, puckered for the recorder, looked too pulpy. Ray realized that he himself had played the boy for years and years. To be sure not when he'd chronologically been a boy, for then he'd been too studious for such posturing. But later, in his twenties and thirties. He saw that all those years of self-absorption had confused him. He had always been looking around to discover if older men were noticing him and he'd been distressed if they were or weren't. He hadn't read or written anything because he hadn't had the calm to submit to other people's thoughts or to summon his own. George had urged him to buy more and more clothes, always in the latest youthful style, and he'd fussed over Ray's work-out, dentistry, haircut, even the state of his fingernails. When they'd doze in the sun on Fire Island, hour after hour George would stroke Ray's oiled back or legs. Ray had been the sultan's favourite. Now he'd changed. Now he was like a straight man. He was the one who admired someone else. He wooed, he paid. At the same time he was the kneeling handmaiden to the Cretan youth, who was the slim-waisted matador. This funny complication suited him.

A journalist came down from Athens to Xania to interview Ralph for an Athens art magazine or maybe it was a paper. Since he was gay, spoke English, and was congenial, Ralph invited him to stay on for the weekehd. The day before Ray was due to fly back to New York, he asked the journalist to translate a letter for him into Greek, something he could give Marco along with the gold necklace he'd bought him, the sort of sleazy bauble all the kids here were wearing. Delighted to be part of the adventure and impressed by the ardour of the letter, the journalist readily accepted the commission. Ralph arranged to be away for a couple of hours on Ray's last night and insisted he bring Marco up to the palace for a farewell between sheets. Covering his friendliness with queenliness, Ralph said, 'How else can you hold on to your nickname, La Grande Horizontale?'

In the palace bedroom that night, just as Marco was about to untie his laces and get down to work, Ray handed him the package and the letter. Before opening the package, Marco read the letter. It said: 'I've asked a visitor from Athens to translate this for me because I have to tell you several things. Tomorrow I'm going back to New York, but I hope to sell my belongings there quickly. I'll be back in Xania within a month. I've already found a house I'd like to buy on Theotocopoulos Street. Perhaps you and I could live there someday or fix it up and run it as a guest house.

'I don't know what you feel for me if anything. For my part, I feel something very deep for you. Nor is it just sexual; the only reason we have so much sex is because we can't speak to each other. But don't worry. When I come back I'll study Greek and, if you like, I'll teach you English.

281

AN ORACLE

'Here's a present. if you don't like it you can exchange it.'

After Marco finished reading the letter (he was sitting on the edge of the bed and Ray had snapped on the overhead light), he hung his head for a full minute. Ray had no idea what he'd say, but the very silence, the full stop, awed him. Then Marco looked at Ray and said in English, in a very quiet voice, 'I know you love me and I love you. But Xania is no good for you. Too small. Do not rest here. You must go.'

Although Ray felt so dizzy he sank into a chair, he summoned up the wit to ask, 'And you? Will you leave Xania one day?' for he was already imagining their life together in New York.

'Yes, one day.' Marco handed the unopened package back to Ray. 'I won't see you again. You must look out for yourself.'

And then he stood, left the room, thudded down the front steps, causing the whole house to rattle, and let himself out the front door. Ray felt blown back in a wind-tunnel of grief and joy. He felt his hair streaming, his face pressed back, the fabric of his pants fluttering. In pop-song phrases he thought this guy had walked out on him, done him wrong, broken his heart – a heart he was happy to feel thumping again with sharp, wounded life. He was blown back on to the bed and he smiled and cried as he'd never yet allowed himself to cry over George, who'd just spoken to him once again through the least likely oracle.

p 279

Who was oracle? look into the classical allusions.

282

Running on Empty

Edmund White

On the charter flight from Paris to New York Luke sat on the aisle. Next to him, in the centre seat, was a man in his mid-twenties from the French Alps, where his parents owned a small hotel for skiers. He said he cooked all winter in the hotel and then took a quite long vacation every spring. This year it was the States, since the dollar was so low.

'Not *that* low,' Luke said, when Sylvain mentioned he had only a hundred dollars with him for a five-week stay.

They were speaking French since Sylvain confessed he couldn't get through even one sentence in English. Sylvain smiled and Luke envied him his looks, his health, even his youth, although that was absurd, since Luke himself was barely twenty-nine.

Next to Sylvain, by the window, sat a nun with an eager, intelligent face. Soon she had joined in the conversation. She was Sister Julia, an American though a member of a French convent for a reason she never explained despite their non-stop chatter for the seven and a half hours they were in the air. Her French was excellent, much better than Luke's. He noticed that Sylvain talked to her with all the grace notes kept in, whereas with Luke he simplified down to the main melody.

It turned out Luke and Sister Julia had both been in France for four years. Of course a convent was a 'total immersion' undreamt of even by Berlitz. Nevertheless Luke was embarrassed to admit to his seat partners that he was a translator. From French to English, to be sure. It was pointless to explain to this handsome, confident Sylvain that a translator must be better in the 'into language', than in the 'out-of language', that a translator must be a stylist in his own tongue.

Sylvain was, in any event, more intrigued by Sister Julia's vows than by Luke's linguistic competence. He asked her right off how a pretty girl like her could give up sex.

'But I'm not a girl,' she said. 'I'm forty-six. This wimple is very handy,' she said with a trace of coquetry, 'for covering up grey hair.'

She was not at all like the stern, bushy-eyebrowed, downy-chinned nuns who'd taught Luke all the way through high school. When Sylvain asked her if she didn't regret never having known a man (and here he even raised his muscular arms, smiled and stretched), she said quite simply, 'But I was married. I know all about men.'

She told them her father had been a composer, she'd grown up an Episcopalian in Providence, Rhode Island, she'd taught music theory at Brown and built harpsichords. Her religious vocation had descended on her swiftly, but she didn't provide them with the conversion scene; she had little sense of the dramatic possibilities her life provided, or perhaps flattening out her own narrative was a penance. Nor was her theology orthodox. She believed in reincarnation. 'Do you?' she asked them.

'I'm an atheist,' Luke said. He'd never said that to a nun before, and he enjoyed saying it, even though Sister Julia wasn't the sort to be shocked or even sorrowed by someone else's lack of faith – she was blessed by the convert's egotism. There was nothing dogmatic about her clear, fresh face, her pretty grey eyes, her way of leaning into the conversation and drinking it up nor her quick nods, sometimes at variance with the crease of doubt across her forehead. When she nodded and frowned at the same time he felt she was disagreeing with his opinions but affirming him as a person.

Sylvain appeared to be enjoying his two Americans. Luke and Sister Julia kept giving him the names and addresses of friends in the States to look up. 'If you're ever in Martha's Vineyard, you must stay with Lucy. She's just lost a lot of weight and hasn't realized yet she's become very beautiful,' the nun said. Luke gave him the names of two gay friends without mentioning they were gay – one in Boston, another in San Francisco. Of course Sylvain was heterosexual, that was obvious, but Luke knew his friends would get a kick out of putting up a handsome foreigner, the sort of blond who's always slightly tanned, the sort of man who looks at his own crotch when he's listening and frames it with his hands when he's replying.

Certainly both Luke and the nun couldn't resist over-responding even to Sylvain's most casual remarks.

When the hostess served them lunch, Sylvain asked her in his funny English where she was from. Then he asked, 'Are all ze womens in Floride as charming like you?'

The hostess pursed her lips in smiling mock-reproach as though he were being a naughty darling and said, 'It's a real nice state. France is nice, too. I'm going to learn French next. I studied Latin in high school.'

Sister Julia said to Sylvain, 'If you can speak English like that you won't need more than a hundred dollars.'

When they all said goodbye at the airport Luke was disappointed. He'd expected something more. Well, he had Sylvain's address and if some day Luke returned to France he'd look him up. Ill as he was, Luke couldn't bear the thought of never seeing France again, which suddenly seemed synonymous with some future rendezvous with Sylvain.

Luke changed money and planes – this time for Dallas. He was getting pretty ill. He could feel it in the heaviness of his bones, in his extreme tiredness, and he almost asked a porter to carry his bags, but he didn't know how to go about it and he feared it would cost too much. He had just two hundred dollars with him – he was half as optimistic as Sylvain and infinitely less appealing. He'd never had enough money, and now he worried he'd end up a charity case or, even worse, dependent on his family. He was terrified of having to call on the mercy of his family.

He'd grown up as the eighth of ten children, all of them small if wiry and agile. His mother was a chicano, but no one ever took her for Mexican (in any event she didn't appear to have much Indian blood and her mother prided herself on being 'Castillian'). His father was a nasty little man with a tweezered moustache who'd worked his whole life as the janitor in a Lubbock, Texas high school. He'd converted to Catholicism to please his wife and enrage his Baptist kin (Lubbock proudly called itself 'the buckle on the Bible Belt'). Luke's father and brothers and sisters all shared a pleasure he'd learned how to name only years later – *Schadenfreude*, which in German means taking malicious pleasure in someone else's pain.

Spite and envy were their ruling sentiments. If someone fell and hurt himself, they'd howl with glee. Their father would regale them with hissing, venomous accounts of the misfortunes of superiors at school. The one sure way to win the family's attention was to act out the humiliation that had befallen Mrs Rodriguez after mass last Sunday or Mr Brown, the principal, during the last PTA meeting. Luke's father grumbled at the TV, mocked the commercials, challenged the newscasters, jeered the politicians. 'Look at him, he thinks he's so great, but he'll look like he's smelled a fart when he sees the final vote.' Everyone would laugh except Luke's mother, who went about her work gravely, like a paid employee eager to finish up and leave.

In high school – not the public high school where his

father worked, but the much smaller parochial school – Luke had emerged as the nuns' favourite. He'd been a brilliant student. Now that his brain was usually fuzzy (and had become an overcooked minestrone during the taxiplasmosis crisis, all swimming and steamy with shreds and lumps rising only to sink again) he regarded his former intelligence with respect. He'd once known the ablative absolute. He'd once read the *Symposium* in Greek without understanding the references to love between men.

Perhaps because of his miserable, mocking family, Luke had always felt unsure of himself. Nevertheless he'd done everything expected of him, everything. He'd been a cross-country champ, he'd stayed entirely virginal, avoiding even masturbation except for rare lapses, in French he'd won the statewide *prix d'honneur*, he'd once correctly and even humorously translated on the spot an entire *Time* magazine article into Latin, though the page had been handed to him only seconds before by the judge of the Cicero Club contest.

In another era he would have grown up to be one of those priests who play basketball in a soutane and whose students complain when he beats them at arm-wrestling ('Jeez, Father Luke . . . ').

He'd only narrowly escaped that fate. He'd found a job in a liberal, primarily Jewish private school just outside New York, and though he'd grown a beard and spouted Saint-Simonism, he hadn't been able to resist becoming the best beloved, most energetic teacher in the history of Dempster Country Day. The kids worshipped him, called him Luke and phoned him in the middle of the night to discuss their abortions, college entrance exams and parents' pending divorces. Several of them had invited him to their parents' mansions where Luke, the gung-ho jock and brain, nose always burned from the soccer field and tweed jacket pocket always misshapen from carrying around Horace's *Odes*, had had to study his own students to discover how to wield an escargot clamp, eat asparagus with fingers only and avoid cutting the nose off the Brie.

What was harder was to keep up that ceaseless, bouncy energy that is always the hallmark of rich people who are also 'social'. Whereas Luke's father had beguiled his brutal brood with tales of other people's folly and chagrin, the Lords of Long Island looked at you with distrust the instant you criticized anyone – especially a superior. Envy proved your own inferiority. Since the parents of Luke's students were usually at the top of their profession or industry, they interpreted carping and quibbles as envy. They usually sided with the object of any attack. With them generosity – like stoicism and pep – had become a sign of good breeding.

Luke learned generosity, too, as easily as he'd mastered snails. The ingredient he added to the package, the personal ingredient, was gratitude. He was grateful to rich people. He was grateful to almost everyone. The gratitude was the humble reverse side of the family's taste for *Schadenfreude*. And yet Luke could express his gratitude in such an earnest, simply way, in his caressing tenor voice with the baritone beginnings and endings of sentences, that no one took it for cringing – no one except Luke himself, who kept seeing his father, hat in hand, talking to the district supervisor.

Luke had left the abjection and exaltation of Dempster and found work as a translator. Working alone was less engrossing than playing Father Luke, but the thrills of wielding power or submitting to it had finally sickened him. As a kid he'd managed to escape from his family through school; he'd stayed in school to consolidate that gain, but now he wanted to be alone, wanted to work alone into the night, listening to the radio, fine-tuning English sentences. Luckily he had a rent-controlled apartment on Cornelia Street in Manhattan, and luckily an older gay man, the king of the translators, had taken him under his wing. He became a translator, joining an honest if underpaid profession.

By subletting his apartment for four times what he paid, Luke had had enough money to live in Paris in a Montmarte hotel on a steep street near Picasso's old studio, a hotel of just eighteen rooms where the proprietor, a hearty woman from the Périgord, watched them as they ate the meals she prepared and urged them to pour wine into their emptied soup bowls and knock it back. 'Chabrol! Chabrol!' she'd say, which was both an order and a toast. She'd point at them unsmilingly if they weren't drinking. She liked it when everyone was slightly tipsy and making conversation from table to table.

He'd never enjoyed gay life as such, at least New York clones had never struck him as sexy. In turn they hadn't liked his look (wire-rim glasses, baggy tweeds, shiny, policeman's shoes), nor his looks. He was small; his eyes mocking or hostilely attentive or wet and grateful; his nose was a red beak; his slim body featureless under the loose pants and outsize jackets but smooth and well built when stripped – the pale, sweated body of a featherweight high-school wrestler. Clones had to work to get to see it.

Luke had sought out sex with working men, straight men or close approximations of that ideal. He'd haunted the building sites, suburban weightlifting gyms, the bar next to the firehouse, the bowling alley across from the police station, the run-down Queens theater that specialized in kung-fu movies. He liked guys who didn't kiss, who had beer bellies, who wore T-shirts that showed through their Dacron short-sleeved shirts, who watched football games, who shook their heads in frustration and muttered, 'Women!' He liked becoming pals with guys who, because they were too boring or too rough or not romantic or cultured enough, had lost their girlfriends.

In Paris he'd befriended a Moroccan boxer down on his luck. But very little of his time went to Ali. He spent his mornings alone in bed, surrounded by his dictionaries, and

strange chandr. likes beer bellies
and medieval relics

listened to the rain and translated. He ate the same Salade
Auvergnate every lunch at the same neighbourhood café. In
the afternoons he often went to the Cluny museum. Luke
liked medieval culture. He knew everything about Roman-
esque fortified churches and dreamed of meeting someone
with a car who could take him on a tour of them.

At night he'd haunt the run-down movie palaces near
Barbès-Rochechouart, the Arab quarter, or in good weather
cruise the steps below Sacré-coeur. That was where you met
his type: men-without-women, chumps too broke or too
dumb to get chicks, guys with girlie calendars tacked on the
inner side of closet doors, guys who practised karate chops as
they talked on the telephone to their mothers.

He didn't want to impersonate that missing girlfriend for
them. No, Luke wanted to be a pal, a sidekick, and more than
once he'd lain in the arms of a CRS (a French cop) who'd
drawn on his Gitane *blonde* and told Luke he was '*un vrai
copain*', a real pal.

That was why he'd been surprised when he of all people
had become ill. It was a gay disease and he scarcely thought
of himself as gay. In fact earlier on he'd once talked it over
with an Irish teacher of English who lived in his hotel, a
paedophile who couldn't get it up for anyone over sixteen.
They'd agreed that neither of them counted as gay.

For him, the worst immediate effect of the disease was that
it sapped his confidence. He felt he'd always lived on nerve,
run on empty. He should have lived the dim life of his
brothers and sisters – one a welfare mother, another a
secretary in a lumber yard, two brothers in the air-
conditioning business, another one an exterminator, another
(the family success) an army officer who'd taken early retire-
ment to run a sporting-goods store with an ex-football
champ. He had another brother, Jeff, an iron worker who'd
dropped out of the union, who lived in Milwaukee with his
girl and travelled as far away as New York State to bend steel

refer to
the beautiful poem
to empty

and put up the frames of buildings. Jeff was a guy who grew his hair long and partied with women executives in their early forties fed up with (or neglected by) their white collar male contemporaries. The last thing Luke had heard, Jeff had broken up with his girl because she'd spent fifty of his bucks hiring a limo to ferry her and two of her girlfriends around Milwaukee just for the rush.

Luke had sprung the family trap. He'd eaten oysters with rich socialists, learned that a 'gentleman' never takes seconds during the cheese course, worried over the right slang equivalents in English of French obscenities – he'd even resisted the temptation to strive to become the headmaster of Dempster Country Day. As the runt of his family, he'd always had to fight when he was a kid to get enough to eat, but even so as an adult he'd chosen freelance insecurity over a dull future with a future.

But all that had taken confidence and now he didn't have any. The translation he was working on would be his last. Translating required a hundred small dares per page in the constant trade-off between fidelity and fluency, and Luke couldn't find the necessary authority.

He never stopped worrying about money. He'd lie in bed working up imaginary budgets. Once he returned to New York, Dempster Country Day might refer students to him for coaching in French, but would the parents worry that their children would be infected? He'd read of the hysteria in America. If his doctor decided he should go on AZT, how would he ever find $12,000 a year to pay for it?

When he landed in Dallas his favourite cousin Beth was there. Growing up he'd called her Elizabeth. Now he was training himself to call her 'Beth' as she preferred. She hadn't been told he was ill and he looked for a sign that his appearance shocked her, but all she said was, 'My goodness, you'll have to go to Weight-Watchers with me before long.' If she'd known how hard he'd worked for every ounce on his

293

bones, she wouldn't joke about it; his paunch, however, he knew, was bloated from the *Cytomegalovirus* in his gut and the bottle of Peptobismol he had to swallow every morning to control his diarrhoea.

Beth's husband Greg had just died. She'd mailed Luke a cassette of the funeral but he'd never listened to it because he hadn't been able to lay his hands on a tape recorder – not a problem that would have occurred to her, she who had a ranch house stocked with self-cleaning ovens, a microwave, two Dustbusters, three TVs, dishwasher, washer and drier and Lord knew what else. So he just patted her back and said, 'It was a beautiful service. I hope you're surviving.'

'I'm doing fine, Luke, just fine.' There was something hard and determined about her that he admired. Beth's bright Texas smile came as a comfort. He told her he'd never seen her in such pretty dark shades of blue.

'Well, *thank* you, Luke. I had my colours done. It was one of the last presents Greg gave me. Have you had yours done yet?'

'No, what is it?'

'You go to this lady, she measures you in all sorts of scientific ways, skin tones and all and then she gives you your fan. I have mine here in my purse, I always carry it, 'cause don't you know I'll see a pretty blouse and pick it up but when I get home with it it doesn't look right at *all* and when I check it out it won't be one of my hues, it will be *close* but not exact.'

Beth snapped open a paper fan. Each segment was painted a different shade. 'Now the dark blue is my strong colour. If I wear it, I always get compliments. You complimented me, you see!'

And she laughed and let her smiling blue eyes dazzle him, as they always had. Her old-fashioned heart-shaped face made him think of Hollywood starlets of the past, as did her slight chubbiness and smile, which looked as though it were shot through gauze.

Her little speech about colours had been an act of courage, at once a pledge that she was going to be cheerful as well as a subtle blend of flirting with him (as she would have flirted with any man) and giving him a beauty tip (as she might have done with another woman). She didn't know any other gay men; she wanted to be nice; she'd found this way to welcome him.

He'd been the ring bearer at her wedding to Greg. They'd been the ideal couple, she a Texas Bluebell, he a football star, she small and blonde, he dark and massive. Now she was just forty-five and already a widow with two sons nearly out of college, both eager to be cattlemen. 'For a while Houston was planning to be a missionary,' Beth was saying, 'but now he thinks he can serve the Lord just by leading a Christian life, and we know there's nothing wrong with that, don't we?' She added an emphatic 'No sirree, Bob,' so he wouldn't have to reply.

Since Luke belonged to the disgraced Catholic side of the family, Beth was careful usually not to bring up religion. Texans were brought up not to discuss religion or politics, the cause of so many gunfights just two generations ago, but Baptists were encouraged to proselytize. Beth was even about to set out on a Baptist mission to England, she said, and she asked Luke for tips about getting along with what she called 'Europeans'. Luke tried to picture her, with her carefully streaked permanent, fan-selected colours from Nieman Marcus, black-leather shoulder-strap Chanel bag and diamond earrings, ringing the bell of a lady in a twinset and pearls in a twee village in the Cotswolds: 'Howdy, are you ready to take the Lord into your heart?' Today she was holding her urge to convert in check. She didn't want to alienate him. She loved family, and he was family, even if he was a sinner lost – damned, for he'd told her ten years ago about his vice.

The programme was that they were to visit relatives in East Texas and then drive over to Lubbock, where Luke would stay with his parents for a week before flying home to New York. He was so worried he might become critically ill while in Lubbock and have to stay there. He felt very uprooted, but New York – scary, expensive – was the closest thing to home. He was eager to consult the doctor awaiting him in New York.

Unlike some of his friends, who'd become resigned and either philosophical or depressed, Luke had taken his own case on and put himself in charge of finding a cure. In Paris he'd worked as a volunteer for the hot line, answering anxious questions and in return finding out the latest information and meeting the best specialists. He had a contact in Sweden who was keeping him abreast of an experiment going on there; through the French he knew the latest results from Zaire. He'd memorized the list of drugs and their side effects: he knew that the side effects of trimethoprim for the pneumonia were kidney damage, depression, loss of appetite, abdominal pain, hepatitis, diarrhoea, headache, neuritis, insomnia, apathy, fever, chills, anaemia, rash, light sensitivity, mouth pain, nausea and vomiting – and those were just the results of a treatment.

The father of one of his former students at Dempster had promised to pay Luke's bills 'until he got better'. Luke felt getting well was a full-time job: he'd even seen all the quacks, swallowed tiny white homoeopathic doses, meditated and 'imaged' healthy cells engulfing foul ones, been massaged on mystic pressure points, done yoga, eaten nothing but brown rice and slimy or pickled vegetables arranged on the plate according to wind and rain principles. The one thing he couldn't bring himself to do was meet with other people who were ill.

They drove in Beth's new beige Cadillac on the beltway skirting Fort Worth and Dallas and headed the hundred miles south to Hershell, where Beth had just buried Greg and where their great-aunts Ruby and Pearl were waiting for them. Once they were out of the city and on to a two-lane road, the Texas he remembered came drifting back – the wild flowers, especially the Indian Blanket and bluebells, covering the grassy slopes, the men with the thick tan necks and off-white straw cowboy hats driving the pick-up trucks, the smell of heat and damp lifting off the fields.

Hershell was just a flyspeck on the road. There were two churches, one Baptist and one Church of Christ, a hardware store where they still sold kerosene lamps and barbed-wire stretchers, a saddle shop where a cousin of theirs by marriage worked the leather as he sipped cold coffee and smoked Luckies, a post office, a grocery store with nearly empty shelves and the 'new' grade school built of red brick in the 1950s. Ruby's house was a yellow-brick single storey with a double garage and a ceiling fan that shook the whole house when it was turned on, as though preparing for lift-off. The paintings – flowers, fruits, fields – had been done long ago by one of her aunts. Luke was given a bedroom with a double bed covered with a handsome thick white chenille bed-spread – *chenille* was a word he'd always said as a child, but only now did he connect it with the French word for *caterpillar*. Beth was given a room across the street with Pearl. Pearl's house had been her parents'. The house was nothing but additions. Her folks had built a one-room cabin and then added rooms on each side as they had the money and inclination to do so. She showed them pictures of their great-grandparents and their twelve children – one of the pale-eyed, square-jawed boys, named Culley, was handsome enough to step out towards them away from his plump, crazed-looking siblings. Pearl's Hershell high-school dip-loma was on the wall. When Luke asked her what the musical notes on it meant, she said, 'Be Sharp, Be Natural but Never Be Flat.'

Pearl said it right out. She was intelligent enough to know how funny it was, but as the local chair of the Texas

Historical Society she took pride in every detail of their heritage. The miles and miles of brand new housing developments Luke had seen on the Dallas–Fort Worth beltway, all with purely arbitrary names such as Mount Vernon or Versailles, had spooked him, made him grateful for these sun-bleached lean-tos, for the irises growing in the creek, for the 'tabernacle', the open-sided, roofed-over meeting place above the town.

He and Beth sat for hours and hours with their great-aunts 'visiting' after their supper of fried chicken and succotash. They drank their sweetened iced tea and traded stories. There were solemn moments, as when the old ladies hugged Beth and told her how courageous she was being. 'That Greg was a *fine* man,' Ruby said, her eyes defiant and sharp as though someone might challenge her judgement. Her enunciation had always been clear (she'd taught elocution for years in high schools all over the state), but she hadn't weeded the country out of her voice.

Then there were the gay moments, as when Luke recounted the latest follies of folks in Paris. 'Well, I declare,' the ladies would exclaim, their voice dipping from pretended excitement down into real indifference. He was careful not to go on too long about a world they didn't know or care about nor to shock them. He noticed they didn't ask him this time when he was going to get hitched up: perhaps he'd gone over that invisible line in their minds and become a 'confirmed' bachelor. They did tease him about his 'bay window', which he patted as though he hadn't noticed it before, which made them laugh.

Beth and he went on a long walk before the light died. They had a look at the folks on the corner they'd heard about who lived like pigs: the old man had gone and shot someone dead and now he was in the pokie for life and the old woman, didn't it beat all, had a garden sale going on every day but who would want that old junk? He and Beth walked

fast, with light hearts. He appreciated their shared views –
they both loved and respected their aunts and they were
both glad to slip away from them.

They walked down to see the old metal swing bridge;
earlier Ruby had shown them a photo of Billy Andrews, in
their class of 1917, swinging from the bridge as a stunt, big
grin on his face, fairly popping out of his graduation suit
with the celluloid collar, his strong calves squeezed into the
knickerbockers.

Oh, Luke ached for sex. He thought that if he could just lie
next to a man one more time, feel once more that someone
wanted him, he could die in peace. All his life he'd been on
the prowl once he'd broken his vows of virginity (in French
he'd learned there were *two* words for boy virgins, neither
comical: *un puceau* and *un rosier*, as though the boy were a
rose bush, blossoms guarded by thorns). He'd lived so fast,
cherished so little, but now he lingered over sexy souvenirs
he'd never even summoned up before, like that time he'd
followed a Cuban nightwatchman into a Park Avenue office
building and they'd fucked in the service elevator and
stopped, just for the hell of it, on every one of the forty-two
floors. Or he remembered sex that hadn't happened, like that
summer when he was twelve, a caddy, and he'd sat next to
one of the older caddies on the bench waiting for a job in the
airless, cricket-shrill heat. He'd moulded his leg so perfectly
to the guy's thigh that finally he'd stood up and said to Luke,
real pissed off, 'What are you, some sort of fuckin' Liberace?'
And he thought of the cop who'd handcuffed him to the
bedstead.

As he and Beth were walking out past a field of cows
standing in the fading light, he started picking a bouquet of
wild flowers for Ruby – he got up to twenty-nine flowers
without repeating a single variety. Beth walked with vigour,
her whole body alert with curiosity. She'd always struck him
as a healthy, sexy woman. He wondered if she'd remarry.

With her religion and all she couldn't just pick up a man in a bar. She'd have to marry again to get laid. But would she want to? How did she keep her appetite in check?

The next day was hot enough to make them all worry what the summer would bring. They were going to the graveyard working ten miles east of Hershell. Once a year the ten or so families who had kin buried there came together to set the tombstones upright, hoe and rake, stick silk or plastic flowers in the soil (real ones burned up right away) and then eat. Ruby and Pearl had both been up since dawn cooking, since after the working everyone shared in a big potluck lunch.

They drove out in Beth's 'fine automobile', as the ladies called the Cadillac. Ruby was wearing a bonnet, one she'd made herself for gardening. The cemetery, which was also named after Hershell since he'd donated the land, was on top of a hill looking over green, rolling farmland. There were ten or eleven cars and pick-up trucks already parked outside the metal palings that guarded the front but not the sides of the cemetery. Big women with lots of kids were already setting up for the lunch, unfolding card tables and stacking them with coolers of iced tea and plates of chicken fried in broken potato-chip batter, potato salad, pickled watermelon rind, whole hams, black-eyed peas, loaves of Wonder Bread, baked beans served right out of the can, pecan pies and apple pies. There weren't more than a hundred graves altogether and all of them had already been decently looked after, thanks to the contributions solicited every year by Ruby, who hired a part-time caretaker.

Luke felt a strange contentment hoeing his grandfather's grave. Pearl had to show him how to hoe and how to rake, but she didn't tease him about being a city slicker. He realized he could do no wrong in her eyes since he was kin. Everyone here was kin. Several of the men had Luke's beaky red nose. He kept seeing his own small, well-knit body on other men – the same narrow shoulders and short legs, hairless forearms, the thinning, shiny hair gone to baldness here and there. Because of the rift in the family he'd met few of these people before and he had little enough in common with them, except he did share the same body-type, possibly the same temperament.

His grandfather had been a Woodsman of the World, whatever that was, and his tomb marker was a stone tree trunk. His wife was buried under a tablet that read, 'She Did The Best She Could.'

Beth was standing in front of Greg's grave, which was still fresh. Luke worried that her mission to England might shake her faith. Wouldn't she see how flimsy, how recent and, well, how corny her religion was once she was in that grey and unpleasant land? They were planning, the Southern Baptists, to fan out over the English countryside. Wouldn't Beth be awed, or at least dismayed, by Gloucester Cathedral, by the polished intricacy of its cloisters? Wouldn't she see how raw, raw as this fresh grave, her beliefs were beside the civilized ironies of the Church of England – it was as though she were trying to introduce Pop-Up Tarts into the land of scones.

During the picnic Beth told Luke that her one worry about her son Houston was that he always seemed so serious and distracted these days, as though dipped and twirled in darkness. 'I tell him, son, you must be *happy* in the Lord. The Bible tells us to be happy in our faith.'

Luke couldn't resist teasing Beth for a moment. He asked her what she thought about the scandals – adultery, group-sex parties, embezzled church funds – surrounding a popular television evangelist and his wife.

'I expected it.'

'You did?'

'Yes, it's good. It's a good sign. It shows that Satan is establishing his rule, which means that we'll live to see the Final Days, the Rapture of the Church.' She spoke faster and with more assurance than usual. Luke realized she probably saw his disease as another proof of Satan's reign or God's punishment. He knew the Texas legislature was considering imprisoning diseased homosexuals who continued having sex.

Ruby came up to them, energized by the event, and asked him if he'd marked off a plot for himself. 'You can, you know. Doesn't cost a penny' (she pronounced it 'pinny'). 'You just put stones around where you want to lie. Up here it's all filling up but out yonder we've got lots to go.'

'No,' Luke said. 'I want to be cremated and put in the Columbarium at Père Lachaise. In Paris.'

'I declare,' Ruby said, 'but you've got years and *years* to reconsider,' and she laughed.

That night, as the ladies visited and told family stories, Luke felt trapped and isolated. Beth sat there nodding and smiling and saying, Auntie Pearl, now you just sit and let me.' But he knew she was lonely, too, and maybe a bit frightened. Other old ladies, all widows, stopped in to visit, and Luke wondered if Beth was ready to join grief's hen club. Girls started out clinging together, whispering secrets and flouncing past boys. Then there was the longish interlude of marriage, followed by the second sorority of widowhood; all these humped necks, bleared eyes, false teeth, the wide-legged sitting posture of countrywomen sipping weak coffee and complaining about one another. 'She wanted to know what I paid for this place and I said, "Well, Jessie, it is so *good* of you to worry about my finances, but I already have Mr Hopkins at Farmers First to look after that for me," and don't you know but that shut her up fast?' On and on into the night, not really vicious but complaining, spontaneously good but studiously petty, often feisty, sometimes coquettish, these women talked on and on. Those who couldn't hear nodded while their eyes timidly wandered, like children dismissed from the table but forbidden to play in their Sunday best.

Luke imagined he and Beth were both longing for a man –
she for Greg, he for one of his men, one of these divorced
cowboys, the sort of heartbroken man Randy Travis or
George Strait sings about . . . They'd met a man like that
during their walk past the old bridge yesterday – a sunburned man whose torso sat comfortably on his hips as
though in a big, roomy saddle. This sunburned rancher had
known who they were: the whole town had been alerted to
their visit. He didn't exactly doff his hat to Beth but he took it
off slowly and stared into it as he spoke. Without his hat on
he looked kinder which, for Luke, made him less sexy. When
he left he swung up into his truck and pulled it into gear all
in one motion. He hadn't been at the graveyard working,
although Luke had looked for him.

The next morning they drove a hundred miles west to
Henderson, where Beth's mother, Aunt Olna, still lived. Her
husband, now dead, had been a brother of Luke's dad –
estranged because Luke's dad had married a Mex and
become an 'old' Catholic (for some reason people hereabouts
always smiled sourly, lifted one eyebrow and said in one
breath, as though it were a bound form, 'old Catholic').
Beth's mother had grown up Church of Christ but had
converted to her husband's religion years after their marriage. One day she'd simply read a pamphlet about what
Baptists believed and she'd said to herself, 'Well, that's what
I believe, too,' and had crossed over on the spot.

Aunt Olna was always harsh to Beth, ordering her around:
'Not that one, Elizabeth.' 'This one which, Mother?' Beth
would wail. Beth's mother was too 'nervous' to specify her
demands. 'Turn here,' she'd say in the car. 'Turn right or left,
Mother? Mother? Right or left?' Olna was also too nervous to
cook. She didn't tremble, as other nervous people did. Luke
figured the nervousness must be a confusion hidden deep in
a body made fat from medication. Because she couldn't cook
she'd taken $300 out of the bank to entertain them. She named

all the menfolk have died. Only women remain

RUNNING ON EMPTY

the sum over and over again. She was proud her husband had left her 'well fixed'. When Beth drove to the store, Olna said, 'Greg left Beth very well fixed. House all bought and paid for. A big *in*-surance policy. She need never worry.'

Just my luck, Luke thought, to have gone husband-hunting among nothing but riff-raff.

Aunt Olna liked Luke. She'd always told everyone Luke was about as good as a person could get. Of course she knew almost nothing about his life, but she'd clung to her enthusiasm over the years and he'd always felt comfortable with her. Not that she was given to gushing. When he'd praised her house, she'd said, 'Everything in it is from the dime store. Always was.' She told him how she'd inherited a dining-room 'suit' but had had to sell it because it was too fine for her house.

Even so he liked the shiny maple furniture in the front parlour, the flimsy metal TV dinner trays on legs used as side tables, the knobbly milkglass candy dishes filled with Hershey's Kisses. He liked the reproduction of the troubadour serenading the white-wigged girl, a sort of East Texas take on Watteau. He liked the fact there was no shower, just a big womanly tub, and that the four-poster bed in his room was so tall you had to climb up to get into it. Best of all he liked leaving his door open on to the night. The rain steamed the sweetness up out of the mown grass and the leaves of the big old shade trees kept up a frying sound; when the rain died down it sounded as though someone had lowered the flame under the skillet. He was surrounded by women and death and yet the rain dripping over an old Texas town of darkened houses made him feel like a boy in his early teens again, a boy dying to slip away to find men. These days, of course, desire entailed hopelessness – he'd learned to match every pant of longing with a sigh of regret.

The next day the heat turned the sweet smell sour, as though spring peas had been replaced with rancid collard greens.

Olna took them to lunch at a barbecue place where they ate ribs and hot biscuits. In the afternoon they drove to a nursing home to visit Olna's sister. That woman remembered having babysat Luke once thirty years ago. 'My, you were a cute little boy. I wish I could see you, honey. I'd give anything to see again. My little house just sits empty and I'd love to go back to it but I can't, I can't see to mind it. I don't know why the good Lord won't gather me in. Not no use to *no*-one.'

The waiting room had a Coke machine and a snack dispenser. One of the machines was making a nasty whine. The woman's hand looked as pale as if it'd been floured through a sifter.

'My husband left me,' she was saying, 'and after that I sold tickets at the movie thee-ay-tur for nine dollars a week, six days a week, on Saturdays from ten till midnight, and when I asked for a raise after ten years Mr Monroe said no.' She smiled. 'But I had my house and cat and I could see.'

In the past, when Luke had paid these calls on relatives in nursing homes he'd felt he was on a field trip to some new and strange kind of slum, but today there was no distance between him and this woman. In a month or a week he could be as blind, less cogent, whiter.

He went for a walk with Beth through the big park the town of Henderson had recently laid out, a good fifty acres of jogging paths, tennis courts, a sports arena, a playground and just open fields gone to weeds and wild flowers. On the way they passed a swimming pool that had been here nearly thirty years ago, that time Luke had served as Beth's ring bearer. Now the pool was filled, clean, sparkling but for some reason without a single swimmer, an unheeded invitation. 'Didn't they used to have a big slide that curved half-way down and that was kept slick with water always pouring down it?' Luke asked.

'Now I believe you are one hundred per cent correct,' Beth said with that slightly prissy agreeableness of Southern ladies. 'What a wonderful memory you have!' She'd been trained to find fascinating even the most banal remarks if a man made them. Luke wasn't used to receiving all the respect due his gender and kept looking for a mote of mockery in Beth's eye, but it wasn't there. Or perhaps she had mockery as much under control as grief or desire.

They walked at the vigorous pace Beth set and went along the cindered jogging path under big mesquite trees; their tiny leaves, immobile, set lacy shadows on the ground.

That sparkling pool, painted an inviting blue-green, and the memory of the flowing water-slide and the smell of chlorine kept coming to mind. He'd played for hours and hours during an endless, cloudless summer day. Play had been rare enough for him who'd always had early morning newspaper delivery jobs, afternoon hardware jobs, weekend lawn-mowing jobs, summer caddying jobs as well as the chores around the house and the hours and hours of homework, those hours his family had ridiculed and tried to put a stop to. But he'd persisted and won.

When he and Beth reached the end of the park, they turned to the left, mounted a slight hill and saw a parked pick-up truck under a tree. Two teenage guys with red caps on were sitting inside and a third was standing unsteadily on the back of the truck, shirtless, jeans down, taking a leak. 'Oh, my goodness,' Beth said, 'just don't look at them, Luke, and let's keep on walking.'

The guys were laughing at Luke and Beth, playing loud music, probably drunk and of course Luke looked. The guy taking a leak was methodically spraying a dark brown circle in the pale dust. He was a redhead, freckled, tall, skinny, and his long body was hairless except where tufted blonde. He looked like a streak of summer lightning.

'But they're not doing any harm,' Luke said with a smile.

'You think not?' Beth spat out. 'Some folks here might think –' but she interrupted herself, mastered herself, smiled her big missionary smile.

Luke felt a rage alarm his tired body and tears – what sort of tears? – sting his eyes.

Tears of humiliation: he was offended that a virus had been permitted to win an argument. He'd been the one to learn, to leave home, break free. He'd cast aside all the old sins, lived freely – but soon Beth could imagine he was having to pay for his follies with his life. It offended him that he would be exposed to her self-righteousness.

Aunt Olna invited them out to a good steak dinner in a fast-food place near the new shopping mall. The girls ordered medium-size T-bones and Luke went for a big one. But then he suffered a terrifying attack of diarrhoea half-way through his meal and had to spend a sweaty, bowl-scorching thirty minutes in the toilet, listening to the piped-in music and the scrapings and flushings of other men. Aunt Olna appeared offended when he finally returned to the table, his shirt drenched and his face pale, until he explained to her he'd caught a nasty bug drinking the polluted Paris water. Then she relaxed and smiled, reassured. When they left the restaurant Olna told the young woman cashier, 'My guests tonight have come here all the way from Paris, France.'

He berated himself for having fallen away from his regime of healthy food, frequent naps, jogging and aerobics, no stress. He was stifling from frustration and anger. When they returned to Olna's it was already dark, but Luke insisted he was going jogging. Olna and Beth didn't offer the slightest objection and he realized that in their eyes he was no longer a boy but a man, a law-giver. Or maybe they were just indifferent. People could accept anything as long as they weren't directly affected.

He ran through the streets over the railroad tracks, past Olna's new Baptist church, down dark streets past houses built on G.I. loans just after the war for $6000 or $7000. Their screened-in porches were dimly lit by yellow, mosquito-repellent bulbs. He smelled something improbably rich and spicy, then remembered Olna had told him people were taking in well-behaved, industrious Vietnamese lodgers studying at the local college – their only fault, apparently, being that they cooked up smelly food at all hours.

The Vietnamese were the only change in this town during the last twenty-five years. Otherwise it was the same houses, the same lawns, the same people playing ping-pong in their garages, voices ricocheting off the cement, the same leashless dogs running out to inspect him, then walking dully away.

There was the big house where Beth had married Greg so many years ago in the backyard among her mother's bushes of huge yellow roses. And there (he could feel his bowels turning over, his breath tightening, his body exuding cold sweat) – there was the house where, when he was fifteen, Luke had met a handsome young man, a doctor's son, five years older and five hundred times richer, a man with black hair on his pale knuckles, a thin nose and blue eyes, a gentle man Luke would never have picked for sex but whom he'd felt he could love, someone he'd always meant to look up again: the front doorbell glowed softly, lit from within. The house was white clapboard with green shutters, which appeared nearly black in the dim street light.

On and on he ran, past the cow palace where he'd watched a rodeo as a kid. Now he was entering the same park where he and Beth had walked today. He could feel his energy going, his legs so weak he could imagine losing control over them and turning an ankle or falling. He knew how quickly a life could be reduced. He dreaded becoming critically ill here in Texas; he didn't want to give his family the satisfaction.

He ran past the unlit swimming pool and again he remembered that one wonderful day of fun and leisure so many years ago. On that single day he'd felt like a normal kid. He'd even struck up a friendship with another boy and they'd gone down the water-slide a hundred times, one behind the other, tobogganing.

Now he was thudding heavily past the spotlit tennis court. No one was playing, it was too hot and still, but two girls in white shorts were sitting on folding chairs at the far end, talking. Then he was on the gravel path under low, over-hanging trees. The crickets chanted slower than his pulse and from time to time seemed to skip a beat. He passed a girl walking her dog and he gasped, 'Howdy,' and she smiled. The smell of honeysuckle was so strong and he thought he'd never really gotten the guys he'd wanted, the big high school jocks, the blonds with loud tenor voices, beer breath, cruel smiles, lean hips, steady, insolent eyes, the guys impossible to befriend if you weren't exactly like them. He thought that with so many millions of people in the world the odds should have favoured the likelihood that at least one guy like that should have gone for him, but things hadn't turned out that way. Of course, even when you had someone, what did you have?

But then what did anyone ever have – the impermanence of sexual possession was a better school than most for the way life would flow through your hands.

In the distance, through the mesquite trees, he could see the lights of occasional cars nosing the dark. Then he remembered that right around here the redhead had pissed a brown circle and Luke looked for traces of that stain under the tree. He even touched the dust, feeling for moisture. He wondered if just entertaining the outrageous thought weren't sufficient for his purposes, but no, he preferred the ceremony of doing something actual. He found the spot, or thought he did, and touched the dirt to his lips. He started running again, chewing the grit as though it might help him to recuperate his past if not his health.

KING ALFRED'S COLLEGE

LIBRARY

What brings these stories together?
they are life stories.
    fictional biographies
    filled with details of past lives. pre - AIDS
lives.   reminisences

Ed White - not full of medical details
The ugliness of the disease does not
touch his stories.